At Sixes & Sevens

Rosie Harris was born in Cardiff and grew up there and in the West Country. After her marriage she resided for some years on Merseyside before moving to Buckinghamshire where she still lives. She has three grown-up children, and six grandchildren, and writes full time. *At Sixes & Sevens* is her eighth novel for Arrow.

At Sixes & Sevens

ROSIE HARRIS

arrow books

Published by Arrow Books in 2005

1 3 5 7 9 10 8 6 4 2

First published in the United Kingdom in 2005 by William Heinemann

Arrow Books
The Random House Group Limited
20 Vauxhall Bridge Road, London, SW1V 2SA

Random House Australia (Pty) Limited
20 Alfred Street, Milsons Point, Sydney,
New South Wales 2061, Australia

Random House New Zealand Limited
18 Poland Road, Glenfield
Auckland 10, New Zealand

Random House (Pty) Limited
Isle of Hougton, Corner of Boundary Road & Carse O'Gowrie,
Houghton 2198, South Africa

The Random House Group Limited Reg. No. 954009

www.randomhouse.co.uk

A CIP catalogue record for this book
is available from the British Library

Papers used by Random House
are natural, recyclable products made from wood grown in
sustainable forests. The manufacturing processes conform to
the environmental regulations of the country of origin

ISBN 978 0 09 946323 8 (from Jan 2007)
ISBN 0 09 946323 7

Typeset by
Palimpsest Book Production Ltd, Polmont, Stirlingshire
Printed and bound in Great Britain by
Bookmarque Ltd, Croydon, Surrey

For Kathryn and Davin with love

ACKNOWLEDGEMENTS

Acknowledgements

My sincere thanks to Georgina Hawtrey-Woore, Justine Taylor and all the other members of the wonderful team at Heinemann/Arrow.

Also to Caroline Sheldon and Rosemary Wills for their helpful support.

Chapter One

Sick with suspense, Rhianon Webster watched helplessly from the doorway as outside on the pavement Pryce Pritchard and Hwyel Barker exchanged punches.

A crowd was already gathering in front of Polly Potter's haberdashery shop in Pontdarw High Street, where Rhianon worked as an assistant, and she wished there was something she could do to stop the two men fighting.

Her heart sank as she saw her sister Sabrina standing in the foreground urging them on, her dark eyes glistening exultantly as the two men traded blows.

Rhianon pushed her way through the knot of onlookers. 'Shush! Don't encourage them, cariad!' she remonstrated, laying a hand on Sabrina's arm in an effort to restrain her sister's excitement as she watched them fight.

Irritably, Sabrina shook her hand away. Straining forward, her voice became hoarse as she continued to urge the two men to even greater antagonism.

Rhianon shuddered. It had been a shock to see Pryce brawling, especially since he was engaged in fisticuffs with her own sister's boyfriend. Normally he was such a gentle giant, not given to scrapping, and loving him as she did she'd hate to see him get hurt.

Hwyel Barker was certainly no match for Pryce Pritchard. Hwyel was thin, slightly built and looked like a schoolboy in comparison with Pryce. Not only was Pryce almost five years older than Hwyel, but his muscles were hardened by years of working as a coal miner. He was strong and powerful-looking with bulging biceps and work-hardened fists, the legacy of swinging a pick for hours at a time in cramped, back-breaking conditions underground.

Hwyel had the soft, lily-white hands of a pen-pusher and the physique to match. Tall and gangling, he looked almost weedy when matched against Pryce's bulk.

As different as Sabrina is from me, Rhianon thought wryly. At seventeen, her younger sister, slimmer than Rhianon, had dark glossy curls, enormous dark brown eyes, a Cupid's bow mouth and long eyelashes. She was also far more voluptuous and a typical flapper. She wore up-to-the-minute styles, dresses that skimmed her figure, their short floating skirts showing her shapely legs to advantage.

Their father, Edwin Webster, a stern-looking angular man in his early sixties, with receding straight dark hair streaked with grey and piercing dark eyes, frowned on such wanton display of flesh. Yet, because he adored Sabrina,

2

he turned a blind eye to her slavish following of the current fashions.

Rhianon was the plain one. Her thick dark hair was straight and nothing she could do would make it curl. When she'd been very little her mother had rolled it up in strips of rag every night. In the morning it would be all frizzy, but an hour or so later it was as straight as ever.

'A plain Jane, that's what you are and no mistake,' her mother had sighed. 'You don't suit pretty dresses either, whatever am I to do about you?'

'Plain as a pikestaff!' her father agreed. 'Let's pray that the Good Lord has imbued her with piety and good sense, since she certainly hasn't been blessed with beauty.'

Her father was right, of course, Rhianon thought resignedly. As she'd grown older she could see that for herself every time she looked in a mirror.

Her dark eyes were too big for her oval face, and her skin so pale it was almost translucent. Even while she was still at school, she looked as though she had the cares of the world on her shoulders.

By then, not only had she accepted that she was a plain Jane but so had everyone else. It was her younger sister who fulfilled all her mother's dreams for a daughter who was as pretty as the little girl on the advertisements for Pears Soap.

As a tiny tot, Sabrina's hair hung in fat

ringlets framing her little round face. She was delightfully dainty and looked adorable in frilly dresses, lacy white socks and patent-leather shoes.

When she was thwarted she pouted so prettily that her tantrum was immediately overlooked. She was never smacked and hardly ever reprimanded. A raised voice would bring crocodile tears, and her rosebud mouth would quiver alarmingly. In next to no time she was swept up, hugged, kissed and forgiven. More often than not it was by her father, whose stern nature seemed to melt like chocolate in the sun where she was concerned.

The two men were still in the roadway fighting, each blow heavy with hatred. Rhianon dreaded what her father would have to say when the news about this fracas reached him. He abhorred physical violence, preferring to assert his authority with harsh words and an overbearing manner.

To the outside world Edwin Webster appeared authoritative and wise, an upright pillar of society with strong religious leanings. A strait-laced man, yet one who was widely respected. Within his own home he was a domineering, hot-tempered bully, intolerant of everyone except Sabrina.

It was a Saturday morning so there were more people than usual to witness what was taking place, including a crowd of children of school age. They were alternately gasping and screaming at the sight of blood, or, like Sabrina, vigorously cheering on the two participants.

There was also a large group of miners. They were watching with mixed feelings, suspecting that the cause of the tussle between the two men had been fuelled by the strike that had just started.

Pryce Pritchard was the Union official at the Pontdarw coal mine where most of the men in the community worked, and he was highly respected for his learning as well as his brawn.

His blue-pitted face might mark him as a miner, but most of his workmates knew that he had ambitions, and that he was studying at night school to become a teacher. Many of the miners thought it would be better if he became a politician. In Parliament he could air his passion for miners' rights to people who might be able to do something positive to change their dreary lot.

'You could tell them exactly how it is, boyo,' they pointed out. 'With your gift of the gab you could make 'em sit up and listen. Let them know what it is really like back here in the Rhondda valley.'

'You could go down to London and give it to them straight from the horse's mouth, mun!'

'Speak out about the shacks most of us have to live in, without water or sanitation, that are pitched perilously on the crumbling mountain-side, boyo!'

'Tell them about the hardships the miners and their families suffer, while the coal bosses live in the lap of luxury.'

'And about the way our young lads have to go down the pits from the age of eight, and work like little slaves. How they have to drag and push the loaded coal trucks along the narrow tunnels, often on their hands and knees.'

'Point out that those youngsters who are too puny to do that have to sit there in the dark, hour after hour, opening and shutting the safety doors to let the wagons pass through. Bloody nightmare for the poor little dabs. Frightened of their own shadows most of them, see!'

'Open their eyes to the hardships a miner's wife has to endure, as well.'

'That's right, mun, and all for a miserly few shillings a week. Not enough to keep body and soul together as you bloody well know.'

Pryce upheld every word they said. The miners' cause was so very dear to his heart that he never tired of listening to them or talking about it.

Rhianon had first been attracted to him by the passion and sincerity she heard in his words, as he talked to a group of fellow students at night school.

When he had singled her out from the crowd, sought her company and confided in her, gradually her admiration had blossomed into love.

'My forebears took part in the Chartist upris-

6

ing in 1839,' he'd told Rhianon proudly the first time he walked home with her after night school. 'Along with colliers from Dukestown, Brynmawr, Nantyglo and a dozen other places, hundreds of them gathered together. Then, at a signal from their convenor, Zephaniah Williams, they marched from Blaenavon to Pontypool where they joined up with another contingent and then marched on to Newport.'

'In support of John Frost, the Chartist leader?' she'd asked in awe.

He'd nodded. 'They carried with them over a million signatures in support of their Charter, but their efforts were scuttled by the intervention of Crawshay Bailey.'

'He was the most powerful Ironmaster of the day, wasn't he?'

Again Pryce had nodded, delighted by her knowledge and interest.

'My great-grandfather was seriously injured in the fierce battle that took place in Newport,' he went on. 'More than twenty men were killed and over fifty men were badly injured in Westgate Square. The military started to fire without warning, see! The soldiers didn't take aim, they just fired at random into the crowd!'

Rhianon soon realised that this bitter memory was one of the reasons why Pryce believed that education, rather than fisticuffs or guns, was a far better solution to the many problems that still beset the mining community.

His attitude was refreshing after listening to

her father's religious bigotry. Despite this, she knew that when challenged, Pryce was ready to physically defend his corner, as he was doing now against Hwyel.

Some of the onlookers, however, aware of local gossip, suspected that there was more than mere politics, or miners' rights, involved between the two men.

Sabrina Webster was a siren. With her big brown eyes, her short skirts and her come-hither looks, it was well known that she would give the glad eye to any man who took her fancy. He didn't even have to be young or handsome. She'd lure her victim into thinking she was infatuated by him. She would delight in leading him on and then, in the twinkling of a smile, or the lowering of her long curling lashes, pretend to be so demure that she was shocked by his advances.

Rhianon was the complete opposite. She was friendly towards one and all, but at the same time so reserved that not one of the men would dream of trying to flirt with her. And, of course, they all knew that she had eyes only for Pryce Pritchard.

Most of the men knew Sabrina was a heart-less minx and could break hearts as skilfully as most of them could hew coal. It didn't stop them trying though. They fluttered about her like moths around a candle, even though they knew that sooner or later they'd get their wings singed.

Once rejected, the men nursed their grievances and suffered the taunts of their mates in sullen silence. They knew that if they made a fuss, or tried to take any retribution, they'd have to contend with the blazing wrath of Edwin Webster.

He would accuse them of lying and threaten them with damnation of the vilest kind. He would even stand up in Capel Bethel and chastise them, because in his eyes Sabrina could do no wrong.

Hwyel Barker was an exception; he had never encountered Edwin Webster's wrath. Hwyel's father, Cledwyn Barker, was an elder at the Capel Bethel where Edwin Webster was a lay reader, and both men thought that the other's offspring was an excellent match for their own child.

Hwyel had never faced going down the pit. His father headed an insurance company and Hwyel had been found a position as a clerk in his office the day he left school.

He'd met Sabrina when she had come to work there as a typist. He'd fallen at once for her pretty face and coquettish manner. What started out as a flirtation became a serious encounter for Sabrina the moment she discovered that Hywel was her boss's son.

It had in no way curbed her delight in flirting, of course. Provocative teasing was second nature to Sabrina. Seeing Pryce striding down the high street, when he would normally have been slaving away underground, had been an opportunity that she couldn't resist. She lost no time in taunting him about lazing around while the rest of the world worked.

It had been this quip that had sparked the fight. Pryce was always ready to pontificate about what the Charter had been trying to do and how even now, with the right inducement, much better conditions could be established.

'This is only the first day, but let me assure you this is going to be the biggest strike this country has ever seen,' he'd told the crowd that gathered round him in the high street. 'Even businessmen can play their part, see,' he'd pronounced, looking straight at Hwyel who was standing on the fringe, Sabrina clinging to his arm.

'You and your dad, for example,' he went on. 'By voting the right man into Parliament, supporting our cause here in the Valleys, you could be invaluable, boyo.'

'Not everyone is a firebrand like you, Pryce Pritchard,' Sabrina responded, laughing and fluttering her eyelashes at him. 'My Hwyel is law-abiding, see!'

'There's no need to break the law, girl,' Pryce told her, 'only to help enforce the regulations that are already law, and then fight to bring in new ones to support our cause.'

'I've never really understood what your cause was,' Sabrina sighed. 'You get paid for what you do the same as Hwyel does.'

The crowd listened in amusement to the spirited exchange between the two of them.

Pryce shook his head. 'Paid, yes, but it is not a fair day's pay for the sort of work we have to do. Your Hwyel, and others like him, wear their white shirts, collars and ties, and sit in comfortable offices. We burrow underground, lying flat on our bellies in muck and water, grappling to make our living.'

Sabrina shrugged prettily. 'You don't have to, no one makes you go down the pit,' she provoked.

'And how else can men here in the Rhondda earn a living? Answer me that?' He looked round at the crowd, which had almost doubled in size since he had started speaking. 'Most of the men have been down the mines since they were mere nippers! They left school long before they could master enough knowledge to do anything other than follow in their own fathers' footsteps.'

'They didn't have to,' Sabrina argued petulantly as the crowd muttered in support and nodded in agreement with Pryce's words. 'They could have stayed on at school longer,' she added lamely.

Pryce shook his head. 'Either you can't understand or won't,' he said impatiently. 'Most of them had to go and work underground because there was no other way they could help support their widowed mother and younger brothers and sisters. Around here the man of the family has usually gone to his grave by the time he is forty! Some die in a fall or an explosion, others are killed by silicosis from the coal dust. As a girl who's lived all her life in Pontdarw you should know all about this without me having to spell it out for you.'

Sabrina shrugged her shapely shoulders. 'That's life, isn't it. If you've got brains then use them and do something else,' she retorted pertly. 'Hwyel never entertained the idea of going down the mine, did you?' she asked, looking towards her boyfriend for support.

'I prefer to use my brain to get a living!'

Pryce regarded him with scorn. 'Darw! Too bloody lily-livered, if you ask me!'

Sabrina bristled. 'Don't let Pryce Pritchard talk to you like that, Hwyel!' she admonished. 'Stick up for yourself, for goodness sake.'

Hwyel smiled smugly. 'I want no truck with riff-raff like him,' he muttered. 'Look where spouting has got him and his workmates. Out on strike, no money, no jobs and no future.'

'So what would you have us do?' Pryce snarled. 'You'd like us to go on being exploited by your kind, I suppose! Parasites who bleed us dry. Your sort exist by preying on other people's fears. They persuade men who have almost nothing to hand over a few coppers out of their meagre earnings each week, so that they can line their own pockets. Oh yes, you assure them that as a result they can rest in their beds at night, knowing that when the end comes at least they won't be tossed into a pauper's grave, because they'll have already paid for their burial!'

The crowd continued to increase, its numbers swelled by men who would normally have been working, but who had found the colliery gates closed and locked when they'd turned up for their shift that morning.

Most of them upheld what Pryce was saying, but there were a few hecklers, men whose plans for the days and weeks ahead had been sabotaged by the strike. Filled with resentment they lent voice to the ensuing argument, stirring up even more anger and indignation.

Rhianon felt deeply troubled. She'd never seen Pryce so fired up before. She had heard him speak so many times, knew how passionate he was about the principles he was fighting for, but now it was as if he was directing all his exasperation at Hwyel. She had lived in Pontdarw all her life and was well able to gauge the mood of the crowd, and she could see they were starting to quarrel amongst themselves as they took sides in the argument going on between Pryce and Hwyel.

For all it was a bright and sunny Saturday morning, the first day of May 1926, when most people were out shopping, or enjoying themselves, the strike was overshadowing their normal pursuits.

Many of the men were waiting for the pubs, or the working men's club, to open around midday. Even though they were hesitant about spending their hard-earned money on drink, since they were unsure of where their next penny was coming from, they knew it was in pub or club that they would be able to garner the latest news about what was happening.

Some of the older men insisted that the strike wouldn't last more than a couple of weeks. Coal was the lifeblood of the nation's industry. Without it factories would be unable to fire their furnaces. Trains needed coal to fuel their engines, the ships down in Cardiff docks relied on coal if they were to sail the oceans. Even the common people in their tiny terraced houses needed coal to keep their fires going in order to warm their homes and to cook their food.

No, the strike couldn't last all that long, they affirmed, but while it did there would be trouble. Men who were idle and without any money became sullen and hot-tempered, bored and bitter. Rhianon was well aware of this, and she was afraid that if other men joined in the spat then a serious brawl could develop.

She tried once more to grab hold of Sabrina's arm and pull her to one side, but again her sister shook her off. Sabrina seemed determined to fuel the discord between Pryce and Hwyel. Rhianon couldn't see the sense of it, couldn't understand why Sabrina was so intent on doing this. Surely she could see that Pryce was by far the stronger of the two men and that Hwyel was bound to get hurt?

The fight deepened in its intensity. The two men were both breathing heavily, their blows becoming more frenzied. Hwyel was delivering short sharp little jabs against Pryce, who stood facing him squarely, and warding them off with a flick of his outstretched arm. It was like watching a puppy yapping at a bulldog, Rhianon thought.

Then suddenly Pryce retaliated. His massive fist shot out and made contact with Hwyel's jaw, stopping the younger man in his tracks.

Hwyel was winded. He fell back, cracking the back of his head against the edge of the pavement.

'You brute! Look what you've done now!' Sabrina screamed, her face chalk white, her deep brown eyes, minutes earlier gleaming with excitement, now dark with horror.

She pulled back, covering her face with her hands, as blood trickled from the corner of Hwyel's mouth.

Responding to Sabrina's hysterical scream, Rhianon pushed her way through the crowd. She looked anxiously at Pryce, but he avoided her eyes. She dropped to her knees to check Hwyel's condition. Her voice was shaking as she looked up.

'He's unconscious. Can someone get a doctor or an ambulance?'

The men standing around began to voice off uneasily.

'Rubbish, girl!'

'Knocked out, poor bugger!'

'That was a cracking blow!'

'Silly bugger should know better than to pick a fight with the likes of Pryce Pritchard!'

'Teach him not to mouth off about things he knows nothing about!'

'Shame on you! Pryce Pritchard's twice his size, mun!'

'That'll teach young Hwyel a lesson he won't forget in a hurry.'

Rhianon tried to shut her ears to their comments. She concentrated on loosening Hwyel's tie and undoing the starched collar of his white shirt.

The commotion increased. Women abandoned their shopping to join their menfolk. Tempers began to erupt. There was pushing and shoving, and more than a few blows exchanged before a policeman came on the scene and restored order.

An uneasy hush prevailed as the ambulance arrived and Hwyel was lifted into it.

'Is anyone coming to hospital with him, then?' the driver asked.

Rhianon looked round for Pryce and her sister, but they were nowhere to be seen.

'You'd better go with them, Rhianon!' someone in the crowd called out. 'Your sister's scarpered and so has that Pryce Pritchard.'

'How can I go! I should be behind the counter in Mrs Potter's shop right now, not out here in the road.'

'She won't mind, she'll understand.'

'Come on, this man needs urgent attention so make your minds up,' the ambulance driver said as he started to close up the doors.

'Dammo di! What a to-do!' Polly Potter exclaimed as she came bustling over to see what was happening. 'It looks serious to me, so you'd better go with them, Rhianon. It's no good hanging around for your sister, she'd never cope, you know that as well as I do.'

'Are you sure?' Rhianon smiled at her gratefully. 'I'll be back as soon as I can,' she promised.

'You do whatever is necessary, girl, and then when you get back you can tell us how he is.'

'Can you get someone to let Mr Barker know what has happened, and could you let my father know as well?' Rhianon asked her.

'They've probably already heard, cariad,' Polly Potter answered. 'Now up into that ambulance and be off with you and get that poor boyo into hospital.'

Pryce Pritchard stood rock still for a few seconds, waiting for Hwyel to get to his feet again. Only his quick deep breathing, making his broad chest rise and fall like some fast-beating pump, gave any indication as to the stress he was under.

When the man lying on the ground made no move to stand up, and Pryce heard Rhianon say they should send for medical help, he elbowed his way through the gawping onlookers and began to walk away down the road.

Sabrina, who had been watching his every movement, chased after him, calling out his name, ordering him to stop, but he paid no attention. He felt ashamed that he had lost his temper and resorted to violence.

There were amused grins from all sides.

'She'll be giving him a taste of her tongue, and no maybe.'

'Duw anwyl! I wouldn't want to be in Pryce Pritchard's shoes!'

'Just wait until she catches up with him, right little fireball she can be, mun.'

'Perhaps someone should go after her then, the temper she's in she might scratch his bloody eyes out.'

'You reckon there might be another fight in the offing, then?'

'It's more than likely, seeing the frenzy she's in!'

'Exploding with anger, I'd say, mun.'

'Leave them to it, I say, it's none of our bloody business.'

'That's right! There's been enough damage done for one day.'

'Pryce Pritchard's a big boyo, he can take care of himself.'

If Sabrina heard them calling her back, or even if she overheard any of their loud-mouthed comments, she paid no attention whatsoever.

18

Chapter Two

All the way to the hospital Rhianon perched uncomfortably on the slatted wooden seat by the side of Hwyel's stretcher. She watched him anxiously. He lay so still, his chest barely rising, his mouth slack, blood still oozing from his head wound.

When the ambulance pulled up in front of the four-storey grey stone building, and Hwyel was trundled inside, she followed down endless bleak corridors.

As he was wheeled into a ward, an officious middle-aged nurse in a stiffly starched green and white uniform, her white cap completely covering her hair and making her face look even more severe, barred Rhianon's way.

'You can't come in here!' she snapped. 'If you wish to wait while we examine him then sit over there,' she ordered, pointing to a row of small uninviting metal chairs in a recess in the corridor.

Time seemed to stand still. The sterile smell of antiseptic made Rhianon's stomach churn.

White-coated doctors, stethoscopes dangling like cumbersome necklets, came hurrying along the corridor, their echoing footsteps breaking the uneasy silence. When they disappeared into the ward, a draught of medicated air wafted out before the doors swung closed.

There was no clock, no way of telling how long she had been sitting there. With each long-drawn-out minute Rhianon's concern because Pryce had left the scene without a word to her, and her fears for Hwyel's welfare, increased.

Her mind was filled alternately with the memory of Hwyel's skinny figure as he'd squared up to Pryce's manly physique, and the memory of his ashen face, with his cut and swollen eye and the blood trickling from one corner of his half-open mouth, as he lay on the ground.

When the ambulance men had lifted him up there had been a pool of blood on the roadway underneath him. She had thought at first that it was from his mouth, following the knock-out blow that had sent him crashing to the ground. As they lifted him she had seen that he had also cut the back of his head when he'd fallen backwards.

She was concerned about how the fight had started. Pryce was such an important part of her life, loving him as she did, that she was fearful of the consequences for him if Hwyel really was seriously injured, especially since what had happened appeared to have been instigated by her sister. She couldn't understand Sabrina's motive, unless it was to try and ruin her relationship with Pryce because she was jealous of their closeness.

Hwyel might be puny, self-opinionated and flashy with his sharp suits and expensive watch, but his father was a man of considerable standing in Pontdarw.

If Hwyel was badly hurt the blame would be placed fair and square on Pryce's shoulders, and Rhianon suspected that Hwyel and his father would exact retribution.

What form that would take she had no idea, but she was pretty certain that Cledwyn Barker would demand justice. Since he could afford to hire a skilled lawyer, the outcome for Pryce seemed bleak. He would not be able to pay a heavy fine, and she shuddered inwardly and refused to contemplate what the alternative might be.

The news of Hwyel's condition, when it did come, was even more dire than Rhianon had anticipated.

'Mr Barker is still unconscious. He has a fractured skull and several serious lacerations to his face as well as a broken jaw,' the stiffly starched nurse informed her curtly.

'Can I see him?' Rhianon asked.

'Are you a relation?'

Rhianon shook her head. 'No, but he is a friend of the family . . .'

'Then I'm afraid it's impossible,' the nurse interrupted brusquely. 'Only his immediate family can visit his bedside. I trust they have been informed about what has happened?'

Before Rhianon could answer there was the sound of hurrying footsteps and Hwyel's father, imposing in his dark pinstripe three-piece suit and highly polished black boots, came striding down the corridor. A pudgy little woman, dressed in a drab navy blue costume buttoned high to her neck, mousy brown hair almost hidden under a coal-scuttle black felt hat, was scurrying along in his wake.

'Rhianon, whatever are you doing here? Where is Sabrina?' Mr Barker asked sharply. Without waiting for her reply he addressed the nurse. 'My son, Hwyel Barker, has been admitted to this ward, so I'd like to see him,' he intoned authoritatively.

'Yes, sir.' Her manner suddenly became deferential. 'If you will come this way, Mr Barker.' She hesitated and looked at the woman who was standing at his side. 'Mrs Barker?'

'Yes, yes, this is my wife. Come along, Mona, don't let's waste any more time,' Cledwyn Barker exclaimed impatiently.

The nurse remained hesitant. 'Your son is still unconscious, and I should warn you that he has received several injuries to his face and head, so . . .'

'Oh, my poor boy, my darling Hwyel!' Mrs Barker tottered ahead, making for the ward doors before the nurse could stop her. Mr Barker and the nurse followed quickly behind.

Rhianon waited anxiously for the nurse to

return. When she did, she told Rhianon briskly, 'There's nothing more you can do here so you may as well go home.'

'Can't I see him just for a moment? He's my sister's boyfriend and I would like to be able to tell her how he is.'

The nurse's starched cap wobbled precariously as she shook her head emphatically. 'Even if I agreed to let you come in and see him I doubt whether his parents would allow it.'

'Couldn't you ask them?' Rhianon pleaded.

'It's quite pointless, he's unconscious. There's nothing more to be said,' the nurse told her abruptly.

Rhianon bit down on her lower lip. 'He . . . he is going to be all right, isn't he? He is going to pull through?'

'You are wasting your time and mine,' the nurse told her impatiently, looking pointedly at the fob watch pinned on the bodice of her uniform. 'There's nothing more I can tell you until he comes round, and that mightn't be for hours, or days even.'

Rhianon stared at her anxiously. 'His other injuries, the cuts, the bleeding . . .'

The nurse shrugged offhandedly. 'I've told you all there is for you to know, now you must leave. There is nothing you can do here at the moment. You can come back later, or some time tomorrow, and ask at the reception desk for news if you wish to do so.'

* * *

The days that followed put a strain on all concerned. Edwin Webster was outspoken in his condemnation of what Pryce had done, and Sabrina vociferously supported her father.

For all that, Rhianon noticed that when Sabrina spoke to her about Pryce her attitude seemed to change. From the look in her sister's eyes it was almost as if she was admiring his prowess.

Rhianon felt utterly confused as she listened to her. Some of the things Sabrina said made no sense to her. It seemed as if Sabrina had some sort of understanding with Pryce that Rhianon didn't share, but she assured herself that this was all nonsense, a figment of her imagination.

When she confided her suspicion to Polly Potter the older woman laughed sardonically.

'Your eyes are open at last, are they, cariad! I've warned you to look to your laurels or that young sister of yours would be taking Pryce Pritchard away from you!'

'That's rubbish, Polly, and you shouldn't say such things,' Rhianon defended. 'Why on earth would she want to do that when she has a boyfriend of her own?'

'There's daft you are, girl! Too trusting for your own good,' Polly scolded. 'Anyone with eyes in their head can see why she'd want to do it. Pryce Pritchard is twice the man Hwyel Barker can ever hope to be.'

'Pryce is years older than Sabrina though, he's five years older than me even.'

'What difference does that make, cariad? In fact, that's probably half the attraction. Man of the world, see! Not a skinny young fellow who is little more than a schoolboy.'

'You're wrong, Polly. Sabrina thinks the world of Hwyel!'

'Of his wallet maybe, and the fun he can offer her, but not of him as a person. Stands to reason she'd sooner be on the arm of a man with a physique like Pryce. It's only human nature, cariad.'

'There's more to it than that, Polly. I can't put my finger on it, but Sabrina seems to change when she's talking to me about Pryce.'

'Then don't let them be in each other's company any more than you can help,' Polly warned her.

Rhianon sighed. 'There's not much chance of that, not unless they meet up in the street. My father has forbidden me to bring Pryce to the house.'

'Because of the fight!' Polly said, her mouth pursed scornfully.

'No, even before that. He's never approved of Pryce's radical views, and now with this strike on he won't hear his name mentioned even. Father takes Mr Barker's side over the fight as well, of course. They both put all the blame on Pryce.'

'The sooner that young Hwyel is out of

25

hospital and can explain what happened the better,' Polly opined. 'It's high time he was on his feet again and up and about.'

'From what Sabrina tells me, and she gets the news straight from Mr Barker each day, Hwyel is not doing at all well. He was unconscious for three hours and even now he is nowhere near back to his normal self.'

'Are you saying that your sister hasn't been in to see him then?'

Rhianon looked uneasy. 'No, not yet. The day after it happened she was very keen to do so, but since then she seems to have changed her mind. Now she says wild horses wouldn't get her in there.'

'Funny girl that one,' Polly murmured, shaking her head from side to side so that the jowls beneath her chin wobbled like a pink blancmange.

Rhianon sighed. 'Father sympathises with her. He says it is because she has such a tender nature. She's told him that she can't bear to see someone she loves in such distress.'

Polly snorted. 'A load of old tripe if ever I heard it! What does her boss think about her refusing to go and see his precious son then?'

Rhianon shook her head. 'I've no idea.'

'And what has Pryce Pritchard got to say for himself? Worried stiff he must be.'

Again Rhianon shook her head. 'I've barely had a chance to ask him, I've hardly seen him alone since it happened. Caught up in this old strike, see! Kept busy he is, drumming up support. As the local Union official he has a lot of organising to do, and he has to speak at so many meetings, not just here in Pontdarw, but throughout the Rhondda, as far afield as Pontypridd and Merthyr.'

'Yes, it's a terrible situation and one that is growing more heated by the day, according to what I hear,' Polly agreed.

'Well, let's hope it is settled soon so that the men can get back to work in the next couple of months,' Rhianon said fervently.

'If they don't then there will be a lot of hardship for their wives and children this coming winter,' Polly Potter declared ominously.

Her concern was echoed by most of the customers who came in over the next few days. Rhianon felt wretched as she listened to them, wondering how it was going to affect her and Pryce. It seemed to be taking up so much of his time that she saw less and less of him.

The strike was still at its height when they received news that Hwyel Barker had taken a turn for the worse.

'Have words with your daughter, and insist she must come to the hospital,' Cledwyn Barker instructed Edwin Webster sternly. 'I've told her countless times that Hwyel is constantly asking for her, but she takes no notice at all.'

Sabrina looked taken aback when her father spoke to her about it, but she remained adamant

27

that she didn't want to visit Hwyel, not while he was in hospital.

For the first time ever, Edwin Webster lost his temper with her. 'You'll go if I have to drag you there,' he thundered. 'How do you think it will reflect on me if you don't go to visit him?' he railed.

'It has nothing to do with you,' Sabrina snuffled.

'Of course it has! You are my daughter. He is the son of one of the elders of Capel Bethel. Now, get your coat on and I'll accompany you to the hospital myself.'

Sabrina hesitated uneasily.

As she saw her father's colour rising and a vein in his forehead pulsing angrily, Rhianon gave Sabrina a warning look. 'Perhaps, Father, it would be better if I was the one who went to the hospital with Sabrina,' she suggested quietly.

Slightly mollified, although he knew it was a face-saving gesture on his elder daughter's part, Edwin Webster grudgingly agreed.

Once they were out of the house, Sabrina again insisted that she had no intention of going to the hospital to see Hwyel.

'You go and see him if you want to,' she told Rhianon. 'I'm going for a walk.'

'You can't do that,' Rhianon exclaimed aghast. 'Surely one visit is not too much to ask! We'll both be in trouble if Father finds out you didn't do as he told you!'

'Then don't tell him. I'm hardly likely to do so, am I?'

'How can you be so hard-hearted, Sabrina? What do I say to Mr and Mrs Barker if they're there? They're bound to ask where you are, because Mr Barker told Father that Hwyel had been asking for you.'

'I simply can't do it, Rhianon, so tell them what you like. If Hwyel's unconscious most of the time then he won't know whether I've been in to see him or not.'

'His parents will know!'

'Then say I'm not feeling well, or that I have a cold and I don't want Hwyel to catch it. Say whatever comes into your head. I'm sure you'll manage to think of something.'

Rhianon worried about it all the way to the hospital. She hated having to tell lies. Mr Barker would be well aware that Sabrina didn't have a cold, otherwise she would be off work. He probably wouldn't even believe her if she said her sister wasn't feeling well.

The problem went right out of her head when she reached the hospital. There was no need for her to make excuses on Sabrina's behalf because much more serious matters were afoot.

The moment she reached the ward and saw Mrs Barker, white-faced and shaking, being brought out supported by a nurse and Mr Barker, and being taken into a side room, she steeled herself for bad news.

'Hwyel has had a relapse, he's unconscious again,' Mr Barker told her.

Relaying the news to her father that Hwyel had relapsed into unconsciousness was distressing for Rhianon.

Her father was deeply shocked. He resorted to quotations from the Bible to cover his dismay and fear of what the eventual outcome might be if Hwyel didn't make a full recovery. The police would be bound to investigate the cause of the skirmish in which Hwyel Barker had been so badly injured, and his daughters would be implicated.

'I'll make a pot of tea,' Rhianon said helplessly. 'You look as though you need one, Father.'

'Yes, yes, do that!' he said dismissively.

'Where's Sabrina?' he asked when she returned with a tray. 'Has she stayed at the hospital?'

'No . . . she went for a walk,' Rhianon said hesitantly.

'And you let her!'

'I thought one of us should remain at the hospital,' she defended, as she poured out the tea.

Chapter Three

It was almost ten o'clock when Sabrina returned home. Rhianon and Edwin Webster were almost out of their minds with worry.

They had no idea where she could be. Her father paced the floor, convinced that Hwyel being injured so badly in the fight, and then being taken off to hospital, had proved too much for Sabrina to bear. He even went as far as to contemplate alerting the police and asking them to search for her, fearing that she might have done something foolish.

Rhianon felt almost as anxious as her father, but for a different reason. He was so upset she felt she couldn't leave him, although she wanted to try and find Pryce and warn him that the police might be looking for him.

Polly Potter's remarks kept surfacing in her mind, as she waited for Sabrina to return. And although she refused to let herself believe that there could be even a grain of truth in Polly's suspicions, she kept wondering if Sabrina had taken it into her head to go and alert Pryce to the situation.

Sabrina had no interest in Pryce or his welfare, Rhianon kept telling herself. Sabrina thought him socially beneath her, a rough miner even though he was studying to better himself. When their father accused him of being a rabble-raiser she'd looked smugly pleased, and was quick to point out that in comparison Hwyel was well bred and had fine prospects.

'In time Hwyel will be head of the Barker Insurance Company,' she'd told them complacently. 'Any day now his father is going to promote him to the position of Accounts Manager.'

She'd got it all planned. Once she had Hwyel's ring on her engagement finger she'd start collecting her trousseau. In a couple of years' time, after a stylish white wedding, she and Hwyel would move into one of the smart new houses that were being built on the outskirts of Pontdarw. A family would follow, but not until she had a well-furnished home that she could be proud of showing off to her friends. But now that dream might possibly be over, Rhianon reminded herself, and all her sister's plans might disintegrate.

Sabrina's explanation was that she had been so overcome by the news that Hwyel was worse that she had gone for a long walk to try and sort things out in her mind, and had lost track of time. This mollified her father.

'Straight off to bed with you, my girl,' he ordered solicitously. 'Rhianon will bring you up a cup of hot milk laced with honey to help you sleep.'

Sabrina smiled complacently, then flung her arms round his neck, and implanted a warm kiss on his stern furrowed cheek.

'You are the kindest, most understanding father in the world,' she breathed softly.

He patted her shoulder, puffed up with pride.

'Run along then and remember, next time you have a problem come and talk to me about it, don't run away. You could have come to some grave harm, you know.'

'Aren't you going to ask if there is any news about Hwyel?' Rhianon queried as her sister moved towards the stairs.

Sabrina paused. 'You went to the hospital?'

'Yes, because you weren't prepared to do so.'

Sabrina shrugged. 'So how is he? Did his dad come and take him home?'

'Mr and Mrs Barker were at the hospital, but they weren't there to take him home. Hwyel has lapsed into unconsciousness again.'

The colour drained from Sabrina's cheeks and her mouth dropped open. 'So what does that mean?'

'It means he is in a very critical condition. Mr Barker has notified the police and they have been looking for Pryce so that they can question him about exactly what happened.'

Sabrina's hand flew up to cover her mouth. She turned quickly and headed for the front door.

'Where are you off to now?' Edwin Webster intervened. 'They won't let you into the hospital

33

at this time of night. Leave it until the morning, there may be better news by then.'

Sabrina's eyes were glistening angrily as she spun round and faced him. 'I'm not going to the hospital. You heard what Rhianon said about Hwyel. If he dies then Pryce will be accused of killing him!'

'And so he should be!' Edwin Webster thundered.

'I know where he is so I'm going to warn him,' Sabrina pronounced.

'What makes you feel you should be the one to do that?' Rhianon exclaimed.

Sabrina gave her a withering look. 'I know Pryce is supposed to be your boyfriend, but you don't appear to be at all worried about what happens to him.'

'That's not true!' Two spots of brilliant red stained Rhianon's pale cheeks. 'I don't just care about him, I love him and he feels the same way about me.'

'Are you sure?' Sabrina's eyebrows lifted. 'It really doesn't show!'

Rhianon bristled. 'You're a fine one to talk, what about your feelings for Hwyel? You haven't even been to visit him in hospital, although he's been asking for you, and you don't seem to be upset by the news that he is worse.'

Sabrina shrugged. 'Nothing I can do about that now, and, as I've said before, if he is unconscious, there's no point in me wasting my time going to see him.'

'Sabrina! You are utterly heartless! I'll try and forget I ever heard you say that,' Rhianon told her sternly.

'Please yourself! Let's hope I manage to find Pryce before the police do,' she retorted.

It took Rhianon's diplomatic pleading, as well as Edwin Webster's adamant stand that it was none of their concern what happened to Pryce Pritchard, to convince Sabrina that she was not going to be allowed to leave the house again that night.

In a furious temper she stormed off upstairs, slamming her bedroom door so hard that the cups on the Welsh dresser clanged against each other like a peal of bells.

Following her father's orders, Rhianon made her own way to bed.

'Leave Sabrina to simmer down. It will all have blown over by breakfast time and then perhaps we can talk some sense into her,' he declared. 'Foolish girl that she is! Too soft-hearted by far!'

Rhianon thought there was much more to it than that. Sabrina's behaviour puzzled her, in particular her remarks concerning Pryce's whereabouts. How could her sister know about his movements when Rhianon herself had barely spoken to him since the incident?

She still couldn't understand why Pryce had walked away before the ambulance had arrived. Perhaps, she thought, he suspected that the blow had done some irreparable damage, and he was concerned about the reaction of the crowd when they discovered this.

Even so, surely by now he would have sought her out to ask about Hwyel. Unless he was deliberately trying to avoid her?

She tried to convince herself that it was because Pryce was preoccupied. The local miners' strike had been only the beginning. Now the TUC had announced a General Strike. Already the effects were beginning to bite and touch all their lives.

There were reports that in the bigger towns and cities like Cardiff and London, clerks and undergraduates were driving buses and trams, and that these were being overturned by strikers whenever they found volunteers at the wheel.

Marches occurred daily, but so far they were mostly peaceful, although everyone feared that couldn't last as the strikers became ever more incensed. Barricades were erected to protect essential services. The Government organised a fleet of private motors and lorries to keep public passenger services flowing and to ensure the transport of goods. At the main ports, sailors were being used as temporary dock-workers. Soldiers were employed as escorts for convoys carrying essential foodstuffs. Two battalions of the guards and ten armoured cars were used to secure food supplies lying in the London docks which were being picketed by strikers.

The Home Secretary, Joynson-Hicks, called for special constables to help the police control the crowds. He inaugurated fifty thousand of them in London alone.

No newspapers were being printed because all the workers involved were on strike, so Joynson-Hicks arranged for the Government to publish a daily *British Gazette*.

Miners hung around outside the pits, many sitting on the ground and playing cards to pass the time. At home their wives pinched and scraped, trying to feed their families on anything they could lay their hands on.

In Pontdarw the men gathered in groups on street corners to discuss the latest developments between the Union officials and pit-owners. Arguments about the rights and wrongs of the strike became heated and bitter, but words, not blows, were exchanged. Marches were planned; fresh resolutions were drawn up; new leaders were constantly being appointed.

There was a feeling of disquiet whenever Pryce put in an appearance, or even when his name was mentioned.

No one disputed that he was the finest speaker they had, or that he could hold his own when it came to debating, handling the hecklers, or confronting the bosses. Even so, remembering the unfortunate outcome of his fight with Hwyel Barker, the people of Pontdarw felt uneasy about the part he was playing in the strike.

It was at the back of all their minds that until Hwyel Barker was fully recovered and out of hospital there was always the possibility that his father might involve the police over the fight. If he did, then since Pryce was their Union representative, it might reflect adversely on the Pontdarw miners.

'If Hwyel doesn't recover, there won't be any question of "if the matter is reported",' they told each other gloomily. 'Once the police are involved then heaven alone knows what will happen. Pryce Pritchard could end up on an assault charge or even be clapped in jail.'

No one had the nerve to say this to Pryce's face, but by avoiding doing so they only increased the general feeling of tension.

Pryce had been keeping away from Rhianon ever since the first day of the strike, when, egged on by Sabrina, he had ended up in a fight with Hwyel Barker. He knew he'd been in the wrong, and that he had been foolish to let Sabrina get under his skin with her flirtatious taunts.

He had so much on his mind. Not only was he partly responsible for the men at Pontdarw colliery being on strike, but he knew the uprising would probably put the hopes and plans for his own future into jeopardy.

He'd studied hard at night school and his final exams were only weeks away. Once he passed them, and was able to begin a new career as a teacher, he would ask Rhianon to marry him.

He loved her deeply and admired the way she had fought back against life's tribulations. Her father was not an easy man to contend with, yet she managed to placate his moods. Ever since her mother's death she had run a home for him and her sister Sabrina, worked at Polly Potter's and also attended night school. Like him, she dreamed of being a teacher one day.

He knew she received no encouragement from her family. Her father was scornful of her ambition, though Pryce was pretty sure he'd be the first to boast once she passed her exams and had her teaching certificate.

Sabrina already had the advantage of commercial training as a typist. She'd probably marry her boss's son and set up in a smart little house. Or she'd find someone with even deeper pockets. She was an inveterate flirt and it was fortunate for her that Hwyel was too egotistical, or too blind, to realise it.

Pryce's blood ran hot every time he thought of the overtures she had made to him, some of them even in Rhianon's presence.

The latest had been right after the fight with Hwyel, an encounter of which he was now bitterly ashamed and which was the main reason why he was avoiding Rhianon.

He'd been overcome with remorse when he saw that Hwyel was being taken off to hospital after he'd punched him, and because of this he'd walked away. Later on, he'd asked around for information, but no one had known very much because the hospital would only allow his family to visit him. Speculation and guess-work filled the air.

When Sabrina came looking for him later he'd been relieved, assuming she would have the latest news about Hwyel.

When she broke down and started sobbing because they wouldn't let anyone in to see Hwyel except his parents, it seemed to be the most natural thing in the world to take her into his arms and try and comfort her.

She'd clung to him, as soft and fragile as a kitten, burying her face against him so trust-ingly that his arms tightened. He wanted to impart some of his strength as well as show her some compassion. At that moment he would have done anything to quieten the sobs that were tearing through her slim body, and the rapid pounding of her heart that he could feel against his own chest.

He'd never been a womaniser, never had the time or the inclination to dally with girls. Rhianon had been different. He'd admired her serenity and wisdom, from the first moment they'd met. His feelings for her were deep, a part of his very being. What he felt for Sabrina was a surge of sympathy, a desire to stop her crying and alleviate the cloud of black misery which was enveloping her.

What happened next was like something in a dream. She looked up into his face, her huge brown eyes two dark unfathomable pools. Her glistening lips parted, inviting his own to take possession of them. The next minute his embrace was no longer one of comfort, but one of passion, of need, the desire of a man for a beautiful woman.

If she had pulled back at that moment, or shown the slightest resistance, nothing more would have happened. She had done neither. She had pressed her body against his, setting him afire.

Their love-making had been savage and primitive. His pent-up frustrations, his unfulfilled desire for Rhianon, combined with Sabrina's need for a real man after Hwyel's boyish fumblings, brought about an explosion of passion that rocked them both.

Chapter Four

The news that Pryce had been taken to the police station came as no surprise to Rhianon.

She had feared that would happen right from the moment Hwyel had been driven away in the ambulance, especially since he had been on the danger list ever since.

Even so, she resented Sabrina bringing her the news and then being so evasive about the time and place of the event.

When she had questioned her, Sabrina had almost bitten her head off.

'What on earth does it matter where he was?' she snapped.

'Well, it doesn't really,' Rhianon agreed. 'It was just that I was wondering if the police took him away from one of his meetings.'

'A lot you care since you never attend any of them,' Sabrina told her scornfully.

Rhianon let it pass. Sabrina was in such a strange mood lately, criticising Pryce one minute and then championing him the next, that she didn't know where she stood with her.

Sabrina still hadn't been to the hospital to see Hwyel, although it was now five days since he'd been taken there and Rhianon thought her excuses very feeble.

'I can't visit him during the day because Mr Barker expects me to be in the office,' Sabrina sighed, her face so full of concern that Rhianon half believed her.

'You could pop along in your lunch hour,' Rhianon suggested.

'What lunch hour? I haven't had a proper midday break all week, we're so busy.'

'Well, after work then, before you come home.'

Sabrina shook her head, her long dark curls bouncing on her shoulders. 'You know how Dad hates it if one of us is late for a meal. "A family that eats together stays together",' she quoted sardonically.

'He'd make an exception under the circumstances, I know he would,' Rhianon protested. 'You needn't stay there very long and I could always delay our meal until you came home.'

'Mess your evening up, wouldn't it, if that happened,' Sabrina jibed. 'It might make you late meeting Pryce.'

Rhianon shrugged. 'That wouldn't matter. We've not had any time to meet up since the strike started. He is too caught up in all these old meetings, see.'

'And you let him get away with it?'

Rhianon sighed. 'He told one of the officials to tell me he's been asked to address meetings at Merthyr, Dowlais, Pontypridd, Tonypandy and even Cardiff, so there's not much chance

43

of him having a free evening in the near future either. He's a good speaker. The men listen to every word he tells them because they know he's studied these things and knows what he's talking about.'

'Surely you should go along and let him see that you support him? Maybe we should go to one of his meetings and hear for ourselves what he has to say, perhaps the next time he's speaking in Pontdarw.'

'Not a lot of point in doing that, cariad, seeing we haven't a vote. Leave the seats for the men, they're the ones who can influence the outcome of this old strike.'

'Wouldn't you like to hear him speak, though?' Sabrina persisted. 'Not on a street corner, but in a proper hall?'

'I know most of the things he's likely to say, I've heard them that many times when he's been spouting off as we walk home after night school.'

Sabrina looked at her wide-eyed. 'Is that the sort of thing you talk about when you're together?'

'Some of the time,' Rhianon admitted. 'Politics and the welfare of the miners mean a great deal to Pryce.'

Sabrina pulled a face. 'I know that, but it's not the sort of conversation you want with your boyfriend, now is it?'

Colour flooded Rhianon's cheeks. 'Well, we don't discuss those sort of things all the time,'

44

she said primly. 'Anyway,' she went on, anxious to change the subject, 'this has nothing to do with you going to see Hwyel.'

'Very true,' Sabrina agreed, 'so what do you say if we call a truce? If you stop quizzing me about what I intend to do about visiting Hwyel, then I'll stop asking you personal questions about you and Pryce.'

'It's not as simple as that though. Father wants to know why you haven't been to see Hwyel. Mr Barker has spoken directly to him about it. He said he's asked you to go to the hospital himself and you've taken no notice.'

Sabrina scowled. Her mildly teasing mood suddenly changed. Spots of angry colour stained her cheeks and her dark eyes narrowed venomously.

'Will you stop nagging and let the matter drop, and don't think you can get Dad to persuade me either. I can't stand hospitals, as you very well know, so I'm not visiting Hwyel no matter who asks me to do so. Have I made myself clear?'

Rhianon sighed as her sister flounced off, muttering exasperatedly as she went upstairs to her bedroom.

She hoped Sabrina would cool off and reappear in a better mood before their father came in, otherwise there would be more arguments and cross-questioning to be endured.

Edwin Webster, however, was too concerned about what was happening to the country to notice his two daughters' frosty manner towards each other when they all sat down for their evening meal.

He did notice that Sabrina was wearing a delicate blue taffeta and chiffon dress, however, and commented on how pretty she looked.

'Let's hope this strike will end soon,' he went on, 'before it ruins all our lives and the future for you young ones. The newspapers are full of gloom-laden stories about what is taking place all over Britain.'

'You mean about troops being needed to help guard convoys of foodstuffs between the docks and shops, and reports that people from all walks of life are still driving the buses, trams and trains,' Sabrina sighed.

'And this is only the beginning,' Edwin Webster intoned solemnly. 'Give it a few weeks and we'll have food riots and general mayhem to contend with, you mark my words.'

'Things may not come to that,' Rhianon said placatingly. 'It may all be over in a week or so.'

'That's hardly likely when there's miscreants like Pryce Pritchard mouthing off and inciting the men to madness,' he barked.

'I'm sure most men can decide for themselves what action they want to take, no matter what Pryce or anyone else says to them,' Rhianon defended.

'There's daft you talk, girl!' he reprimanded her sharply. 'The men are idle, standing around on street corners or sitting on the ground outside the pits, their minds a void waiting to be filled. Easily led they are when whipped into a frenzy by the wild tongue of a firebrand like Pryce Pritchard.' He glared across at Rhianon. 'You've not been seeing him, I hope? Stay clear of that blackguard, you understand!'

'I haven't spoken to him since the strike started,' Rhianon murmured.

'Only because he hasn't had any time for you because he's been too busy attending meetings,' Sabrina commented with a sly little laugh.

Rhianon's anger surged, but she bit her lip and said nothing. She refused to let her sister goad her into a row that she knew she had no hope of winning.

Sabrina flouted authority, even that of their father, who was well known throughout the Valleys for his severity. He was a deeply religious man, strict to the point of harshness with everyone he came into contact with.

Whilst he would reproach Rhianon for the slightest fault, even now when she was almost twenty and old enough to be married with a family of her own, he readily forgave Sabrina for her indiscretions.

Rhianon sighed. Life had not been easy since her mam had died of TB seven years earlier. Her father had looked on it as God's intervention and from then on devoted himself to his church activities. He expected Rhianon to run their home with the same proficiency that he had demanded from his wife.

As a result she had always been in awe and fear of her father, obeying his every wish and command. Sabrina, however, had not only disobeyed all his rules but had been able to twist him round her little finger.

He had never taken off his leather belt to her, no matter what misdemeanours she committed. He had never scoffed at her ambitions as he had done when Rhianon told him she would like to stay on at school and study to be a schoolteacher. He had been proud when Sabrina told him she was walking out with Hwyel Barker, but scornful when Rhianon had brought Pryce home to meet him.

'That man is nothing but a rabble-raiser,' he told her contemptuously, 'inciting his fellow workers to be dissatisfied with the role the Lord has ordained they should fulfil.'

He had forbidden her to bring him to the house ever again. Since then she'd had to confine their meetings to when their classes ended after night school, and he walked her home.

At first Pryce had talked mostly about their studies, and then about his dream of improving conditions for his fellow mine-workers. With the passing of time their friendship had deepened. Contrary to her father's opinion she found that Pryce was a highly sensitive, deep-thinking man. He was passionate about his beliefs and determined to do something to improve working conditions for miners, despite the opposition of those in authority.

He could also be equally passionate in expressing his feelings for her. No one, before Pryce, had shown her affection or tenderness since her mother had died. Rhianon felt the colour creeping up her neck and flooding her face as she remembered the blissful times in his strong arms, the touch of his firm lips on her own.

The sweet words he whispered to her made her feel so special, such an important part of his life, just as he was of hers. Often last thing at night, as she settled down in bed, she would bring those words to mind and let them lull her to sleep.

The minute their meal was finished, Sabrina pushed her chair back from the table, smoothed down her dress and then walked over and kissed her father on the cheek.

'What was that for, my dear?' he asked, his hand reaching out and grasping her arm before she could move away.

'I'm going out,' she said, smiling, 'and you will probably be in bed by the time I come home.'

He frowned. 'Why will you be so late?'

'I'm going to a concert in Pontypridd with two of the girls from work.'

Seeing his disapproving look Sabrina added quickly, 'The father of one of the girls is coming with us, so there is nothing at all for you to be worried about. It's a very important concert.

It's to celebrate the Silver Jubilee of King George V. Her father bought the tickets as a special surprise treat because it's her birthday.'

'That sounds very enjoyable, my lovely, but shouldn't you be visiting poor Hwyel in hospital?' he admonished gently.

Sabrina sighed soulfully. 'I would have forgone the evening if I thought I could do any good by going to see him.' Her voice dropped to a petulant whimper as she dabbed at her eyes with a scrap of lace-edged cambric. 'His dad wanted me to go with him, but when he said Hwyel doesn't even know when people are there, I told him I couldn't stand that, it would make me feel so miserable, and he seemed to understand.'

'There, there! Don't take on so, my lovely. We all know how unhappy you are about what has happened.' He patted her arm understandingly.

A large tear rolled down her cheek. 'It is so very sad! I thought this outing might take my mind off things, since there is nothing at all I can do for Hwyel. I won't go tonight if you think it would be heartless of me to do so.'

Edwin Webster shook his head benignly. 'No, you go, cariad. As you say, there is very little you can do for Hwyel at the moment.'

'Are you quite sure? You don't think it would upset the Barkers if they heard I'd gone to a concert?' she pressed.

Edwin Webster shook his head again, his face grave. 'Let's hope that Cledwyn Barker doesn't find out, because he is almost out of his mind with worry and he tells me that Hwyel's mother is quite demented.'

Sabrina nodded in agreement, lowering her eyes and biting down on her full lower lip as if trying to hold back her tears.

'Hurt they are, mind, that you haven't been along to the hospital. You will go tomorrow, Sabrina, now promise me that.'

'Yes, Dad!' she whispered. 'Of course I will, I give you my word.'

Her father nodded, then his expression changed as he looked across at Rhianon. 'You'll see that she doesn't forget,' he ordered curtly.

'I told you I would,' Sabrina intervened huffily, looking at him through tear-stained lashes. 'There's no need to ask Rhianon to remind me!' She dropped another kiss on his cheek before speedily making for the door, giving Rhianon a self-satisfied grin as she passed her.

Chapter Five

'Well now, boyo, what you been up to this time then?' Bryn Richards, the sergeant designated to interview Pryce Pritchard, asked as they sat down facing each other in the interview room at Pontdarw police station. He opened his notebook and placed it on the table between them.

'I've written down your name and age since I know those as well as I know my own, so now all I need from you is an account of what took place.'

'You probably know what happened even better than I do, since you had your spies there,' Pryce told him.

'That's as maybe, but in all fairness we like to give the criminal the chance to tell the story in his own words,' Bryn grinned. 'So shall we get on with it?'

The two men were equally matched in every way. Of similar build, both with a Celtic appearance, they had been lifelong acquaintances.

As raggedy-trousered young boys with no shoes on their feet, and not a brass farthing between them, they'd played together on the slag heaps that dotted the landscape around Pontdarw.

They'd lived side by side in identical two-up two-down terraced cottages that, built straight onto the pavement, clung to the mountainside like snails to an old flower pot.

They'd sat side by side at school, cribbed and copied each other's work, and been caned for each other's mistakes and misdeeds.

Not until the day when Pryce's father had been killed in an underground explosion, at the pit where he worked as a hewer, had their paths started to deviate. Pryce had been forced to leave school and take his father's place as breadwinner, to help his mam provide for his three younger sisters.

She'd hated everyone and everything, blamed the world for the burden she'd been left to shoulder. He couldn't remember her ever kissing any of them. True, her life had been hard, but she'd been so cold and distant that at times it had been frightening.

Even after his sisters were working and bringing home money, so that between all of them they were probably better off than most of their neighbours, she still hadn't been happy or satisfied.

In the end the girls had all left home. Two of them had married and the third had gone as a skivvy to a wealthy family in the English Midlands. The last time Pryce had heard from her she'd risen from kitchenmaid to assistant cook.

Once the girls had gone, it was as if his

mother felt her work was finished. The death certificate said pneumonia, but it had happened so suddenly that he'd often wondered whether she really had died from natural causes.

Bryn had been more fortunate. He'd stayed on at school, passed his exams, gone to the technical college in Cardiff.

Pryce had envied him. He blamed his own lack of learning on everything that went wrong in his life. If he had enjoyed a decent education, perhaps he would have been the first of the Pritchard men not to work underground in the pits.

If he'd had the right education he could still have retained the family tradition of being involved with the pits – if he felt that was where his destiny lay.

I could have worked there in some other capacity, not spent my days toiling underground, Pryce thought bitterly. Surely the sacrifice my forebears made at the time of the Chartist uprising should have been enough for generations to come.

Bryn's dad had been a miner, but he'd been invalided out. His lungs were so impregnated with coal dust that he hawked and spat from the moment he woke up in the morning until he went to bed at night.

Though not educated above primary standards himself he'd seen the futility of such a life, and pushed Bryn to work hard at his books.

Bryn had badly wanted to accompany Pryce when he started work at the pit. He'd had sense enough to listen to his old man, though, and stay on at school.

When he'd gone to the technical college in Cardiff, he'd liked the bright lights and the smell of prosperity in the city. In next to no time he'd taken up with a young shop girl and before anyone knew what was happening, he'd married her. Then he'd taken the plunge and joined the police force.

Pryce had taunted him when he'd first heard the news. 'Never thought of you as a blackleg,' he jibed.

'That's because I'm not! Upholder of peace and order, boyo, that's what I aim to be.'

'You'll be on the other side the next time the miners go on strike,' Pryce pointed out.

'Then don't go on strike, mun, it's as simple as that.'

It wasn't simple for Pryce. It was a tradition in his family, and had been for generations, to uphold the miners' rights. Like his forebears he was prepared to fight for those rights whenever necessary.

In those days Pryce never tired of reminding Bryn of this, and pointing out that such loyalty to the cause went right back to the Chartists.

'Never forget,' Pryce told him over and over again, 'my great-grandfather was killed when, without warning, the soldiers turned their fire on the marchers.'

Over the years Bryn lost interest. He had no time for that sort of loyalty. He was too busy carving a career in the police force and looking after his family, his wife, his young son and baby daughter.

As Pryce had grown older he'd realised, from the things Bryn told him, the senselessness of trying to outrank the government of the day. They had not only the police, but the military behind them too, so he'd modified his approach to authority.

Words, not guns, made better weapons, he decided. In some ways they were just as lethal. Words could ruin a man's reputation, and deprive him of his livelihood, but this would be achieved without bloodshed.

That was when he'd decided to change direction, if he possibly could. He opted to go to night school. Sometimes he felt so exhausted at the end of a long shift that it took him every ounce of inner strength to do so. Strangely enough, once in the classroom, concentrating on the lectures, he found that his tiredness seemed to vanish.

It was almost as if he were two persons in one. A manual worker whose daytime job required brawn and muscle, and then at night a thinker who used brain and reasoning.

It was at night school that he had met Rhianon. She wasn't glamorous or even beautiful, but he thought she was the most wonderful woman he had ever encountered. She was always so

56

calm and smiling, willing to listen to his problems as well as his dreams.

He had never known anyone as caring as Rhianon was. For all the responsibility that rested on her slim shoulders, she never became snappy or moody. Her warmth was all-encompassing. Her lilting voice was soft and attractive. Even when she was attempting to control her sister's exuberant outbursts, or persuade Sabrina to obey their father's strict rules, her voice, though firm, was always quiet and controlled.

Attractive though these attributes were, it was Rhianon's ability to listen that he found so engaging.

Most women, even if they did pay attention to what a chap was saying, soon became bored if the subject wasn't of interest to them. When they did pretend to listen they had nothing to say afterwards, not even when a decision was called for, but only made some silly or light-hearted comment.

Rhianon was so different. She listened in silence, but with rapt attention. Afterwards, when they discussed what was involved, her comments were always apt.

He should know. He'd run so many of his dreams and ideas past her. Some, she tactfully pointed out, were not feasible, not unless they were changed or adapted. Those that she thought to be good she praised highly, offering both support and encouragement.

She'd make a wonderful schoolteacher! He'd told her that time and time again, although he was the only person to do so. Her father opposed her because he was concerned that her change of career would distract her from running their home and taking care of his needs and comfort.

Sabrina was afraid that it would mean she would be asked to help around the home. At the moment, as far as Pryce could see, she was not expected to do anything or ever give a hand. Polly Potter, Rhianon's employer, was the only other source of support, even though she was loath to lose a first-class assistant.

Pryce considered Rhianon's companionship and understanding so important to him that for a long time he'd been afraid to let her know that what had started out as friendship had become love: sweet protective love. He wanted to spend the rest of his life with her. She would provide a tranquil refuge, an escape from the harsh realities of the world.

Finally he could stand it no longer. He had to know what her feelings for him were.

Their first kiss had wiped every vestige of doubt from his mind. The declaration of their passion had been a revelation for both of them. Rhianon was shy and reticent about such matters, but it had made their relationship even more precious.

The only impediment was her father's reaction to their courtship. When Rhianon took

Pryce home and introduced him as a very special friend from night school, Edwin Webster had been cold and calculating. A deeply religious person himself, he deemed that everyone had a duty to fulfil according to the role they had been given. He had been shocked that a man who was courting his daughter talked of rights for the workers, and openly discussed miners' wages and conditions.

Pryce had heard later, although Rhianon with her kind heart had tried to conceal it from him, that Edwin Webster had dubbed him a rabble-raiser and had forbidden her to bring him to their home ever again.

Pryce knew it had made her unhappy, but he was relieved to find that it made no difference to her feelings for him and certainly not to his for her. As he came to know Rhianon better, Pryce became ever more astounded by her forbearance, in view of all her personal commitments.

Her father was the most intolerant man he had ever met, and her sister the most outrageous flirt. While Rhianon did all the housework, Sabrina seemed to do little more than prettify herself and expect everyone to admire her and take care of her.

She was beautiful, of course. Men were immediately charmed by her presence.

Every man he worked with thought she was a stunner, especially when she was attired in one of her floaty little dresses that rippled over her curves. Most men would have sold their soul to the devil for the chance to take her out.

Right from the moment they first met she flirted with Pryce disgracefully, but because she was Rhianon's sister he'd refused to rise to her bait.

Well, he had until she'd come looking for him after the fight to tell him how seriously hurt Hwyel was.

He wasn't proud of what had happened that night. He blamed it all on the fact that he was keyed up by the strike, and the rush of adrenaline that resulted from the fight. His defences had been down and he'd let lust rule his mind and body. Like Adam in the Garden of Eden he'd succumbed to temptation. Now he felt so ashamed of what had happened between the pair of them that he was avoiding Rhianon. He was sure she must be suspicious, and would see guilt written all over him.

Pryce had thought about this over and over again since his brawl with Hwyel Barker. He had known that trouble would follow the moment he had landed the punch that sent Hwyel reeling backwards, and he'd heard the dull thud as Hwyel's head hit the ground. He'd been waiting for the repercussions to start, but hadn't anticipated the form they'd eventually taken.

This was why his dalliance with Sabrina sickened him so much, and caused him such anguish. He knew that he had let Rhianon down and he fervently hoped that she would never find out. He wasn't sure, though, that he could trust Sabrina to keep what had happened between them a secret.

The matter would have weighed even more heavily on his conscience if it had not been for the strike. It was the biggest ever known and was affecting the entire country. As a Union official he was involved in it up to his neck. Every day, morning, afternoon and evening, there were meetings where he was expected to speak.

This occupied his mind, but it didn't ease his conscience. Even if she didn't know it, he'd betrayed Rhianon. What he had done was completely unforgivable. He would have given anything to turn the clock back, but he knew that was impossible.

As Pryce completed his statement for the police about the fight with Hwyel, he reminded Bryn that he had Union duties to attend to.

'You're not keeping me penned up here in one of your blasted cells, are you? I've got a list as long as your arm of meetings to address over the next couple of weeks.'

'We won't be keeping you in today, but if that boyo in hospital kicks the bucket then without doubt we will have to pull you in.'

'You mean it would be considered as murder?'

'No, it would be manslaughter, not murder. Mind you,' Bryn added gloomily, 'there's not all that much difference in the punishment.'

'They don't hang you for manslaughter, do they?' Pryce asked in alarm.

'No, but you'd probably get life, and in some ways that is worse!' He shook his head solemnly. 'The conditions in some of the jails where the lifers are kept are beyond belief!'

'I don't suppose they are any worse than working down the pit.'

Bryn shrugged his wide shoulders. 'Perhaps not, but at least when you're a miner you are allowed home at the end of each day. You sleep in a decent bed and have food that is fit to eat.'

'Well let's hope it won't come to that then,' Pryce said, with an air of bravado he didn't really feel.

'I hope so too,' Bryn affirmed, 'but the news about Hwyel isn't all that good, is it?'

'I'm not too sure. I understand from his girl-friend, Sabrina Webster, that no one outside the family is allowed in to see him.'

'Not much point in them doing so now, is there, since most of the time he's unconscious,' Bryn commented.

'That's not what I heard. I was told he'd rallied.'

'Only for a short while, and then he blacked out again, and he's been out for the count more or less ever since. Some punch you threw, boyo! Twice the size of him you are, mun! His falling backwards like he did, that's probably what did the damage.'

'In that case then it's not really my fault if he

doesn't come round, now is it. If it was all because of the way he fell . . .'

Bryn looked sceptical. 'You can try that one out on the judge if it ever comes to court. I hope for your sake he does pull through, mind, because I don't think you have a leg to stand on if he doesn't. His father is already sounding off about retribution and so forth. He's a man of some standing, as you well know. If he does make an official complaint it will be treated very seriously. Apparently Hwyel was about to be married, so that will have to be taken into consideration as well.'

Pryce felt the colour staining his cheeks and he avoided Bryn's penetrating stare. The less he said, the better it would be for him in the long run, he decided.

Chapter Six

The ink had barely dried on Pryce Pritchard's statement when the news broke. It was something they'd all feared. Hwyel Barker was dead!

People sighed; raised their eyebrows in horror; shed a few tears; or merely nodded sagely as if they had known all along that this would happen.

'He died without ever regaining consciousness, without ever speaking a consoling word to his mother, who has haunted his bedside day and night ever since he's been in hospital,' Cledwyn Barker told Edwin Webster dolefully.

He shook his head and turned away despairingly when Edwin, by way of consolation, murmured, 'We must all pray that he's safe with the Good Lord now.'

By coincidence, the news that Hwyel had died came almost simultaneously with the announcement that the General Strike was being called off. The TUC had withdrawn its support and said that all the men, including the miners, must return to work immediately. Furthermore, they must accept that no changes would be made to either their conditions or wages.

The miners resolved to stay out.

Pryce Pritchard dashed from one meeting to the next, exhorting the miners to stand up for their rights, whipping up their loyalty to the cause. He begged them not to let the sacrifice they'd already made be wasted.

'It will be if you return to the pits, your tails between your legs, to become once more the slaves of the coal masters,' he warned them.

His enthusiasm was double-edged. He believed passionately in the cause they were striking for, but throwing himself heart and soul into the campaign also helped to block out from his mind the alarming news about Hwyel.

The next day, two policemen appeared at the meeting he was addressing in Tonypandy. Before he had time even to finish speaking they arrested him.

The crowd, most of whom hadn't yet heard that Hwyel Barker had died, believed it to be because of the things Pryce had been saying, and they were outraged. They believed that the police interference was because they opposed the strike, and so they fought back.

The two policemen were overpowered, and were forced to call up reserves. The melee that ensued ended with Pryce being bundled into the back of a Black Maria. He was driven back to Pontdarw police station where they read him his rights, and then told that he would appear before a magistrate the next day on a manslaughter charge. His arguments and demand for bail were ignored.

'Once a date for your trial is fixed, you'll probably end up in Cardiff jail until your case comes to court, so think yourself lucky that at least you'll be in a cell on your own tonight,' Bryn Richards told him. 'Make the most of it, boyo, it might be the last good night's sleep you'll have for a long time.'

'Come off it, Bryn! What about bail? As the sergeant in charge here surely you can arrange that, mun! For old times' sake use the bit of power those stripes on your arm give you!'

Bryn shook his head and laughed ruefully as he refused. 'My orders are to keep you locked up out of harm's way. We don't want any more riots!'

The evening meal at the Websters' house that Thursday was overshadowed by the sad news that Hwyel had died late the previous night.

Edwin Webster held forth about justice, rabble-raisers like Pryce Pritchard, and how they should be dealt with, until Rhianon thought her head would split. Sabrina remained completely silent, concentrating on the food on her plate. Rhianon assumed she was grieving for Hwyel and felt sorry for her, and ached to say, or do, something to comfort her.

'Can we talk about something else, please, Father,' she intervened at last.

'Your conscience troubling you is it, daughter?' Edwin retorted grimly. 'Thinking of the heartache your young sister is suffering because of that villain Pryce Pritchard, are you? Seventeen and her life lies in tatters. All her plans will come to naught. Her heart is broken. I wonder she can bear to sit at the same table as you.'

Rhianon bit her lip. Sabrina was obviously upset, but not to the extent her father claimed. She'd eaten everything that had been put before her. She had even had a second helping of the baked apple pie which Rhianon had made because it was Sabrina's favourite pudding.

Rhianon looked across the table, hoping her sister would back her up and ask their father to stop going on about Hwyel's death, and the part Pryce had played in it. Sabrina kept her eyes down, her long dark lashes resting on her cheeks. From her demure attitude it was almost as if she was silently praying.

'Remove the used dishes, Rhianon, and then all three of us will go to Capel Bethel and offer up prayers for poor Hwyel. I have sent word to the Barkers and asked them to join us there.'

As Rhianon began clearing the table, Edwin Webster spoke cajolingly to his younger daughter.

'Come Sabrina, you must change from that dress into something more appropriate,' he advised. 'Red is not the colour of mourning, my child. Remember, Capel Bethel will be packed and all eyes will be on you. They know that your loss is equally as painful as that of the

Barkers and so they will expect to see you dressed accordingly.'

As he had foreseen, the chapel was crowded. News of the unscheduled service had snowballed. People who rarely went there, as well as those who attended regularly, had come out of curiosity.

It was common knowledge that both Edwin Webster and his daughters were closely connected with the tragedy. It was like being an exhibit at a peep show, Rhianon thought, as strangers, as well as people she'd known all her life, nudged each other, whispered together and stared at her and Sabrina. She knew they were waiting to hear what her father had to say about both Hwyel Barker and Pryce Pritchard.

She felt angry and resentful, but Sabrina played to the gallery to perfection. In a neat little black suit, which she'd bought when she'd gone for her interview at Barker's Insurance Company, her dark curls brushed back from her face and confined under a black velvet cloche hat, she looked suitably grief-stricken.

Her occasional little sob, accompanied by the application of a lace-edged lawn handkerchief to her eyes, had hearts melting for her.

Many looked at Rhianon with dismay, some even with hatred in their eyes. It was as if they were suggesting that her relationship with Pryce Pritchard had resulted in Hwyel's death.

Edwin Webster's address did nothing to absolve her. He praised Hwyel fulsomely, exploiting his virtues as a God-fearing, well-brought-up young man, who could rightly expect a long and happy life. He emphasised the bright future he'd had ahead of him, both as his father's son and as Sabrina's husband. Then, without pausing, he spoke slightingly of Pryce, and his Trade Union connections, but was careful to make no mention of his friendship with Rhianon.

Rhianon wished she could register her disapproval of what her father was saying by getting up and walking out. She was sitting in one of the front pews, though, and, realising the disturbance this would cause, she didn't quite dare to do it.

It would only make tongues wag all the more, she told herself. It might even stir up greater animosity towards Pryce than her father's words had already done, if that was possible.

She waited until the service was over, and then taking Sabrina's arm said softly, 'I think you should go and speak to the Barkers. Poor Mrs Barker looks absolutely devastated. I'm sure that a few words from you would be of great comfort to her, since you were so very much part of Hwyel's life.'

Sabrina shook her arm away irritably. 'If they want to talk to me they can come over here. I shall probably miss Hwyel far more than they will!'

'Then tell his mother how you feel, cariad.

Share your sorrow, and grieve with her. It may help to lighten the blow for both of you.'

'You sanctimonious bitch!' Sabrina spat, her dark eyes flaming. 'It was your boyfriend that killed him, or have you conveniently forgotten about that?'

'I know only too well,' Rhianon said sadly. 'There is nothing I can do about it now, though, is there?'

'Only hold your tongue and leave me alone.'

'Please go and speak to the Barkers, that's all I'm asking you to do, Sabrina. It will be expected of you,' Rhianon persisted. 'I'll come with you if you like.'

'That would only make things worse, wouldn't it,' Sabrina flared. 'They know all about you and Pryce Pritchard. They're hardly likely to want to chat to the girlfriend of the man who killed their only son, now are they?'

Rhianon felt mortified. She searched her mind for the right words, not wanting to say anything that might inflame Sabrina further. Before she could speak, however, Sabrina had flounced away. Rhianon was relieved to see her approaching the Barkers, and then sighed resignedly as she spotted her father following hot on Sabrina's heels.

Rhianon's heart went out to Hwyel's mother. Mrs Barker's face was ravaged by hours of weeping. Even now, although she was trying to control herself and listen to what Sabrina was saying, sobs continually shook her dumpy figure, and she surreptitiously wiped away the tears that ran in rivulets down her cheeks.

Mr Barker's face looked as grey as the pinstriped suit he was wearing. He was trying hard to hold himself erect, but there was an air of dejection about the droop of his shoulders that revealed the inner torment he was suffering.

Feeling it might be better if she made herself scarce, Rhianon decided to go home on her own.

As she left Capel Bethel she was conscious of the way people drew to one side to let her pass. Those she smiled at, or spoke to, barely acknowledged her. Some even turned away pointedly, mutely signalling that they wanted nothing to do with her.

Unhappily she made her way through the town, oblivious to the stares and nudges from people she passed, her mind otherwise occupied.

As she approached the police station she hesitated, then, on impulse, she went inside.

'Yes, miss. How can I help you?'

The middle-aged policeman on duty regarded her sternly, almost as if she was a stranger, even though he had known her all her life.

'It . . . it's about Pryce Pritchard,' she stuttered. 'Is he here? Can I see him?'

'Of course you can't see him! He's been taken into custody. You should know better than to ask.' The officer scowled.

'Can you tell me what is going to happen to him then? Please, Constable Jenkins, set my mind at rest. Tell me if there is anything I can do to help him.'

'Duw anwyl! We don't know anything for sure until he appears before the magistrate, so how can I tell you what is going to happen to him?'

'Is there nothing more you can tell me?' she pleaded.

'It's all the information we have.' His voice softened. 'I think I would cut along home if I were you, Rhianon. It mightn't be very safe for you to be out on the streets by yourself tonight, if you know what I mean,' he cautioned.

Although she knew she wouldn't sleep, Rhianon went home and straight up to her room. It was almost an hour before she heard her father and Sabrina coming in.

She could hear them having a long discussion, but she couldn't make out what they were saying. She heard Sabrina's voice falter, and then give way to sobs, as she said goodnight to her father and came upstairs to bed.

As Sabrina's sobs became louder and louder Rhianon wondered if she should go in and try and comfort her. Evidently she had been wrong in thinking that Sabrina hadn't been very affected by what had happened to Hwyel.

Now, or so it seemed, the effort of putting a brave face on things earlier was beginning to take its toll. Either that, or Sabrina had only just realised the full implication of what had happened.

Pulling on her dressing gown, Rhianon walked softly to her sister's bedroom door. It was tightly shut so she knocked gently, calling her name very quietly.

Only a choked hiccup of suppressed crying broke the silence.

Rhianon tried the door, but found that it was locked. 'Let me in, Sabrina,' she whispered. 'You might feel better if we talk things over.'

There was no response.

'It's all right, I do understand,' she said softly. 'Perhaps we can talk things over in the morning, but only if you want to do so, of course. Try and sleep, cariad.'

Rhianon waited for a moment or two longer, but there was still no response from her sister. She retreated to her own room with a sense of overwhelming sadness.

What was there for them to talk over, she asked herself. Everything and nothing. The past couldn't be changed in any way and there was no knowing what problems lay ahead.

What did the future hold for either of them now, she pondered. Hwyel was dead and Pryce was in jail. There seemed very little doubt that he would end up being found guilty of manslaughter.

All she knew for certain, she thought hopelessly, was that her own life would never be quite the same again.

Chapter Seven

Sabrina heard her father come upstairs, and his bedroom door click shut. She listened patiently until she judged that he was in bed before striking a match and relighting the candle by her bedside.

She wasn't sure if her sister was asleep or not, since there was no light showing under Rhianon's bedroom door. The only way of making certain would be to go and tap on it and call out her name, but that will alert her to the fact that I am still wide awake, Sabrina reasoned.

She pulled aside the curtains and peered out of her bedroom window. The street outside was deserted, except for a stray black and white cat foraging in the gutter. She tried telling herself that since it was probably well past midnight most people would be tucked up in bed and asleep. She made up her mind that she must act quickly. There was no time to spare, she had to move fast if she was to get as far away from Pontdarw as possible before morning.

Gingerly she pulled a brown fibre suitcase down from the top of the cupboard and rested it on her bed. She tipped out the miscellany of bits and pieces that were inside it, piling them up haphazardly in a corner of the room. Then she began cramming as many of her clothes into the suitcase as she could.

Where should she go? Merthyr Tydfil, Bridgend, Swansea, Pontypridd? Were any of them big enough? She wanted to hide from the world, especially from her own family and from Hwyel's.

The only person she didn't want to hide from was Pryce Pritchard, but he had been taken into custody and was locked up inside Pontdarw police station.

Everyone was sure that when he appeared before the magistrate in the morning he'd be remanded in jail, so since there was no possibility of them being together it really didn't matter where she went.

She leaned heavily on the lid of the case, struggling to shut it, then sat back on her heels quite breathless with the exertion. When she stood up and lifted the case off the bed, she staggered under its weight.

For one wild moment she thought of leaving without it, simply going in the clothes she stood up in. She was still in the dark suit she'd worn to chapel. She hated it, it was so plain and ordinary, so the thought of leaving all her pretty dresses behind made her grit her teeth and brace herself to carry the heavy suitcase.

Negotiating the stairs, balancing the case step by step, she crept out of the house. The loud click as she shut the front door startled her. She froze to the spot, expecting that at any moment a bedroom window would be thrown up and her father would peer out to see what was happening.

When nothing stirred, some of her flagging courage returned. Picking up the suitcase she walked away from her home, still not knowing where her destination was to be.

The furthest she'd ever been was to Swansea on a Sunday school outing. She'd sat next to Rhianon on the charabanc, scared half out of her mind by the speed they were travelling at.

The seaside had been like a new world: the gulls, boats, sand, beach huts and the crowds of people all enjoying themselves. There'd been middle-aged women sitting on the sand with their dresses pulled up to their knees, baring their legs to the sun, and paunchy men with their jackets off sitting there with their braces showing. Some of them had knotted their handkerchiefs at all four corners and placed them on top of their bald heads to protect them from the heat of the sun.

Children armed with buckets and spades played barefoot on the sand. Some of the older ones built sandcastles with a moat around them. Then they ran down to the sea's edge, filled their tiny buckets with water, brought it back and poured it into the moat.

Rhianon had taken off her shoes and socks and made her do the same, and then they'd walked right down to the sea, leaving their footprints in the damp sand as they squelched over it.

At first she'd been afraid even to put a toe in the sparkling water that crept closer and closer with each breaking wave. When she did, the cold shock had taken her breath away. Then she became braver. Tucking the skirt of her pink cotton dress into her knickers, and holding on tight to Rhianon's hand, she'd ventured out until the sea was up over her knees.

She would have liked to stay there for ever. But no sooner had they eaten their sandwiches, and the slices of bara brith that Rhianon had brought with them in a tin box, than it was time to get back on the charabanc and start the journey home.

This time the speed didn't bother her, she was too busy thinking about all the wonders they'd seen. The fresh air and all the excitement had tired her out and by the time they reached Pontdarw she was sound asleep, her head resting on Rhianon's lap.

The only other time she had been away from Pontdarw was when she went with Rhianon to hear her father speak at the Capel Bethel in Merthyr Tydfil. They'd both had to wear their Sunday clothes so that they looked respectable and he could be proud of them, and they'd had to be on their best behaviour. Sabrina remembered it well because she had been wearing new black shoes and they'd hurt her feet and rubbed her heels.

It had been hot and stuffy in the chapel and her father's voice had droned on and on until she was afraid of falling asleep. He'd preached about sin and damnation, just the same as when he stood up and addressed the congregation in their own Bethel.

That had not been as memorable a day out, and she hadn't liked Merthyr Tydfil because it had been very similar to Pontdarw. A main street full of shops and chapels, and then row after row of bleak terraced streets stacked up the side of a mountain.

Somehow, neither of those places seemed to be the right destination for her now. She'd prefer not to spoil her wonderful memories of the sea and sand at Swansea, and Merthyr Tydfil was only another mining town.

No, she decided, she'd go to Cardiff, since that was where everyone seemed to think that Pryce would be held in custody. Even if he wasn't, it certainly would be where his trial would be held. For something as grave as manslaughter he'd be brought before the County Court in Cardiff, so that was where she must go.

She'd heard that it was a huge city, with hundreds of streets, and thousands of inhabitants, so no one would know her or recognise her if she went there. She'd surely be able to find work as a typist in a place that big and prosperous. Even more importantly, she'd be right on the spot and able to follow Pryce's trial when it came to court.

She wouldn't rest until she knew the outcome of that. She didn't know what she would do if Pryce was found guilty, because to some extent it was all her fault. If she hadn't egged him and Hwyel on to fight then none of this would have happened, and Hwyel would still be alive.

If the truth ever came out, she might be judged to be as guilty as Pryce Pritchard, she thought worriedly. Guilty by association, or implication, or some such phrase she'd heard. The association between them, of course, had happened after Pryce had delivered the fatal blow, but did that exonerate her?

She kept asking herself how she could have had such strong feelings for both men when they'd been so totally different.

Pryce had a body like one of the Greek heroes or Roman gods that they'd been told about in history lessons at school. He was clever as well as handsome, a deep thinker and a persuasive, knowledgeable speaker who could draw the crowds. The fact that he earned his living as a miner only added to his appeal.

Hwyel was good-looking, but no one would mistake him for a man who worked underground even though he was thin and wiry, having inherited the physique of a typical miner. Fate, or rather his father's sharp business sense and good fortune, had made him into an astute young businessman, and a money-loving social climber.

Perhaps that had been the attraction, the fact

that the two men were such opposites in both build and character. Another factor had been her resentment of the way Pryce seemed to worship the ground Rhianon walked on, evidently preferring her sister's docile uninspiring company to her own.

Until the fight Pryce had practically ignored her, despite the many flirtatious glances she'd sent in his direction, and her efforts to intrigue him with her bright chatter. It had been a challenge!

She'd been wrong to use the miners' strike in the way she had to incite the two men to fight. She could see that now, but at the time it had been thrilling. While it was happening she'd even fantasised that they were fighting over her.

She hadn't wanted it to end the way it had, of course. It was sheer bad luck that Pryce's knock-out punch had floored Hwyel; sent him crashing backwards to the ground. That was what had done the damage, not Pryce's fist, she kept reminding herself.

Still, there was no point in dwelling on what had happened, it was impossible to turn the clock back. Hwyel was dead and Pryce was in custody and nothing would ever be the same again for any of them.

The fight alone mightn't have mattered so much, it was what had happened later on between her and Pryce that had been so gloriously shameful.

She didn't regret one moment of it, though. She'd been thrilled by his love-making! Their encounter had put everything else out of her head, it had been so exciting!

She'd known as they lay in each other's arms afterwards that there was no other man in the world for her.

If Hwyel had recovered she would have been forced to break off the understanding between them. She could never have married him, even though she knew he would have kept her in luxury and supplied her every need – with one exception! Having slept with Pryce, she knew that there was only one man who would be able to satisfy her.

How could she ever start to tell Rhianon about what had happened, let alone explain to her father why Pryce Pritchard's future meant so much to her?

Rhianon would be hurt and tearful. She'd never understand about the tremendous passion there was between the two of them.

Her father would be shocked and disbelieving. He'd consider it a sin that she had fallen in love with her sister's boyfriend, and an even greater sin that it was Pryce Pritchard. He'd rant on about wickedness and damnation, as if that would make any difference to her feelings. All she wanted was the man who was capable of creating sensations that were thrillingly turbulent; passion that made her feel more deliciously alive than ever before.

She sighed, realising with astonishment how much she had been missing in the past. Simply thinking of Pryce sent a tingly feeling rippling through her.

She felt repelled by the memory of Hwyel's tentative fumbling, his soft moist kisses, the eager demanding look on his face. It had all been so raw, so immature. Selfish too, he'd never asked about her feelings, he'd only been concerned with his own satisfaction.

Pryce had wanted her as a real man needs a woman.

Hwyel would have been able to offer her most of the things that money could buy, she reminded herself again. He would have been able to make her life comfortable and secure. What were material things, though, compared with the sort of love, and the ecstasy of unbridled passion, that she'd shared with Pryce?

Pryce had promised her nothing, of course. She would gladly take her chance, though, accepting whatever fate might throw at them, as long as they were together.

It couldn't possibly be the same between him and Rhianon. Her sister was far too tranquil and self-controlled ever to become impassioned. She was too reserved to throw caution to the wind and abandon herself to his demands for sensual fulfilment.

Their love-making had made her certain that she and Pryce were destined to be together. She only wished he could assure her that he was as bewitched as she was.

Her decision to leave home was the right one, she was sure about that. She could only begin to sort out this complicated situation by getting right away, not only from Pontdarw, but from her family and everyone else she knew.

She had to start a new life on her own so that she could be free to make her own decisions. Being set on a pedestal by her father, and watched over and smothered by Rhianon, had hampered her long enough, and led to a kind of irresponsibility.

She didn't want to be in the bosom of her family when the case came to court and to have to listen to her father pontificating about Pryce's character.

She couldn't bear the thought of Pryce being in prison. If that was what resulted when he was brought to trial then she'd wait for him until he came out, no matter how long that might be.

The thought that Rhianon might also do the same was something she refused even to contemplate. Prison would disgrace Pryce in Rhianon's eyes, she told herself. She wouldn't want a jailbird for a husband! She was too prim and respectable in her neat dark clothes, her straight no-nonsense haircut, her sensible hats and serviceable shoes. She wouldn't be able to live with such a stigma hanging over her.

No, Rhianon's future lay in realising her

dream of becoming a teacher and educating other people's children. Such a future was not only orderly and controllable, but, above all, highly respectable.

Chapter Eight

Rhianon felt concerned next morning when Sabrina didn't put in an appearance at breakfast time.

'Take her up a cup of tea,' her father ordered. 'Poor child, she's probably still feeling upset by the dreadful news about Hwyel. It's been a harrowing experience for her, you know.'

'I wonder if she is going into work today? Did Mr Barker say whether or not she had to when you were talking to him last night?'

Edwin Webster shook his grizzled head. 'No!' he said shortly. 'And while we are on the subject of last night, I thought it very rude and unfeeling of you to walk off like you did without saying a word to the Barkers.'

Rhianon looked at him in astonishment, her colour rising. 'I did it because I thought they might not want to talk to me, since I'm the girlfriend of the man who accidentally caused their son's death.'

'Girlfriend! Stop talking so foolishly, Rhianon! Never let me hear you make a claim like that ever again, do you understand? Pryce Pritchard is a most undesirable character. I told you that the first time I met him.' His voice rose harshly.

'Never let me hear you describe yourself as anything more than a mere acquaintance of that man, someone you met by chance at night school, more's the pity.'

Rhianon bit her lip, knowing how unwise it was to argue with her father, but unable to accept what he said.

'That would be a lie. We mean a great deal to each other and . . .'

Her father cut her short. 'The sooner you put all thoughts of him out of your mind the better,' he snapped. 'Now, go on upstairs with that tea for Sabrina!'

The shock of finding Sabrina's room empty, the bed not slept in, and her clothes missing, filled Rhianon with alarm.

Edwin Webster was equally apprehensive when she hurried back downstairs to tell him.

'Haven't you any idea where she is, or where she might be?' he growled.

'None at all. Not unless she's decided to go into the office early. Perhaps she wanted to catch up with some work or something.'

'You said that her clothes were missing. She wouldn't take them to work with her, now would she?' he said peevishly.

Rhianon shook her head. 'No, I wouldn't think so, but I can't think where else she might be.'

'She can't just vanish into thin air. Have you looked to see if she's left a note?'

'I didn't see one.'

'Did you look? Properly, I mean. Out of the

way.' He pushed past her and clumped up the stairs. Rhianon stayed where she was, contemplatively drinking the tea she'd poured out.

She pondered Sabrina's disappearance. They had no relations, and, as far as she knew, Sabrina had no friends that she might have decided to turn to. So where was she, and why on earth had she left home without a word to anyone?

It must be a reaction because of what had happened to Hwyel, there could be no other reason, she told herself, but what was behind it? Had the Barkers said something last night to upset her? Was that why she had gone straight to her room when she came home, without saying goodnight, and why she had been sobbing and refused to answer her door? Or was it because Hwyel had died as a result of the fight with Pryce, and Sabrina felt she could no longer bear to live with her sister, Pryce's girlfriend?

When her father came back downstairs, Rhianon wondered if she should mention her fears to him, but he looked so devastated, so heartbroken, that she kept her own counsel.

'I must hurry or I will be late for work,' she murmured as she began clearing the table. 'Had you finished your breakfast?'

'Yes, yes!' He pushed the plate of half-eaten toast towards her. 'How do you expect me to eat with Sabrina's absence hanging over my head?'

Rhianon turned away in silence, not knowing what to say. He never considered her opinion or feelings of value, in any case.

'You are going into work, even though your sister is missing, I take it,' he said angrily.

'Well, yes. I can't let Polly down, can I? I'll ask her if I can take the morning off though, if you would like me to be here.'

'And what will you do if you take the morning off? Sit around the house moping, or trudge the streets looking for your sister, eh?'

'Well, I thought perhaps you wanted me to be here with you.'

'What good will that do? No,' he went on in exasperated tones, 'you go to work, perhaps someone will come into your shop and divulge where she is, or tell you that they have seen her. Meanwhile I'll go to the police and report her missing.'

'The police!'

'Indeed! That's what they're there for, as well as taking criminals like Pryce Pritchard into custody. The harm that man has done to this family is so immense that it doesn't bear thinking about. The Good Lord will wreak his vengeance on him, never fear. Hellfire and brimstone will be his lot, mark my words!'

'I don't see how that will serve any purpose, or what it has to do with finding Sabrina . . .'

'We wouldn't be looking for Sabrina if Pryce Pritchard hadn't murdered the man your sister was planning to marry!' Edwin Webster thundered. 'He's the root cause of all this worry and upset.'

In a more modified way, Polly Potter was in agreement with Edwin Webster when Rhianon told her what had happened.

'Oh, cariad, there's sorry I am for all the worry you've got on your young shoulders,' she sympathised. 'Like your father I think there is a connection, but not in quite the same way as he does.'

Rhianon frowned. 'What are you hinting at now, Polly?'

'Look at the facts, girl! What started the fight between those two boyos in the first place?'

'The miners' strike, I suppose. Tempers were raised and silly words flying.'

'Duw anwyl! That was only the half of it! The reason they were fighting was because your Sabrina had been stirring things up between them.'

'Surely . . .'

'Oh yes she was, so don't you try and tell me otherwise,' Polly interrupted quickly when she saw Rhianon was about to dispute this. 'When I nipped out to the grocer's before the fight started, I heard her chivvying the pair of them. She was taunting and teasing them, and throwing those provocative glances of hers at Pryce Pritchard.'

'And you think that is what started it?'

'Judging by the look on Hwyel Barker's face it most certainly did! His dander was up and well it might be. Wicked little flirt, your Sabrina, and well you know it. She'd make eyes at anything in trousers. I don't say she went any further than to tease them, see, but she'd picked the wrong day. The miners' strike began it – her behaviour was the final straw.'

'Maybe you're right,' Rhianon said cautiously, 'but where do you think she might be now? My father is out of his mind with worry.'

'Duw anwyl, she's seventeen, she can look after herself! Probably only run off to attract attention and make sure she gets everyone's sympathy. She'll be back in time for Hwyel's funeral, you mark my words!'

'The funeral!' Rhianon clapped a hand over her mouth. 'I'd forgotten all about that. I don't even know when it will be. I don't imagine she does either, so how will she know when to come back?'

Polly shrugged her plump shoulders. 'She'll know, she'll find out, I'm sure of it.'

Rhianon didn't argue with her, but she didn't believe her either.

The news that Hwyel Barker was dead and that Sabrina Webster had vanished spread like butter left out in the sun. There was a constant stream of customers coming into the shop for a reel of thread, or a few pins, simply to have the opportunity to ask Rhianon what had happened to her sister. One and all they promised to come straight back if they saw her or heard any news about her.

A great number of them did return later in the day, but it wasn't with news of Sabrina. They came back to let Rhianon know that Pryce had appeared in the magistrate's court.

The outcome had been that he was now officially on a manslaughter charge. He would be taken to Cardiff and kept in custody in the jail there until the day of his trial. The date of that hadn't yet been fixed, so it could be weeks or months away.

Dry-eyed and stony-faced, Rhianon listened to them. It was as if her tears, and indeed all her emotions, had suddenly petrified. Her mind was numb. She could only nod as they sympathised or condemned.

She dreaded going home. She knew that once again she would be forced to listen to an impassioned harangue from her father about Pryce and the aura of evil he insisted surrounded him.

She didn't need to hear any comments about what a terrible catastrophe it all was. She kept telling herself that none of it was her fault, no matter what her father might say, or anyone else if it came to that.

Though her reasoning might have been sound, it did nothing at all to ease her conscience. She was tempted to do as Sabrina had done and get right away from Pontdarw to a place where no one knew her, or anything about what had happened to her family.

The vicious accusations, the disparaging

comments, even the well-meaning condolences, were all equally unbearable.

There was still no news of Sabrina when she arrived home that night. Her father had been to the police, but they told him there wasn't much they could do, not at the moment anyway.

'She's not been gone twenty-four hours yet,' they had pointed out. 'She's probably only gone for a long walk to be on her own and sort things out in her mind.'

'And taken a suitcase with all her clothes in it?' Edwin Webster asked in withering tones.

'People do funny things when they're distressed, and your young girl has had more than her fair share of worry over the past couple of weeks.'

When Rhianon asked her father if he knew when Hwyel's funeral would be, he accused her of being morbid. When she told him that Pryce had been remanded in custody he replied that he hoped Pryce would be hanged or rot in jail. He also reminded her in a threatening voice that he never wanted Pryce Pritchard's name mentioned in their home again.

'And don't go sneaking off and trying to visit him,' he thundered. 'The man is evil personified, the cause of all our troubles, and don't you *ever* forget it.'

She knew she ought to take a stand, to speak up and defend Pryce. She should be reminding her father that he wasn't a criminal, not until he had been proven guilty in a court of law, but her father looked so careworn, so defeated, that she felt sorry for him. He was so desperately worried about Sabrina's absence that she couldn't bring herself to make matters worse for him.

She spent the early part of the evening turning over Sabrina's room from top to bottom, hoping to find some clue as to where she had gone. There was not the slightest vestige of evidence.

Her father stood moodily watching her from the doorway, vainly hoping Sabrina might have left them a note that had dropped down somewhere.

They listened for any footstep, any sound that might herald her homecoming.

By midnight, Rhianon felt utterly exhausted by the strain they were both under.

'I'm going to bed and you should do the same,' she told her father. 'There's nothing else we can do, only wait and hope.'

'Wait and hope!' He repeated her words scornfully. 'Yes, wait and hope, and if my little girl comes to any harm may the wrath of God come down on your head. You are the one who has brought trouble to this house!' he added savagely.

Chapter Nine

As the train pulled into Cardiff General, obliterating the buildings that ran alongside the track with its billowing smoke, some of the euphoria Sabrina had felt earlier disappeared.

As she handed over her one-way ticket, she was taken aback to find that miners, acting as pickets, were handing out leaflets about the strike to passengers leaving the train.

Although the TUC had said that the strike was over, and that men must return to work, the miners were still disobeying this directive. They knew they were putting their jobs and their livelihood in jeopardy, but there was a principle at stake, and one which they were not prepared to abandon.

Since she was a mere woman, and a young one at that, the pickets ignored her, but their presence brought memories of Pryce rushing to her mind.

If it hadn't been for the strike he wouldn't be in trouble, there would have been no meeting in the centre of Pontdarw, no fight, no punch that had proved fatal for Hwyel Barker. Yet if that hadn't happened, she reminded herself, she would never have discovered that Pryce was the only man in the world for her.

As she emerged from the station into Wood Street she stared around her bewildered, wondering which way she should go. Slightly to her right and ahead of her she could see a street of towering buildings that looked like huge shops. To her left was a road that seemed to lead to a bridge, and beyond that, busy but less imposing streets.

She felt lost and confused. She had no idea where to look for somewhere to stay. She couldn't afford anywhere very expensive, although she had brought all her savings with her. She'd been planning to spend this money on pretty clothes for herself, as well as things Hwyel and she would need for their new home when they were married.

Her first priority, she decided, was to find a room for the night. She would take it, no matter what it cost. One night in a smart hotel wouldn't break her. She couldn't go looking around Cardiff carrying her heavy case, so it was the sensible thing to do. One night, that was all, just to give her enough time to scout for lodgings she could afford.

The first hotel she came to looked so grand that she didn't dare go inside. Instead she lugged her suitcase further along the road and then, in sheer desperation, went into the Royal Hotel.

The receptionist was very snooty and spoke

to her so condescendingly that Sabrina almost turned tail and ran from the place. The pain in her arm from carrying the case decided her, however, and she boldly stated, 'A room please for one night.'

'Double or single?'

That was a funny way of asking if you were married or not, she thought as she replied, 'Single. Does it matter?'

'Well, a single room is much cheaper than a double one,' the girl pointed out.

'Oh.' Dismayed by her misunderstanding, and ignorance of such matters as booking a room, Sabrina said no more. She looked round tentatively at the thick red carpets, the expensive red damask curtains and the mahogany reception desk. Again she wondered if she was doing the right thing in staying there, even if it was only to be for one night.

Before she could summon up the courage to say, 'It doesn't matter' or 'I've changed my mind', and to pick up her suitcase and walk out, the receptionist had assigned her a room. With a snap of her fingers she summoned a uniformed bellboy and handed him the key.

'Follow me, miss,' he said, picking up her case.

The room, though small, was pleasantly furnished. The bed had a white wrought-iron bedhead, and was covered by a quilt in gold brocade. There were curtains of the same material at the tall narrow window that looked out onto the back of the building. There was also a mahogany chest of drawers with a mirror above it, and a matching wardrobe.

The bellboy placed her case on the rack at the foot of the bed and looked at her expectantly. It took her a minute to realise that he was waiting for a tip, and she quickly delved into her handbag for some coins. Not at all sure how much it ought to be, she handed him a threepenny piece.

'Thank you, miss!' With a funny sort of bow he withdrew so quickly that she was sure she had given him too much.

She looked round the room again, then lay down on the bed. She was feeling giddy, the room was spinning round her, and her heart was beating like a sledgehammer. She felt terrified by what was happening, but excited at the same time. She stared up at the pristine white ceiling and tried to marshal her thoughts and plan what she ought to do next.

She tried making a list: somewhere to stay, something to eat, find some work. No, perhaps the most important thing was to take a look around Cardiff. She had no idea what the place was like, and until she knew something about it she wouldn't know where to start looking for lodgings or work. Getting something to eat was even more urgent than that, she told herself.

She picked up the glossy white card from her bedside table and studied it. She saw it was possible to call for room service and they would deliver food to her room, or a newspaper, or a drink.

Perhaps that was what she ought to do, ask them to send up some breakfast. The memory of the sharp-faced bellboy, and the smug look on his face when she'd given him a threepenny bit, stopped her. She didn't know what was expected of her, so it would be better to go and buy breakfast somewhere outside the hotel. There must be several cafés nearby.

She took her suitcase off the stand at the bottom of her bed and stood it on end inside the wardrobe. Then she locked the wardrobe door and secreted the key under the mattress. Her money, every penny of it, was in her hand-bag and she clutched that firmly under her arm.

She read the notice again about leaving the key to her room at the desk if she went out. It seemed silly to do that, she would have preferred to take it with her. Still, she told herself, her possessions were all safely locked away so she'd better comply with their wishes. As an added precaution, she retrieved the wardrobe key from where she'd hidden it and put it in her handbag.

The streets were busy with shop and office workers hurrying to their various destinations. She walked the full length of St Mary Street, marvelling at all the wonderful things displayed for sale. She gazed in awe at the grey stone castle with its crenellated outer walls that looked like some medieval bulwark at the far end of St Mary Street. She followed the main road until the Civic Centre rose up like some Eastern palace. The gleaming white city hall, with its impressive clock tower and huge dragon crouched over the entrance portico, sparkled in the morning light. She walked past it and into Cathays Park, which had the cenotaph in its centre. Facing it on the other side of the tree-lined road were the law courts.

The law courts! She shivered at the thought that one day, quite soon, Pryce would be summoned to appear there. He would have to stand in the dock before a judge who'd be wearing a wig and gown, and be questioned by lawyers about a crime he had never intended to commit.

She turned back, unable to bring herself to walk past the actual building, and returned to the busy shopping area. The clanging of the trams and the roar of the traffic deafened her. She took refuge in one of the Victorian-style arcades where it was so quiet it was almost as if she was hiding away from the rest of the world.

She found a café, went inside and sat at a table near the window. She ordered a pot of tea and some Welsh cakes and stared out unseeingly at the people walking by, each intent on his or her own business, until the food was placed in front of her.

As she assuaged her hunger her sense of calm

returned, and she also became aware that no one took a second look at her. She was a stranger amongst strangers.

After another cup of tea she began to think again about her future and what she must do.

Work and lodgings were the next priority. She was a competent typist so she should be able to find a job in an office, only she had no idea how to go about doing this. She'd never had to apply for the position at Barker's Insurance. The day after she left business school she had reported to Mr Barker's office and that was that.

It had all been too easy, she reflected. She wished she'd gone for an interview, like other girls had done, in order to get a job. At least it would have prepared her for what lay ahead now.

Instead, everything had been handed to her on a plate. Even Mr Barker had been especially easy-going and ignored all her early typing mistakes because of his friendship with her father.

If she hadn't gone to work there she would never have met Hwyel, or been encouraged in her friendship with him because her father had thought he was such a good catch.

She must have been stupid to go along with the idea when she'd realised from the very first that he was uninspiring company. He had money to spend, of course, and he'd given her a good time. Even though he was so dull and predictable, she would probably have married him if Pryce had never come into her life.

If only she'd met Pryce first she would have known what a real man was like, and what a feeble creature Hwyel was.

Even so, she wished things hadn't ended the way they had. It was like being in the middle of a nightmare, only she knew it wasn't, and that it was happening right this minute. She didn't want to think about the future, but she had to if she was to survive.

How did you go about finding lodgings and a job in a big city like this, she wondered. Back at home she would simply have asked around. Everyone in Pontdarw knew everybody else's business, more or less. If someone had a room they wanted to rent out then the news spread by word of mouth. It was the same with jobs. There weren't many of them going, but whenever someone was leaving it was the talk of the place, and somebody quickly came forward to step into their shoes.

Because she worked in a shop in the high street, Rhianon had always heard all the news and gossip. The realisation that she couldn't talk to Rhianon, share her problems with her, stabbed at her like a knife. She had always turned to her sister for advice and comfort.

Ever since she had been a very small girl, Rhianon had been like a mother to her, and deep down Sabrina felt terrible about the way she was treating her. She tried not to think about it, but she knew that Rhianon must be grieving about what had happened to Pryce, just as she was.

She hadn't meant to hurt her sister, and she had never intended to fall in love with the same man as Rhianon, but that wasn't really her fault, it was fate.

Now, so it seemed, he was lost to both of them, unless some miracle happened and he was able to talk his way out of the predicament he was in.

Why did life have to be so complicated, Sabrina wondered. She drained her cup and put it back in the saucer, and began collecting up her belongings ready to leave.

She noticed that the girl who came to give her the bill and clear the table was not much older than herself. As she handed her the money, she plucked up the courage to ask her how she could find out about a room and a job.

The girl raised her thick eyebrows and shrugged expressively. 'There's a daft question!' she giggled. 'You could try looking in the *Echo*, mind.'

'The *Echo*?'

'The evening paper!'

Sabrina's face fell. 'What time does that come out then?'

'Not until about four o'clock. You can see yesterday's in the public library. It's only along the road. Go out of here, turn left when you leave the arcade, and then left again, and there it is. You can't miss it. Big tall building it is, standing all on its own in the middle of William Street. Go into the Reading Room. They have all the papers there, see.'

Sabrina found three jobs that she thought she could do. One was in Splott, one at Cardiff Docks, and one in The Hayes. She looked the places up on a street directory displayed in the library, and decided to try the one in The Hayes, because that was the nearest to where she was at the moment.

The company was called Ferdinands and they were importers of goods from Holland, everything from tulips to gin. The manager, Mr Meyer, was a pompous, portly little man with a square face, small tight mouth, dark beady eyes and sallow skin.

At first he was dubious about whether at her age she had enough experience for the job. When she told him she had worked in an insurance office he agreed to give her a trial, since she would only be typing invoices. He offered her seven shillings a week. Hesitantly she told him that it was not nearly as much as she'd been earning in Pontdarw. Frowning, he promised her a rise after a month, if she was any good at the job.

When he asked her for her address she wasn't sure what to say. She didn't want to tell him that she was staying at an expensive hotel in St Mary Street.

'I'm still looking for somewhere to live,' she explained.

To her surprise he gave her an address to try.

'Grangetown is only about twenty minutes' walk away, so when the weather is good you won't need to take a tram,' he told her.

'Thank you.' She took the slip of paper he'd written the address on and went to put it in her handbag.

'You'd better cut along and see if it's still vacant,' he advised. 'If so, get yourself fixed up and then you can start here tomorrow morning. Eight thirty sharp, half an hour for lunch, finish at six thirty and at one o'clock on Saturdays,' he said briskly.

Sabrina checked the address he had given her. 'How do I get to Corporation Road from here?'

He frowned. 'Haven't you ever been to Cardiff before today?'

She shook her head. 'No, never!'

She sensed he was about to ask her more questions, but she wasn't prepared to answer them, so she quickly made for the door.

'Hold on, I haven't told you how to get there yet! You arrived by train?'

Sabrina nodded.

'Right, well go back to the station, then instead of turning right and coming towards St Mary Street, turn the other way, down Wood Street. Continue along Penarth Road, then left along the Taff Embankment until you come to Aber Street. Turn up there and you'll find yourself in Corporation Road. Do you think you can manage that?'

'I'll find it,' she said stiffly. 'I've got a tongue in my head. I can always ask if I get lost.'

Chapter Ten

Even the national newspapers carried banner headlines about Hwyel Barker's death.

'Tragic casualty of the miners' strike'

'Union official accused of dealing a fatal blow'

'Innocent bystander killed by feuding miners'

'Knock-out blow proves fatal'

These were just some of the screaming headlines of what had happened on that fateful first day of the strike – Saturday 1st May 1926.

The reports all described Pryce Pritchard as a zealot who was fanatical about the rights of miners. They claimed that he was inflamed by what he saw as the injustice caused by the coal owners to the men who spent their lives working underground in appalling conditions. Many of the reports also described him as a powerful fighter, in every sense of the word.

Rhianon wept as she read them all. She longed to see Pryce, to find out if there was anything she could do to help him, but Constable Jenkins had warned her that it was pointless trying.

'Going all the way down to Cardiff jail won't do you a scrap of good, my lovely,' he told her.

'They might have let you have a few words with him if the pair of you'd been married, but as a mere friend they won't even give you the time of day.'

'If I write a letter to him, then, do you think he will get it?'

Constable Jenkins lifted his broad shoulders in a barely perceptible shrug. 'No harm in trying, cariad, but don't be disappointed if you get no answer. They might let him read it, but even if they do I doubt if they will let him write back to you.'

'Can you find out if Pryce will be represented when he appears in court, and then perhaps I could speak to whoever that will be?'

He nodded kindly. 'Leave it with me, cariad, but don't build up your hopes.'

Build up my hopes, Rhianon thought bitterly, she had no hopes, none at all. In one week she had lost not only Pryce, but her sister and her sister's boyfriend. Hope was the last thing she had.

Each morning she waited for a letter from Sabrina, but nothing came, there was no news at all about her. She'd asked everyone she could think of if they had any idea where Sabrina could be. She'd even gone to the Barkers' house to ask them, but they told her they hadn't seen or heard from her since she'd been in chapel the night after Hwyel died.

'We thought that at least she would come and see us even if she didn't turn up for work,'

Cledwyn Barker said stiffly. 'Is she coming to Hwyel's funeral? People will think it is very strange if she doesn't.'

Rhianon knew this, she had heard it so many times from her father that it resounded in her head over and over again like a dirge. He felt it was a terrible slur on their name that Sabrina had absconded and no one knew where she was.

'Don't fret about it, cariad,' Polly Potter told her. 'She'll be back for Hwyel's funeral, you'll see.'

'How can you be so sure about that? She won't have any idea when it is to be.'

'Don't talk daft girl, it's in every newspaper you pick up! She'd have a job not to know when it is, if you ask me!'

The funeral date was fixed for Thursday 20th May at midday, and the whole of Pontdarw seemed to be intent on attending. Some of the shops had even decided to close.

Right up until the very last minute Rhianon hoped and prayed that Sabrina would put in an appearance. Her father had already left for Capel Bethel, and finally, knowing that she would be late, and that would cause him even more pain, Rhianon locked the front door and hurried to the chapel.

All the way there she kept telling herself that Sabrina would already be at the chapel when she arrived. As Polly said, she would have read about when it was to take place and she would go straight there.

When she reached Capel Bethel, though, she knew from the way heads turned, and people stared at her as though surprised to see that she was on her own, that Sabrina hadn't appeared.

She felt in a complete daze as she sat through her father's overlong address; the drone of his voice was like a saw rasping away inside her head.

Numb with grief she followed the cortège to the small hillside cemetery and stood by the graveside with the other chief mourners, but it was Pryce, not Hwyel, that she was thinking about.

Pryce was still alive, yet in some ways he might as well be dead. His name had been blackened, his career as a teacher doomed. When his case came to court there was no doubt at all that he would be given a prison sentence. His freedom would be taken from him for such a long time that his spirit would be broken by the time he was released.

Her own future was in ruins, too, she reminded herself. Years of loneliness lay ahead. She would wait for Pryce, of course, but what if he didn't want her when he was free?

That was why it was so important that she should see him and talk to him. What was she to believe? Everyone seemed to have conflicting opinions. Sometimes she was sure they said what they thought she wanted to hear rather than telling her the truth, or even what they really thought.

She and Sabrina were so very different that Pryce couldn't possibly be in love with both of them. Had he been tempted by Sabrina, fleetingly, or had he fallen for her? If only she could talk to him, or to Sabrina. If only both of them weren't completely out of reach.

Pryce had such dreams for the future. He'd worked so hard to become a qualified teacher, and now, if he was sent to prison, all that hard work would be wasted.

She thought of the enthusiasm he had put into his work for his fellow miners. His duties as a Trade Union official had taken up much of his energy, and there had been little time left over for them to enjoy each other's company. She hadn't minded. She'd admired the way he was so whole-hearted about all his undertakings. For her that was part of his attraction.

After the service and interment ended, Rhianon went over to speak to Mr and Mrs Barker, but she felt deeply hurt by their reaction. Their faces were stony, and they simply nodded when she expressed her condolences, then turned away and ignored her.

Blinded by tears she left and went home, even though she knew that would only incense her father. She suspected that she would have to listen to a tirade from him later in the evening about her behaviour.

Perhaps Sabrina had not only left home straight after Hwyel's death, but stayed away ever since, because she hadn't wanted to listen to her father's sanctimonious sentiments about Hwyel? The ordeal of facing Hwyel's parents would have been another reason for her to go. Or was it because she was ashamed of the fact that she had been the catalyst between the two men, the spark that had ignited the fire that was destroying so many lives?

Perhaps Sabrina had been the clever one. By vanishing, she'd freed herself and escaped both from her father and from the Barkers.

And perhaps I ought to do the same, Rhianon mused.

What was there left for her in Pontdarw except her job? Her ambition to become a teacher was faltering without Pryce there to urge her on, which meant she was in danger of remaining a shop assistant for ever. She was fond of Polly Potter, but to spend the rest of her life behind a counter in a haberdashery shop in Pontdarw was a stifling prospect.

Perhaps the time had come for her to spread her wings and find out what went on in the outside world. She should begin a new life, put the past behind her.

There was her father to consider, but why should she put him first in her life and sacrifice her future for him? The truth was she couldn't bear the thought of being alone in the house with him, and having to listen to his ponderous deliberations.

She wouldn't leave him completely in the lurch. She couldn't simply disappear like

Sabrina had done. Before she left she'd make sure that he was going to be properly looked after. There were plenty of women who would come in to cook and clean for him. They'd be only too pleased to earn some money, especially if the strike went on for much longer. Even if it ended tomorrow, it would take months for most people to get back on their feet. Whoever was working for her father wouldn't relinquish the job lightly, not even if he drove them to distraction with his preaching.

She'd write to him regularly and keep him fully acquainted with where she was and what she was doing. She'd visit him, too, from time to time.

Where to go, that was the problem. It had to be somewhere where she'd be able to find work, and her only experience was as a shop assistant. So it would have to be a large town, not some small place like Pontdarw where jobs were filled before they even became vacant.

The largest place she could think of was Cardiff. She'd never been there, but people who knew it said that it was a city with many fine buildings, the centre being full of big shops. With her years of experience as a counter assistant she shouldn't have any trouble finding work there.

Her mood lifted, and she became almost excited as she thought more and more about her decision. Cardiff was where they had taken

Pryce. It would be where his trial was held. If she went there, and found work in one of the shops, then she'd be close to him.

They mightn't let her visit him while he was in custody, but they couldn't stop her from going along to the trial. Leastways she didn't think they could. And if he was found guilty, as everyone thought he would be, if he was kept in Cardiff jail, then surely she'd be able to visit him.

What was more, if she was living in Cardiff she could carry on with her night-school lessons. She might eventually qualify as a teacher after all.

She told her father of her decision to leave home the moment he arrived back after the funeral. She knew it was insensitive of her, but she also knew that if she didn't act right away then her courage would fail her.

'If that is what you think is best for you, daughter. You are obviously without conscience, just like your sister, so presumably you'll go ahead and do it even though it means you will be leaving me here desolate and alone.'

'I shall make sure that you're taken care of, Father. I'll arrange for someone to come in and cook for you and clean the house.'

He waved his hand imperiously. 'Now that I'm an old man, my two daughters, who have both brought disgrace on our family name, are deserting me. My days on this earth are numbered, so be prepared not ever to see me again once you walk out of that door. I shall die lonely and neglected.'

'That's not true, Father, and you know it,' Rhianon defended. 'You have plenty of friends of your own. You have your position at Capel Bethel . . .' Tears misted her eyes at the unfairness of his accusations.

Over the next few days she planned for her own future. She also made arrangements to ensure that her father was well looked after. He did everything in his power to stop her, but Rhianon's mind was made up. She was determined that nothing he said, or did, would deflect her from her purpose.

She told Polly Potter what she was planning to do, but agreed to carry on working until the very last minute.

'I worry that I am going to leave you in the lurch,' she said with concern.

'Not a bit of it, my lovely! There's plenty of miners' wives around who will be only too glad to come in and give a hand if I ask them. The women will do just about anything to get enough money to keep their kiddies from going hungry.'

Things didn't work out as Rhianon had planned. The morning she braced herself to tell her father that she was definitely leaving Pontdarw she found him sitting in his armchair, bent forward with his hands on his knees, his face grey and drawn.

'Whatever is the matter, Father?' she asked

in alarm. 'Can I get you anything? A drink of water?'

He waved her aside. 'I'll be all right again in a few minutes. Having one of my attacks, that's all.'

'Attacks? What attacks?'

'My heart.' He lifted his hand and patted his chest shakily.

'You've never said there is anything wrong with your heart before. Shall I send for the doctor?'

'There's nothing more he can do,' Edwin Webster gasped breathlessly. 'I went to see him last week and he gave me a thorough examination. He prescribed some new tablets, but they don't seem to be doing much good, though I suppose it is early days yet.'

Rhianon looked at him in disbelief. 'You've never mentioned that there was anything wrong before,' she repeated. 'You've always boasted that you're as strong as an ox.'

Her father smiled wistfully. 'I was, but I am not any longer, or so it would seem.'

'You've never said a word about being on any sort of tablets, either,' Rhianon persisted.

He shook his head. 'You've been so wrapped up in all the other things that have been happening that I thought it best not to mention it. There's nothing that you or anyone else can do.'

'Did the doctor tell you what has caused this problem with your heart, then?'

'Getting myself upset and worried, that's what he said brought it on. It's all happened over the last couple of weeks. Perplexed about that stupid fight between Pryce Pritchard and Hwyel Barker, and then Hwyel dying like he did. Worrying about Sabrina running off like she has. It all puts a strain on the heart when it is as old as mine.

'And now, as if that isn't enough, you're saying you are going to leave home, the same as Sabrina. Knowing that any day now I'll be all on my own here, with only strangers to do things for me, isn't helping!'

Rhianon placed a hand on his shoulder consolingly. 'I had no idea you were unwell. Of course I won't go away. I wouldn't dream of leaving you here on your own if you're ill.'

Chapter Eleven

As soon as her interview was over Sabrina went back to the hotel, collected her suitcase and paid her bill. Following the directions she'd been given she walked down Penarth Road and then along the Taff Embankment, keeping the grey waters of the River Taff on her left. The suitcase seemed to grow heavier and heavier and she kept having to stop and rest.

She wished she'd left it at the hotel, found the place in Corporation Road, and then gone back to collect it. Her arms were aching, and she was out of breath, by the time she reached Aber Street. She cut through it and found herself in a busy main road where there were trams passing up and down every few minutes.

The woman who answered the door was extremely tall, broad-shouldered and statuesque. Her blonde hair was in a thick plait that was wound around her head emphasising the broadness of her face, her pale blue eyes and fresh complexion. She wore a mid-blue cotton dress partially covered with a crossover apron in blue and white gingham.

'Yah?'

'I was told you had a room I could rent,'

Sabrina told her nervously, dropping her heavy suitcase onto the donkey-stoned doorstep.

The woman shook her head emphatically, pressing her thick pink lips together firmly. 'No room,' she said curtly.

Sabrina frowned as she stared down at the scrap of paper in her hand, checking the address written there. There was no name given, only the house number, but it corresponded exactly with the number plate on the centre of the door.

'Sorry,' she picked up her suitcase and took a step back, 'Mr Meyer told me there was . . .'

'Wait! You said Meyer? Hans Meyer? Hans Meyer from Ferdinands who have offices at The Hayes?'

'Yes, that's right.'

The woman's moon face softened, she beamed a warm welcome, displaying a mouthful of large white teeth. 'You should have said who told you about it! If you want a room and Hans Meyer sent you then of course there is a room. Come along in.'

She opened the door wide in a welcoming gesture. Grabbing hold of Sabrina's suitcase she ushered her down the passageway into the big living room at the rear of the house.

'I am Helga van Amudsen, but you can call me Helga. Come, I show you the room. It is the middle room of the house and it is lovely. It has a door out into the yard and you walk across that to the kitchen, which we will share together. Understand?'

Sabrina nodded.

'That is good. You will like it here. Hans Meyer tell you it is good here, yes?'

Sabrina was not too sure what to say. She assumed they were talking about the same person. Hans must be his Christian name, or a Dutch form of address, she told herself as she followed Helga into the adjoining room.

As Helga had said, it was a nice room. It was quite large, much bigger than her room at home. The single bed was tucked away at one end and the blue and white bedspread matched the floor-length curtains hanging at the glass-panelled outside door.

At that end of the room there was an armchair, a small round table, and an upright chair. Sabrina walked over to the glass door and looked out onto a small paved yard of spotless red tiles. She could see the door to the back part of the house, which she assumed led to the kitchen as Helga had explained.

She looked round her with interest. There was a built-in floor-to-ceiling cupboard on one side of the fireplace, and a set of shelves holding china above a smaller cupboard on the other side.

'This is for your food and things like that,' Helga told her, waving a hand to the shelves stacked with blue and yellow china, and then opening one of the cupboard doors underneath. 'This,' she opened the door to the full-length cupboard on the other side, 'is for your clothes and personal belongings. There is a lavatory out in the yard, the other side of the kitchen, which you can use.'

'Where . . . where do I get washed?'

'Right here, of course. You bring water from the kitchen in a bowl, and then you tip it away down the drain outside afterwards. Yes?'

Sabrina nodded and smiled a little uncertainly.

'Is there anything else you must ask?'

'No, no! It all seems to be very nice indeed . . . except . . .' She paused and looked helplessly at Helga. How could she explain that she had never cooked herself a meal in her life, and had no idea how to start?

Her father had always insisted that Rhianon was the one who should take care of all that sort of thing. Rhianon did the shopping, cooked the meals and kept the house clean. Rhianon changed the sheets on their beds, washed and ironed Sabrina's clothes, did her mending and even bought her new stockings, vests, and things like that, when she needed them. The only shopping she'd ever done in her life was for new clothes.

Taking a deep breath she explained, 'It . . . it's about meals. Do I have to cook them myself?'

Helga looked at her in astonishment, her wide mouth agape. 'You do not like the cooking?'

'Well, it's not that, I won't have much time to shop for food if I am out working all day.'

'You are saying that you want me to cook for

you, is that it? You would like me to prepare a meal for you each evening, perhaps, yes?'

'That would be wonderful!'

'It would cost you extra,' Helga warned. 'The room will be five shillings a week and an evening meal will be another one shilling a night, so that will be twelve shillings a week.' She watched Sabrina's face as she heard this, and quickly added, 'and there will be a charge of another one shilling and sixpence each week for clean sheets. So it will be thirteen shillings and sixpence a week and you must pay it in advance.'

Sabrina looked worried. The wage Mr Meyer was paying her was only half that amount. She did have her savings to fall back on, she reminded herself. Also, Mr Meyer had promised her a rise after she had completed a month's trial.

She chewed on the inside of her mouth as she tried to make her decision. She had to live somewhere and she couldn't afford to stay on at the hotel. Reluctantly she counted out her first week's payment in advance.

The meal Helga served was plain but sustaining. Even so, Sabrina decided she couldn't exist on only one meal a day. She would have to budget very carefully if she was to make her money last out until she received the promised rise.

Sabrina found her days at Ferdinands far more arduous than when she had been working for

Mr Barker. She had always found him very easy-going and suspected that he treated her leniently because she was Hwyel's girlfriend. Mr Meyer acted very differently! He believed in extracting the last ounce of work from his employees. He was a slave-driver who tolerated no talking or time-wasting, and who demanded the utmost accuracy and neatness in everybody's work.

By the end of the first week Sabrina felt absolutely exhausted. The walk to and from Corporation Road was tiring, yet she didn't want to waste money on a tram – not while the weather was fine – preferring to buy herself something to eat at midday.

She wasn't sleeping as well as she had at home. Although her room was not at the front of the house the sounds of the trams clanking up and down Corporation Road, from early morning until well after midnight, disturbed her sleep. So, too, did all the other noises in the house. Several times she had woken in the middle of the night to hear people moving about and had been unable to get back to sleep again afterwards.

Sabrina also found she was missing her father. She wished his stern authoritative figure was still there in the background, telling her what she should and should not do. Above all, she missed Rhianon.

For the first time in her life, Sabrina appreciated how wonderful her sister had been. She had been able to tell her anything, knowing that she would understand. Rhianon had cared for her so well that now, without her presence, Sabrina felt neglected.

She also missed having Hwyel dancing attendance on her, pampering her, and humouring her every whim.

Although she refused to let herself think about Pryce, she scanned the billboards every day for news of when his case was coming to court.

From things she heard discussed in the office, it seemed the seamen had gone back to work, and so had the postmen and most of the other workers. It was only the miners who remained on strike, still demanding that their cause should be heard.

'Get this fellow Pryce Pritchard up in court and sentenced and then they'll cave in,' one of the visitors to the office told Hans Meyer. 'His sort want shooting! They'll have all the rest of us out of work as well as themselves, given half a chance.'

'Well, I don't think they'll shoot him, but they might well hang him,' Hans Meyer rejoined. 'He killed a man, and here in this country the punishment for that is to hang, is it not?'

'The chap he thumped didn't die right away though, did he! Technically, it was only manslaughter, and because of that he might get away with a life sentence.'

'Given the chance of a life sentence, or hanging, I know which one I would choose!' Hans

Meyer stated. 'If they hang you then it's all over and done with. If you're given a life sentence then in some ways it is a far greater punishment. The conditions in prison are terrible, especially for lifers, the others give them hell.'

The two of them argued the pros and cons until Sabrina felt she would scream. Neither of them ever mentioned that Pryce Pritchard might get off altogether, she noticed.

She wondered how Rhianon was bearing up. She could well imagine her father's ponderous lectures about sin and evil, and how Pryce deserved to be brought to justice.

Poor Pryce, he must be suffering more than any of us, she thought miserably. Why couldn't they have discovered their feelings for each other without any of this happening? If only he had met her before he'd taken up with Rhianon, before she had met Hwyel. They could have been together and Hwyel would still be alive, too.

Shut away from the world, were Pryce's thoughts of Rhianon or of her? His passion had been so intense that she was sure he must be thinking of her. He was certainly never out of her thoughts! She dreamed about him at night, she thought about him on her daily walk to work, and again on her walk back in the evening.

He even came between her and her work. Sometimes her hands would hover over the typewriter keys, but she wasn't sitting there in a stuffy poky little office, with all the noise and bustle of city life going on outside the window. She was back in Pontdarw, in Pryce's arms.

In her mind she could feel his mouth covering hers, his weight pressing the breath from her body as his strong lean hands explored her burning flesh, stirring her senses to fever pitch.

She found it desperately hard to keep her mind on her work, and she sensed that Hans Meyer was aware of this. Several times she had come out of one of her daydreams to find him watching her, his hard beady eyes speculative. She expected him to say something, reprimand her even, but although his small mouth would tighten ominously, he remained silent.

As the days passed her feeling of loneliness, of isolation, became greater. There were no other girls at the Ferdinands office, and both the men who worked there permanently were middle-aged and dour. They rarely spoke to her, and they conversed with each other in a language which she didn't understand, but she assumed to be Dutch.

There were frequent visitors to see Hans Meyer. Some were blond and plump like himself, others dark and saturnine-looking. Although they stared at her inquisitively they never spoke to her. Within minutes of their arrival they were closeted away in Hans Meyer's private office. Once their business was transacted he escorted them to the door, shook hands with them and they departed.

Exactly what the nature of their business was she had no idea, but she assumed it was something connected with the import and export trade that Ferdinands conducted.

She was rarely asked to type any correspondence. Some of the invoices she typed were for bulbs, wines, spirits and tobacco products. Others had the products in some form of key or code word, which she didn't understand, and she was instructed to leave the name and address section blank. Hans Meyer filled these in himself in ink. The counterfoils to these particular invoices were kept in a locked drawer in his office.

On her second Sunday in Cardiff Sabrina felt so homesick that she was very tempted to take the train to Pontdarw to see Rhianon. She might even have some news of Pryce, she told herself.

When she calculated the inroads the trip would make on her rapidly dwindling savings, she gave up the idea. Her resources had almost gone and now every penny counted.

As the weather was warm and sunny she spent the day walking round Cathays Park, in the centre of the city, marvelling at the magnificence of the Temple of Peace and wishing Rhianon was there to share it all with her. As soon as she got her rise, she promised herself, she would go to Pontdarw, even if it was only for one day.

Chapter Twelve

Rhianon was beside herself with worry over Sabrina's disappearance. Every time a customer came into the shop she looked up expectantly, hoping it might be her sister. If there was a knock on the door at night, her heart raced as she went to open it.

'If only she'd left a note,' she said over and over again to both her father and to Polly Potter. 'If only we knew where she was, and that she was safe and sound.'

'The devil looks after his own,' her father told her dourly, 'and a more wicked young woman would be hard to find. All these years I've been nurturing an evil spirit in the bosom of my family. I blame you, Rhianon. You were responsible for bringing her up. She has learnt her wicked ways from you. I knew no good would come from your association with that, that . . . man, and my premonitions have come true.'

'Pryce has nothing whatever to do with Sabrina's disappearance,' Rhianon replied defensively. 'Pryce is in prison, and no one is allowed to visit him, so how could he have persuaded Sabrina to leave home?'

Edwin Webster's colour heightened in anger.

'Don't argue with me, girl! He is implicated, he is the root cause of all our troubles,' he insisted.

Rhianon regarded him sorrowfully. She could see that the worry of it all had turned him into a pitiful old man. The spark had gone out of him, even his voice had lost its dominant fervour. His eyes had sunk back into his lined face and his steel-grey hair had become lank. His clothes hung on him as though they were made for a bigger man altogether.

His appetite, too, had been affected. Normally he enjoyed his food. Even though he never praised her cooking skills he always left a clean plate, but this was no longer the case. He picked at his food and pushed it away half eaten, even though she had begun to serve him smaller portions, and to cook only the dishes she knew to be his favourites.

'He's probably feeling guilty about the way things have turned out, cariad,' Polly Potter commented. 'He spoilt your Sabrina from the day her mother died, now didn't he. He never made her lift a finger to help you in the house, but pandered to her every whim, and let her have her own way over everything.'

'She was only nine years old when Mam died, and it wasn't an easy time for any of us,' Rhianon sighed. 'I suppose he was doing what he thought was right and trying to be both mother and father to her.'

'She didn't need him to be a mother to her, she had you,' Polly stated. 'Sacrificed yourself to her you have, my lovely, and well you know it! You're more like a mother than a sister to her, and that's a fact.'

'I've not made a very good job of it then, have I?' Rhianon said ruefully.

She knew Polly was trying to be kind, but it seemed that in the last few weeks her entire life had changed drastically. Nothing, she thought glumly, would ever be the same again.

Her father had always been critical of whatever she did, but now there was a tinge of hatred in his voice. His eyes, when they met hers, seemed to reject her very presence.

She knew he blamed her for Sabrina's disappearance, but he didn't seem to understand that she was as worried as he was, perhaps even more so. She knew better than he did how naïve and inexperienced Sabrina was when it came to looking after herself. Perhaps she had been wrong to do so much for her. It might have been kinder to have forced her to do her share of the housework, and to take care of her own washing, ironing and mending, but it was too late to rectify matters now.

Sabrina had always been able to wheedle her into doing things for her, and because Rhianon loved her so much she simply accepted it as her responsibility to agree without making a fuss.

If her father had been stricter with Sabrina, not allowed her to wear such provocative clothes, then perhaps she wouldn't have become such a flirt. There were so many 'ifs', and now it was too late to act upon any of them.

Her father was so inconsistent in his attitude towards Sabrina, she reflected. Look at the way he had encouraged her to go out with Hwyel from the moment she went to work for the Barkers.

This was one of the reasons why Rhianon couldn't believe that Sabrina had suddenly become interested in Pryce. Why should she when she already had a boyfriend, and they were making plans to be married? Polly reckoned it was jealousy or spite, but Rhianon wasn't convinced by that argument. Hwyel had more money and probably a far more prosperous future ahead of him than Pryce would ever have. Ever since she was a small child, material things had mattered a great deal to Sabrina. She liked nice clothes, going to the pictures, having money to spend on lipstick and silk stockings and chocolates.

Rhianon knew her sister was a flirt, but she had never taken her mischievous glances at Pryce, or the provocative quips she made to him, as anything more than Sabrina showing off. She had never dreamed that there was anything serious going on between the two of them. Yet Polly had, and she'd warned her time and time again to keep her eye on the way Sabrina was flirting with Pryce before things went too far.

Mr Barker had paid Sabrina far more than

she could possibly earn anywhere else. When she'd once mentioned this Sabrina had looked annoyed. 'I'm worth every penny he pays me,' she'd argued. 'You're only saying that because you are envious that I earn twice as much as you do, serving behind a counter.'

Even with her generous wage packet, Sabrina never had enough money for all the things she wanted. She was always borrowing stockings or shampoo, and cadging a loan for something or other. Yet Hwyel had always paid for everything whenever he took her out, and she had never been asked to hand over any money at home for her keep.

Annoying though this had been at times, Rhianon would still have given anything to have her back at home, or at least to find out where she was. She didn't know which was worse, her concern about Sabrina or her anguish over what was going to happen to Pryce when his case came to court.

The strike had fizzled out like a damp squib, except for the miners. Fortunately for their wives and children, it was summer so they were able to manage on less food and they didn't need warm clothes. Later in the year, as Christmas approached, if the miners were still out there would be real hardship as their meagre savings dwindled to nothing.

In Pontdarw, as in most of the mining villages, there was an air of despondency that even the summer sun couldn't disperse.

Weekend picnics were out of the question. Even the youngest children sensed that no one was in the mood for fun. Men hung around in small groups, looking unhappy and scanning the headlines in other people's newspapers whenever they got the chance, because they couldn't afford to waste money on such things themselves.

Some of them were blacklegging, working as delivery men in towns near Pontdarw, or as casual labourers in the building trade. They were ready to do anything to make a few extra shillings to help eke out their savings.

The pubs and the club were still half full. The men sat over half a pint of beer for hours at a time, exchanging views, culling news, or playing dominoes to help pass the day away.

Without Pryce Pritchard there to chivvy them into action, most of them were like lost souls. They were not sure what they ought to be doing, and half-hoping that the strike would end and they could all go back to work again. Most of them were now willing to do so, even if it was at the same wage as they'd been earning when the strike began.

The coal bosses knew this and they were prepared to sit the workers out. They had lost money during the strike and they needed to recoup this loss on behalf of their shareholders. When the men did return to work, as they surely must once the cold weather set in, then the bosses would only accept their labour if they took a lower wage. The cause that Pryce, along with all the other union officials, had been fighting so hard for was already doomed.

Pryce, too, was doomed, Rhianon thought worriedly. There was a great deal of speculation about the sort of punishment that would be meted out to him. Everybody seemed to have a different opinion, some more vindictive than others.

The Barkers wanted him to hang. 'Why should he live when our Hwyel is dead?' Mr Barker had demanded bitterly the day Rhianon had gone along to ask him if he had any news of Sabrina.

'I would have thought you would feel the same way,' he went on, 'since he has caused such a rift between you and your sister. My heart goes out to your poor father. It must be an unbearable burden for him, a man of such strong faith, to know that his favourite child has become involved with a man of Pritchard's reputation and strayed into such evil ways.'

Rhianon didn't tell her father anything about this conversation, or about Mr Barker's views as to what had happened. She didn't even mention her visit to him. Tentatively she did suggest to her father that perhaps they should report Sabrina's absence to the police again and let them see if they could find her, but he had been incensed at the idea.

'She's brought enough dishonour on my name as it is without adding fuel to the fire,' he ranted. 'If we ask the police to find her now after the recent developments, news of it will spread everywhere. Wicked things they'll say about my girl, and though they may well be true I don't want them aired to the whole wide world. She's already disgraced our family by her actions, and by now she has probably sunk as low as it is possible to get.'

'Surely that worries you?' Rhianon argued. 'Where is your Christian spirit of forgiveness?'

His eyes were steely as he stared back at her. 'How can I ever forgive Sabrina for the shame she has brought on my name? Nor will I ever absolve you, Rhianon, for your sinful wickedness in leading her into temptation,' he said grimly.

Rhianon remained silent, her thoughts in turmoil. She felt resentful that her father blamed her for Sabrina's selfish nature, which was due to his spoiling and indulgence. Sabrina had taken advantage of his favouritism and had laid claim to everything that took her fancy. If Rhianon had treasured something, Sabrina had wanted it all the more. This was probably one of the reasons she had made a play for Pryce, Rhianon reasoned. She'd snatched him away, just as she used to take Rhianon's favourite doll or pretty hair ribbons when they were small.

Rhianon had tried hard to fill the void after their mother had died, but it had not been easy because her father had always taken Sabrina's side. This was the first time she had ever heard him say a word against her, and even now he was blaming her for her sister's transgression.

Perhaps she should have been stronger and gone ahead with her plans to leave and try and start a new life, ready for the day when she and Pryce would be together again.

Now she was trapped. Pryce had yet to come to trial, and until he did it seemed there was no way she could get in touch with him. Sabrina had vanished, and she was left to look after her sick father and listen to his continual tirades of blame and reproach.

Chapter Thirteen

Sabrina was eagerly looking forward to Friday 18th June because it would be her fourth payday since she had started working at Ferdinands. According to her calculations, this meant that she had completed her trial period and was now due to receive the rise Hans Meyer had promised her.

When he handed over her sealed brown wage envelope at the end of the day she opened it quickly, anxious to see how much there was. Then her heart sank because there was still only a measly seven shillings inside it.

Tears of anger, as well as frustration, brimmed in her eyes as she tipped the coins out into her hand and recounted them. Bristling with indignation, she rapped on Meyer's office door.

Her employer's face was impassive as he listened to what she had to say. Then with the merest shrug of his shoulders he turned his attention back to the work in front of him.

'Yes, I agree you have now completed your first month here so I will give the matter my consideration,' he told her dismissively. 'Don't let me keep you from your work, we will discuss this sometime next week,' he added brusquely.

'You don't understand! I was expecting that there would be more money in my wage packet this week,' Sabrina persisted. 'I need it to pay Mrs Amudsen. She charges me such a lot!'

'You've managed quite well up until now, so why suddenly such a fuss?' he asked impatiently.

Sabrina sighed unhappily. 'She is charging me twice what I earn here! I've had to make up the difference out of the money I had saved up before I came to Cardiff. Now that is all gone,' she told him agitatedly. 'I can't afford to go out anywhere or even take a tram to come to work, not even when it is raining. I wanted to go home for the day on Sunday.

'I haven't seen my sister or any of my family for over a month,' she continued in genuine distress, 'but I can't afford the train fare to Pontdarw,' she added, even though she knew he was no longer listening to her.

'Next week, next week. I'll sort it all out next week,' he snapped.

Sabrina left Hans Meyer's office not sure whether she had won her argument for a pay rise, or whether he was merely procrastinating because he had no interest in her problems.

There was an enormous pile of invoices awaiting her so she was late finishing that evening, and unable to go to the library to look for a job elsewhere.

That evening Helga Amudsen reminded her somewhat sharply about the overdue rent.

Next day, Sabrina was waiting to speak to Hans Meyer about his promise of a rise the minute he arrived at the office.

'This is not the time for us to talk about such matters. I said I would consider it, but since I have to be out of the office most of next week it will have to wait until I return,' he snapped, waving her away impatiently.

'That's not good enough,' she protested. 'I already owe Helga Amudsen for last week and she has threatened to throw me out into the street if I don't find the money. I'm really desperate!' she wailed, fat tears rolling down her cheeks.

'Don't worry about Helga, I'll deal with her,' he said curtly.

She looked at him in astonishment. 'How will you do that?' she gulped.

'Perhaps the answer, Miss Webster, is for you to have another job.'

Sabrina stiffened. She sniffed unhappily and then dabbed at her eyes to give herself time to think.

'Are you telling me to leave?' she blurted out, sniffing even more loudly.

Hans Meyer gave a sharp laugh. 'Not at all. I meant extra work.'

Sabrina's heart sank at the thought of longer hours. She was already working from eight in the morning until after six in the evening, and until one o'clock on Saturday.

'I did not mean here in the office,' Hans Meyer told her. 'I meant something you can do in the evening, work that is like play, yes?'

She looked puzzled.

'I have not the time to discuss the matter at the moment,' he told her abruptly. 'The invoicing is far more important.'

'Helga said that if I didn't . . .'

'Leave her to me,' he snapped, avoiding her eyes. 'You get that invoicing finished and I will deal with Helga Amudsen. You need not worry. Everything can be sorted out next week if you are prepared to co-operate over doing some extra work.'

Sabrina tried to concentrate on the invoices, but it was difficult. When she returned to Corporation Road she told Helga what had been discussed and was stunned by her reaction. She accepted the news that Hans Meyer would contact her in an extremely cordial manner. Sabrina found her as pleasant and as welcoming as she'd been on the night of her arrival. Helga even offered her a second helping of her special hot apple cake.

Sabrina was still not convinced that everything was going to be all right. She was puzzled about what Hans Meyer had meant about doing some extra work. She was already undertaking more than she had ever done in her life, and yet she had far less to show for it, she thought ruefully.

To make matters worse it was a wet weekend,

and having no money to spend Sabrina found it one of the longest she had ever known. By Sunday evening, because it was very warm and muggy, her room felt more like a prison than a comfortable bedsit. Being forced to stay confined there had given her plenty of time to think and to take stock of her situation.

It was now almost two months since the fight between Hwyel and Pryce, six weeks since Hwyel had died, a month since his funeral and five weeks since she had left Pontdarw and come to Cardiff.

By now, she decided, she should have established a fresh life for herself. She ought to have made some new friends and be going out enjoying herself. Instead all she did was go to work, come home and sit in her room every night, and walk around the streets on a Sunday. She'd not been able to go to the pictures, buy anything new or spend any time pleasantly relaxing.

She couldn't even afford to buy the right sort of clothes for work. When she had gone for her interview she had been wearing her dark suit. It was the only really sober outfit she owned, and it was far too hot and formal now that the weather was so much warmer.

Mr Meyer had glowered disapprovingly when she wore one of her flimsy floaty dresses, and obviously didn't think it was appropriate wear for the office. In fact, he had even gone as far as to tell her so when she had arrived in a white chiffon dress with a short pleated skirt.

'Are you coming in to work, or are you on your way to play tennis?' he'd scowled.

Both the other men in the office, Claud Ernst and Jakob Samuels, had guffawed heartily at his remark. They'd made comments to each other in Dutch. Although she didn't understand what they were saying she was quite sure it was something rude, because of the way they'd looked at each other and laughed.

She realised now that leaving home hadn't been a good idea at all. Even so, she couldn't bring herself to admit defeat and go back to Pontdarw. Rhianon would probably welcome her with open arms. As soon as she heard what a hard time she'd been having her sister would forgive her and do everything possible to make things right for her again.

She wasn't too sure, though, what her father's attitude would be. In the past he had treated her like some precious prodigy who could do no wrong, but she thought it unlikely that his feelings would be the same after all that had happened.

Hwyel had, after all, been the son of one of his closest friends, and by now her father had probably been made aware of her part in encouraging the fight between Hwyel and Pryce. Such behaviour would go against his principles. He would be so angry about the reflection on his good name that it would not be easy to placate him.

Perhaps, in time, he would find forgiveness

in his heart and welcome her home again, but she was sure it was far too soon to risk putting it to the test.

What also made her miserable was the fact that there was no definite news about what was happening to Pryce. As far as she knew he was still in custody in Cardiff, but when she had tried to make an enquiry at the local police station about the date of his trial she had been rebuffed.

Sabrina didn't sleep at all well on Sunday night. There was a violent thunderstorm, and by the time that abated she felt wide awake. She lay there in the dark planning all the things she was going to say to Hans Meyer first thing on Monday morning.

She'd make it quite clear that she wasn't prepared to do extra work of any kind whatsoever. She worked hard enough as it was. She wanted a proper rate for what she was already doing. She would demand that there was an increase in her next pay packet on the following Friday. What was more, she would ask him to pay her extra for the past week as well, so that she could give Helga the money she owed her.

Her plans were immediately scuttled when she found that Hans Meyer wasn't in the office on Monday. Claud Ernst told her that he wouldn't be back until Friday at the earliest, and that until then she was to take her orders from him.

Sabrina racked her brains to think of some

way out of her dilemma. In the end, she decided that the obvious answer was to go ahead and find herself another job. If she did that then she would be able to force Hans Meyer into giving her a worthwhile rise, otherwise she'd tell him she was leaving.

That evening, instead of going straight back to her room she went to the public library. That was where she had found the job at Ferdinands, and what she could do once she could do again, she told herself firmly.

As she made a note of four vacancies that seemed eminently suitable, Sabrina wished she had looked at the newspaper in her lunch break. All the offices would be closed now, and she would have to wait until the next day before she could apply to any of them.

On Wednesday morning, she found that three of the four vacancies had already been filled. The fourth job was in Tiger Bay, and she had heard so much about how dangerous it could be in that area that she decided not to go after it.

She had already been out of the office for most of the morning, and as she hurried towards The Hayes she tried to think of some reason she could give to explain her absence.

Both Claud and Jakob were displeased with her for coming in so late. They insisted that she must stay on that evening in order to catch up with the invoicing before Mr Meyer returned. There seemed to be no way she could get out of doing so, and that meant she couldn't reach the library before it closed.

Hans Meyer was already in the office when Sabrina arrived the following morning. He gave her a mountain of additional work so not only was she unable even to leave the office all day, but she was late finishing that evening as well.

On Friday her wage packet still had only seven shillings in it, and she simply didn't have enough to pay Helga anything, because she needed money for lunches and train fares as well as new stockings.

'I will pay you as soon as I can,' she told her. 'Mr Meyer has been out of the office all week and I've not had a chance to talk to him about my wages.'

To her surprise, Helga accepted what she told her with an expressive shrug. 'Until Monday, yah? No later, though. Understand?'

Chapter Fourteen

The following Monday Hans Meyer was in and out of the office all day like a jack-in-the-box.

During his spasmodic moments at his desk he generated enough work to keep Sabrina frantically tapping away at the keys of her typewriter.

When she grumbled that she wasn't going to have time to go out for her lunch break, he sent out for a cheese sandwich for her so that she wouldn't have any excuse to leave her desk. When she tried to speak to him about the promised pay rise, which she'd now been worrying about for well over a week, he waved her aside. Infuriated by his cavalier attitude, she kept her head down with the intention of leaving the office promptly, and visiting the library.

At the last minute she realised that the library wasn't open on a Monday, so although she had cleared her desk on time it was pointless going to William Street. There was only one thing for it, she decided, she'd buy an evening paper rather than wait until next day.

She glanced through it as she walked home along the Taff Embankment, feeling more and more depressed as she found there was nothing that she could apply for with her limited experience.

By the time she reached Aber Street her mood was as grey as the river as she headed for Corporation Road. Once again she would have to come up with an excuse for not paying Helga the money she owed her.

She considered sneaking in as quietly as possible so that she would avoid seeing Helga, and then staying in her room all night. The appetising aroma of cooking, even before she opened the front door, made her realise that if she did that it would mean going without her evening meal. It was such a long time since she'd eaten the sandwich at midday that she decided this would be impossible.

Helga came rushing into the hallway the moment Sabrina stepped inside, her round face beaming a welcome.

Sabrina gulped and tried to find the right words to explain about the money she owed. Before she could utter a word Helga said, 'Hurry up, I'm ready to dish up the meal and I want you to come and join me tonight and not eat alone. We have a guest, someone who will be a happy surprise for you, yah?'

Sabrina's heart quickened. Could it be Rhianon, she wondered. Rhianon was the person she wanted to see most in the world. Well, apart from Pryce, of course. It couldn't possibly be him because he was still in prison awaiting his trial.

'Are you ready, yah?' Helga asked impatiently.

'I will be in a moment. As soon as I've had a minute to tidy myself,' Sabrina told her. 'Who is going to join us?'

Helga smiled broadly. 'Hurry and then you will see,' she replied mysteriously.

Sabrina noticed that for the first time since she had known her Helga did not have on one of her print overalls. The dress she was wearing was a soft blue almost the same colour as her eyes, with a deep white piqué collar and matching trims on the elbow-length sleeves.

As she walked into Helga's living room Sabrina stopped in surprise. She had only been in there once before, on the day when she had come to ask for a room. Now the table in the centre was covered by a white damask tablecloth and laid with cutlery and glasses for three people. Sitting at the table, almost as if he owned the place, was Hans Meyer.

'Come along, Sabrina, we've been waiting for you to join us. Isn't that so, Helga?'

'Yah, yah!' Helga nodded enthusiastically. 'Now will I serve up our meal, yah?' she asked, looking at Hans for approval.

Sabrina hardly noticed what she was eating, she was so surprised to find Hans Meyer there. She was equally astounded by the air of familiarity between him and Helga. What puzzled her was that they seemed to know each other so well. Apart from giving her Helga's address, when she'd been looking for somewhere to stay, he'd barely mentioned her.

As if he realised her confusion, Hans Meyer explained, 'You perhaps did not know that Helga is my elder sister. Her husband, Jan Amudsen, was a seaman, and he was drowned when his ship was torpedoed during the very last days of the war. Since then, Helga has stayed on here in Cardiff, making a living by accommodating my business acquaintances when they come over from Holland.'

'I see! So that is why you knew there was a room here!'

'Yes, indeed. And it was why I was quite sure that no matter what she said, Helga would not throw you out into the street because you were behind with your rent,' he told her.

'I didn't realise that there was anyone else staying here,' Sabrina said in surprise. 'Although,' she added thoughtfully, 'once or twice I have heard people here late at night.'

Hans Meyer shrugged. 'They come and they go. Lately it has not been so busy. Having a permanent lodger is something quite new, especially a lady. Never before has Helga taken in a woman, it has always been men. Travellers and businessmen.'

Sabrina nodded, but she wasn't sure how that affected her or the money she owed Helga. She was not left in doubt for much longer, however.

'My sister is no longer a young woman,' Hans Meyer went on, as Helga cleared away the plates after their main course, and served up her apple-cake speciality. 'This is why I thought you might be interested in some evening work to help her out.'

Sabrina stiffened. If Hans and Helga thought that she could supplement the meagre wage he paid her at Ferdinands by washing up and doing other types of housework, then they were very much mistaken. She had never lifted a finger to help Rhianon when she'd been living at home, so she certainly wasn't going to start doing so now for complete strangers.

She finished her apple cake in silence, noticing that this time Helga had served it with thick cream instead of the usual custard, as if it was a special occasion. She had to admit that it was truly delicious, but it still wasn't going to make her change her mind.

Afterwards, when Helga set out cups of dark bitter coffee, and tiny glasses that she filled with a deep red liqueur, Sabrina decided to excuse herself and go to her room.

'No, no!' Hans Meyer extended a restraining hand. 'You must join us, we are going to drink a very special toast . . . to you, and to the success of our scheme, your evening work. That, of course, is if you agree with our plans.'

Sabrina looked from one to the other of them uncomfortably. 'If you think I am going to do housework for you then you can forget it,' she blustered.

'Housework?' Helga looked puzzled.

Hans laughed heartily. 'That is not at all what we had in mind,' he chortled. 'Housework! A pretty girl like you!'

Sabrina relaxed. If it wasn't housework then what did he have in mind, she wondered.

Seeing her puzzled expression, Hans Meyer spread his hands wide as he started to explain. 'As I told you, Helga is my sister, and often when customers, or company representatives, come over from Holland they stay here. They prefer Helga to look after them rather than stay at a hotel where they know no one and would feel lost and miserable. You understand?'

He paused and looked searchingly at Sabrina, and waited for her to nod before going on. 'In the past, Helga has entertained them for me, but she no longer wants to do so. We both thought you might like to do it on our behalf.'

'You mean take them out to a restaurant, that sort of thing?'

Hans Meyer shrugged expressively. 'Sometimes, maybe, but for the most part they prefer their favourite dishes cooked by Helga, rather than the sort of food they are served in restaurants. However, I digress, that is not what you are interested in hearing. After they have eaten they like to be entertained.'

'So you are suggesting that I should take them out to the cinema, or sometimes to go dancing, things like that?'

He smiled broadly. 'Well, you did complain

to me that you cannot afford to do any of these things yourself. If you were willing to accompany my clients, if that is what they wish to do, then you would be able to enjoy such occasions without it costing you anything. So, now what do you think about doing some extra work in the evenings?'

'That's hardly work, is it,' Sabrina smiled. 'That would be enjoying myself.'

'Then you agree to do it?' Hans asked quickly.

'I would love to do it, but it doesn't take care of my living expenses,' Sabrina pointed out pragmatically. 'The wages you pay me do not cover the charge your sister makes for my rent and food each week.'

Hans and Helga exchanged glances. 'That will be taken care of,' Hans told her. 'You will not need to pay any more rent from now on. I will see to all that for you.'

'I can live rent-free instead of being given any wages, you mean?'

'You will receive your seven shillings a week, Sabrina, the same as you do now, but you will not have to pay anything to Helga for rent or food. A very handsome rise, is it not? Especially when you will also be reimbursed for any money you spend, on taking the clients out in the evening.'

Sabrina did some quick mental calculations. She could hardly contain her excitement at the wonderful offer, but she was careful not to let it show.

'It sounds like an interesting arrangement, but when does it all start?' she asked cautiously.

'The financial arrangements start right away. The money that you already owe to Helga will be cancelled. You have no need to worry any more about that. The entertaining will begin the next time we have clients staying here with Helga. That will not be for a few weeks, or perhaps a little longer. Helga will give you plenty of warning, and you will also know from what is going on in the office.'

Hans rose to his feet and refilled their liqueur glasses. 'Now, shall we drink to that? And to the future?'

As they clinked glasses, Sabrina felt a surge of relief and excitement. This was very much a change for the better. Pontdarw, and all that had happened since the fight between Hwyel and Pryce, began to fade into the background as she contemplated the wonderful time ahead of her. She wouldn't forget about Pryce of course, but her new way of life would make waiting for him very much easier, she decided.

Chapter Fifteen

It was late August before Pryce Pritchard's trial came to court, but when it did the news spread rapidly. Everyone was talking about it, not only in Cardiff and the Valleys, where the miners were still on strike, but as far away as London and Liverpool.

Sabrina was determined to attend the trial, in the hope that she might have a chance to speak to Pryce. She told Hans Meyer that she wasn't feeling too well and that she needed a few days off.

He was most concerned. 'You have been rather subdued the last couple of days,' he agreed, his beady eyes sharp with concern. 'We have some important clients arriving at the beginning of September, are you going to be better in time to entertain them?'

Sabrina smiled wanly. 'I hope so! A couple of days off is what I need.'

Hans Meyer pursed his small mouth. 'Helga tells me you are not eating as you should be. She says that you have been sick several times recently.'

'Yes, I have. It is some sort of stomach upset. There's a lot of it about. I think they call it gastric flu. It would probably be better if I wasn't in the office until I am over it. It would be awful if you caught it when you have those important clients coming soon.'

'Yes, you're right!' He moved away from her. 'You run along home and go to bed. You should tell Helga to send for a doctor . . .'

'No, no!' Sabrina said quickly. 'It's best that I'm out of the house, in case it's catching. You don't want Helga getting it! I'll go home to Pontdarw for a few days. My sister will look after me.'

For a moment Hans Meyer seemed reluctant to agree to that. She waited tensely, afraid he was going to ruin all her plans. Then he nodded. 'That probably is the best idea,' he said at last. 'I don't want Helga to be ill. She will have enough to do with all the preparation and extra work and cooking.'

Sabrina went back to Corporation Road and told Helga about the arrangement she had made with Hans Meyer.

'I'm taking my suitcase so that I can bring back the rest of my clothes,' she said. 'I've only brought my summer dresses with me to Cardiff, and lately I've been feeling quite cold first thing in the morning and coming home at night.'

'Yah? You should have told me! Here,' Helga peeled off the drab blue woollen cardigan she was wearing and wrapped it round Sabrina's shoulders. 'You wear this until you have your own warm coat,' she insisted.

Sabrina took a tram to the centre of the city. The three nights that she had said she would be at home in Pontdarw she intended spending in a bed and breakfast place in Cathays. She'd located a rooming house in Wyvern Road that suited her purpose perfectly, because it was within walking distance of Cardiff Law Courts.

An hour and a half later she was sitting in the public gallery there and listening to the case against Pryce Pritchard.

Knowing there might be people from Pontdarw attending, she'd taken care to change her appearance as much as possible, so that no one, not even Pryce, would recognise her.

She had on a close-fitting cloche hat, pulled down over her ears, and she'd pushed her dark curls up inside it. Instead of the floaty feminine dress she'd been wearing when she left Corporation Road she now had on a dowdy brown skirt that reached almost to her ankles. Over it she wore Helga's blue knitted cardigan which she'd buttoned up to the neck, and which drooped down baggily over the skirt.

She saw Mr and Mrs Barker sitting in the well of the court and hoped they wouldn't look up into the public gallery. Even if they did, she assured herself, it was doubtful if they would recognise her. In her drab clothes she appeared so different from the smartly turned-out girl they had known when in Pontdarw.

She looked for her father or Rhianon, but couldn't see either of them. Mostly the court seemed to be full of officials of one kind or another.

As well as barristers in white wigs and black gowns there were a number of the TUC and Union officials, part of the group Pryce worked with. Some of them had been in the crowd on that fateful Saturday.

The trial lasted two days and Sabrina found that because of the legal jargon, many of the arguments were difficult to follow. She listened intently to the barrister putting forward evidence in Pryce's favour. It was so compelling that she became more and more convinced that Pryce would either be let off or receive a very lenient sentence.

The main factor seemed to be the medical evidence. It had been discovered that Hwyel had a heart condition and that the blow to his head, and his subsequent fall, might have caused a heart attack.

At the end of the second day the jury brought in a verdict of manslaughter, as expected. The judge in his summing up reinforced the possibility that Hwyel's death could have been the result of his heart condition.

The outcome was a greatly reduced sentence.

Sabrina shuddered as the judge pronounced, in sonorous tones, that Pryce was to be sent to prison for three years.

Three years was a light sentence, she knew that, but it was still a long, long time to wait before they could be together again. The thought of having to continue, until then, working for Hans Meyer and living in Helga Amudsen's house, filled her with dismay.

Rhianon was relieved yet shocked by the length of Pryce's sentence. She had sat in the court throughout the entire trial, her gaze fixed on Pryce as he stood tall and straight in the dock. His voice had been firm and controlled as he answered the questions that were fired at him. His words told her nothing she didn't already know, but only added to her sadness about what had led to Hwyel's death.

After Pryce had been sentenced and taken down to the cells under the dock, Rhianon begged an official to be allowed to see him.

'Please! Even if it is only for a few minutes.'

'Are you a relative?'

Her heart sank the moment she heard the question. She knew full well that when she admitted she was only a friend, her request would be refused.

'You can always try again later, miss. What you need to do is apply for visiting privileges once he's a prison inmate,' the man advised kindly.

She stood outside the court, watching the Barkers leave. Mrs Barker was crying, Mr Barker was looking dour and dissatisfied by the outcome.

Rhianon had been surprised that her own father hadn't wanted to attend, if only to see justice done. It left her in no doubt about how much he hated Pryce, which was why she hadn't told him she was coming to Cardiff each day to attend the trial.

Polly had been very co-operative. She'd not only let her take the time off, but promised to tell no one about where she was going.

'Mind you, cariad,' she warned, 'there's bound to be someone in court who will recognise you, and like as not tell your father that you were there.'

'I know,' Rhianon agreed, 'but it's a risk I must take.'

Even though she'd guessed they wouldn't let her speak to Pryce, she had thought the journey worthwhile. She'd also hoped that Sabrina would have heard about the trial, and that she might be there.

She'd looked round the courtroom hopefully each day. She'd also waited outside the court afterwards, hoping to spot her sister amongst the crowd as everyone left.

Most of the people attending, though, were either from Pontdarw, and known to her by sight, or connected with the miners' union in some way. The only complete stranger was a drab-looking young woman in the public gallery. It wasn't until she was leaving the court on the final day, and saw this person in front of her, that Rhianon thought for one brief moment that it could be Sabrina. She was about to run after her, but then she looked again and realised she was imagining things. The woman's figure was far more substantial than Sabrina's, and she was wearing such shapeless clothes.

Pryce Pritchard had mixed feelings as he was taken from the court back to the prison cells. He knew he had been very lucky. From what his barrister had said, he had not expected to be charged with murder, but he knew that manslaughter could result in a life sentence. To have only been given three years had surprised him. The other shock had been learning that young Hwyel Barker had a heart condition.

Pryce had had plenty of time to think back over the incident since he'd been in custody. He would never be able to forgive himself for what had happened with Sabrina afterwards. He must have been mad to risk losing Rhianon for the sake of a brief burst of lust. That was all it had been, after all. Sheer lust! Nothing at all like the deep tender feelings he had for Rhianon. She was the woman he wanted to spend the rest of his life with, but he feared that the possibility of that was now in jeopardy.

He had watched her in court, following every word of the trial. He could see she was concentrating hard, looking just like she did when she listened to him explaining the miners' cause to her in the weeks preceding the strike.

In her leaf-green cotton dress and loose matching coat, her straight brown hair shining under the brim of her little cream straw hat, she'd looked as lovely and composed as he remembered her. Everything about her was so modest and serene. She was so different to Sabrina that it was hard to believe they were sisters.

He remembered clearly the dress Sabrina had been wearing on the day of the fight. It had been low-cut, flimsy, and so provocatively styled. Added to that, her flirtatious manner towards him, the jibes, and then the way she had urged him and Hwyel to pit their fists against each other, had stirred his blood.

He had been so keyed up that he hadn't really known what he was doing. He blamed the excitement of the moment for what had happened afterwards. He'd been carried away. He'd lost control. Sabrina had happened to be there. He had no real feelings for her, he'd simply given way to his basest instincts.

How could he face Rhianon after that? She would be horrified when she knew what he had done. He couldn't bear to see the hurt in her eyes, or hear the reproach in her voice.

He'd concentrated on union matters, making that his excuse for not having time to see her. Then, before he had regained his common sense, and worked out how he was going to put the madness of a moment behind him, he'd found himself in custody.

Once they had him under lock and key, he was utterly powerless. He wasn't allowed visitors, or permitted to communicate with anyone.

It seemed like a lifetime ago that he'd been separated from the outside world, endless months that had changed so many lives, as well as his own.

He'd serve his sentence, forever regretting a fight sparked off by a taunting jibe, to which he had retaliated instead of ignoring it.

He could only hope that when he was eventually allowed to see Rhianon, she would understand the dilemma he'd had to face. The question was, would she forgive him for what had happened between him and Sabrina?

Chapter Sixteen

Three years! The judge's solemn voice as he'd intoned Pryce's punishment echoed repeatedly in Sabrina's head as she left the grandeur of the law courts, and made her way back to Wyvern Road.

It seemed merely a silly dream on her part, that Pryce might get off. Yet she'd felt even more positive of this outcome when it was revealed that Hwyel had a weak heart.

The very thought of that sent shivers rippling through her. If she had known about it she would broken off with Hwyel ages ago. Supposing he'd dropped dead when they'd been somewhere on their own? She would have been terrified. What was more, she might even have been questioned about it. People might have thought it was her fault!

Once clear of the civic centre she pulled off the horrible little hat and shook her head vigorously, running her hands through her brown curls to free them.

Although it was late afternoon the sun was shining from a clear blue sky. It felt so warm that she peeled off the thick blue cardigan, and rolled it up into a bundle. She would have happily tossed it away, or dropped it in the gutter, but then she would have had to explain to Helga why it was missing.

As she hurried along Senghennydd Road on her way to the room she was renting in Cathays, she folded the waistband of the brown skirt over a couple of times until the hemline reached barely to her knees. Even though it made an uncomfortable bunch around her waist she immediately felt she looked less dowdy.

Her step became quite jaunty until she caught sight of her reflection in a window. She bit her lip in dismay, shocked at how fat and frumpy she looked.

She blamed Helga's cooking. She wasn't used to eating so much rich food, it upset her stomach. Lately she had felt really sick and queasy when she woke up in the morning. She wasn't sure if it was the food, or the worry about what was going to happen to Pryce.

Well, she knew Pryce's fate now. If she was to go on living with Helga and her cooking for the next three years she'd have to change her diet in some way, she decided.

But by the time she reached Wyvern Road she was in utter despair about her own future. She felt so weary that all she wanted to do was lie down on the hard narrow bed, and take a rest.

She closed her eyes and refused to think about her situation. Instead she fantasised about being back in Pontdarw, at home with

163

her father and Rhianon, getting ready to be taken out for the evening by Hwyel.

In spite of being in unfamiliar surroundings, Sabrina drifted off to sleep. She slept so soundly that the next thing she knew was the landlady banging on her door and telling her that she was too late for breakfast.

'Don't forget you have to vacate your room before midday or else pay for another night's stay!'

It took Sabrina several minutes to gather her senses and remember where she was. She couldn't believe that she'd been asleep since the previous afternoon.

The moment she realised that she should be at work, she leapt out of bed. When her feet touched the ground the room spun round and she felt nauseous and weak. She sat down on the edge of the bed for a minute, hoping the queasy sensation would soon pass. Cautiously she dressed and packed her belongings into her suitcase.

'I'll be fine once I get out in the fresh air,' she told herself out loud.

She studied her reflection in the mirror and was daunted by what she saw. Her hair seemed to have lost its shine. Her face was puffy and pale. Even the pretty pink pleated skirt and jumper-blouse she was wearing didn't look nearly as flattering as usual, because it was so tight around the waist.

The fresh air didn't seem to make any

difference to how she felt, either! She was still feeling unwell, even after she'd walked from Wyvern Road to a tram stop in Newport Road.

Once she'd boarded the tram, the lurching and swaying made her feel really ill. As soon as the tram had turned into St Mary Street she decided she'd better get off and walk the rest of the way to The Hayes.

Hans Meyer was relieved to see her, but very annoyed that she was so late.

'I give you a holiday and then you don't come back on time, and there's a mountain of invoicing waiting to be done,' he grumbled.

'I missed the early train and had to wait nearly three hours for the next one,' she told him as convincingly as she could. 'As it is I've come straight here from the station. I didn't even go back to Corporation Road with my suitcase.'

'Well, I suppose these things do happen,' he conceded, slightly mollified by her explanation.

'Don't worry, I'll get all the invoicing up to date. I'll even stay late tonight if necessary,' Sabrina promised.

He looked sceptical. 'I don't want you to make yourself ill again,' he said, tetchily. 'I must say you are still not looking as well as you should. Are you feeling any better?'

'Yes, the break from work has done wonders. I'll be fine.'

'I hope so, since we have such a busy week ahead. You haven't forgotten that clients from

Amsterdam arrive tomorrow? You have undertaken to help to entertain them, and I am depending on you to do so.'

'I haven't forgotten. That's why I said I would make sure that the invoicing is up to date before I go home this evening.'

'Very well, I will send Jakob out to get you some sandwiches,' he promised.

By the time that happened Sabrina was ravenous. She ate the meat sandwiches sitting at her desk, still working. She felt much better afterwards. The reason she'd felt so ill earlier, she decided, was because she'd had nothing to eat that morning or the previous evening.

Helga welcomed her back with a hearty stew and one of her steamed puddings to follow. As she sat back, replete, Sabrina remembered her intention to cut down on the amount of food she was eating.

She sighed. She wouldn't be able to do that if the clients she was entertaining for Hans Meyer asked to be taken out for a meal. If they did, she'd start cutting down next week, she vowed, or as soon as they had left.

The three men who arrived the next day spoke very little English, but talked vociferously to Helga in Dutch. Two of them were short, square-built, smooth-faced and overweight, like Hans Meyer. The other man was taller and slimmer, with dark hair and eyes, and lean saturnine features. For some reason she couldn't quite fathom, Sabrina felt frightened of him.

Escorting them to the Ferdinands office at The Hayes the next morning was simple enough. Once they arrived there Hans Meyer and Jakob took over, and she was free to get on with her work.

At the end of the first day, when Hans asked her to escort the clients back to Corporation Road, she made no attempt to converse with them. She simply indicated the route they were to take when they needed to cross into Aber Street to reach the house.

Sabrina felt mystified by the whole arrangement. Why on earth couldn't Hans Meyer entertain them in the evening? Surely he could have taken them out somewhere, or even invited them back to his house. If he was married, then his wife, if she was also Dutch, would probably have been delighted at the opportunity to talk to some of her own countrymen.

When she arrived back at Corporation Road that evening with the three visitors she found Helga waiting for them. The table was laid with crisp white linen, sparkling glassware and the best china. The meal she served up met with loud approval from all three men.

'If the rest of the evening is as enjoyable as this, then we will be well satisfied,' Marc, the dark, saturnine man, commented.

'What do you wish to do?' Sabrina asked as he drained the liqueur Helga had poured for all of them. 'Would you like to go to the pictures or the theatre? Or would you sooner go dancing?'

The three men exchanged amused glances, eyebrows raised, mouths twisted into wry smiles.

'We prefer to enjoy the entertainment here,' Marc told her.

Sabrina frowned and looked across the table at Helga questioningly, but the older woman avoided her eyes.

'I must see to things in the kitchen and you must entertain Marc and his friends on your own, Sabrina,' she said firmly.

'They haven't said what they want to do?'

'This way and then you will find out!' Marc's lean hand closed firmly around Sabrina's elbow as he helped her from her chair. Smiling, he guided her out of the living room towards the hall.

As she tried to resist, his grip tightened. Her heart beat faster as he propelled her up the stairs, ignoring her protests and hesitation, steadying her when she stumbled.

She was aware that the other two men were lumbering up behind them. Her breath caught in her throat as Marc pushed open the door of the main front bedroom and forced her inside.

She had never been in any of the upstairs rooms in the house, and she was taken aback by what she saw. The room was so opulent that she wondered if she was still in Helga's house. She had never seen anything like it, not even when she went to the pictures.

There were heavy red velvet curtains at the

bow window, and a luxuriously thick red carpet on the floor. The huge bed, which dominated the room, was covered with a brocade bedspread patterned in red and gold. On it, piled up against the padded red velvet head-board, was a varied assortment of red and gold velvet cushions.

Sabrina tore her gaze away to study the rest of the room. Suspended from the centre of the ceiling was a glittering glass chandelier. The most astonishing feature of all was the pair of enormous gilt-framed floor-to-ceiling mirrors facing each other on the walls flanking the bed.

In a flash their purpose snapped into Sabrina's mind. At the same moment, the realisation of what the men had meant by entertainment hit her like a fist.

She looked from one to the other of them and saw the anticipation, the lustful eagerness on all their faces.

Quickly she moved sideways, one of her hands seeking the door, intent on making her escape.

'Come, you are not going to be a tease and pretend to be reluctant, are you?' Marc said with derision. 'Hans promised us much enjoyable entertainment! He told us that you would provide us with a night we would never forget. You are not going to disappoint us, are you?'

Sick with apprehension, Sabrina smiled nervously. Conscious of the cruel twist to Marc's mouth, she felt like a rabbit faced by a fox as his dark eyes stared into hers.

Feverishly she tried to think of a way out of this dilemma. Admittedly, she was an avid flirt, with a reputation for giving provocative looks and making teasing remarks. She even enjoyed kissing and cuddling, but she liked it to be with the man of her choice. She certainly didn't want to partake in an orgy of love-making with these three men! She hardly knew them and she most certainly didn't like any of them.

She wondered where Helga was. Would she come to her aid if she screamed? She was quite sure from the set-up that Helga knew what was likely to happen, and that she wanted no part of it.

She understood now what Hans had meant when he said that Helga was getting too old for entertaining his clients. It had obviously been one of her duties in the past.

That Hans Meyer should expect her to do such a thing frightened her. Yet she should have realised that when he said he would take care of her rent, he would expect something in return. This was to be his way of making her earn it!

She felt trapped. Somehow she had to get out of the room, and out of the house, before one of these men, or all of them, violated her.

Chapter Seventeen

It was October before Rhianon was allowed to visit Pryce in Cardiff jail.

As her train drew in at Cardiff General station she felt apprehensive. All the way from Pontdarw she had been thinking back to the last time she had made this journey. That had been in late August, to attend Pryce's trial.

Countless times since then she had brooded over the frumpy young woman who had also been at Cardiff Crown Court. She kept wishing that she'd taken her courage in both hands and spoken to her. The more she thought about it, the more convinced she became that it had been Sabrina. Yet, if this was so, why hadn't the young woman spoken to her? Surely she had seen her!

When she'd talked this over with Polly, and listened to her opinion, she'd felt more convinced than ever that it had been Sabrina.

'Mind, what I can't understand was why she was dressed in such a strange way.'

'That's easy, cariad,' Polly laughed. 'Your Sabrina didn't want anyone from Pontdarw to recognise her.'

'Why not?' Rhianon frowned, concentrating on the hanks of wool she was sorting out.

'Stands to reason, doesn't it, my lovely,' Polly said sagely. 'She knows only too well that she had a hand in Pryce Pritchard ending up in that dock.'

'You are convinced that was the reason why she ran away in the first place?'

'What do you think, cariad?'

Rhianon shook her head. 'I don't know, Polly. My mind has been in a whirl ever since it happened.' She pushed her hair back from her forehead irritably. 'One way and another that damned old strike has ruined my life, hasn't it?'

'It's ruined a lot of people's lives, cariad,' Polly agreed sadly. 'Without your Pryce here to lead them, and to tell them what to do, all the Pontdarw miners are at sixes and sevens. Most of them are refusing to go back to work out of loyalty to him.'

'Well, there's nothing he can do to help them, not when he's locked up like he is. They won't even let anyone in to see him!'

'They will, now he's been sentenced,' Polly assured her. 'You'll have to go through the right channels, mind. You'll have to apply to the authorities, and they'll want to know every damn thing about you! Mind you, that shouldn't be any problem, not for someone who has led as blameless a life as you have, my lovely.'

As usual, Polly had been right. Getting a pass

to visit Pryce had been time-consuming, and at times frustrating, but she'd managed it in the end.

Rhianon left the station and followed the directions she'd been given. As she walked past the Custom House, across the top of Bute Road, along Bute Terrace and then on into Adam Street she felt more and more nervous. By the time she reached the entrance to the prison, she was shaking so much that she didn't realise that the people standing there were waiting for the doors to open. She was completely taken by surprise when a heavily-built woman angrily told her off for pushing in front of them all.

Meekly she took her place at the end of the long queue, astonished at how many there were ahead of her. By the time all their passes were checked, and they were inside, half the visiting time would be over, she thought unhappily.

While she stood in line she tried to keep her mind occupied by going over all the things she wanted to ask Pryce. Above all she must try and find out if he knew any reason why Sabrina had run away from home, because the shame and the gossip were making her father ill. He'd lost weight, he looked dejected, and the fire had gone out of him.

He claimed it was because of his bad heart, but she thought he was grieving because he suspected that there was some truth in the rumours, and that his beloved Sabrina was in some way responsible for the fight that had led to Hwyel's death.

To add to her father's distress Cledwyn Barker, as an elder of Capel Bethel, was talking of making sure her father was suspended as a lay preacher. For Edwin Webster the shame of being banned from the pulpit was a bitter pill.

Rhianon hated to see her father suffering in stony silence, refusing to air his feelings to her or anyone else. He had declined to attend Pryce's trial, and he'd banned all newspapers, with their banner headlines about the outcome, from the house.

Rhianon had read them though, every word. Polly had saved the *News Chronicle* and the *Western Mail* for her. She had bought the *Cardiff Echo* herself each day and read the report in it over and over on the train back to Pontdarw, until every word was imprinted on her mind. Then she had carefully cut out all the reports and placed them in a tin box, which she'd secreted at Polly's shop.

Her father had never mentioned the trial, but then he never mentioned Sabrina, either. Rhianon knew, though, that every morning he waited for the postman, hoping there might be a postcard, or letter, from her. Each time there was a knock on the door an expectant look flitted across his face, as if he hoped it might be Sabrina or someone with news of her whereabouts.

She had wondered whether or not she should tell him that she intended to go and visit Pryce in prison, but Polly had advised against it.

'Whatever will you do if he forbids you to go there, my lovely?'

'I'll still go, of course,' Rhianon assured her.

'Which will upset him even more! What is the point of defying him, cariad?' Polly asked gently. 'Of course you must go and visit Pryce, but your father doesn't have to know.'

'He's bound to find out!'

'Nonsense! Visiting is only one afternoon a month. Your dad will never miss you. Simply tell him you are working. No one except me will know that you've nipped down to Cardiff.'

'Someone might spot me at the railway station, or even see me on the train! You know how it is when you don't want anyone to know.'

'So what if they do? You are going to Cardiff to collect some stock for me, what is wrong with that?'

Rhianon smiled broadly as the full concept of the ruse sank in. Impulsively she flung her arms around Polly and hugged her.

Now she was here, and as the queue began to edge forward slowly her heart thumped in anticipation. She would be seeing Pryce again after all the long months of separation. She didn't count seeing him in the dock in August, because he had been just like a stranger. She hadn't even managed to catch his eye.

Anxiously she showed her papers to the officer on duty as she entered the grim building, praying inwardly that they were all in order.

Everything was strange and forbidding. Sounds were magnified, and echoed hollowly. Gates clanged, keys jangled, the sound of footsteps bounced back.

Then they were admitted to a room filled with lines of chairs set out in front of small windows with bars in front of them. Behind each grille a prisoner was sitting.

She was asked for the identification number of the prisoner she was visiting, and then she was directed to a window in the middle of the row.

For a moment she didn't recognise Pryce in the harsh lighting, and thought there had been some mistake. His hair had been cropped close to his skull, giving him a sinister look. There were deep furrows either side of his nose, and his mouth was set in a hard tight line.

In his drab prison uniform he looked so different from the good-looking chap who had walked her home after night school – nothing like the man who had shared his ambitions and explained his political creed to her with such enthusiasm.

As she sat down in front of the window his whole face lit up, his eyes brightened, shining with pleasure at seeing her. As Rhianon stretched out her hand through the dividing grille to touch his, she felt an overpowering surge of love at being close to him once again.

She had never loved him more than she did at that moment. She was trembling, tears of happiness filling her eyes so that she could hardly see him.

'Oh, Pryce! I've missed you so much.'

His grip on her hand tightened, then was abruptly withdrawn as a patrolling prison officer tapped sharply on his wrist with his truncheon, indicating that physical contact was not permitted.

As well as telling Pryce how much she loved him and missed him, there were so many other things she wanted to say. Yet now that she had the opportunity to do so she felt tongue-tied. The grille separating them was a barricade that seemed to make them strangers.

She waited for him to speak, to tell her he loved her, as well as ask her the countless questions he must have stored up since they had been apart.

'How are you, Pryce?' she asked nervously.

He shrugged. 'We get enough to eat, and the screws aren't nearly as vicious as I'd expected, but it is so claustrophobic in here. There are days when I think I will go out of my mind if I can't get outside and breathe fresh air.'

She nodded understandingly. What she felt about them being separated was painful enough, but he had almost three more years of being confined behind bars. How was he going to stand it, she wondered.

'And you? How are you?'

She smiled deprecatingly. 'I'm all right. Very worried about you, of course. We all are.'

'I can't believe that! I'm quite sure your father isn't worried about me! Most likely he thinks I am exactly where I should be, where I should always have been,' he said bitterly.

Rhianon bit down on her bottom lip. Pryce was quite right, of course, so there didn't seem to be any point in denying it.

'Polly sends her best wishes,' she said brightly. 'She's very kindly let me have time off so that I can come and see you.'

'Good old Polly, she always did have a heart of gold.'

'Yes, she's been a tremendous support,' Rhianon added lamely.

The conversation between them seemed to wither and die. Rhianon searched her mind feverishly for another safe topic.

'They wouldn't let me bring you in any food or cigarettes,' she said at last.

He gave a short derisory grunt. 'Did they say what we could, or could not, talk about?'

'No, of course not!'

'Then shouldn't you be telling me all the news from Pontdarw, especially the gossip?'

'There's not a lot to tell . . .'

'Oh come on, Rhianon,' he exclaimed tetchily, 'what is happening about the strike?'

'Well, the men are still out. The miners are, at any rate. You know that the TUC called off the strike and all the other workers have gone back?'

'Damn fools! Working for such low pay, most

of them,' he said angrily. 'The only way they'll ever improve their lot is by solidarity. The miners know this, that's why they are still staying out.'

'It's biting in though, Pryce. The women and children are already starting to feel the pinch. When the weather gets colder things are going to be terribly hard for them. Without money coming in each week how can they put food on the table, or keep the children warm?'

'Are the men speaking out and making themselves heard, though?'

'Not in Pontdarw they're not. Sitting around on the street corners most of them, playing cards, would you believe. No one to guide them, see, Pryce, not with you locked away in here.'

She saw the anger and pain her words caused, but it was the truth, and she felt he should know it.

'Perhaps if you gave me a message to take back to the men, they might see sense and return to work,' she suggested tentatively.

'If they cave in now then everything we've fought for will be lost,' he said stubbornly. 'What other news is there?'

'Your time is up! Your visitor must leave now, Pritchard!' The prison officer who had been standing only a few feet away, keeping an eye on Pryce and Rhianon to see that they didn't try to make contact again through the grille, said sharply.

'I have to go?' Rhianon whispered.

'I'm afraid so. Is there anything else you want to tell me?'

She shook her head. 'I don't think so.' Her mind was in such a turmoil she couldn't think clearly. The thought of having to leave him, still locked away from the rest of the world, distressed her.

'Nothing?' His voice cut through her muddled thoughts and she looked at him questioningly.

'What else is there that you want to know?'

His face tightened. 'You've not mentioned your sister!'

She felt uncomfortable. 'No, I didn't mention Sabrina because she has been missing since the day you were arrested,' she said awkwardly.

Pryce stared at her in amazement. 'You've not seen Sabrina since then! That's almost five months ago!'

Rhianon nodded. 'I know, but there's not been a word from her. She didn't even come to Hwyel's funeral.'

'Have you made any enquiries or looked for her?'

Rhianon nodded. 'Everywhere I can think of, but there's no trace of her. I've asked every customer who comes into Polly's shop, but none of them have seen or heard of her since then.'

'What about the Barkers? Haven't they any idea where she might be?'

'They won't have anything to do with me, or my father! Cledwyn Barker has even taken steps to see that my father is no longer a lay preacher at Capel Bethel.'

Pryce ran a hand over his cropped head in a gesture of bewilderment. 'You weren't even going to mention any of this, were you?' he said accusingly.

'What was the point? You aren't in a position to do anything about it! I'm worried out of my mind. It has made an old man of my father, and now he refuses to even mention her name.'

'Why, for heaven's sake? He doted on her!'

Before Rhianon could reply the prison officer intervened. 'You leave by the same door you came in, miss. You,' he poked Pryce in the ribs with his truncheon, 'back to your cell!'

Chapter Eighteen

As Rhianon left the prison and came out into Knox Street she felt not only dazed and bewildered, but filled with self-doubt about the things she had said to Pryce.

The look of utter dejection on his face as she was ordered to leave had highlighted the reality of his imprisonment. It had touched a raw nerve, and no matter how much she tried to do so she couldn't shut his expression out of her mind.

She shuddered at the thought of him being taken back into a cold bare cell and locked in. Even worse was knowing this was the sort of existence he would have to endure for the next three years.

She felt that going to see him had probably done more harm than good. She would have given anything to be able to go back inside the prison and start her visit all over again.

What on earth had she been thinking about, telling Pryce so much dire news? That wasn't what he needed. She should have been saying things to cheer him up, and comfort him in some way. Instead, she had probably made him feel guilty by pointing out that the men were missing his guidance, and reminding him about all the ill effects the strike was having on the women and children in Pontdarw.

She'd even alerted him to the fact that Sabrina was missing, and that was something she'd never intended to mention at all. From the way she had told him, it was more than likely that he would think she was blaming him for this.

It might have been better if she'd done as her father had instructed and stayed well away from Cardiff prison, and from Pryce. How could she possibly do that, though, when she was the only person ever likely to visit him, his only contact with the outside world? To leave him shut up in there for three long years without any news, or the sight of a friendly face, would not only be cruel, but would make his plight intolerable.

No, she told herself, she had done the right thing. She was convinced of that, and she would try to visit him as often as she could for the rest of the time he was in prison. But would he want to see her again, she wondered.

Rhianon was so absorbed in her uneasy thoughts that she barely noticed where she was going. She'd assumed that she was taking the same roads back to the railway station that she had come along earlier in the day. Now she was suddenly aware that she didn't know where she was, and she felt alarmed.

Although she was in a busy street, full of traffic and trams clanging their way up and down, she didn't recognise it. It certainly wasn't one of the main roads she had walked down on her way to the prison.

Rhianon looked around her anxiously, hoping to see someone she could ask for directions. To her consternation there seemed to be only men about, and most of them seemed to be foreign.

Panic surged through her – she had no idea where she was, or which way she should be going. It was like being in a foreign land. Already the street lamps were lighted and the October dusk was closing in.

'Calm down, calm down! Count to ten and stop panicking! Keep walking! You'll be safe enough as long as you stay on a main road,' she whispered to comfort herself.

She forced herself to concentrate on her surroundings. Since she was on a busy main road, it must lead to somewhere important. The sensible thing to do was to stay on it and keep walking.

When she reached the next tram stop, she might even be able to work out from the destination board exactly where she was, she consoled herself. If she was going in the wrong direction, a tram would take her back to where she should be.

She tried to keep her pace steady, although her instincts were to break into a run because she was so frightened. There were so many foreign-looking men that she felt threatened. She had no idea what she would do if one of them stopped her, or even spoke to her.

Hold your head up and try and walk confidently, as though you know exactly where you're going, she told herself over and over again.

The road began to change. Prosperous city offices gave way to dingy run-down buildings that looked like warehouses.

She started to check the names of the streets running off the main road. Maria Street, Sophia Street, Loudon Place. The names meant nothing to her, but then that was not surprising since she had only been to Cardiff four times. On three of those occasions it had been for Pryce's trial, which had taken place in the heart of the city centre.

She took a deep breath and resolved to ask directions from the very next person she met. Well, the very next woman. It mightn't be safe to ask a strange man, especially a foreign one.

Rhianon had reached Mount Stewart Square before she saw a woman come out of a side road ahead of her. Shaking with relief, she walked quickly to catch her up.

'Excuse me, could you direct me to . . .' The words died on her lips. 'Sabrina?'

The young woman stepped back and turned sharply as if she was going to hurry away.

Rhianon reached out and grabbed her arm, her eyes fixed on the brown curls, the lovely face, the huge brown eyes that she knew so well. Even the dress she was wearing, although it was grubby and the hem was coming down in one place, was familiar because it was one she had made for her sister.

'Sabrina, it is you! I know it is! Speak to me!'

'Hello,' Sabrina muttered. 'What are you doing here? Are you spying on me?'

'Spying on you? I had no idea where you were. Oh, Sabrina!' Rhianon held out her hands.

After a moment's hesitation Sabrina flung herself into Rhianon's arms and returned her sister's embrace.

'Oh, Sabrina, you'll never know what a miracle this is,' Rhianon exclaimed in wonder. 'I thought we had lost you for ever!'

She hugged her close again, almost smothering her. Then she smoothed her sister's brown curls back, and holding Sabrina's face between her hands kissed her on the cheeks and brow.

She looked puzzled. 'I was going to say you had lost weight because your face is so thin, yet the rest of you doesn't feel thin!'

As she stepped back she gave a shocked gasp. 'Oh, Sabrina, you're pregnant! Duw anwyl! Was that why you ran away? Oh, cariad, why on earth did you have to do something like that?'

'Why do you think?' Sabrina snuffled.

'Surely you knew you could confide in me, my lovely. I would have stood by you!'

Sabrina shook her head, sniffing back her tears.

'Oh, cariad! Why didn't you tell me? Or you could have told Mr Barker. We would all have understood. Everybody would have rallied round and done everything possible to help you.'

'Even Dad?'

Rhianon shrugged uneasily. 'Well, he mightn't have been quite so understanding,' she admitted. 'Under the circumstances, with Hwyel dying so unexpectedly like that, but he would have come round given time.'

'I doubt it!'

'Oh, he would have done, Sabrina. You were always so precious to him, he thought the world of you. You know you could never do any wrong in his eyes!'

'He wouldn't have been able to accept something like this,' Sabrina said miserably, patting her extended stomach. 'Think of what all the people at the Capel Bethel would have said.'

'No one would have thought any the worse of you, since you and Hwyel were practically married.'

'No we weren't!'

'Well, you had plans, so you would have been in a few months' time.'

Sabrina shrugged. 'Perhaps! Who can be sure of anything? None of us knew that Hwyel had a bad heart, or that he was going to die suddenly, now did we?'

'I know, but all that was almost six months ago,' Rhianon rushed on. 'So what are you then, six or seven months pregnant?'

'Six months.'

'Oh, Sabrina, how unlucky. Hwyel didn't even know that there was to be a baby, then?'

'No, he didn't know,' her sister snapped.

'Even so, I'm sure his parents will be delighted. Come back to Pontdarw with me; they'll be so pleased, you'll see.'

Sabrina shook her head, her face impassive.

'Come on,' Rhianon urged. 'Even if they aren't willing to help you, I'll look out for you. I'll take care of you and the baby, I promise.'

Sabrina once again shook her head emphatically. 'I don't think you will . . .'

'If you think I'm afraid of how Father will react then don't worry, I'll soon talk him round,' Rhianon assured her.

'I wasn't thinking of Dad, Rhianon, I was thinking of you.'

'I've already told you that I'll stand by you, no matter what anyone else says or thinks . . .'

'I doubt it,' Sabrina interrupted, 'not when I tell you the rest.'

Rhianon felt cold fingers of fear clutching at her heart as she looked at Sabrina's ravaged face. 'Go on, what is it that I'm not going to like hearing?'

'It's not Hwyel's baby I'm expecting.'

'Not Hwyel's!' Rhianon looked astounded. 'Then whose baby is it?'

Sabrina shook her head, avoiding her sister's eyes. 'Does that really matter?'

'No, I don't suppose it does,' Rhianon agreed hesitantly. 'I think you should tell me though.'

'Sorry! I can't do that.'

Rhianon looked at Sabrina's clenched mouth and her determined expression, and shrugged. 'As you like. Perhaps in time you'll feel ready to confide in me, but, as you say, it doesn't really matter. It's your baby, my little niece or nephew, that's all that matters.'

She took hold of her sister's arm. 'I feel like a cup of tea, how about you?'

'If you like, there's a café near here.'

'Wouldn't it be better if we went back to your lodgings?' Rhianon suggested. 'Surely it's not all that far away? Come on, I'd like to see where you're living and to make sure you are comfortable.'

Sabrina stiffened. 'I don't think that's a good idea, either,' she protested.

'Well, I do,' Rhianon said firmly. 'I've heaps to tell you and I'm sure you have a lot to tell me as well. We don't want to have that sort of a talk in a café, now do we?'

Rhianon knew it wasn't what Sabrina wanted, but she was intent on finding out as much as possible about her sister's new life. Determinedly she ignored her reluctance.

'Show me the way then, you know I'm completely lost!' she smiled.

'What are you doing here in Cardiff anyway?' Sabrina asked suspiciously.

'I came to . . . to do a message for Polly Potter, and somehow when I came out of the building my mind was on other things and I got lost. I was trying to find my way back to the station, but I must have turned in the wrong direction. It was a good thing I bumped into you when I did, wasn't it!'

'You are miles away from the main station,' Sabrina told her.

'I thought I must be, but I couldn't see anyone to ask. All the way down this road there seemed to be only men about and a lot of them were foreigners, so I was afraid to ask any of them. It's a funny sort of area for you to be living in, isn't it?'

Sabrina no longer attempted to hold back her tears. Within a few seconds she was crying so hard that Rhianon couldn't understand what she was saying.

She put her arm around Sabrina's shoulder and pulled her close to her side, murmuring words of comfort as they walked along.

'Hush, hush! Leave it for now, we can talk about it later, cariad. Tell me all about what has happened over a nice cup of tea when we get back to your place, my lovely.'

Chapter Nineteen

After they left the main road, which Sabrina said was Bute Street, they criss-crossed a great many different side streets. Rhianon began to wonder if her sister was taking her on some wild goose chase, or deliberately trying to lose her.

As the district became grimmer and grimmer, the clanking of the trams was left behind. In their place there was the sound of ships' hooters and klaxons, and the scream of gulls as they swooped overhead. The houses became more and more slummy. They made even the poorest part of Pontdarw, where most of the miners lived in two-up, two-down, back-to-back terraced houses, seem attractive by comparison.

When Rhianon thought things couldn't get much worse, Sabrina took her along a muddy footpath by the side of an evil-smelling canal. A couple of barges, reeking of fish and diesel oil, were tied up there. A few hundred yards along they turned into Margaret Street. The front doors of the dreary looking houses opened straight onto the pavement. Some were ajar, and cooking smells, mostly of boiled cabbage and frying, wafted out into the street.

Although it was a chilly October afternoon,

two barefoot children were playing in the puddles in the gutter. One of them, a boy of about three years old, was poking amongst the accumulated mud and grime with a stick. A fair-haired girl, who had a dummy in her mouth, was crouched down on the edge of the pavement watching him. Neither child looked up or took any notice as Sabrina approached one of the paint-scarred doors, pushed it open and led Rhianon into a dingy hallway.

Immediately a door at the far end of the passage opened. A big brawny woman, her hair in curlers, a half-smoked cigarette dangling from her lips, appeared. She stood in the doorway, arms akimbo, glaring at them with such hostility that Rhianon wondered if they had come into the wrong house.

'Well, and who is this then that you're bringing back here without asking if you could?' the woman demanded aggressively.

'This is my sister, Mrs Jones.'

'Your sister is it, indeed!' the woman snapped. 'So what's her name then?'

'Rhianon. Rhianon Webster.'

The woman took a long drag on her cigarette as she looked Rhianon up and down.

'Well Rhianon Webster, I'm Nellie Jones and I'm your sister's landlady. I've been waiting to meet you so that I can give you a piece of my mind!'

Rhianon frowned. 'I'm afraid I don't understand, Mrs Jones?'

'Duw anwyl! You're a po-faced bitch and no mistake! Fancy having the nerve to come here now, and pretend to be all friendly with your sister, when you haven't been near her for the past three months or longer. She'd have starved to death if it hadn't been for me and my big heart.' Her voice rose higher and higher as she spoke until she was almost screaming.

Rhianon took a deep breath and tried to answer her calmly. Inwardly she was quaking, terrified by this raging Amazon.

'Mrs Jones, until about half an hour ago, when I accidentally bumped into Sabrina, I had no idea where she was living.'

Nellie Jones sniffed disbelievingly.

'I've come back here with my sister so that we can have a quiet cup of tea and a good long talk. We need to tell each other all that's been happening over the past few months. If that's not acceptable to you then we can go somewhere else.'

'Duw! You've got a polished tongue on you, girl! Sabrina said her dad was a preacher and it seems to have brushed off on you and no mistake.'

There was an electrifying silence as the three of them stood uneasily in the narrow passageway.

'Well, if it's tea you're wanting then I'd better put the kettle on,' Nellie Jones said at last and turned back into the kitchen. 'You'd both better sit down and wait for it to boil,' she added over her shoulder.

Rhianon caught hold of Sabrina's arm. 'Do we have to stay down here, can't we go to your room?'

Sabrina shook her head. 'We wouldn't be on our own there,' she whispered. 'Nellie's daughter is up there getting ready for her stint as an usherette at the Gaumont. She shares the room with me,' she added by way of explanation.

Rhianon gazed in disbelief as she followed her sister into the kitchen.

A square wooden table dominated the room. It was piled high with dirty dishes, old newspapers and an assortment of other rubbish. There was a narrow window that looked out onto a brick wall with a padded bench seat underneath it. At the far end of the room there was a kitchen range, and at one side of that a door opening onto some steps down into a back kitchen. Rhianon could see Nellie Jones in there, pouring boiling water into a large brown teapot.

'Right, sit yourselves down then,' Nellie ordered, coming into the room with the teapot. She placed it on a corner of the table and pulled a bright red knitted tea cosy over it. She then swept all the dirty dishes to the far end of the table so that she could set out cups and saucers for the three of them.

'Are you joining us then, Mrs Jones?' Rhianon questioned.

'Duw anwyl! I wouldn't miss this cosy reunion for the world, girl!' she said positively.

'We were hoping for a private sisterly chat,'

Rhianon persisted. 'You know, just the two of us, since we haven't seen each other for quite a long time.'

Nellie cackled harshly. 'Yes, it's been a long time, you are right about that! Your sister has been living here for over two months, and there's never been a sound from you. So why this sudden interest?'

'Please, Nellie, stay if you must, but let us do the talking,' Sabrina begged. 'There is so much we have to say to each other.'

'That there is!' Nellie agreed, ignoring Sabrina's request. 'So when did you last see each other then?' she demanded as she began pouring out the tea. 'You want milk and sugar in yours?' she asked Rhianon as she pushed a cup towards Sabrina.

'Yes, please.'

'Right! Well come on then, girl, when did you last see your sister?'

Rhianon chewed her lip uneasily. 'Not since May, if you must know. Not that it's any business of yours,' she added spiritedly.

'Rhianon, please!' Sabrina reached out and touched her sister's arm. 'Nellie means well. She's been so good to me. She's only asking because she cares.'

Rhianon shrugged exasperatedly. 'Perhaps you should be the one to explain things, then. You can start by telling me why you ran away like you did, and what has been happening to you ever since.'

Sabrina picked up her cup of tea in both hands and took a tentative sip.

'Come on then, cariad! Get on with it,' Nellie urged. 'There's probably things I don't know, stuff you haven't told me, so spit it out, girl! Cards on the table!'

Nellie and Rhianon listened in silence as Sabrina told them of her decision to leave Pontdarw, and how she came to Cardiff and found work at Ferdinands.

Rhianon shuddered when her sister described the arrangement Hans Meyer and his sister Helga wanted to make.

'When I refused to entertain his clients the way he expected me to, Hans Meyer threw me out into the street,' Sabrina said flatly.

'Are you telling us that you lost your job and your lodgings at a stroke?' Rhianon gasped.

Sabrina nodded. 'When I told them that I was pregnant they couldn't get rid of me quickly enough. I had only a few bob and the clothes I stood up in, and nowhere to go.'

'And that's when I found her wandering down Bute Street bawling her eyes out. I was on the way home from the offices I clean in Mount Stewart Square . . .'

'And Nellie brought me back here and said I could share her daughter's room,' Sabrina interrupted. 'She even found me some work.'

'What sort of work?' Rhianon asked suspiciously.

'Charring of course, that's all I'm able to get.

Even here in Tiger Bay the back-street shops and pubs don't want you working for them in my condition,' Sabrina added bitterly.

'You shouldn't be charring! Not when you're pregnant,' Rhianon said aghast.

'How else is she going to exist, then?' Nellie demanded. 'I'm not charging her any rent, but she has to dib up a few bob for her food.'

'Yes, of course,' Rhianon said hastily. 'It's very kind of you to have taken her in and to have done so much to help her.'

'What about the future though?' Nellie demanded. 'What's going to happen once the babby's born? She can't go on sharing a bedroom with my Olwen. It wouldn't be fair on my girl to have a young baby squalling and keeping her awake. Anyway, your sister won't be able to work for weeks once the baby's here, so where's the money coming from for her to live on?'

Rhianon shook her head, overwhelmed by all the problems that were being thrown up. 'You'll have to come back home with me, Sabrina, there's nothing else for it,' she said at last.

'Are you mad! I'd have Dad preaching and going on about me bringing the wrath of God down on my head every minute of the day.'

'You will have to let the Barkers help you, then. They may be a bit frosty at first, but they'll come round, you'll see.'

Sabrina shook her head vehemently.

'Think about it, cariad. It will be their only

grandchild, remember, and they wouldn't want it to suffer in any way.'

'I've already told you, Hwyel isn't the father.'

'You really meant that? Then you'd better tell me who is,' Rhianon said.

Sabrina shook her head, letting her tangle of brown curls fall over her face so that her expression was completely hidden.

'Well, if you won't, you won't, I suppose,' Rhianon said resignedly. 'I must go. Are you going to come to the tram stop with me, Sabrina?'

'So you're walking out and leaving her with me, are you?' Nellie snapped angrily.

'Only for the moment, Mrs Jones. I must go home now, my father will be expecting me. I promise I will be back and I'm sure I can manage to arrange something for my sister.'

'Mmm! Well we'll see, won't we,' Nellie Jones intoned dubiously. 'You haven't got that much time, mind. She don't look all that strong to me, so if you want my opinion I think the baby may be premature.'

Startled, Rhianon looked at her sister with new eyes. Her distended stomach gave an entirely false impression of well-being. You only had to look at her legs and arms, Rhianon realised, to see how thin and undernourished she really was.

'I do understand, Mrs Jones. I will be back again as soon as I possibly can. In the meantime, I'd be grateful if you'd keep an eye on my sister. If you need me in a hurry then you can always contact me at the shop where I work. If you have a piece of paper I'll write it all down for you.'

'Time's running out, remember that,' Nellie Jones repeated ominously, as she took the scrap of paper and stuck it behind a jug on the shelf over the range. 'Another thing, your sister hasn't got a single solitary bit of clothing for this baby.'

'Don't worry about that,' Rhianon assured her quickly. 'I work in a haberdashery shop. I'll get some baby clothes and other bits and pieces together, and I'll bring them with me the next time I come.'

'Make sure there's some blankets and bedding and napkins, things like that, not silly fancy clothes to doll it up in.'

'I understand. I'll see to it all,' Rhianon promised.

Nellie Jones's mouth tightened. 'Let's hope you do!'

Rhianon turned to her sister. 'Don't you worry either, cariad, I'll organise things. Now, are you going to walk to the tram stop with me?'

'You'd best take her down to the Pier Head, Sabrina, you're sure to be able to get on one there,' Mrs Jones advised.

Rhianon found the walk through the heart of Tiger Bay frightening. She had never seen so much squalor. Even though it was getting dark and the street lamps were on, ragged barefoot children were everywhere, playing in the gutter, swinging on ropes from lampposts, or playing hopscotch amongst the litter on the dirty pavements. There seemed to be every nationality under the sun. No one spoke to them or accosted them, but Rhianon still felt that the place was evil. She hated the idea of Sabrina living there, or even being left to walk all the way back to Margaret Street on her own.

There was a tram about to leave when they reached the Pier Head. 'Ask the conductor to put you off at the Custom House stop,' Sabrina told her as they kissed goodbye.

'Will you be all right walking home on your own?' Rhianon asked anxiously.

'Of course I will,' Sabrina grinned. 'I've been living here for months, I know how to take care of myself.'

Rhianon shook her head. 'I can't help worrying about you, cariad. I am so glad I've found you. I will be back, as soon as I possibly can,' she added as the tram began to start up.

'We'll see.' Sabrina shrugged.

'I've said I'll be back, so I will. What makes you doubt my word?'

Sabrina looked uncertain. 'You wanted to know who the father is and I'm not going to tell you, so are you still going to come back?'

Chapter Twenty

Rhianon's head was buzzing, her senses reeling as the tram started to pull away. She remained on the platform, swaying precariously, staring down at Sabrina who was standing on the edge of the pavement and looking defiantly up at her.

As she grabbed at an overhead strap and stumbled into a seat, Rhianon asked herself over and over again why Sabrina was being so secretive and refusing to name the father of the baby she was expecting.

She found a window seat on the train and sat staring out as she tried desperately to remember the dates when the troubles in Pontdarw had begun. The strike had started on 1st May, she knew that well enough. It was all the events afterwards that were so muddled in her mind.

The day the strike began was the day that Hwyel had been taken to hospital, but whether Sabrina had run away before he died, or afterwards, she wasn't too sure. She knew it was before the funeral because there had been recriminations about her absence, but she couldn't be certain if it was before Pryce was arrested, though she thought it was. Everything was so jumbled up in her mind at the moment, but she was sure Sabrina couldn't have been seeing anyone other than Hwyel because they were rarely apart.

Sometimes they even went out straight from work. On Sundays Sabrina had to attend Capel Bethel, just as Rhianon did. Hwyel was always there as well, and afterwards he and Sabrina walked home together.

The more Rhianon thought about it, the more bewildered she became. By the time the train pulled into Pontdarw she had come to no conclusion. It *must* be Hwyel's baby. Yet Sabrina said it wasn't, and surely she wouldn't lie about a thing like that!

Perhaps that was really what the fight had been about. If Hwyel suspected that she was seeing someone behind his back, when Sabrina started flirting with Pryce he might have decided it was Pryce who was his rival. Maybe Hwyel had been trying to defend what he considered to be his.

If only she could recall the incident in greater detail! It had taken place right outside Polly Potter's shop, and Rhianon knew she herself had been one of the first on the scene. She had no idea, though, which of the two men had thrown the first punch. Nor could she remember if there had been any verbal exchanges between them.

At the time she had thought it was a dreadful

thing to find them fighting each other. Now she was more concerned about the outcome when her father learnt the real reason why Sabrina had run away from home.

She thought back to her visit to Cardiff prison to see Pryce, and how he had asked her for news of Sabrina. Her blood ran cold. If he knew about the baby, then she wondered who else did. Perhaps he even knew who the father was.

Common sense told her he couldn't possibly know, because he had now been in either police custody, or prison, since almost the beginning of May, and that was five months ago. Sabrina claimed she was barely six months pregnant, so she wouldn't have known she was expecting when the fight took place.

Unless Sabrina wasn't telling the truth about how many months pregnant she was? Nellie Jones had hinted that there wasn't much time left for them to make arrangements. When she'd said the baby might be premature, had she been trying to warn her that really Sabrina's pregnancy was far more advanced than she had admitted?

Rhianon sighed. No, that couldn't be the case. Nellie Jones wasn't the sort of woman to be tactful, so she must think Sabrina was telling the truth.

As she walked from Pontdarw station back to Polly's flat up over the shop to change into her plain working dress, Rhianon wondered why she was bothering to cover up what she'd been doing.

Lies, lies, it was all lies. If she told her father that she'd found Sabrina in Cardiff, then he'd want to know what she'd been doing down there. If she told him she'd been looking for Sabrina, that would be another lie to add to the mountain of untruths already told.

Perhaps the time had come to tell the truth and shame the devil, as her mam had been fond of saying. Time to admit to her father that she had been visiting Pryce in prison.

Polly Potter took one look at Rhianon's face and knew that there was something very wrong.

'Come on in, the kettle's on the boil. You look as though you need a cuppa, cariad,' she greeted her affectionately.

'Well, did they let you in to see Pryce?' she asked as she brought cups and saucers to the table. 'There's daft, asking you something like that. The time you've been gone, of course they let you in. Late back, aren't you, I've been expecting you for hours. Did you miss your train or something?'

'I met up with Sabrina.'

'Duw anwyl! You never did, girl! Where did you see her then? She wasn't at the prison, was she?'

'Of course not! Why would she be there?' Rhianon said sharply.

'Oh, I don't know. I've always had it in the

back of my mind that she'd gone to Cardiff because she knew that's where the trial would be,' Polly said lamely.

Rhianon stared at her curiously. 'Do you know something about Sabrina and Pryce that I don't?' she asked bluntly.

'Dammo di, of course I don't,' Polly blustered. 'Why on earth should I?'

'What made you ask if I'd met up with her at the prison?'

Polly looked flummoxed. 'I don't know, cariad. Me and my big mouth. It just came out, but I didn't mean anything by it. Cardiff is such a big place, and since you'd run into her, I thought it must have been at the prison.'

'Well, you're wrong, but I'd still like to know why you thought she might be visiting Pryce,' Rhianon persisted.

Polly's mouth tightened. 'We seem to be at cross purposes. Here,' she pushed a cup of tea into Rhianon's hand. 'Drink that and then tell me all about it from the very beginning.'

Rhianon took the tea, but placed it down on the table nearby. 'It's all so silly, Polly. I'm so mixed up I don't know if I'm coming or going.'

'You'd better start talking and put me in the picture then, hadn't you, girl,' Polly advised. 'Until I know what you are on about I can't help.'

Rhianon shook her head wearily. 'It's all such a muddle,' she moaned. She picked up the tea and took a long drink, then put it back on the table.

'Sabrina is pregnant!'

'Duw anwyl!' Polly exclaimed, her eyes widening. 'Oh the poor dab! Terrible wicked goings-on, mind you, in Cardiff, or so I've heard.'

'It's nothing to do with being in Cardiff. It's why she went there.'

Polly's mouth dropped open. 'You mean she ran away after poor Hwyel died because she was in the family way!' she exclaimed aghast.

Rhianon swept her hair back from her face. 'That's the trouble, Polly, I can't remember if she ran off before he died or afterwards.'

'We can soon work it out,' Polly assured her. 'Does it matter to a day anyway?'

'Yes, it does matter.'

Polly frowned. 'Because of Hwyel dying? What difference does that make? Are you trying to say he didn't know she was expecting?'

'He didn't know, Polly, and what is more to the point Sabrina says it isn't his.'

'Dammo di! This gets worse with the telling. If it isn't Hwyel's child then who else's can it be? Those two have been a pigeon pair ever since she started work in Barker's office. You never saw them apart. I thought that she'd run away because she was heartbroken about what had happened. She'd been down there with the crowd urging them on to fight that Saturday morning, if you remember.'

'Yes, but why were Pryce and Hwyel fighting and why was she egging them on?'

Polly looked at her, bewildered. 'In heaven's name how would I know?'

'I thought she was wanting Hwyel to win, but now I'm not so sure,' Rhianon went on. She wiped her face with both hands, as a child might, trying to clear her mind.

'What are you getting at, my lovely?' Polly frowned. 'What's any of this got to do with the fact that your Sabrina is expecting?'

'She won't tell me who the father is,' Rhianon answered dully.

'You're surely not thinking that it could be Pryce!' Polly sounded both shocked and astounded.

'You did warn me that she was making up to him, but I took no notice,' Rhianon went on bitterly.

'Flirting with him, yes. Then your Sabrina would flirt with absolutely anyone, you know that for a fact. With her pretty hair, and lovely face, she only had to smile at any man and he was smitten. That's all I meant about watching out for the way she was carrying on with Pryce,' Polly babbled.

Rhianon laughed dryly. 'Well, there could have been a lot more to it than flirting.'

'Rubbish, cariad! She always was something of a tease, she likes to get you worked up, it's her idea of fun.'

'Not any more, Polly. She's living in a slum that would make your stomach turn. She's had a hard time of it since she's been in Cardiff, things seem to have gone from bad to worse for her. She's sharing a bedroom with the daughter of some rough old woman in Tiger Bay. The woman, Nellie Jones, has been good to her, mind. It's a pig of a place though, and Nellie says she can't let her stay on after the baby arrives.'

'So what's going to happen? Why didn't you bring her back home? You should have done, this is where she belongs.'

'I know that, Polly, but I'll need to talk to my father first, and find out his opinion about it all.'

'Humph! You know the answer to that before you ask!'

'I'll have to tell him the truth though, or else he will be dashing over to see Cledwyn Barker, and blaming Hwyel for Sabrina's condition. Think of the trouble that would cause!'

'Yes, I suppose you're right. Proper old muddle, isn't it. Anyway, my lovely, what do you feel about it all?'

'Me? I just want to do whatever's best for Sabrina. I can't leave her there in that slummy hole!' Rhianon's face hardened. 'I'm so churned up inside, Polly, that I don't really want to talk about it.'

'You'll have to, my lovely. You can't sweep it under the carpet and forget it. You need to have things out in the open, believe me! It's one of those things that won't go away.'

* * *

Edwin Webster's face became as black as thunder as he listened to Rhianon's account of her trip to Cardiff to visit Pryce.

'So you defied me, daughter, and went against my wishes! If you visit the devil then you must expect to be blackened not only in my eyes, but in the eyes of all God-fearing people.'

'Yes, Father, but because of what I did it also meant that I found Sabrina,' she explained.

'Sabrina! My miscreant daughter, the jezebel! The little hellcat who broke my heart before she turned her back on me! Why should that please me?'

'You must have been worrying about her, wondering where she was? We've both been longing for the day when she would come home again.'

The silence was threatening. Drawing himself up to his full height and trying to straighten his bowed shoulders, Edwin Webster bellowed with a cry that was torn from deep in his chest, 'Never mention her name in my presence ever again!'

'Father, please listen. Sabrina is in serious trouble. She's expecting a baby!'

His face became puce. 'Then let her go to the Barkers for help,' he snapped.

'She says Hwyel isn't the father.'

As colour flooded his face and his eyes bulged, Rhianon was afraid he was about to have a seizure, but she felt she had to go on and try to persuade him to be reconciled with her sister. 'She needs us! Surely you want her to come home so that we can take care of her, and of the baby, when it arrives,' Rhianon pleaded.

'I've spoken my last word on the matter.'

'I can't abandon her,' Rhianon protested.

'No? Why not? Is it because you are ridden with guilt? She is the way she is now because of how you raised her. I trusted you to be a mother to her. I put her into your care and look where it has led. She now carries a bastard, and it is all your fault, girl,' he thundered.

Rhianon stared at him in dismay. Spittle shone like white foam on his twisted lips. Losing Sabrina seems to have turned his brain, she thought apprehensively. How many more lives were going to be drawn into this maelstrom and destroyed?

'I feel responsible for her,' she protested.

'Then go to her. Desert me as she has done. Leave me here to mourn the loss of not one daughter, but of two.'

'You could be celebrating the joy of having a grandchild,' she said gently.

'Spawned in evil! Offspring of a harlot! I want no part in this scurrilous travesty. Go to her if your guilt makes you feel you must, but if you do then never darken my door again.'

'What about Christian charity and forgiveness, Father?' Rhianon persisted, trembling at defying him but determined to do so. 'It's not too late.'

He shook his head. 'It's too late to save her . . . or you. The pair of you are damned, and may both of you rot in hell for all the disgrace you've heaped on my head.'

'Please Father, think it over. I know you're angry and upset at the moment, but if Sabrina comes home then we can be a family again.'

Edwin Webster didn't answer, but the look he gave her spoke volumes. Then, without a word, he picked up his hat, rammed it on his head and walked out of the house, slamming the door behind him.

Rhianon felt the tension between herself and her father permeating their home like a dark cloud. She knew that deep down he was as concerned about Sabrina as she was.

He barely spoke to her and avoided eye contact as much as possible. She desperately wanted to talk to him about Sabrina, and about how they might help her, but he remained unco-operative.

She realised he must be devastated about the news that Sabrina was pregnant. She wished he could see further ahead than the shame it was bringing on his name. He must realise that they couldn't leave her in Cardiff on her own. There was no way that Sabrina could provide for herself as her pregnancy advanced, or for the baby when it arrived.

She wasn't sure who he thought was the father of the baby, and her own uncertainty continued to preoccupy her. Sabrina insisted that it wasn't Hwyel's, but Rhianon couldn't bring herself to believe that it could be anyone else's. She kept telling herself it was the sort of thing Sabrina would say, simply to shock.

Polly was non-committal whenever she mentioned it.

'Your Sabrina's made her bed so she's got to lie on it. There's no sense in you worrying yourself silly over something you can't do anything about,' she commented pragmatically.

'That's the point, though, I feel I must do something about it. Sabrina won't be able to work for much longer.'

'Rubbish! Women go on working right up to the last minute, now don't they, girl?'

'Around the home, perhaps. They don't go out charring, though, do they!'

'She's young and strong, she'll be all right, my lovely, so you stop worrying about her.'

Rhianon tried her best to do so, but Sabrina and her problems haunted her, especially in bed at night. She had promised to return with things for the baby, but she kept putting it off in the hope that her father would let Sabrina come home. Time and again she tried to discuss this with him, but he turned a deaf ear to her entreaties.

Matters came to a head early in November when the miners from the Rhondda marched to Cardiff to try and draw attention to their situation. The following week, one of the men came into Polly Potter's shop to tell Rhianon that he'd seen Sabrina.

'Your sister was standing there, as large as life, as we walked down St Mary Street, see.'

'Did you speak to her?'

'Well, not really. I called out to her, like, but we was all marching, see, so I couldn't stop for a chat. Rough she looked, I thought. You know she's pregnant, I suppose? Belly on her like a bloody balloon! Be dropping it any day, I should think.'

Rhianon felt distraught. Once again she tackled her father, begging him to reconsider his decision, pleading with him to let Sabrina come home.

'I'll look after her, she'll be no trouble, I promise you. It will set both our minds at rest to know she's back here safe and sound.'

Whatever she said made no difference at all. Edwin Webster remained adamant that he wanted nothing more to do with Sabrina. She'd contravened his rules, disgraced herself and brought shame on his name. His decision was final.

'One more word and I'll turn you out as well,' he threatened.

'You've no need to do so,' she told him sharply. 'If you won't let Sabrina come home then I'm going to Cardiff to take care of her.'

Chapter Twenty-One

Rhianon placed two large suitcases down on the pavement outside the front door in Rhoslyn Terrace. Then she went back inside to take one last look around the house that had been her home since the day she'd been born.

There were tears in her eyes, and an ache in her heart, when she came back out and forced herself to pick up the cases.

They were so heavy that she stumbled as she tried to carry them. She'd packed all her own clothes and also those that Sabrina had left behind. There was a bundle of baby clothes, two shawls and two little blankets. Polly Potter had insisted on giving her those when Rhianon had told her that she'd decided to go to Cardiff so she could be with Sabrina.

'Keep in touch and remember, if you change your mind and want to come back to Pontdarw there will always be a job waiting for you here,' Polly told her as she hugged her and kissed her goodbye.

'Thank you Polly, I'll always be grateful for all you've done for me, and I'm sorry to be leaving you in the lurch like this.'

'Dammo di, there's nothing to be sorry about,

cariad. I can soon find someone else. Once it gets around that you've left, girls and women will be queuing up to fill your shoes, no problem at all. They'll not be as good as you, mind, but I'll manage.'

'I'll write and let you know my address as soon as I have one, so that you can keep in touch and let me know how my father is.'

'If that is what you want. Old devil that he is, he doesn't deserve to have you worrying about him.'

Rhianon hated saying goodbye to Polly. She'd hoped that even then, at the eleventh hour, her father might relent and tell her that he didn't want her to go, and that she could bring Sabrina back home.

His silence had been icy and unrelenting. He hadn't even answered her that morning when she'd said she was definitely leaving.

As she boarded the train, turning her back on the world she knew, Rhianon wondered when she would see Pontdarw again.

Nellie Jones were very taken aback to find Rhianon on the doorstep.

'This isn't a lodging house, you know, so I don't know where you think you are going to put those two great suitcases, or yourself if it comes to that,' Nellie Jones sniffed.

'I had no intention of asking you to put me up,' Rhianon told her primly. 'If I can leave the cases here, though, for a couple of hours, while

215

I look for somewhere to stay, I would be very grateful. I'll come straight back and get them so they won't be in your way for very long, Mrs Jones. I suppose you don't happen to know where I can get a room?'

'Damnedigaeth! Not when it's sprung on me out of the blue without a moment's notice, I don't! You'd better come in and have a cup of tea and that will give me breathing space to think,' Nellie told her. 'Was it for you on your own or are you taking Sabrina along with you?'

'For both of us, of course! You said Sabrina couldn't stay here after the baby was born . . .'

'What I said and what I meant is two different things,' Nellie scowled. 'I said it wouldn't be fair on my Olwen for her to have to go on sharing a bedroom with Sabrina and a squalling young baby. If you were sharing a room here with your sister, then I suppose that would be a different kettle of fish.'

Rhianon looked puzzled.

'I've got another bedroom, you daft ha'p'orth! I lets that out. The fellow who's in there at the moment is moving on in a week's time, so if you can afford to pay the rent then the pair of you can have that room. It's twice the size of the one your sister is sharing with my Olwen. You'd have plenty of space, even after the babba arrives and you have a cot in there.'

Rhianon thought quickly. It certainly wasn't what she'd intended to do, but it seemed to be the perfect answer. Nellie Jones might be rough

216

and ready, but she was good-hearted; she'd proved that by taking Sabrina in and looking after her.

If it didn't work out she could always look for somewhere else after the baby was born. It would give her a chance to be with Sabrina, to get a job and find her bearings. By that time they might even be able to move to a better district.

She smiled her thanks. 'That sounds first-rate, Mrs Jones! I intend to find work right away so I will certainly be able to afford the rent.'

'Well, that's settled then! The name's Nellie, so no more of this Mrs Jones! There is one snag, mind.'

'What's that, Mrs Jo— Nellie?'

'My present lodger doesn't move out until the end of next week, so you two can't have the room until then.'

Rhianon's spirits sank. She had only a very limited amount of money and she was hoping to hang onto it, knowing Sabrina was bound to need extra things when the baby was born.

'If you don't mind sleeping on a couch for the next few nights, mind, I can put you up temporary like in my best front room.'

'That sounds fine, but are you quite sure that won't be inconvenient for you?'

'The room is only used on special occasions, it's more like a damn museum than anything else.' Nelly laughed. She stood up. 'Come on and see for yourself and tell me what you think.'

Nellie was right, Rhianon decided. The room was stuffy and airless and so full of furniture it was difficult to move around in it. There were two china cabinets filled with a miscellany of souvenirs, a piano, table and chairs and a sofa, covered in black imitation leather. It looked as solid as a rock! She could see at a glance that it would be uncomfortable, but since it was only for a few nights she accepted the offer.

'Come and have that cup of tea and then we'll move those great suitcases out of the hallway and put them in the front room. Make it a bit of a tight squeeze for you but it's not for long,' Nellie told her cheerfully.

Finding work proved much more difficult for Rhianon than it had been to find somewhere to live.

Nellie suggested that Currans might be her best bet, because they paid top wages. 'It's the factory where they make pots and pans and all sorts of other enamel stuff,' she said airily. 'You'd do well there, I shouldn't wonder.'

Rhianon went there first. Even before she arrived at the factory gates, though, the obnoxious smell was so overpowering that she found herself almost choking, and she turned away.

She'd try somewhere else first, she decided. She could always come back to Currans if there was no other sort of work going. She would prefer shop work, and Polly Potter had written a glowing reference for her.

None of the large department stores in the city centre showed the slightest interest in granting her an interview. There didn't seem to be many small haberdashery shops, either in the centre or in the surrounding area.

She hated the thought of going back to Currans, but there was nothing else for it. It looked as though they were her only hope.

She felt exhausted, and realised that she'd had nothing to eat or drink since early morning. It was now mid-afternoon, so she went into a café on the corner of Bute Street and Loudon Place.

'Please sit down and I will bring your order to you,' the smiling Italian behind the counter told her. Ten minutes later he still hadn't brought the cup of tea, and poached egg on toast, that she had requested. She began to wonder if she would have time to wait for them, if she was to get back to Currans before they closed.

Finally, in desperation, she went back to the counter to cancel her order.

The Italian looked so woebegone when she told him that she found herself not only apologising, but explaining why she was being impatient.

'You are looking for a job?' He seemed puzzled. 'Why go to work in a factory? A pretty young lady like you shouldn't be shut away in a place like that, wrapping your hair up in a scarf and having to wear overalls. No, no!' He smiled broadly, displaying big white teeth, some with gold fillings. 'Why do you not come and work here for me, Gino?'

'Work here? Do you mean doing the cooking?'

He shrugged. 'Some cooking if that is what you really want to do, but I would like that you wait on the customers, and serve behind the counter. No matter, whatever you like to do best I will be happy. So what do you say?'

Rhianon was so taken aback she couldn't answer.

'I pay you well,' he added quickly when he saw her hesitate. 'Not quite so much as in the Currans factory, perhaps, but it will be more pleasant for you. You will not work as hard. You will meet people, smile and talk with them. You will be keeping them happy because they no longer will have to wait a long time for the food they have ordered. You say yes?'

'Well . . .' Rhianon didn't know what to say. She'd never thought about doing the sort of work that Gino was offering her.

Gino patted her on the shoulder. 'You sit over there and think about it while you enjoy your cup of tea and poached egg, yes?'

Rhianon studied the menu card on the table as she ate. It was all fairly basic home cooking, except for the Italian dishes, which were marked as specialities.

She looked round her thoughtfully. The place was spotlessly clean, and Gino seemed hard-working and easy enough to get on with. What were the drawbacks, she wondered. There must be something he hadn't mentioned, or why would he be needing a waitress?

As she finished eating, he came over to collect her used dishes.

'You like my food?'

'Yes, it was good. I was very hungry.'

'Then you can eat one of my Italian specialities, a very special sweet. You taste and try and tell me if you like, yes?'

'No, no thank you.' She had seen the price of his special dishes and felt it would be extravagant to indulge in one after she'd already eaten.

'Nonsense! I insist. It will be my treat!'

He was gone before she could protest further. He returned with a glass dish which held a concoction of fruit, ice cream and cream that looked so delicious she hadn't the heart to refuse.

'I leave you to eat, then I come back again and we talk more about you coming to work here, yes?'

So he's trying to sweeten me up, Rhianon thought. Well, it won't work. Before I even consider taking the job I want to know exactly what all my duties will be.

'It is exactly as I have already said,' Gino told her when she asked for an outline of what the work entailed. 'What else is there that you need to know?'

'Who does the washing-up?'

He looked at her in silence, shaking his head as though amused by her question.

'So I would be the one who had to stand at the sink, up to my elbows in hot greasy dirty water? That would be part of my duties as well, even though you have forgotten to mention it?'

He shook his head, laughing so much that his rolls of fat wobbled. 'No, no, no! Gino not expect a pretty lady like you to do work of that sort!' he told her.

'You are quite sure?'

'I already have a woman in the kitchen who does all that, and she prepares all the vegetables and fruit that I use each day. My wife, she does some of the cooking, but she does not like being out here serving customers. That is why I have to cope both in the kitchen and out here, and that is why the orders are so slow . . .'

Rhianon gave a sigh of relief. 'So really, all you want me to do is serve behind the counter and wait on the customers?'

He beamed at her. 'That is exactly so! That would be good, very good!'

'If that is what the job consists of, then it will suit me very well,' she agreed. 'No work at all in the kitchen, mind!'

'So when is it that you will be able to come and begin working here?'

'I could start tomorrow, but you haven't told me what the hours are, or what my wages will be.'

Half an hour later, Rhianon was on her way back to Margaret Street feeling well satisfied with her deal. She couldn't wait to tell Sabrina, and to be able to assure Nellie Jones that there would be no problem about paying for the room she'd offered them.

Chapter Twenty-Two

It took Rhianon quite a while to settle into her new job at Gino's café because everything seemed so strange to her. She'd been used to starting work at nine and finishing at six each day. Now she didn't need to be at the café until half past ten, but she didn't finish until eight or even nine o'clock in the evening.

Even so, she enjoyed working there. She found both Gino and his wife, Maria, easy to get on with and anxious to help her adjust to her role of waiting on customers. She even liked Adda, the stick-thin Nepalese woman who worked in the kitchen. What she didn't like were some of the customers.

Most of them were all right, they placed their order, waited patiently for her to serve them, thanked her and that was that. It was the others, men who seemed to eat her up with their eyes as they studied her every movement, who made her uncomfortable.

Some of them tried to hold her gaze, their lustful eyes signalling their desires. Others avoided eye contact, but they would slyly brush against her as she was leaning over the table to put down their order, or as they passed her when they were leaving the café.

In the busy, brightly lit environment of the café none of this bothered her too much. But afterwards, when she left work and had to walk all the way down Bute Street, and through the side roads that led back to Margaret Street, she always felt uneasy, fearing she might meet one of them.

Supposing one or other of them waited outside for her to leave – they all knew what time the café closed – what would she do then, she asked herself.

Common sense told her that such an obvious ploy would be unlikely. If they did intend to waylay her, they would do it when she reached one of the dark side roads, not in the well-lit main street bustling with people.

Even so, she began to vary her journey. Some nights she would catch a tram to the Pier Head and walk to Margaret Street from there. At other times she would thread her way through different side roads, hoping to avoid anyone who might be lying in wait for her.

Apart from that, she was happy with her work. The hours were long, but the money was quite good. Added to that, she was allowed to eat whatever she liked and often when she was leaving for home there would be a leftover pie, or some cakes that wouldn't keep until next day, for her to take back for Sabrina and Nellie.

Nellie had kept to her promise, and as soon

as the lodger left she'd moved Rhianon and Sabrina into the big front bedroom.

Sabrina was very restless at night, because she found it difficult to get comfortable. Despite that, even though she had to share the double bed with her, Rhianon found it heaven after the nights she'd had to spend on the rock-hard sofa in Nellie's best parlour.

She had thought that Sabrina would be well pleased with the new arrangement, but she seemed listless and far from happy. It was obvious that something was preying on her mind, and Rhianon felt there was a lot she still didn't know. She tried to persuade Sabrina to talk to her about it, but her sister clammed up immediately at any overture of this kind.

Halfway through November came the news that the miners had given in, and gone back to work. The strike that Pryce had set such great store by had collapsed. They had not achieved any of the aims for which he had been fighting. Worse still, they had not only returned to the pits but had agreed to a cut in their wages.

It would be a bitter blow to everyone in Pontdarw, Rhianon thought sadly. Yet, with winter setting in, the wives would secretly rejoice because once more there would be some money coming in to buy food and warmth for themselves and their children.

She wondered if Pryce had heard the news. No doubt the warders would tell him. They'd take a delight in taunting him with the fact that his hopes for better working conditions had been dashed.

'Bloody fools for going on strike in the first place,' Nellie remarked, when she heard Rhianon telling Sabrina the news. 'The daft buggers should know they can't beat the bosses, and now that they've caved in the bosses will make their life hell.'

Sabrina seemed to be completely disinterested and made no comment at all. She concentrated on hemming some cot sheets she was making from old sheets Nellie had given her to cut up.

As soon as Rhianon started earning a wage, Nellie suggested that Sabrina should give up her charring job.

'It's heavy work, see, for someone in her condition, and she doesn't look all that strong to me,' she told Rhianon.

'Yes, you're probably right, but she's going to get pretty fed up sitting here on her own all day doing nothing,' Rhianon pointed out.

'Oh there's plenty to keep her occupied, cariad. She can help around the house for one thing. Anyway, it's about time she made a start getting stuff ready for the babba. I know you brought a bundle of baby clothes with you from Pontdarw, but there's lots of other things she needs to do.'

Sabrina didn't argue, nor did she seem pleased in any way by the arrangement.

'Take no notice, it's her condition,' Nellie stated dismissively.

Despite all her private worries, Rhianon found the time flew by because they were always so busy at the café. It seemed no time at all before it was Christmas.

She kept thinking that perhaps she ought to go home to Pontdarw over the holiday to see how her father was managing. Polly had written to her saying she saw him in the street occasionally, but he never spoke to her, not even to acknowledge her greeting.

Christmas Day 1926 was on a Saturday and Gino had promised some of his regular customers, men who had no homes, but lived in lodging houses, that he would be providing Christmas dinners. As a result, he wanted Rhianon to work.

'I'll pay you extra money, of course. A really good bonus! We'll be through by four o'clock, so there will be plenty of time for you to celebrate with your sister and friends.'

Knowing that Sabrina still needed several expensive items, such as a cot and a pram, for the baby, Rhianon agreed. She wrote a long letter to her father explaining the situation. She promised to visit him the following weekend. At the back of her mind was the hope that since it would be the start of a new year he might be in a forgiving mood, and agree that Sabrina could come home.

The following weekend, however, Gino made

a similar request for her to work over the New Year to help him and his customers greet 1927 in festive style.

Rhianon reluctantly agreed to think about it. Nellie had promised to ask around and see if anyone had a pram or cot for sale. Rhianon didn't really want to buy second-hand items, so with the extra money she would earn she would be able to buy new ones. It did mean, however, that she wouldn't be able to visit her father as she'd planned.

Sabrina didn't seem to care what she did, one way or another. All she wanted was for the baby to be born so that she would be free to lead her own life again.

In the middle of the week Rhianon received a letter and recognised her father's handwriting on the envelope. Her hopes soared as she opened it, praying that he was sending them good wishes and asking them to come home.

Inside, unopened, was the letter she had written to him. Quickly she scanned the outside of the envelope to make sure that it was his handwriting, and not someone returning her letter because something had happened to him. She saw the scrawl in his handwriting on the outside of the returned letter. It read 'Not wanted!'

She felt so stunned that she couldn't even cry.

'I've asked Patrick Nelson to walk you home,' Gino told Rhianon, as she helped him and

Maria clear away after the New Year's Eve festivities at the café ended.

'That's not necessary, I'll be all right.'

'No, no, there's still a lot of celebrating going on and the streets will be full of men who have had far too much to drink. Patrick is returning to his ship, so he's going your way. It is no trouble for him to walk you home.'

Rhianon smiled her thanks. She felt too tired to argue, and she knew what Gino said was true. Even from inside the café they could hear boisterous singing as sailors made their way back to their ships, and local men to their homes.

She knew she would be safe with Patrick Nelson. A quietly spoken man, in his late thirties, he was a long-standing friend of Gino and Maria, and visited them whenever his ship docked in Cardiff.

He was tall, broad-shouldered and had clear blue eyes and receding fair hair. He looked very authoritative in his smart midshipman's uniform, and she was glad of his presence as they made their way through side streets packed with revellers.

She saw the surprise on his face when they reached Margaret Street, where people were still celebrating, and she introduced him to Nellie and Sabrina.

He didn't stay or accept the drink Nellie offered him. 'I have to be back on board ship, as we sail on the morning tide,' he explained.

After he'd gone, Rhianon reflected that she really must try and make a fresh start. This wasn't the sort of place where she and Sabrina should be living. They'd suffered a great many setbacks in 1926, but now it was a new year and time to put all that behind them, she told herself resolutely.

The first thing she was going to do was visit Pryce again and try and sort things out with him. When she mentioned this to Sabrina her mood seemed to darken, and she became more and more sullen as the time for the visit approached.

Rhianon felt under a terrible strain. Her suspicions that Polly might have been right, and that there had been something between Sabrina and Pryce, even before the fight, became stronger. She had to know the truth, and she wondered what Pryce's reaction would be when she told him about the baby. If Sabrina was to be believed and it was not Hwyel's child, would Pryce be able to tell her who the father was?

Was she the right person to deal with this, she asked herself over and over again. If only Sabrina would talk to her, let her know exactly what had gone on.

Because she was still very much in love with Pryce herself, Rhianon found it hard to accept that he could know about the baby. If he did, then the sooner that was out in the open the better, however much it might upset her.

Matters came to a head the night before she was due to make the prison visit. She'd arranged with Gino that she could take a day off, although she hadn't told him why she wanted to do so.

As she made her way home that evening she came to a decision. She couldn't go to the prison weighed down with so much doubt. She would insist that Sabrina talked to her. She'd make her tell the truth whether she wanted to or not.

Her plans were thwarted the moment she reached Margaret Street.

From the roadway outside she could hear Sabrina screaming in agony. As she hurried indoors she found Nellie doing all she could to quieten her.

'I've sent Olwen for Morfa Edwards and she should be here any minute,' Nellie told Rhianon. 'I wanted Sabrina to go upstairs and get into bed, but she says she can't move she's in such pain.'

'I'll see if I can persuade her,' Rhianon said. 'I'd better run up and get the bed ready first though.'

'I've done that, girl. It's all protected with newspapers and an old blanket and sheets. Everything else is all ready for Morfa when she gets here. It's just a case of persuading Sabrina to get up there.'

'Leave her to me!' Half lifting, half dragging Sabrina from the wooden armchair in Nellie's kitchen, Rhianon propelled her sister towards the stairs.

'Come on, no fuss now, cariad! You must be brave, you're going to be a mother within the next couple of hours.'

Angrily Sabrina tried to resist. 'Leave me alone, let me be. I don't want you telling me what I should do. You know nothing about the agony I'm in. This baby is killing me, I'm going to die, I know I am,' she screamed hysterically.

'Nonsense! You've got to expect some discomfort, but Morfa will be here to help you as soon as we get you upstairs.'

'Discomfort! What do you know about it?' Sabrina howled. She collapsed at the bottom of the stairs, her shoulders heaving, sobbing as though her heart would break.

'Duw anwyl, you'd think she was the only woman in the world to give birth!' Nellie exclaimed. 'Can't you reason with your sister, Rhianon? Dammo di! Try and talk some sense into her. A bit of co-operation is what we need, we're doing our damnedest to help her.'

Sabrina raised her tear-streaked face and stared at them both, her huge eyes dark with hatred. 'I don't want this bloody kid, can't either of you understand that? I want my life as it used to be. Twelve months ago I was going to work at Barkers every day, going out with Hwyel at night and planning to get married. Now look at me, fat and bloated and in agonies of pain! What's more, I'm going to spend the rest of my life bringing up a child that everyone knows is a bastard.'

'Sabrina!' Rhianon looked at her in horror. 'I thought you were pleased about having this baby,' she said lamely.

'I might be if Pryce was here with me,' her sister muttered.

Rhianon froze. 'Pryce! Why would you want him here?'

'He's the baby's father, that's why!' she screamed frenziedly, as a fresh wave of pain twisted her body.

The damp flannel that she'd been using to mop at Sabrina's forehead dropped from Rhianon's hand as Polly's warnings rang inside her head.

It was true, then! Sabrina was intent on taking Pryce away from her. For all that Rhianon had defended her sister when Polly had insisted that was what was happening, the truth was out at last. But even Polly hadn't thought Sabrina capable of this.

What had she done, she asked herself. Why had she given up her comfortable home and good job to be in Cardiff? She'd gone against her father's express wishes so that she could be with Sabrina.

She couldn't believe her own foolishness. To have abandoned her life in Pontdarw in order to come here to Cardiff and live in a slum. How Sabrina must be laughing at her!

Her sister had done everything in her power to steal Pryce from her. She'd obviously slept with him! Sabrina was having his baby, and Rhianon had sacrificed everything she held dear to help her.

A lot of good it would do either of them, she thought bitterly. Pryce would be incarcerated for almost another three years. It was a lifetime sentence for both Rhianon and Sabrina, too.

The child would be a toddler by the time Pryce was released! It would be walking and talking, yet its father would be a stranger to him.

A further scream of anguish from Sabrina brought Rhianon sharply back to the present. All those matters would have to be resolved, but for the moment there were more important things at stake. The baby's birth was imminent and that must take precedence over everything else, including her own feelings.

Chapter Twenty-Three

Sabrina's baby was born at three minutes past midnight on 11th January 1927. He was a scraggy, mewling little bundle. In his tiny, wrinkled face it was not possible to see any resemblance to anyone.

Her travail over, Sabrina took one look at the baby, after Morfa had cleaned him up, then pushed him away. Turning on her side, she buried her face in the pillow and settled down to sleep.

Nellie went downstairs to make a pot of tea while Rhianon helped Morfa to tidy up the bedroom.

They worked in silence, both of them feeling exhausted. Rhianon was also nonplussed by Sabrina's reaction. She fully realised that her sister had been through a tremendous ordeal, but her complete lack of interest in the child seemed incredible. It was almost inhuman, Rhianon reflected. She wondered what the two other women felt about it.

She was not left in doubt for very long. As they closed the bedroom door and went downstairs Morfa did not even try to conceal her surprise.

'I've delivered hundreds of babies,' she told the other two as they all sat round the table in Nellie's kitchen, 'but I've never seen any new mother act the way your sister has, Rhianon! To push her babba to one side and reject it like that!'

'She's very young,' Rhianon said apologetically. 'It's been a terrible ordeal for her! You can see how weary she is.'

'You say that, but most new mothers won't let their babba out of their sight no matter how difficult the birth has been,' Nellie insisted.

Rhianon tried to shut her ears to their lengthy criticisms of her sister. Deep down she was also wondering how Sabrina could have been so dismissive of the baby, and what sort of mother she was going to make.

As soon as she could, Rhianon left the two women to their gossip. Morfa was in her element, describing the many deliveries she had attended and the problems she'd encountered at each one of them.

When she went back upstairs Rhianon found the baby was crying, making a weak mewling sound like a starving kitten.

Sabrina was sound asleep. Her face was flushed, her brown curls spread across the pillow, her lips slightly apart almost as if she was smiling.

Hardening her heart, Rhianon put a hand on Sabrina's shoulder, shaking her and repeating her name until she woke up. The smile faded and a look of irritation settled on Sabrina's face as she finally opened her eyes.

'Your baby is crying and he needs feeding,' Rhianon told her quietly.

'You see to it then,' Sabrina muttered, shaking her sister's hand away, and pulling the eiderdown up to her chin.

Rhianon shook her again. 'Come on, cariad, I can't feed him, now can I! Only you can do that!'

Sabrina threw back the covers and half pulled herself up in bed. Smoothing her hair back she stared at her sister, a blank puzzled look on her face.

Rhianon lifted the baby from its makeshift cot and settled it against Sabrina. 'There you are!'

Sabrina pushed it away with the back of her hand. 'I don't want it anywhere near me!'

'Sabrina! You have to feed it!'

'Not me! I'm not having that thing gnawing away at me. Ugh!' She shuddered violently.

Rhianon felt outraged. She knew it would take a heated argument to change her sister's mind, and in this instance she wasn't sure that she would succeed.

The baby's crying became more distressed, a pitiful squalling noise that touched her heartstrings, but appeared to merely irritate Sabrina.

Rhianon rocked the child in her arms, trying to pacify it, but to no avail. As a last resort she took the baby downstairs, hoping that Morfa was still there and could tell her what to do.

'She won't feed it!' Nellie exclaimed. 'Dammo di! I've never heard anything like it in the whole of my life!'

'She may come round, given time,' Morfa said hopefully.

'What do we do in the meantime though?' Rhianon asked worriedly.

'Put it on a bottle, I suppose, that's the only thing you can do.'

'I haven't got one!' Rhianon said hopelessly. 'It wasn't one of the things we bought, was it Nellie?'

'No, cariad, it certainly wasn't. I never for one moment thought we would need one, not right away, mind.'

'So what can we do, Morfa? She won't even try to feed it, and the poor little thing is crying with hunger.'

'Wait a minute!' Nellie pulled herself out of her chair, went over to one of the cupboards and rummaged around inside it, clanking and clattering amongst the bottles and jars.

'Ah! Here's what I want,' she said triumphantly, turning to face them with a half-pint bottle of stout in her hand.

'Stout! The baby can't drink that,' Rhianon exclaimed in alarm.

'Damnio! I'm not that stupid, girl,' Nellie said huffily. She tipped the contents of the bottle into a glass, then took the bottle to the sink in the scullery and began to rinse it out.

She brought it back into the room and held it out to Morfa. 'Sniff that, cariad. Clean enough for you?'

'That'll do!'

'Right! Well then fish one of them rubber teats out of your bag of tricks, I know you always carry a few spares with you, and I'll heat up some milk and water.'

Rhianon watched in disbelief as Nellie half filled the bottle with warm watered-down milk, and fitted a feeding teat onto it before handing it to Morfa.

'Pass me the babba, then, Rhianon. Mind you, I'm not sure it will work, but it's worth a try.'

Holding the baby in the crook of her arm, Morfa waggled the teat gently across his lips. For a moment the crying ceased, but then he turned his head away and began grizzling again.

Morfa tipped the bottle, shaking it until a drop of milk dripped through and lay suspended on the teat. This time she parted the baby's lips and pushed the teat into his mouth. For a moment he resisted, then slowly, awkwardly began to suck on it and settled down to feed.

'There you are, it's working, see! Not such a stupid idea as you thought, Rhianon!' Nellie exclaimed delightedly as she drank the last of the stout.

'Yes, he's completely worn out so he should sleep for a few hours now his little belly's full,'

Morfa agreed. 'Come to that, so am I!' she added with a deep yawn.

She handed the baby over to Rhianon. 'Put him back in his crib and get off to bed yourself, girl. By the look of things you are going to have your hands full from now on, so you'll need all the sleep you can get. In fact,' she added ominously, 'I think it would be a good idea if you gave him a name or got him christened, whatever you are thinking of doing, as he doesn't look that strong to me.'

Sabrina appeared to be asleep when Rhianon carried the baby back upstairs, but she roused her nevertheless.

'So what name have you got in mind, then, for this little one?'

Sabrina groaned. 'Go away! Leave me alone, can't you!'

'You've got to give him a name. Are you going to call him after his father?' she asked tentatively, her heart pounding, afraid of what the answer would be.

Sabrina scowled. 'You give him a name. Call him whatever you like. I couldn't care less.'

Rather than tempt fate, Rhianon decided on a name that wasn't connected to them in any way. 'I like the name Davyn,' she said tentatively.

'Then call him that,' Sabrina muttered, and once more buried herself under the covers.

Pryce Pritchard paced up and down the cell he

shared with three other men. He was counting the hours, even the minutes, until he would be collected by a warder and taken to the visitors' room to see Rhianon.

Sitting behind a grille, not being allowed even to hold her hand, was a torment in itself. Even so, breathing the same air as her, being able to look into the warmth of her eyes, watch the emotions flitting across her face as she talked, sustained his very soul.

The months dragged by, day by day, the hours, the minutes, all leaden. It was so claustrophobic! The nights were the worst of all, when he was kept awake by the snores and grunts of his three cellmates.

He tried to live within his head, to ignore the activities going on all around him, but it was impossible. The routine, the indignities, the frustrations expanded inside his head until he felt it would burst. He hated every moment. He couldn't breathe, his space was constantly invaded. He ached to climb the mountains around Pontdarw, he would even be glad to be underground, working in the pits beneath the town. Prison life was far more confining than the narrow shafts and tunnels of the mines had ever been.

He tried to keep his brain active, fighting against the day-by-day blankness. The lack of reading matter frustrated him, as did the fact that he was no longer able to counsel and guide other men.

Most of all, though, he missed Rhianon.

From the first moment he'd met her he'd known she was special. Her calmness, her quiet manner, the intelligence in her dark eyes, her warm sweet voice and her deep understanding of his aims and ideals – all these qualities made up the unique woman who meant so much to him.

She was the one who stood to lose most by the nightmare that had evolved since the fight. This made him all the more bitterly ashamed of what had taken place between him and Sabrina.

It couldn't be undone, but he knew he should explain it all to Rhianon. It would ease his soul and his conscience. He wished he'd told her everything the first time she'd come to visit him. He'd held back not only for fear of hurting her, but because he was afraid that once she knew she might not want to see him again.

Her knowledge of the situation was bound to put a severe test on their relationship. Yet his silence was causing an even greater strain. And matters would be made even worse if she found out from someone else.

He'd tell her today. He would try and explain it all, calmly and unemotionally. He must convince her that there was nothing of a passionate nature involved between him and Sabrina, despite what had taken place. He would make it clear that she had thrown herself into his arms, that the fight had brought a rush of adrenaline and he'd reacted instinctively.

Pryce dropped his head into his hands. 'Duw anwyl,' he groaned aloud. What sort of a story was that? It sounded the weakest excuse he'd ever heard. He didn't even believe it himself!

If only he could get out of this place and take Rhianon out for an evening. He needed the opportunity to clarify everything over a meal in civilised surroundings. Afterwards, he could physically prove his love for her and how much she meant to him.

He was so deep in his thoughts that the warder called his name twice before he heard him. As he was frogmarched down to the visitors' room, his doubts about whether this was the moment for confessing increased until he could no longer think rationally.

Rhianon seemed so tense that he immediately wondered if she knew the truth. Perhaps Sabrina had come back and told all. Or someone had thrown out hints. Anything was possible, that was why it was so important to tell Rhianon the truth. He must be the one to clear the air, so that she was able to judge the situation for herself.

Before he could summon up the nerve to do so, Rhianon startled him by saying, 'There's something I have to tell you . . . about Sabrina.'

'Perhaps I should tell you something first . . .'

'No! I have been going over in my mind what to say to you, so let me speak first.' She chewed anxiously on her lip. Her eyes, as they met his, were deeply searching, and filled with concern.

'There's a lot that you know nothing about,' Rhianon stated uncomfortably. 'Things that have happened since you've been in here, things I should have talked to you about the first time I came to see you . . .'

Her voice trailed off, and she gulped almost as if she was choking. Then, squaring her shoulders, she continued in a hard flat tone that sounded completely unlike her.

'I told you that Sabrina ran away after Hwyel died and that none of us knew where she went. Then you were arrested, and it was impossible to ask you if the rumours about her being seen with you after the fight were true or not.

'Polly said Sabrina was bound to turn up for Hwyel's funeral, but she was wrong. My father was so angry that he disowned her, because he felt she'd shamed the family name.

'Polly suggested I should come to your trial because she was pretty sure Sabrina would be there as well. On the last day I thought I saw her leaving the court, but I wasn't sure.

'Then, the very first time I came to visit you, I accidentally bumped into her when I left here. I found out that she was almost destitute and living down in Tiger Bay. It's a long story how she ended up there.'

He nodded, his mouth tightening as he struggled to collect his thoughts.

'The shocking thing was that she was

pregnant. I wanted to take her home, but she knew Father wouldn't make her welcome. I was right about that!' She shuddered. 'He said some cruel things when I told him about where she was living and the state she was in.'

'So what has happened?'

'She wouldn't go back to Pontdarw and she wouldn't let me tell the Barkers that she was pregnant. A couple of weeks before Christmas I moved here to Cardiff to look after her.'

'Has Sabrina had the baby?' he asked in a strained voice.

'Yes, and it's a boy. We've called him Davyn. The trouble is she not only refuses to nurse him, but she says she doesn't want him.' Her gaze held his for a long silent moment before she added in a shaky voice, 'She claims that you are the father, Pryce.'

Her eyes appealed to him to deny it, but all Pryce could do was drop his head into his hands. His shoulders were shaking, and when he looked up there was utter desolation in his eyes.

'Tell me it's not true!' she whispered, her face drained of colour.

'I can explain . . . It's you I love, Rhianon!'

He struggled to tell her about what had happened, but before he could finish a warder came to say that their time was up.

'I love you, Rhianon, trust me,' he pleaded as the warder poked him in the ribs to make him stand up and move.

'Rhianon, you must believe me!' Pryce called back desperately over his shoulder as he was frogmarched back to his cell.

Chapter Twenty-Four

Stunned by Pryce's mute admission that he was the father of Davyn, Rhianon watched him being led back to his cell. She felt as if the ground had dropped away beneath her feet.

Pryce looked so dejected that she longed to run after him, throw her arms around him, and reassure him that although she didn't understand what had happened between him and Sabrina, it made no difference to the way she felt about him. Things would work out for them, she'd make sure of that. She would still be waiting for him when he got out of prison.

As the realisation of what had taken place between him and Sabrina hit home, though, she felt utterly confused. It was all very well Pryce claiming she was the one he loved, but which of them did he really want, she asked herself. Was it her or Sabrina?

She walked out of the prison in a daze. She decided not to go back to Margaret Street, at least not right away. She needed to be on her own for a while to sort things out in her mind, and try and plan for the future.

The thought of the mewling baby, of Nellie fussing and tutting over it, of the dirty muddled state she'd been living in ever since she had come to Cardiff, was all too much. Worst of all, though, was the thought of facing Sabrina, knowing for certain now that she'd been carrying on with Pryce behind her back.

What else could go wrong in her life, she wondered. Blindly she walked up St Mary Street, automatically avoiding other pedestrians. She ignored the attractive shop windows filled with beautiful things that at any other time she would have stopped to admire.

The bitter east wind pierced through her coat, but she hardly noticed the cold as she made her way to Cathays Park. She'd instinctively sought out the green oasis in the middle of the busy city, hoping that there, away from the crowds, she could come to terms with what lay ahead.

She found the park was almost as desolate as her thoughts. Even the grass had been shrivelled up by the cold. Wearily she turned and made her way back. As she walked through the arcade that would take her into St Mary Street, she paused outside a café. On impulse she went inside and ordered herself a pot of tea and a round of toast.

The warmth of the place was comforting. For the first time that day she found herself relaxing. Mentally she lined up her many problems, and as she sipped the hot tea tried to deal with each of them in turn.

Sabrina had had her baby and rejected it, so who was going to be responsible for its welfare and bringing it up? She herself couldn't look after it and go out to work. She was sure that once the novelty wore off Nellie wouldn't want to look after it, either. Anyway, Nellie's house was not suitable for a baby, any more than Tiger Bay was the right surroundings for the child to grow up in.

What was the alternative? It seemed that Pryce was the father, but how could he care for his son? He couldn't even provide any money to help with bringing Davyn up, not until he came out of prison. The child would be well over two years old before that happened.

Was there a chance that by now her father would have relented, she wondered. Perhaps it was time to return to Pontdarw and take Sabrina, and the baby, with her.

As she left the café and started to make her way back to Margaret Street, her mind was full of this new idea, the possibility that they could all be a family again.

First, though, she decided, she wanted everything out in the open with her sister. Sabrina would have to promise to play her part. She would have to co-operate, and help look after the baby, if they were going to return to Pontdarw.

Sorting out the future in her head was one thing, but it was nowhere near as easy when it came to reality. The moment she entered the house Nellie was waiting for her, scowling indignantly.

'Duw anwyl! You two must think I'm weak in the head,' she stormed. 'The pair of you just walk out of the place and leave that babba squalling with hunger. What's the matter with you both?'

'I'm sorry, Nellie. I did tell you I was taking a day off work because there was something I had to attend to,' Rhianon reminded her.

'That was before the baby arrived. Surely you could have changed your plans once that happened?'

'No! It was quite impossible. Anyway, I was hoping that Sabrina would look after the baby and feed it now that it was on the bottle.'

'Not her! She's as bloody stubborn and self-ish as you are, girl,' Nellie muttered scathingly. 'She refuses to lift a finger to help with it. Won't even hold the poor little dab!'

Rhianon removed her coat and hat. 'I'll go upstairs and talk to her,' she said wearily.

'Waste of time that will be, so save yourself the effort.'

'Don't worry, I'll make her see sense,' Rhianon promised.

'Dammo di!' Nellie exploded. 'Do you ever listen to a word I say? Your bloody sister's not upstairs!'

Rhianon stopped and gaped at Nellie. 'Where is she then?' she demanded.

'How the hell should I know? She marched out around midday, not long after you left the house, without a word to me and Olwen about where she was going. Dressed up to the nines she was! She left that poor little scrap howling his head off because he needed a feed. Hard-hearted little bitch she is, and that's a fact!'

'She went out!' Rhianon stared at Nellie in disbelief. 'Surely she should have stayed in bed,' she said in alarm.

'Of course she should have done,' Nellie snapped. 'Heaven knows what harm she will do to herself, gadding about so soon after giving birth.'

'And you have no idea where she's gone?'

'All I know is she left the babba lying up there crying, screaming his lungs out. Out of the goodness of my heart, and because I couldn't stand the racket he was making, I brought him down here and fed him.'

'That was kind of you, Nellie, and I'm truly grateful.'

'Yes, well, I can't go on looking after him. It's your sister's responsibility to do that, he's her child.'

'It was good of you to tend to him, Nellie,' Rhianon repeated placatingly. 'Shall I take him back upstairs out of your way?'

'No, you'd better leave the poor little dab where he is on the couch while he's sleeping,' Nellie said grudgingly.

'You say you've no idea where Sabrina went?'

'None at all, but believe me, cariad, I intend to give her a piece of my mind when she gets back, I can tell you.'

It was late evening before Sabrina returned, and she was on the point of collapse.

'Duw anwyl! There's mad you are,' Nellie scolded. 'Fancy going out in your condition! After all the screaming and performance we had from you a couple of days ago, the least you could have done was rest up.'

'I had to go out, I had some business to attend to,' Sabrina defended sulkily.

'Nothing that couldn't have waited for a week or ten days,' Nellie argued, as she stalked out of the room, banging the door behind her.

'That's where you're wrong. I've been to see about having the baby adopted. They like to have them when they are just a few days old because it is easier to place them. Now do you see that it was something that had to be done as quickly as possible?'

'You've done what?' The colour drained from Rhianon's face as she looked at her sister. 'You're planning to have your baby adopted?'

'I told you right from the moment it was born that I wanted nothing to do with it,' Sabrina reminded her. 'I want my life back. I want to be able to go dancing, and be free to enjoy myself. I'll never be able to do that if I'm lumbered with a kid, now will I?'

Rhianon shook her head in despair. 'You can't do this, Sabrina. You can't give him away! He's your own flesh and blood and . . .' she choked as she forced herself to say it, 'and Pryce is his father,' she ended in a strained whisper.

Sabrina stared at her. 'So you do believe me at last,' she said balefully.

'I went to the prison today to see Pryce,' Rhianon admitted, a tremor in her voice. 'I told him you'd had the baby, and what you said about him being the father.'

Sabrina's sulky expression vanished, and for a moment she looked quite animated. 'What did he say?' she asked eagerly.

'He looked shocked, but he made no effort to deny that it was his baby,' Rhianon told her numbly.

'So now you believe me!'

'Yes, I suppose so, but that's not the end of the matter by any means, Sabrina. I want to know the whole story.'

Sabrina's eyes narrowed. 'There's nothing to tell. The kid was a mistake, I don't want it, that's all there is to say. The sooner it's adopted and I can put it all behind me the better, as far as I'm concerned.'

'No! Davyn is not going to be adopted, Sabrina. I won't allow it,' Rhianon flared, her eyes blazing. 'He's part of our family no matter who his father is, now is that understood?'

Sabrina shrugged. 'If that's the way you want things, but on your head be it. I'm not having any part in raising him, so don't expect me to lift a finger to help. Is that clear?'

'So who is going to look after him, then?' Rhianon asked exasperatedly.

'You are, presumably, since you're the one

who wants to keep him. I tell you what,' suddenly Sabrina's eyes were shining and a broad smile spread across her face, 'how about you staying at home and looking after him and I'll go out to work! How does that sound?'

'Sabrina! Do you know what you are saying?'

'Of course I do! I'll earn the money, but you stay home and look after the baby. You can even adopt him if you like,' she challenged.

'You are talking utter nonsense, Sabrina.'

'No, it makes sense if you are so keen that he becomes part of the family. Admit it!'

Rhianon sighed exasperatedly. 'Well, I suppose it would be a better arrangement than for him to go to strangers. In a year or so, when you are over this silly stage, you can be responsible for him again.'

'Oh no! If you want to keep him, then you adopt him and he stays yours,' Sabrina insisted. 'I want nothing to do with him, now or ever. I want my own life,' she added emphatically.

'It's not that easy, Sabrina. We need money to pay Nellie for our room, and for our food. There will be all sorts of extra things we'll be needing for the baby as well.'

Sabrina pulled a face. 'Stop making it all sound so impossible. We've managed all right up to now!'

'We've coped because I've been working so hard! It's taken every penny I've earned to keep us going. Are you prepared to make that sort of commitment?'

'I've said I will, haven't I,' Sabrina retorted sulkily.

'I'll think about it, then,' Rhianon promised. 'One problem is that it may take you ages to get a job. If I give up at the café and stay home to look after Davyn, we'll have no money at all coming in for a while.'

'Why don't we swop places?' Sabrina grinned.

Rhianon frowned. 'What do you mean?'

'You stay here and look after the kid and I'll do your job at the café.'

'How can you possibly do that, Sabrina! You're in no fit state to be on your feet all day.'

'Give me a few days and I will be,' Sabrina told her eagerly. 'It will give you time to explain to Gino what is happening. You can get him used to the idea that I'm the one who is going to be working there in future, not you.'

'Sabrina, this is utter nonsense. Gino may not agree to it. You have no experience of that sort of work.'

'Neither had you before you went there. Come on, at least ask Gino if he will agree to the idea. Either that or the baby goes for adoption.'

'That's blackmail!' Rhianon said furiously.

'No, I'm offering you a fair deal. It's a way for us to solve this problem and for both of us to get what we want.'

Gino threw up his hands in alarm when Rhianon broached the idea. Maria shrugged expressively to convey her astonishment, but said nothing. Then the two of them went into a huddle, waving their hands and gesticulating. Their voices rose higher and higher and Rhianon wished she understood Italian so that she knew what they were saying.

As she was leaving that night, Gino suggested, 'Perhaps you should bring your sister in to meet us and then we will talk about it again, yes?'

A week later Sabrina, wearing one of her smartest frocks under her uniform, her brown curls gleaming and her huge eyes shining with excitement, was the one carrying the trays in Gino's café, and Rhianon was at home looking after the baby.

Davyn was now nearly two weeks old and he was taking milk regularly, so his face and limbs were beginning to fill out. His wrinkled scrawny appearance had vanished and he was sleeping soundly between each feed.

The bond between Rhianon and her nephew strengthened daily. The feel of his small warm body nestling into hers as she held him close while he took his bottle stirred emotions previously unknown to her.

All she wanted now was to erase the bad feeling between herself and her father. If she took the baby to Pontdarw, she felt sure her father's heart would melt the moment he saw little Davyn. She was confident that he would wish them to move back home.

'I think you're mad, but if that's what you want to do then go ahead and visit him,' Sabrina told her. 'Count me out. I'll be too busy working. I can't afford to take time off and risk losing my job, now can I?'

Chapter Twenty-Five

It was a bitterly cold March day and it was sleeting as Rhianon left the train at Pontdarw station. Pulling the collar of her coat as high as it would go, she draped the shawl Davyn was wrapped in so that he was completely covered. Then, picking up her suitcase with her free hand, she headed for Rhoslyn Terrace.

By the time she reached it the sleet had turned into snow, and both her coat and the shawl were coated in white flakes.

To her surprise the front door was locked. When she slipped her hand through the letter box for the piece of string with a key on the end of it, that had hung there for as long as she could remember, it was missing. Puzzled, she banged on the door, but there was no reply.

She knew she should have written to let her father know she was coming with the baby, but she'd been afraid he might write back refusing to see them or return the letter unread like last time.

Davyn stirred in his cocoon of shawls and began to whimper. It was time for him to have a feed, but how could she give it to him out here in the street, Rhianon thought worriedly.

She hammered hard again on the front door. When there was still no sound of anyone coming to answer it, she opened the letter box and shouted through it. The sound echoed back, but there was no movement at all from inside.

Desperate, Rhianon picked up her suitcase again, and after a moment's hesitation headed for the high street. She was sure Polly would let her go into the little room at the back of the shop so that she could feed Davyn.

Polly was ecstatic at seeing her.

'Darw! There's good it is to have you back, my lovely,' she exclaimed, her plump face wreathed in a huge smile.

As she made to hug her, Rhianon dropped her suitcase and put out her hand to hold Polly back, pointing to the bundle in the crook of her arm.

Polly's eyes widened as she heard the whimpering cry. 'Sabrina's babba?' she breathed.

Rhianon nodded. 'He's called Davyn.'

'Come on through, then, my lovely,' Polly urged, pushing Rhianon towards the rear of the shop.

'Now let me hold him for you while you take off your wet coat,' Polly insisted.

'Daro! The little love,' she murmured tenderly as Rhianon passed the baby over to her, and she began peeling away the snow-bespattered shawl. 'Shush now, shush!' she soothed, as his crying became more intense.

'He's hungry, he needs a feed,' Rhianon told

her. 'I have it all ready.' She opened the suit-case and took out a feeding bottle wrapped in several layers of towelling. 'It should still be warm,' she added, placing the bottle against her cheek to test it.

'Here, cariad, let me feed him,' Polly said eagerly.

Rhianon hesitated. 'The shop, what happens if a customer comes in?'

'You'll have to serve them won't you, my lovely, since I'm here on my own nowadays! You haven't forgotten how to do that, have you?'

'Oh, Polly, it seems a lifetime ago that I was working here,' Rhianon smiled. 'Some of the happiest days of my life, only I didn't realise it at the time,' she added wistfully.

'You've had lots of adventures since then, I've no doubt,' Polly said sagely. 'You'd better put the kettle on and then start telling me all about them. Have you come back for a visit, or for good?'

Rhianon sighed. 'I'm not sure, not until I've seen my father. I've been to the house but there's no one there. It's all locked up.'

'He'll be out walking. He does a lot of that these days.'

'Really? He never used to do anything like that. I thought he must be at Capel Bethel.'

Polly gave her a quizzical look. 'He's not been telling you anything about what's been going on lately, then?'

'I haven't heard from him since I went to Cardiff,' Rhianon admitted. 'Why? Is there something I should know about?'

'Your dad and the Barkers have fallen out completely, cariad. It was talked about all over Pontdarw. It seems that Cledwyn Barker called a meeting of the deacons of Capel Bethel, and the outcome was they stopped your dad from going there any more. Very cut up about it he is, I can tell you!'

'That's terrible news! Preaching was his whole life!'

'Oh, I know, and it's put years on him, there's no doubt about that! He's lost weight and he walks round in a trance looking demented most of the time. I feel quite sorry for him, in fact.'

'So where does he go for these walks then?' Rhianon frowned.

'Up to the pitface most of the time. Up and down three or four times a day, rain or shine. When he first started doing it the strike was still on and the pickets thought he was out to cause trouble, but after a while they took no notice of him.'

'So do you think that's where I should go and look for him?'

'Have your cup of tea first, cariad. The snow may have stopped by then. Come on, tell me all about what's been happening to you and that Sabrina while you've been down in Cardiff.'

'Well, Sabrina's had the baby, as you can see!' Rhianon smiled. 'Lovely little boyo, isn't he!'

'Oh he's beautiful,' Polly agreed, looking down at the baby, who had now finished his bottle and was lying quietly in her arms, his eyes closed. 'Why are you the one bringing him to see his granddad?'

'Sabrina's working. We came to this arrangement that she'd go out to work and I'd look after the baby,' Rhianon explained.

'Oh yes, and what sort of work is she doing then?'

'She's a waitress in a café.'

'One of these Nippys we read about, is she? Fancy little white apron and a tiny starched cap perched on her head? She'll love that!'

'No, she's not working in a Lyons Corner House, she's a waitress in one of the cafés in Tiger Bay.'

'Dammo di!' Polly looked shocked. 'Tell me you are having me on, Rhianon. Working in Tiger Bay! Duw anwyl! A den of iniquity, that place. I wonder you even go near there. All foreigners, from what I hear. You can get your throat cut just walking down the road!'

'That's all nonsense, Polly. It's pretty rough and run-down, and of course there are people of every nationality under the sun living in the area. There's good and bad amongst them, the same as there is in Pontdarw.'

Polly shook her head in disbelief. 'If you say so, cariad. I've heard dreadful tales though. And to think you've left your Sabrina there on her own!'

'She was there on her own before I went down to look after her,' Rhianon reminded her sharply.

'Yes, I suppose she was, and if she could survive then she'll manage to do so now. Take no notice of me, my lovely. Small-minded, see! With always living here where you know everybody and you don't even need to lock your doors at night, you get this way. Do you know, even when the strike was on, and half the folks were starving, there wasn't any thieving or break-ins. Not a single one!'

'Well, we've never been threatened, attacked or had anything stolen from us since we've been living in Tiger Bay,' Rhianon defended.

'I'm glad to hear it! So what else have you to tell me, my lovely? Have you heard anything more from that Pryce Pritchard?'

'I've been to see him in prison a couple of times.'

Polly frowned. 'I shouldn't tell your dad that piece of news,' she warned. 'Terrible things he's said about Pryce Pritchard and no mistake. When he heard he'd got three years he wanted to get up a petition, remember, to try and have his sentence extended.'

'He never did like Pryce,' Rhianon said sadly. 'I'm in two minds about whether to tell him that Pryce is Davyn's father.'

Polly looked shocked. 'So it's true! You did wonder the last time I saw you but . . .'

'I know,' Rhianon said sadly.

'Well, you can't let him think that it is Hwyel Barker's child! If you don't tell him the truth he'll be round at the Barkers causing even more trouble,' Polly warned.

'He knows the baby isn't Hwyel's. It's a job to know what to do for the best though,' Rhianon frowned. 'I should have listened to you all along, you did warn me that something was going on between Sabrina and Pryce. Could I leave Davyn here for half an hour while I go and see my father and break the ice?' she asked tentatively, looking at Polly hopefully.

'Of course he can stay here,' Polly assured her. 'It sounds like a good idea to me. You leave your suitcase here and take your time. There's no need to rush things, cariad. I'm sure he'll be pleased to see you, but it may take a while to talk things over. Mind you soften him up a bit before you mention Sabrina or the baby. Cut right to the quick, he was, about her not coming to the funeral, as you know, and that old Cledwyn Barker made things a damn sight worse, I can tell you.'

The look on Edward Webster's face was so cold and impassive when he finally opened the door that Rhianon wondered if he had recognised her.

'Hello, Father! How are you?'

Polly had warned her that she would see a change in him, but even so, she was shocked at how frail and careworn he looked. His hair was now completely grey and so scant that his scalp shone through in places. His face was deeply lined, but what brought a lump to her throat was the way his shoulders drooped. He looked so thin that she wondered when he had last had a decent meal.

'Aren't you going to ask me in, Father?'

Stony-faced, he stared at her in silence. She waited so long for him to speak that she felt tears pricking her eyes. She feared that without a word he would slam the door shut and cut her out of his life for ever.

When he turned and shuffled back inside the house, leaving the door open, she wasn't sure whether he wanted her to follow him or not.

Gritting her teeth she stepped into the hallway, determined to set matters straight between them. It would be daft to come all this way in such weather and then go back to Cardiff without having things out with him, she told herself.

In the living room he stood leaning against the mantelshelf as he looked her up and down. 'Well? What is it you want?' he muttered. He picked up the wrought-iron poker and jabbed viciously at the heart of the fire.

'I thought it was time I came to see you,' she said awkwardly. 'I've so much to tell you . . .'

'Things I don't want to hear,' he interrupted. He waved a gnarled hand. 'As far as I'm concerned you're nothing to me any more, nor your sister either. I want no further truck with either of you.'

Rhianon remembered what Polly had told her about how her father had changed, and her suggestion that she should soften him up before mentioning the baby. There didn't seem to be any possibility of doing that, so she decided to tell him the bare facts straight out.

'You have a grandson,' she stated flatly. 'Sabrina's baby was born two months ago. He's called Davyn. Do you want to see him?'

He shook his head. 'No! Nor do I want to see her . . . or you.'

'Oh, please, Father! Isn't it time to forgive, time for us to be a family again?' she pleaded. 'Surely you must want that, too?'

He stared at her from rheumy eyes, and she shuddered at the coldness in his glance. He had never been a warm-hearted or demonstrative man, except when it came to Sabrina. She had always found favour in his eyes and been very special, but now he seemed to have set his face against her.

'I've brought Davyn to Pontdarw so that you can see him,' Rhianon persisted. 'I called here earlier, but you were out, so I went round to see Polly Potter. I've left Davyn with her, shall I go and fetch him?'

For a moment she thought he was going to refuse to see the baby, but she waited patiently, determined not to be browbeaten by his attitude.

'Your sister's not with you then?'

Rhianon shook her head. 'No, Sabrina is still in Cardiff. She couldn't get time off work. I came because I thought you would like to see the baby. I wanted to see you, too, and make sure you were managing all right on your own.'

'I've had to manage on my own ever since you walked out,' he snapped.

'I had to go, Father. Sabrina needed looking after. Now she's had the baby I can come back if . . .'

'What you mean is you're expecting me to give you a home and provide for the brat she's spawned,' he said contemptuously.

'No, not at all!' She spoke sharply, angry that his opinion of her was so low. 'I already have somewhere to live in Cardiff, and I only intended staying here for a day or two. I told you, I wanted to make sure you were all right and also to let you meet your grandson. I can go straight back now if that is your wish.'

'You want me to turn you out into the snow, give rise to more spiteful gossip and recriminations!' he sneered.

'There won't be any gossip because no one except Polly Potter knows that I am here. She won't breathe a word about my visit to anyone if I ask her not to.'

He hesitated so long that Rhianon was on the point of walking out. It was only because she could see how hard he was struggling inwardly that she waited hopefully and patiently for his answer.

'Go and fetch the child. You can stay then if that's what you want to do, as long as it is only for a day or two,' Edwin Webster muttered. 'I'm too old to have a squalling baby around the place. I don't sleep well as it is,' he added grumpily.

Chapter Twenty-Six

Rhianon returned to Cardiff the following Wednesday. It was a cold bleak day, very grey and overcast. She would have liked to stay on for a few more days in the warm comfort of Rhoslyn Terrace, but it wasn't possible. She was planning to see Pryce at the end of the week, so she wanted to be back in Cardiff in good time for her visit.

The time she'd spent with her father had given her a chance to catch up on jobs around his house that needed doing. It had also been an opportunity to wash and mend his clothes and stock up his food cupboards.

After his initial hostility things had settled down. He had even seemed to be pleased that she was back, and there had been no more arguments or recriminations.

Bearing in mind what Polly had told her, Rhianon made no mention of Capel Bethel. Instead she waited patiently for him to tell her about what had happened between him and the Barkers.

She waited in vain. Even on Sunday, when normally they would have put on their best clothes to attend chapel, and he would have fired up the congregation with one of his powerful sermons, the topic was completely ignored.

He seemed to mellow towards her over the weekend, but he remained a sad old man, cut off from the life around him. He had no interest in what was going on in Pontdarw, and this worried her deeply.

By the time she left Rhoslyn Terrace he was not only talking to her again, but, more importantly, he had listened while she explained to him why Sabrina had run away from home. Grudgingly, he had seemed to come to terms with all that had happened, and accepted Davyn as his grandson.

'You can come back for good and bring the little boyo with you any time you want to do so,' he told her gruffly as he bid them both goodbye. 'It would be far better for him to grow up here in Pontdarw than down in Cardiff, you know!'

'Thank you, Father!' She pressed his hand. 'I'll think about it, but I'm not sure if I'd be doing the right thing. It would mean leaving Sabrina all alone in Cardiff to fend for herself, see.'

He shrugged. 'She could come back as well, I suppose. Only if she wanted to do so, of course,' he added quickly. 'There's bound to be a bit of trouble at first, mind, with the Barkers. You'd better warn her that she'd have to face up to them, as well as live down all the other malicious gossip and tittle-tattle!'

'I'm not sure if she will want to go through all that,' Rhianon warned him, 'but I will ask her and see what she says.'

'Yes, very well. You are going to bring the young boyo back again, though, even if she doesn't want to come?'

'Of course! I'll pay you another visit quite soon and I'll certainly bring Davyn with me. I worry about you being here on your own, Father, and I want to make sure that Cara Jenkins is doing a good job of looking after you.'

'I'll be all right. She tries her best. She doesn't keep the place as clean as you did, and she's not as good as you were at making cawl, mind. What is more, her bara brith is nowhere near as tasty, either, but don't worry, I'll manage.'

Sabrina was out when Rhianon arrived back at Margaret Street. Nellie seemed to be in a prickly mood and shrugged her shoulders when Rhianon asked her if she knew where she was.

Rhianon gave Davyn his bottle, and then took him upstairs and settled him in his crib. By the time she'd unpacked her case, and put her clothes away, he was sound asleep.

'What about the two of us sitting down and having a cup of tea then, Nellie?' she suggested when she went back downstairs.

'Cup of tea, is it! You think that will put everything right, do you?'

'I thought it would give us a chance to catch up with all that has been happening while I've been away,' Rhianon said, as Nellie made no move to put the kettle on or lay out the cups.

'Humph! Dammo di! Plenty went on and that's for sure. You won't like what I have to tell you, I know that for a fact.'

Rhianon looked at her in surprise. 'Oh? How can you be so certain?'

'Because most of it is about your Sabrina and it's bad! Terrible, see, most of it.'

'Come on, Nellie, let's have that tea and you get it off your chest. I could tell there was something up the minute I came in the house, you were as prickly as an old hairbrush.'

'Prickly! Duw anwyl! How do you expect me to be, cariad, after the way that sister of yours has been carrying on!'

'What do you mean? I have no idea what you are talking about.'

'Fellas! That's what I'm talking about! Bringing them back here to my house, what's more.'

'When did she do that?'

'One night! She let him stay until the early hours of the morning, too. Creeping out at goodness knows what time, he was, like some dirty old tomcat that's been on the tiles.'

'You mean Sabrina brought a man back here after she finished work at Gino's?' Rhianon exclaimed in dismay.

Her mind flashed back to some of the customers who had tried to get friendly with her when she'd worked there, and a shudder went through her.

'I don't know where she picked him up. I shouldn't think it was at that Gino's place, though, because she's not working there any longer now, is she!'

Rhianon stared at her in disbelief. 'What on earth are you talking about, Nellie?'

'Sabrina packed it in the day after you went off to Pontdarw.'

The colour drained from Rhianon's face. 'She left Gino in the lurch after he was so good about letting her have the job? Surely you've made a mistake, Nellie?'

'No, not a bit of it. Ask her yourself when she comes in if you don't believe me.'

'Yes, I will. I can hardly credit that she would do such a thing.'

'Dammo di! Why ever not? Do either of you two girls ever think about anyone except yourselves?' Nellie said furiously.

'Oh come on, Nellie, that's not fair. What harm have I ever done you?'

'It's not you I'm angry with, cariad, it's that sister of yours! She shows no consideration for other people at all. What about the reputation of my family? What about my daughter? It's her home too, you know! It's not fair on her that your Sabrina is treating my place as a bawdy house. Have you thought what people will say about my Olwen? They might even think she is tarred with the same brush!'

'Nellie, I can't tell you how sorry I am that this has happened. Don't worry, I'll have it out with Sabrina as soon as she gets home, and make her see sense. You'll have no more trouble from her, I promise.'

'That's not all you don't know about,' Nellie smirked. 'She's been visiting some bloke in Cardiff jail. That's the sort of company she keeps!'

'Cardiff prison?'

'Daro! That's wiped the smile off your face, now hasn't it!' Nellie crowed. 'She's really gone off the rails, I can tell you. Got a jailbird for a friend, see! Now what have you to say about that?'

'I'll wait and see what she has to tell me,' Rhianon said stiffly. She pushed away her unfinished cup of tea. 'In fact, I feel pretty tired after my journey so I think I'll have an early night.'

'Oh, do you! Well *I* think you should wait down here until Sabrina gets in. You need to have a talk with your sister and put her straight on one or two things, do you understand?'

'I've already promised that I will talk to her, Nellie. I can do it upstairs just as well as here in your kitchen,' Rhianon said cuttingly.

It was well after midnight before Sabrina came home. She was incensed when she heard that Nellie had told Rhianon about what had been going on.

'Silly old cow!' she railed. 'What business is it of hers who I see or what I do?'

'Show some sense, Sabrina. Of course Nellie

is going to be concerned when you bring a strange man back to her house. Why did you have to do something like this the moment I left you on your own? Who was he anyway, some casual pick-up?'

'No, as a matter of fact it was someone called Patrick Nelson, and he was looking for you! A rather good-looking midshipman, so I'm sure you know the chap I'm talking about,' she said sarcastically. 'He's the bloke you met at Gino's. You introduced me and Nellie to him, remember? Well, he walked me back home and stayed and chatted for a while, before he went off to catch his boat.'

'Gino asked him to walk me home on New Year's Eve, that's how I know him,' Rhianon told her dismissively. 'Now, what about the rest of the things Nellie has told me? For a start she said you had left Gino's.'

'I told you, I want my life back. That's why I wanted to have Davyn adopted. That is what should have happened. It's not too late even now,' she added quickly. 'I've been to see the adoption people again and they say they accept kids up to six months old. Any older than that and it's a case of putting them into an orphanage.'

'Sabrina!' Rhianon clamped her hands over her ears. 'I don't want to hear this. Davyn is not being parted from us, not under any circumstance.'

'Pryce believes differently. He knows the

kid'll never amount to anything if he's dragged up here in Tiger Bay. He thinks that he should be put up for adoption and have a proper upbringing in a decent home. If he's lucky, and gets adopted by people with money, and gets an education, then he might turn out all right.'

'Stop making things up, Sabrina. Pryce would never say anything of the sort.'

'I went to see him in prison while you were in Pontdarw.'

'You went to the prison?' Rhianon shook her head in despair. Nellie had been right, after all. Even so, she couldn't understand how Sabrina had managed to get in to see Pryce, when it had taken her months to get a visiting permit.

Sabrina gave a self-satisfied smirk as she saw the puzzled look on Rhianon's face.

'And they let you in?' Rhianon persisted.

'You left your visiting permit behind so I used it,' Sabrina told her triumphantly.

'You mean you pretended to be me?'

'That's right!' She giggled. 'Pryce was a bit surprised to see me, I can tell you. He was pleased, mind. I told him all about having the kid adopted and he agreed with me. He thought that it would be the best thing to do for all of us. If he was adopted then he'd have a proper home, and we could all start our lives afresh.'

'Sabrina, I don't believe a word of what you are saying!'

'Well, it's true. He told me to go ahead and make whatever arrangements were necessary.'

'No! There's not going to be any adoption.'

'Don't talk so daft, Rhianon! Someone's got to be responsible for Davyn's future, because I'm not going to look after him. I don't want him and Pryce doesn't want him either!'

'Then in that case I really will go ahead and adopt him,' Rhianon told her grimly.

'Please yourself. You'd better make sure you can afford to bring him up, though, because I don't intend to hand over any money to help.'

'Why ever did you pack in your job at Gino's? It was a dreadful thing for you to do. He was kind enough to give you a job and you turn round and let him down without even giving him time to get a replacement.'

'You're too soft, Rhianon. Gino was exploiting us, you as well as me.'

'Rubbish! Gino and Maria were good to us. I found him a wonderful employer. Look how helpful he was when you wanted to go back to work. What other boss would have let you step into my shoes like that?'

'He wasn't paying us the right wage for the hours we had to work,' Sabrina insisted sulkily.

'I agreed to what he offered me. I thought it was a very fair wage, since I had no experience of that sort of work. Look how generous he was with all the food he gave me to bring home, as well.'

'He was exploiting you and he thought he could do the same with me, but I wasn't having any,' Sabrina countered belligerently. 'I told him so before I walked out, so it's no good thinking you can go crawling back there and make amends!'

'So where are you working now?'

Sabrina grinned. 'Somewhere where they appreciate what I have to offer. One of Gino's customers owns a nightclub and he offered me a job as a hostess.' She tossed back her long dark curls and wiggled her hips defiantly. 'I have my own spot as well.'

'Spot? What does that mean?'

Sabrina giggled. 'I dance to entertain the customers and they love it!'

Rhianon shuddered. She could imagine the sort of dancing that would be, and it horrified her. How, she asked herself, in such a short time, a matter of a few days, could Sabrina have changed her entire way of life so dramatically?

She could see that persuading her to return to Pontdarw would be a complete waste of time. All the same, she wondered if she and Davyn should go back there and leave Sabrina to her own life in Cardiff.

Sleep was out of the question. Rhianon tossed and turned all night. The many problems she had found on her return haunted her like macabre nightmares.

By morning, hollow-eyed and tense from lack of sleep, Rhianon had worked out what she was going to say to Pryce when she went to visit him.

She was determined not to let Davyn be taken away from her. She intended to convince Pryce that it would be wrong to have him adopted, and persuade him to back her up over this.

She also wanted him to know that she still loved him. Despite everything, she would be waiting to make a home for him and his son when he was released from prison.

Chapter Twenty-Seven

Over the next few weeks Rhianon felt as if her entire world was crumbling away and there was nothing she could do to stop it.

Her visit to Pryce had resulted in them disagreeing over just about everything. He was aggrieved because Sabrina had been in to visit him.

'After I had told you about what had happened between us, what on earth made you think that I would want to see her?' he exploded.

'I had no idea she had been to see you until I came back from Pontdarw,' Rhianon assured him.

'You must have done,' he argued angrily. 'She used your visiting permit!'

'So I understand. She did it without my consent or knowledge, though.'

'In that case, you ought to report her for using your pass.'

'Don't be so ridiculous!' Rhianon exclaimed. 'Why on earth should I want to do that? I know it was wrong of her, deceitful, in fact, and I've given her a good telling-off. I certainly don't want to get her into any trouble, though.'

'If you don't report it and the prison authorities find out, they'll take the pass off you,' he warned. 'It's an offence to let anyone else use it.'

'At least it meant you had a visitor,' she told him tartly.

Pryce shook his head. 'Yes, one I would have sooner not had.' His dark eyes held hers. 'She was complaining you've done everything possible to stop her coming to see me up until now. She was in tears about it.'

'That's utter rubbish.' Rhianon bristled. 'Anyway, I thought you said you didn't want to see her and there was nothing between you . . .'

'There isn't, but, as she kept reminding me, she is the mother of my kid! I suppose I owe her some consideration,' he admitted grudgingly. 'She says you're fighting her all the time over how she should be bringing him up. Is that right?'

'Fighting her!' Rhianon's face flooded with colour. 'I've done everything possible to help her. I gave up my job and left my father to fend for himself in order to be here in Cardiff with her when the baby was born.'

'I know all about that, and the problems it has caused you. Why won't you agree to her plan and have the kid adopted, then the pair of you can live normal lives again?'

'You talk as though Davyn was a pair of old boots you want to pass on to someone else.' Rhianon glared at him. 'He's a child, a precious little baby! He's now part of our family, not something to be discarded because he's too much trouble to look after.'

'He's nothing to you, Rhianon! It's not up to you to make decisions about his future. That's for me and Sabrina to do.'

Rhianon's mouth tightened. She felt deeply hurt by what Pryce was saying. She'd done everything she could to help Sabrina.

She'd been prepared to overlook the past and Pryce's momentary lapse with Sabrina because she still loved him, and believed him when he said that despite everything he still loved her. She had hoped that after he had served his sentence they could start a new life together. She had every intention of having Davyn to live with them so that they could be a proper family.

Now, finding that he had let Sabrina talk him into believing that Davyn should be adopted sent all those plans crashing.

'So you agree with Sabrina and you want to have your child adopted, do you?' she said coldly.

Pryce ran a hand over his shorn head. There was a look of bewilderment on his face as he said, 'I don't know, Rhianon. I'm shut up in here, with no possibility of being able to support him. Would he want a father who'd been sent to prison for killing a man? After listening to Sabrina it seems to me that it's the best thing for everyone if Davyn is adopted.'

'Simply throw him out with the rubbish,' she said caustically.

Pryce groaned. 'Don't say that, it is not what I meant. Surely it will be better for him to have a proper home, be well looked after and brought up as part of a family?'

'And you don't think that would be the case if I looked after him until you finish your sentence? I hoped that then we could bring him up together.'

Pryce looked taken aback. 'I'm sure you'd do your best for him, but could you ever forget that Sabrina was his real mam?'

Rhianon was dumbfounded. 'Why would I need to? What would that have to do with it?'

'You'd never be able to look at him without remembering that he was the result of a stupid fling between me and Sabrina.'

She stared at him in alarm. 'You said it meant nothing to you . . .'

'It didn't, but as Sabrina pointed out you would never be able to forget that it had happened.'

Rhianon shook her head. 'That's nonsense. I've forgotten about it already.'

'Well, I can't,' Pryce admitted. 'I doubt if you have, either. It will always be there, something for you to drag up every time we have an argument, something for you to hold over my head.'

'If that's the way you feel about it, then you had better not take the risk,' Rhianon snapped as she pushed back her chair.

He looked at her in surprise. 'You're not leaving already, are you?'

'There's not much point in sitting here arguing with each other, is there!'

'Do we have to row?' he pleaded. 'Why not let Sabrina do what she wants about the kid. Let her go ahead and have it adopted. Afterwards we might be able to put the whole incident out of our minds and start afresh.'

'My life includes Davyn, now and in the future. If you and Sabrina want to be rid of him then, as I've already told her, I'll adopt him.'

'Don't talk such rot!' he exploded. 'How on earth can you afford to bring him up? And I can't. I've at least another two years to serve and when I come out I'll have no job, no money and no home!'

The problems of their existence at Nellie's increased until the three of them were barely speaking. When they did it was usually to carp or argue about something or other.

Nellie constantly complained about Davyn's crying. 'Every night it's the same,' she grumbled. 'Grizzling away he is, stopping me and my Olwen from getting a good night's sleep.'

She also continued to gripe about how late Sabrina came home every night.

'She slams the front door and makes such a racket as she comes upstairs that it disturbs our rest as well! If it isn't the babba then it's her. Darw! It can't go on like this, something has got to be done.'

Rhianon tried to explain that Sabrina couldn't

get home any earlier because she was working in a nightclub. 'She doesn't finish work until after midnight, that's why she's so late.'

'Nightclub!' Nellie's lip curled disdainfully. 'You mean a brothel, don't you? The only kind of job she's interested in is tarting herself up to attract men.'

'You shouldn't say wicked things like that about her, Nellie, not even when you're angry,' Rhianon told her crossly.

'Dammo di! I know what I'm talking about. She'd have turned my place into a bloody brothel if I hadn't put my foot down, I'll have you know!'

'You complained that she brought a chap back here with her, but I can assure you there was no harm in it at all. He was a friend of mine, Patrick Nelson. As a matter of fact you'd met him before, when he walked me home on New Year's Eve. He accompanied Sabrina back because it was so late and he wanted to make sure she got home safely.'

'And then tucked her up into bed and himself alongside her,' Nellie sneered. 'Duw! You must think I was born yesterday and that I'm as blind as a bat or a gullible fool.'

'No, I don't think anything of the sort, Nellie. I know you only mentioned it because you were worried and you didn't want Sabrina to come to any harm,' Rhianon told her placatingly. 'All they did, though, was sit and chat until it was time for him to get back to his ship.'

A couple of weeks later their uncomfortable truce ended abruptly in a violent row. Sabrina, dolled up to the nines for the evening in one of her floaty little low-cut dresses, silk stockings and high-heeled shoes, was about to leave the house when Dai Rogers, the boyfriend of Nellie's daughter Olwen, arrived on the doorstep. Instead of calling out to let either Nellie or Olwen know that he was there, Sabrina couldn't resist fluttering her eyelashes and chatting flirtatiously to him.

Hearing voices, and recognising that one of them belonged to Dai, Nellie came out from her kitchen to see what was going on. She arrived in the passageway in time to see Sabrina giving Dai a hearty farewell kiss on the cheek, and her blood boiled.

'Slut! Tart! Bitch!' she yelled at the top of her voice, advancing on Sabrina with her hand raised ready to slap her.

Hearing all the commotion, Olwen, who was in her room getting ready to go out, appeared at the top of the stairs. It was at exactly the same moment as Sabrina defiantly kissed Dai again.

Screaming with jealous rage, Olwen joined her mother in the hallway. Tears streaming down her face, and yelling like a banshee, she upbraided Dai for his unfaithfulness. Nellie continued to shout abuse at Sabrina, who was standing on the pavement smirking.

Rhianon rushed down the stairs to try and

restore peace. Before she reached the hallway Sabrina blew a kiss to them all and strutted off down the road, her high heels clicking and clacking defiantly.

'Since you can't control that little whore, the pair of you can get out of my house,' Nellie screeched at Rhianon angrily.

'She didn't mean to upset any of you, she was simply being . . . being playful.'

'Playful!' Nellie's face turned deep red with anger. 'You call flirting with my Olwen's boyfriend, brazenly kissing him in front of us, being playful!'

'Aggravating, then. You know what a tease Sabrina can be,' Rhianon said weakly.

'Oh she's a tease all right, but not the innocent sort of little tease you'd have us all believe. That sister of yours is a wicked little bitch! She's bad all the way through. Men are easily fooled because she has a pretty face and a figure that makes her look like an It girl, but believe me she's evil.'

'Look Nellie, I'm sorry if Sabrina's upset Olwen by pretending to flirt with Dai. I'll speak to her about it when she comes home and it won't happen again,' Rhianon promised.

'You're dead right about that, girl!' Nellie declared furiously as she pulled herself up to her full height and glared at Rhianon. 'It won't happen again because both of you can get out of my house. I've put up with you long enough.'

Rhianon stood her ground, refusing to be

intimidated. 'You can't simply turn us out into the street, Nellie. If you want us to leave then you've got to give us time to find somewhere else to live.'

'I haven't got to do anything of the sort,' Nellie blustered. 'Since I suppose none of this is your fault, though, I'll be reasonable about things. The pair of you can stay until the end of the week. That will give you plenty of time to find somewhere else, now won't it?'

Rhianon realised that it was pointless arguing the matter any further. Secretly she hoped that in another day or so both Nellie and Olwen would have calmed down, and no more would be said about them leaving.

She could hear Davyn crying and knew he was due for a feed, so she made her way back up to her bedroom. She was halfway up the stairs when she heard Nellie call her name.

'Hang on a minute,' Nellie said. She delved into the pocket of her overall and brought out a letter. 'You'd better have this.'

Rhianon frowned as she looked at the envelope and recognised Polly Potter's writing. She ripped open the envelope and read the brief note inside, 'When did this arrive, Nellie?' she asked sharply.

Nellie shrugged. 'Yesterday, or the day before. I can't remember. I picked it up and meant to give it to you, but you've been gadding in and out of the house like a blue-arsed fly so I forgot about it. It's not important, is it?'

'It's to let me know that my father is ill, he's had a stroke,' Rhianon told her curtly. 'I only hope I can get back to Pontdarw before it is too late,' she added ominously.

Her heart was thundering. Polly would not have written to her unless it was serious. Anxiously she began trying to plan ahead.

'It's too late to go tonight,' she told Nellie, 'so I'll have to leave first thing tomorrow morning and catch the earliest train I can.'

'Well, remember to take all your bits and pieces with you,' Nellie retorted unfeelingly.

Rhianon looked at her in amazement. 'Surely we can leave things as they are for the moment, Nellie! My father's been taken ill . . .'

'I meant what I said. I want you and that sister of yours out of my house before the end of the week!' she stated, her mouth tightening.

'Nellie, don't be like that,' Rhianon pleaded. 'I can't stop to find anywhere else for us to live. I must get back to Pontdarw and see what is wrong with my father.'

'I know that, you've already said so. And I'm telling you again to take all your belongings with you because I damn well want you out of my house.'

'Sabrina won't be coming to Pontdarw with me . . .'

'Then she'd better find somewhere else to stay, hadn't she, because I certainly don't want her here.'

Chapter Twenty-Eight

Friday 25th October 1929 was a special day for Pryce Pritchard. He'd been counting the months, the weeks and the days to his release. Now, it was only a matter of hours and minutes. Finally he was out of the grim building where he'd been incarcerated for the past three years. He walked through the prison gates and breathed deeply of the cold fresh air as it whistled round the corner of Knox Street and Adam Street. He savoured its coldness on his face, letting it cleanse away the fetid air of Cardiff jail.

Freedom! Clutching a canvas bag that held his few possessions, he squared his shoulders, turned his back on the jail and walked away.

Never again would he endure being shut up inside a place like that, he vowed.

Yet, in many ways it had been an education. It had given him time to think. Time to unravel the muddled thoughts in his mind without being pressed or coerced by other people's opinions. His sentence had, without doubt, changed the course of his life. The stain on his character meant that his chances of becoming a teacher had been forfeited, and that his years at night school had been wasted. Or had they? Was learning ever wasted? Even the three years inside had taught him many things.

His zeal for campaigning had dimmed. Never again would he fight a battle he wasn't sure he was going to win. Standing up to the bosses, the coal owners and the like, was a waste of energy. They had the power and the whip hand. If they chose to withhold work or money from the lower orders, there was very little the ordinary working man could do to combat their decision. As far as he was concerned, the fight was over.

He hadn't lost, he wouldn't admit to that, he preferred to think that he had retreated strategically. Nor was he licking his wounds. He had seen the futility of such tussles and, during the last three years, he had experienced firsthand what could happen when you set yourself up against the law.

From now on Pryce wanted a quiet existence. Above all he longed to be reunited with Rhianon. His love for her had deepened while he had been inside and now he was determined to spend the rest of his life atoning for the wrong he had done her, and helping her to fulfil her dreams of a loving marriage and a happy home life.

He deplored his fling with Sabrina. It had been so pointless, so stupid, and must have caused Rhianon tremendous anguish. That was, of course, he reflected, if Rhianon still felt the same way about him as he did about her. She had neither visited him nor contacted him in any way since the day when she'd walked out of the jail in anger.

From then on he had been completely isolated from those he knew. He'd had no visitors, no news, only the mental and physical torment of incarceration in the hellhole of prison.

He squared his shoulders. He'd been so determined that on his release his first point of call would be Pontdarw, to try and find Rhianon. He'd dreamed about this, of being free and able to tell her what he felt about her, and how much she meant to him. He cherished the hope that she would forgive and forget the past, and agree that they could start a new life together.

Now he didn't feel so sure. As his doubts clouded his resolve he tried to decide whether to head straight for the railway station and take a train back to Pontdarw, or to remain in Cardiff. Perhaps he should stay and find himself some work and prove himself responsible and worthy of her.

He felt a hand tugging at his sleeve. It brought him back to reality and he spun round in alarm. 'What the hell are you doing here?' he exclaimed in surprise when he found Sabrina clinging to his arm.

She was dressed fetchingly in a dark red coat with a white fur collar that was fastened high at the neck with two fur pompoms. At a jaunty angle on her dark curls was a red beret trimmed with matching white pompoms on top. She looked so smart and chic that he was suddenly conscious of his own scruffy appearance. The grey flannels and dark jacket that he'd been wearing when he was arrested three years ago were creased and threadbare.

Sabrina pouted provocatively, fluttering her long lashes as she looked up at him. 'That's not a very friendly greeting. I went to a lot of trouble to find out when you were to be released so that I could be here to meet you.'

He stared at her in uneasy silence. She was the last person he wanted to see. He thought he'd made it perfectly plain when she'd come to visit him in jail that it was Rhianon he was in love with and hoped to marry, not her.

'Come on, let's find a café and get a hot drink,' she said, linking her arm through his possessively. 'I've been freezing hanging about waiting for you,' she added huffily when he made no response.

'No one asked you to come, Sabrina!' he said ungraciously.

'Better than having nobody to meet you,' she retorted pertly. 'I thought you'd find things pretty strange, seeing you've been shut away from the real world for three years. There's been an awful lot happening, you know.'

'What do you mean?' His thoughts were immediately of Rhianon. His senses spun. Was she hinting that Rhianon had got married?

'Well,' she pursed her bright red lips, 'women over twenty-one now have the vote. We've got new pound and ten-shilling notes. There's a new Labour government. Oh, and yesterday there was a terrible to-do in America when some place called Wall Street crashed.'

His mouth twisted cynically as he looked down at her. 'Learned all that like a bloody parrot to try and impress me, did you. Well, you needn't have bothered. I might have been in jail, but those sort of things are still talked about even in there. Anyway, I don't suppose they mean anything to you! Your head's too full of clothes and the stuff you put on your face.'

'That's not true!' Sabrina's eyes glistened with tears. 'I've been counting the days until you would be out.'

'Why?' He stared at her uneasily. 'I thought I made it clear when you came to visit me a couple of years ago that there was absolutely nothing between us. We had a fling! It was a mistake! It was all over even before I was arrested.'

'Pryce!' Sabrina gasped dramatically. 'How can you say that! You must remember the passion there was between us!'

'Passion?' Pryce gave a short harsh laugh. 'You mean lust, don't you?'

Sabrina clutched at the front of his jacket. 'You killed my boyfriend because of your feelings for me,' she reminded him, gazing into his face earnestly. 'I would have been married to Hwyel by now if you hadn't done that.'

'For God's sake, Sabrina!' He shook her hand

away from his arm. 'I've served time for what I did, even though it was an accident. The whole matter is over and done with.'

'Not for me it isn't,' she whispered throatily. She placed a hand on his chest. 'You mean the world to me, Pryce Pritchard.'

He backed away angrily.

'I've waited three long years for you . . .'

Pryce held up his hand to silence her. 'Yes, Sabrina, it's been three years, I'm three years older and three years wiser. I've had a lot of time to ponder my future as well as mull over my past . . .'

'And think about your son?'

Pryce ran a hand over his chin. 'My son . . .' He looked shaken. 'Where is he?' he demanded.

For a second Sabrina seemed taken aback, then she gave a shrill laugh. 'You didn't think I was going to bring him with me in this weather? Poor little boyo, he would have been frozen to death in this wind!'

'So where is he?' he repeated.

'Being looked after, of course. You don't think I'd leave him on his own, do you?'

Pryce stared at her in silence. This was a new obstacle, but one that had to be faced and dealt with conscientiously. He had been so busy planning a new life for himself and Rhianon that he'd given no thought to the child. Yet there was a little boy to consider. His son! A child he had never even seen.

He pushed his hand through his hair, staring

down at Sabrina, trying to work out what she had in mind. His throat felt parched, his head muzzy. What a mess! How could he hope to win Rhianon back when her own sister was the mother of his child?

He had to pull himself together. He had to take the situation slowly. He must watch what he said and keep his head clear, or Sabrina would trap him into setting up a home for her and the boy. She might deserve such consideration, but it was not what he had dreamed of all these years.

The only thing that had kept him sane while he had been in prison was the thought that Rhianon was out there waiting for him. He loved her so intensely that he found his mind constantly wandering to thoughts of her, to the exclusion of all else. He never stopped hoping that once he could prove how much he'd changed while he'd been in prison, Rhianon would take him back.

He shivered. 'Where's this café you're talking about then?' he asked, pulling up the collar of his jacket.

Confident that she'd won him over, Sabrina smiled complacently. 'Not very far away,' she assured him cheerfully.

'Right, let's go there then and get inside somewhere warm. I can't think straight out here in this freezing cold wind.'

He still couldn't think clearly even when he was in the warmth of the café, but the walk had given him time to assess the situation. He sat opposite Sabrina, with his hands wrapped round a steaming mug of tea, and began slowly and carefully to tell her about his future plans.

She listened in silence. He noticed a little smirk on her face when he told her he was not going back to mining, but would look for some other kind of job.

'Well, you've got no choice, have you?' she smiled. 'They wouldn't have you back, not after what you did.'

'Possibly not.'

'So you're going to stay here in Cardiff, are you?' she asked, sipping her mug of tea and looking at him provocatively from over the rim of it.

He took a minute to consider this. 'No, I was on my way to get a train to Pontdarw. I want to see Rhianon as soon as possible.'

Sabrina shook her head. 'I don't think that's a good idea. She hates your guts.'

'No she doesn't. She came to see me in jail.'

Sabrina laughed cynically. 'Ages ago. A couple of months after Davyn was born, and he's over two and a half years old now!'

He frowned and concentrated on his tea. 'Well, that's what I intend to do,' he reiterated stubbornly.

'If you set foot in Pontdarw they'll hound you down,' she warned. 'Hwyel's dad said he'd kill you if he ever saw you again. Ruined all his dreams for the future, you did, when you threw that punch! No one there has a kind word to say for you.'

Pryce sighed. 'I realise that, but it is something I must face up to, isn't it? Mr Barker probably spoke in heat, while he was still feeling bitter about the loss of his son. Possibly it was before he knew that Hwyel had a heart condition that contributed to his death. We all mellow, with time.'

'Oh yes?' A smile flitted across her mouth. 'Have you mellowed, then?'

He shrugged. 'No, but I would like to think that I am a more mature, responsible person than I was before I went to prison. I certainly know what I want from life.'

'In that case then, Pryce Pritchard, perhaps you should face up to your responsibilities,' she snapped. 'You have a son called Davyn to bring up, remember.'

'I thought you were planning to have him adopted,' he said uneasily.

'Rhianon wouldn't let me go ahead with it. I thought she told you so the last time she came to visit you.'

'That was a very long time ago, as you pointed out,' he muttered.

'And you didn't have the guts to insist that the kid should go, so I've been lumbered with him ever since!'

'I will do whatever I can to help,' Pryce promised. 'He won't want for anything.'

'You mean you'll marry me and give him a proper family life?'

Pryce felt anger bubbling inside him. Sabrina knew that wasn't what he meant and she was trying to trap him. He'd already told her that he loved Rhianon, had always loved her, and that he wanted to start his new life married to her.

'A child needs to live at home with its parents,' Sabrina pressed. 'There's only one way you can give Davyn that life, now isn't that right?'

'I don't love you, Sabrina. What sort of family life would he have?'

'Well, bach, that would be up to you, wouldn't it,' she said huffily. 'It would work if you put Rhianon right out of your mind, and out of our life. I'm the one who was outside the prison waiting for you when you came out today, remember, not her!'

Pryce groaned, holding his head between his hands. How could he even consider what Sabrina was suggesting? He raised his head and stared across the table at her. Many men would envy him the opportunity he was being offered. She was young and she was lovely. She had a splendid figure and she was as bright as a button. Too bright! She'd twist him round her little finger, he thought wryly. That didn't daunt him, but he didn't love her. He wanted Rhianon, no one could ever take her place in his heart. She was the only woman he would ever truly love.

Rhianon wasn't a pert, brittle show-off like her sister, but calmer, kindlier, warm and considerate. She shared many of his interests and ideals. Their life together would be so rewarding that he was convinced they could be blissfully happy. If only . . .

'Remember, you are the father of my little boy,' Sabrina persisted softly. 'If you want to put things right, Pryce, then surely that's where you should start. A home for your son . . . and for his mother!'

He shook his head. 'This is not what I planned. I need time to think, Sabrina. There's no doubt in my mind, though, that the first thing I have to do is to go to Pontdarw and talk to Rhianon.'

'No!' Her face hardened. 'I've already warned you that the Barkers will have you lynched if you so much as set foot in the place!'

He spread his hands helplessly. 'Then perhaps I'd better stay here for a while.'

'You mean you'll move in with me?' she said jubilantly.

'No!' He shook his head firmly. 'I want to be on my own. I need to concentrate on what is involved and to decide what to do for the best.'

Sabrina's face fell. 'What about me? I've waited for you all this time, remember. What am I supposed to do?'

Pryce shook his head despairingly. 'I don't know what to say to you, Sabrina. I can't promise you anything. You've made a life for yourself, haven't you? I've never contemplated marrying you, you know that!'

'Not even for your son's sake?' she jibed.

He scraped back his chair and stood up. 'I'll keep in touch,' he said brusquely.

'Hold on!' She grabbed at his sleeve. 'Where will I find you? Where are you going to live if you won't come back and stay with me?'

'I'll look for some digs.'

'You can't afford them, you've no money and no job,' she pointed out spitefully.

'Then I'll go to one of the hostels for down-and-outs in Bute Street. Give me time, a couple of weeks to try and find work.'

'So I simply have to go on waiting, do I?' Sabrina said bitterly.

Pryce shrugged. 'Wait or carry on as before . . . I don't know. This isn't what I'd planned, Sabrina. I'll meet you back here in a couple of weeks' time.'

'That's far too vague,' she scowled. 'For all I know you may be planning to scarper and leave me all on my own to bring up your kid!' she snapped.

'No,' he said firmly. 'No matter where I go I'll always provide for my child. That's a responsibility I will always face up to and honour!'

Chapter Twenty-Nine

Rhianon quietly tiptoed out of her father's bedroom, holding a finger up to her lips when Davyn came running towards her.

'Ssh!' she warned. 'Granpy's sleeping. Come on, we'll go downstairs and play with your toys only we mustn't make any noise,' she told him.

He nodded solemnly, a sturdy little toddler with thick dark hair and big brown eyes, and a smile that displayed small even teeth.

Hand in hand they went into the living room. It was warm and comfortable. A fire glowed in the black-leaded range, and the steel fender and fireguard were burnished to a silver gleam that reflected the flames.

Rhianon sat down in the armchair at the side of the fireplace and lifted Davyn onto her lap. Hugging him tightly, she closed her eyes. After another disturbed night she felt so tired that she was sure she could sleep the clock round.

For a few seconds the child sat quietly, enjoying the cuddle, then he began to squirm and reluctantly she opened her eyes.

'Right! What is it to be, then? A story?' She leaned down and picked up his picture book from the floor.

Davyn curled into the warmth of her body, put his thumb in his mouth and settled to listen.

Within minutes his thick dark lashes were sweeping down over his cheeks as his breathing became slow and rhythmical. Cautiously Rhianon removed his thumb from his mouth. He stirred slightly, so she rocked him gently until he settled back into sleep.

Smothering a yawn, she stood up and carefully carried him across to the sofa. Then she covered him over with the shawl she kept handy to slip on whenever she had to go outside for coal or wood.

With both Davyn and her father asleep, she wondered if she dared have a nap herself. Then she thought guiltily of the mountain of chores that were waiting to be done, and decided she'd better get on with them.

As she spread a thick piece of old blanket over one end of the dining table, and covered it with old clean sheeting, ready to do some ironing, there was a knock on the front door.

Rhianon frowned, wondering who it could be. Quickly she went to answer it, before whoever it was banged again and woke Davyn up.

She was shocked when she opened the door and found Sabrina standing there. She had only seen her sister twice in the two years since she'd left Cardiff and returned to Pontdarw to look after their father, bringing Davyn with her.

'This is a surprise!'

'Well, it's not easy to take time off work. I'm not free to come and go as I please, like you.' Sabrina said balefully. She came into the living room, removing her fur-trimmed red coat as she did so. 'You've certainly got it nice and warm in here, haven't you,' she commented. 'It's like an oven!'

Her voice was loud and critical, disturbing the sleeping child. He sat up, pushing the shawl away and sliding off the sofa onto the floor.

'I have to keep the house as warm as possible because Father feels the cold,' Rhianon explained.

Sabrina looked round expectantly. 'Where is Dad then?'

'Upstairs in bed, he's still asleep. He had a very restless night so he's no good for anything today.'

'We've got to keep very quiet because Granpy's having a sleep, haven't we, Davyn,' Rhianon said, smiling at the little boy who was watching them wide-eyed. 'Look who's come to see you! Come and say hello, then.'

Timidly he moved towards them, then stuck his thumb in his mouth and clung onto Rhianon's dress.

'Not very friendly, is he!' Sabrina commented disparagingly.

'He's shy. He'll come round in a minute or two. Sit down then and I'll make a pot of tea, and you can tell me all your news and why you're here. I take it there is a reason?'

'Yes, there certainly is! I wouldn't have come all this way on a freezing day simply for the pleasure of a visit,' was the caustic reply.

As she went into the scullery Rhianon wondered what was on her sister's mind. She felt a flicker of fear. Did this visit mean Sabrina wanted to take Davyn away?

Whatever happened she wouldn't let her do that. It might be a desperate struggle to make ends meet because the only money they had to keep them in food and coal was her father's dwindling savings, but she'd manage somehow.

She'd found a way to make a few shillings, by undertaking knitting for Polly's customers. It didn't amount to much, but it was one of the few things she could do at home and she was glad of anything to supplement their money. Because of her father's failing health she was afraid to leave the house for more than the half-hour or so when she did the shopping each day.

Even then, she was uneasy the entire time, worrying in case he came to any harm. She tried to go out when he was still in bed and asleep, but there was always the chance that he would wake up while she wasn't there, attempt to get out of bed and have a fall. He was so frail, so unsteady on his feet, and so pitifully thin, that her heart ached for him.

She wondered what Sabrina would think when she saw him. It was over six months since her last visit, and he had deteriorated considerably since then.

Davyn followed her into the kitchen and was still holding onto her dress as she went back into the living room with a tray of tea things.

'Isn't it time he stopped clinging to you like a limpet?' Sabrina said disdainfully.

'He doesn't usually,' Rhianon defended. 'He's shy because he doesn't know you.'

'Doesn't know me!' Sabrina exclaimed, her dark eyes widening incredulously.

'He's little more than a baby, and he hasn't seen you for six months,' Rhianon reminded her. 'He'll be all right in a few minutes if you take no notice.'

'Don't worry, I'm not going to pay any attention to him! Don't expect me to pick him up and nurse him, either,' she added sharply, smoothing down her smart black skirt.

'So why have you come? Obviously not to see Davyn, so it must be Father you're worried about.'

Sabrina shrugged. 'Not really!' She took out a fancy cigarette case and matching lighter, selected a cigarette and lit up. 'No!' She blew out a plume of blue smoke. 'I came because there is something you need to know.'

'Oh?' Rhianon wafted the smoke away with her hand. She knew Sabrina shouldn't be smoking there, not with a small child and a sick man in the house, but she felt it would be uncivil to point this out to her. 'What is it that you think I need to know?'

'I saw Pryce Pritchard last week.'

Rhianon looked annoyed. 'You're still visiting him in prison then, despite what we agreed!'

'No, I haven't been in that horrible place, I didn't need to, he's out.'

Rhianon clapped her hand over her mouth in dismay. Of course! She had had so much on her mind she'd forgotten that his release was at the end of October. She'd intended to be at the prison gates to meet him when he came out, but so many other things had needed her attention that she'd overlooked the date.

'So how is he?' she asked cautiously.

'How would you think? He's three years older, grim-faced, hardened, disillusioned, shabby and out of work,' Sabrina said acidly.

Rhianon found she was unable to speak because of the lump in her throat. Pryce was so much in her thoughts, and yet at the very moment when he needed her most she'd failed him. She tried to imagine what it was like, coming back into the world after three years shut away in jail.

'He's had plenty of time to think,' Sabrina went on, 'and he knows what he wants from life.'

'He does?' Rhianon exclaimed in surprise, a tremor in her voice.

'Yes, he wants me,' Sabrina told her triumphantly. 'He says that he doesn't want to see you ever again. All that is in the past. Do you understand?'

Rhianon shook her head. The colour drained from her cheeks, her shoulders drooped. 'You don't know what you're saying. He can't mean that, you must have misunderstood what he said!' she choked out in a whisper.

'Those were his exact words,' Sabrina insisted. 'We're going to set up home together,' she added smugly.

'You're getting married!'

Sabrina shrugged. 'Perhaps. One day.'

'What . . . what about Davyn?' Rhianon's hand went out blindly to the child still clinging to her dress, and she buried her fingers in his thick mop of hair. Tears misted her eyes as she stared at her sister. 'You've come to take him from me, but I won't let you! You've not a scrap of love in your heart for him, admit it!'

'Take Davyn away! Don't talk ridiculous! Of course I've not come to do that. You're more than welcome to him. I came to tell you that Pryce doesn't wish to see you again, that's all. As long as you keep away from him you can keep the kid,' she added. 'Remember that!'

'Is that a threat?' Rhianon challenged

'No, but it is sound advice and you'd do well not to forget it.'

'What does Pryce say about this? Supposing he wants him back? Davyn is his son, remember!'

'I've told you, all that is in the past. We're starting a new life together and we don't want to be weighed down by memories of our mistakes. Now,' she parried, 'let's have that cup of tea and then I must be off.'

'You're going back to Cardiff right away?'

'Of course I am! You didn't think I was going to stay overnight, did you?' she asked with sour amusement.

Rhianon shook her head uneasily. 'No, I suppose not. You haven't seen Father yet though.'

Sabrina sipped at her tea, frowning darkly. 'Do I have to?'

Rhianon looked aghast. 'Of course you must!'

'He probably won't want to see me, so why tell him I'm here? Leave him if he's sleeping. I'll be off as soon as I've drunk this and he need never know I've even been here.'

Rhianon shook her head. 'No, you must see him, Sabrina. I can hear him stirring, so he'll be down in a minute. I must go up and help him, he can't manage the stairs on his own.'

'I'd rather not be involved,' Sabrina scowled.

'Please, Sabrina. He's your father! He's very frail, and rather depressed. A visit from you might help to cheer him up.'

Sabrina shrugged resignedly. 'Very well, if I must, but if he is anywhere near as ill as you say then he probably won't even know who I am.'

Edwin Webster looked surprised to see his younger daughter. He peered at her through rheumy eyes, and for a moment it looked as though Sabrina was going to be proved right, as he showed no sign of recognition.

'It's Sabrina, Father. She's come up from Cardiff to see how you are,' Rhianon told him.

'From Cardiff.' He frowned. 'What was she doing in Cardiff?'

'She lives there now, don't you remember?'

He shook his head, clutching the arms of his chair as he sat down at the table, and staring at Sabrina in a bewildered way.

Rhianon placed a bowl of soup and a plate holding two small slices of bread in front of him.

'Is that all you're giving him?' Sabrina asked critically. 'It's not much of a meal!'

'He hasn't a very good appetite these days,' Rhianon explained.

'Maybe not, but shouldn't he be having something more substantial? Chicken, meat . . . I don't know.'

'We rarely have meat, or chicken, they're far too expensive,' Rhianon told her as she poured a cup of weak tea for her father.

Sabrina looked round the room as if seeing it for the first time.

'Where are all the ornaments we used to have? The place looks bare! Why have you put them all away? I suppose it's because you can't be bothered dusting them,' she said critically.

'They've not been put away,' Rhianon told her sadly, 'they've been sold.'

Sabrina's eyes widened. 'Sold?'

'Food and medicine for Dad are more important than ornaments,' Rhianon said with some exasperation.

Sabrina looked shocked. 'You mean you are that hard up?'

Rhianon nodded. 'Father's savings are practically gone, and I can't work while I have him and Davyn to care for, now can I? I manage to earn a few shillings now and again by doing knitting for Polly, but it doesn't amount to very much.'

A crafty look came into Sabrina's face. 'I had no idea. Perhaps we can come to some arrangement. I tell you what I'll do, I'll send you money every week as long as you stay away from Pryce. You've got to promise, though, not to come between us or try and prevent him from marrying me.'

Rhianon started to say that she had no intention of contacting Pryce ever again, not if he had said he didn't want to see her. She mightn't have very much, but she did still have her pride.

Then, as she realised the implication of what Sabrina was saying, she clamped her lips together. If her sister could afford to send her money each week, why not take advantage of the situation?

'Do you agree to my terms?' Sabrina challenged.

Rhianon gave a forlorn nod. She looked around at the bare room, at Davyn playing with some buttons and old cotton reels, at her ailing father and then at her smartly dressed sister, and knew she had no alternative.

Chapter Thirty

Rhianon didn't know which she found more hurtful, the news that Pryce didn't want to see her again, or that he wanted nothing whatsoever to do with his son.

The fact that he wished for no further contact with her she could understand. She had probably brought this on herself when she stopped visiting him in prison, but the fact that he was Davyn's father had left her utterly devastated.

Looking back, she wished she'd not been so hasty, so condemning, but at the time she had felt as if her heart had been broken. For him to have slept with her own sister seemed unforgivable, even though she suspected that Sabrina had more than likely been the instigator.

Ever since I was quite small Sabrina has always been jealous of everything I've ever had, she thought sadly. No matter how much I tried to care for her I never made her completely happy.

As Rhianon relived those traumatic months in Cardiff up until the time Davyn had been born, she wondered why she had tolerated Sabrina's disgruntled attitude. Perhaps I should have been stronger and walked away from her, she thought uncertainly. Things might have turned out better if I'd left her to arrange her own life and that of the baby she was expecting.

The knowledge that Sabrina would get rid of it, one way or the other, was what had stopped her. She'd been afraid that if Sabrina went ahead and had a back-street abortion, as she wanted to, she might ruin her health, or even die in the process.

Then, after the baby was born, she couldn't bear the thought of it being given up for adoption and brought up by strangers. Not when it was Pryce's baby!

It had been a terrible shock to discover that Pryce agreed with Sabrina and that he thought the best future for the child was to have him adopted. She couldn't believe he could be so heartless. She couldn't accept his excuse, that it was the only way the child would be able to grow up untainted by the fact that his father had been jailed for killing a man.

If that had been the sole reason for the decision then perhaps she could have understood, even agreed to it. In her heart, though, she was sure that he had been persuaded to take this attitude by Sabrina, because she wanted to be rid of the responsibility of bringing up a baby.

Pryce was a strong-willed man, with firm principles about what was right and what was wrong. The very fact that Sabrina could influence his decision could only mean one thing, that he was so much in love with her that he would agree to anything she said.

Sabrina might be lovely to look at, but inwardly she was shallow and selfish. To her, even now, Davyn was a burden, a nuisance she didn't want encroaching on her life. She had not one scrap of love in her heart for the child, no sense of true responsibility for him or his future.

Rhianon was fully aware that the money Sabrina had promised to send was a form of coercion. It was probably also a way to assuage her feeling of guilt, because she knew she wasn't taking her fair share of the burden. She was no more interested in their father's welfare than she was in Davyn's, yet she had been the apple of his eye when she was growing up. In those days, life in Rhoslyn Terrace had centred round Sabrina and what she wanted.

She'd seen the look of contempt on Sabrina's face as she looked round the living room and saw the chipped paintwork, the scuffed door, the faded curtains, the cracked linoleum and the threadbare rug in front of the fireplace.

The furnishings had been there since they were small children. All of them now reflected the many years of hard wear and tear to which they'd been subjected. They should all have been replaced a long time ago, as one by one they began to grow shabby. To renew them at the moment was out of the question.

She couldn't even afford a tin of paint to

touch up the woodwork. Every penny that came into her hands went on coal and food. Sometimes she was hard pressed to decide which of those two was the more important. Her father needed nourishment, but his blood was so thin that he shivered uncontrollably if there was the slightest draught, so from necessity she had to keep the place warm.

Davyn was growing rapidly, but because she couldn't afford to buy him new winter clothes he also needed the place to be kept warm.

She sighed. It was a dilemma that kept her awake at night. There was nothing left in the house that she could pawn or sell. All her mother's ornaments and bits and pieces, even the fancy boxes she'd kept her handkerchiefs in, had gone. She used mainly elbow grease to keep the floors scrubbed and the furniture shining, since there was no money to waste on polish or cleaning materials. The emery paper that she used to keep the steel fender burnished was almost worn out, and when that was gone there was no more to replace it.

Davyn's few toys and picture books had all been given to him by the neighbours. They were ones which their own kids had outgrown, and, battered though they often were, they provided him with endless enjoyment.

Christmas was coming, and unless Sabrina kept her word and sent some money there would be nothing better than sausages and mash for their Christmas dinner. Rhianon knew she would be lucky if she could afford an apple and an orange to put in Davyn's stocking for when he woke up on Christmas morning. His only hope of a present of any kind was if Polly bought him one.

Polly had been such a stalwart friend. She'd helped her so much since she'd come back to Pontdarw that she felt guilty about taking anything more from her.

Sabrina was feeling quite smug as she sat on the train that was taking her back to Cardiff. She'd put things as plainly as she possibly could to Rhianon, and she was pretty sure she'd managed to convince her that Pryce wanted nothing more to do with her.

Even if Rhianon did have any doubts, or thought she would like to see Pryce and hear it all from his own lips, Sabrina was confident that her sister would resist making contact. She was too much in need of the money Sabrina had promised to send, providing Rhianon kept to her part of the bargain.

She smiled to herself. What a dope Rhianon was. Imagine taking on someone else's kid when they weren't paying you to look after it! And fancy her going back to Pontdarw to look after her dad, considering the way he'd treated her when she was growing up!

From the day Mother died she had to take care of me, Sabrina reflected, and I played her up something silly.

She remembered how her dad had spoken to Rhianon in those days. He'd treated her almost as if she'd been a servant, ordering her to do this and do that. He'd expected her to wait on him hand and foot. She'd had to have his meals ready to put on the table the minute he walked in the door. He'd also expected her to scrub and polish, as well as doing all the washing and ironing, as if she was the woman of the house.

He hadn't been like that with her. No, she'd been his little pet, unable to do a thing wrong! He'd even paid for her to study shorthand and typing when she'd left school. And then he'd arranged for her to have a plum job with the Barkers the minute she was qualified.

Remembering Hwyel made her sigh. It was a sigh of relief. Since he'd died she'd really started to live and enjoy herself. She was now well aware that if she had married him her life would have been almost as dull and monotonous as the one Rhianon was living.

She wouldn't have been hard up, of course. Hwyel would have been able to provide her with a nice house, lovely furniture and as much money for housekeeping and spending on herself as she needed. She smiled to herself, reflectively. She would have been comfortably off, but it would have been nothing like her present existence.

She loved working at the Dragon Club. She enjoyed being the centre of attention and revelled in the way the fellows eyed her up and down. She could flirt, tease and tantalise them all as much as she liked. They could look, but they knew they couldn't touch, not unless she invited them to do so.

The money was good, and there was always plenty of it. That was important to her, and combined with the excitement of the job she was more than happy with her lot.

She lived well, too. A handsomely decorated couple of rooms above the Dragon Club, furnished exactly the way she wanted them to be. She had a wardrobe overflowing with smart clothes. Good ones at that, not things picked up off the market or in cheap shops! She had plenty of money in her pocket to spend on herself. She could buy anything that took her fancy.

Rhianon had looked so grateful when she'd promised to send her a couple of pounds each week to help out that she'd almost laughed in her face. If her sister knew how much she was pulling in each night, she'd have wanted a lot more than an extra quid or so.

Still, if that was all it needed to keep Rhianon from contacting Pryce it was a good investment, and she didn't grudge her a single penny piece of it. In fact, she'd even send her an extra fiver at Christmas. She'd tell her to use it to treat herself to a new dress or something a bit special. The trouble was, knowing how soft-hearted Rhianon was, she'd use it to buy something for the kid.

All she had to do now was convince Pryce

that Rhianon had said she didn't want to see him ever again, or have anything more to do with him. That mightn't be quite so easy. He wasn't as gullible as her sister. If what he said was true, he couldn't put Rhianon out of his mind.

She'd really have to convince him that a great many people in Pontdarw still hated his guts for killing Hwyel, and that they'd crucify him if he ever returned there. If she managed that, given time things should work out the way she wanted them to.

Rhianon would never be able to afford to come to Cardiff to look for him, she'd make quite sure of that! What was more, now that he was out of prison and living in dosshouses in Tiger Bay, Rhianon wouldn't have the faintest idea of how to trace him.

Why did she want Pryce Pritchard, she asked herself. She didn't need him. There were plenty of attractive men willing to give her a good time. They were wealthy, too, and eager to spend money on her.

The only reason was that Pryce meant something special to her. She hungered for him. She'd wanted him for herself ever since the first time she'd seen him with Rhianon. He was so different from other men. He was so strong-minded, so unfazed by her looks, or her figure, that she'd always been determined to win him.

It had been Rhianon's brains that had attracted him to her sister, she was sure of that.

There couldn't be any other reason. Rhianon was so dull, so conservative in her approach to life. Pryce had always been a hothead, a fighter, a believer that every man was as good as the next. He despised the bosses and the way they ground down the workers and kept them in their place.

Leastwise, he had. Three years in prison seemed to have changed his views slightly. He still held that no man was any better than he was, but he was no longer eager to defend the rights of others. All the energy he had devoted to fighting for the miners' cause had calcified into hate against the system and the world in general.

Sabrina smiled to herself. She'd been keeping tabs on him through her many contacts. She was piqued that he wouldn't accept her offer to move in with her, but she hadn't given up yet. He would, in time.

So far, according to the reports she'd had, he'd only been able to afford the cheapest of dosshouses. He hadn't managed to find any work, and every day was taking its toll on him. Each time he was turned down for a job he became more bitterly angry, more depressed. Very soon now he would be reduced to such despair that he'd be ready to accept help from anyone who held out a hand.

As far as Sabrina was concerned, this was good news. It was what she'd hoped would happen. She wanted his spirit to be broken because she had his future all planned out. She was well aware, though, that he would have to be on his uppers before he would ever accept help from her.

When she felt the time was right she'd step in and offer to help him, but not before. There was a job ready and waiting for him. It would only be as a doorman at the Dragon Club, but it would be the first step on the ladder.

After that, it was up to him. He could fall in with her plans or he could stay grovelling in the mire. If that was his decision then she'd walk away from him, but she didn't want to have to do that. She still wanted him, but only at her price. She would be the dominant one: he would be her slave, in mind and body.

It would be a long haul, but if he played the game her way he'd rise up the ladder so fast that he'd be dizzy. She had big plans for the future, but she needed a man to act as a front. Someone to make the hard boys realise that she really was a force to be reckoned with, not merely a jumped-up tart.

The club they'd eventually own would set tongues wagging. Its attractions would outdo everything else in Tiger Bay. If he fell in with her plans they would be running it together, and it would lay the foundations for a wonderful life.

Was there any need to mention Davyn, she mused. She'd been so evasive about where he was and who was looking after him that Pryce had stopped asking about him. He probably thought she'd had him adopted after all and didn't want to admit to the fact. If she said nothing, he might never bring the matter up again.

Once Pryce let her find him a job he'd be so indebted to her that he'd be afraid of upsetting her if he asked after the kid, so he'd say nothing. If he did start asking questions about what had happened, she would play the maternal card and say it broke her heart to talk about it. Dissolving into tears would soon shut him up.

With their own club established and Pryce enjoying the high life, he wouldn't want to risk losing any of it. He wouldn't pursue the matter, he'd be too concerned with staying on the right side of her and making sure that they kept their business dealings, the drink, the drugs and everything else that would be on offer, within the law.

Chapter Thirty-One

Pryce Pritchard soon found that the economy had worsened considerably while he'd been in prison. Even so, he found it hard to believe that unemployment could be so rampant in a busy shipping and shipbuilding port like Cardiff.

He'd thought that when the miners went on strike to try and force the coal bosses to pay them a living wage, things for the working man had sunk as low as they could possibly go. In the weeks since his release, though, he'd discovered that there were a greater number of men than ever before out of work in Cardiff.

What was equally depressing was the fact that the bosses' position had been strengthened yet further. It was as if they were still punishing the workers for holding them to ransom by going on strike – working conditions were harsher than they'd ever been.

Pryce's first impulse was to pitch in and battle for the rights of his fellow men. Then common sense took over, and he remembered he was now a marked man. If he was arrested again, whatever it was for, he'd be the one in the wrong. With his record, no matter what he said or did, he'd never be able to prove his innocence. If he was found guilty of causing a disturbance his punishment would be severe.

Three years in Cardiff jail had hardened him, and had also instilled in him the necessity of putting number one first. His resolve now was to look after his own interests and mind his own business.

He'd tried once to help a fellow prisoner, to speak up for him and persuade some of the other inmates to support him in a plea to the screws, and through them to the Governor. His good deed had brought him nothing but trouble.

Fellow prisoners who had encouraged him to be the spokesman, and who had promised to support him, had disappeared into the woodwork. His punishment had been three days in solitary confinement because he was considered to be a troublemaker. He'd been put on bread and water. That had taught him a lesson he'd vowed never to forget.

Furthermore, he'd been permanently marked down as a troublemaker, probably because the crime that had brought him into prison had not been so very different. He had been publicly upholding the rights of his fellow miners when the fight between himself and Hwyel Baker had broken out.

He could still remember how most of the men in the crowd he'd been addressing had been yelling at him to trade blows with Hwyel. Yet, when the police asked for witnesses, not one of them had spoken up. Not one of them had come forward to give the true version of what had happened.

He promised himself that he'd never put himself in that sort of situation again.

While he was inside he'd had plenty of time to think and consider all aspects of life. He had changed many of his aims and modified his outlook. All he wanted in future, he decided, was a quiet existence, ideally back in Pontdarw and married to Rhianon.

He knew he had treated her badly. He regretted that he had made her so angry that she'd walked out on her last visit, and not come to see him again. He'd tried writing to her countless times, but then decided that the words he'd put down on paper nowhere near conveyed what was in his heart, so he'd scrapped them. He'd never stopped hoping to hear from her, longing for a visit, a message or a letter, but none had come.

To find Sabrina waiting outside the prison for him when he was released had been a shock, one he resented. It brought back the reason why he'd been incarcerated, and he wanted to put the memory of his fight with Hwyel behind him. He'd served his sentence, wiped the slate clean, and now was the time to start afresh.

To find that Sabrina was still hankering after him had also been unwelcome. His future, as well as his dreams, lay with Rhianon, not Sabrina.

Sabrina had been trouble from the moment he'd first met her, a bright young flapper intent on flirting with every man she met. She'd done her best to come between him and Rhianon, and finally she'd succeeded. He would never understand why he had slept with her, it had been unforgivable, and he knew that nothing he said, or did, could ever erase the hurt he had inflicted on Rhianon.

It was all very well Sabrina telling him that Rhianon never wanted to see him again, that the people of Pontdarw would lynch him if he ever set foot in the place, but Rhianon still held him in thrall. His heart was still hers, he loved her as he had never loved any other woman, she was all he wanted.

Somehow, even if it took him the rest of his life, he was determined to make things right between them.

There were plenty of unemployed miners, like him, hanging around Cardiff docks, unable to find work. They weren't wanted because, unlike the Lascars and countless other foreign men, they demanded proper wages and fair working hours. Agreeing to work for a pittance that was less than a living wage was against Pryce's principles, against everything he had fought for all his life.

Since manual work on the dockside seemed to be out of the question, his only hope was that his other skills might lead to employment. Years of attending night school, training to be a teacher, meant he was both numerate and erudite.

He didn't want to be a clerk, but if that was all that was available he'd do the work willingly and efficiently. All he longed for was to prove to Rhianon that he could provide for her if, despite Sabrina's words, she was eventually willing to marry him.

He found that no one would even consider employing him in any office capacity whatsoever, once they heard about his prison record.

As the days passed he became desperate. The few shillings they'd given him when he'd come out of jail were almost gone. He knew from what he had witnessed that if he couldn't pay in advance for his night's lodgings, he would be out on the street.

He was down to his last few coppers, and so hungry that he scavenged for food from the refuse bins outside the backs of cafés before he finally found work. It was with a shady character called Felinde, a weasel-faced Spaniard who owned a gambling den in Bute Street.

Felinde was willing to use him as a debt collector. The debts had mostly been accrued by betting on the horses. Among the men who had run up a card and then defaulted were some of the toughest characters to be found in Tiger Bay. Felinde told Pryce that it was only his reputation as a man who had done time for killing that gave him the necessary kudos and made him suitable for the job.

There were no regular hours of work, no agreed wages. Felinde promised Pryce that he would give him a percentage of the monies he brought in. Each day he was handed a list of names and addresses and left to devise his own method of collection.

In the early days the work seemed easy, if rather unpleasant. The names on his list were 'newcomers', which meant it was the first time they'd been approached. Most of them were sufficiently intimidated to pay up what they owed without any fuss.

At the end of the first week Pryce had five pounds in his pocket and a spring in his step. He didn't like the work, but it was better than begging. It would give him a chance to get on his feet and then he'd look around for something more suitable.

He wanted to move out of the flea-infested, bug-ridden room that was little more than a glorified cell, only not so clean as the one he'd occupied in Cardiff jail. Once he'd found some respectable digs he'd buy himself some decent clothes so that he looked presentable. After that he'd be ready to go and see Rhianon, he promised himself.

His optimism was short-lived. When his initiation period was over, the names on his list changed from first offenders to hardened borrowers. They were tougher. They knew all the scams when it came to avoiding paying their debts.

The five pounds he had been earning during the first two weeks dwindled until he was only managing to collect a few coppers in commission. The returns he was able to make were so pitiable that eventually Felinde called him into his office.

'You are completely and utterly useless,' he told him contemptuously. 'There's the door, bugger off.'

'Give us a chance, I've got to live, mun,' Pryce pleaded. 'I proved myself the first few weeks I was working for you.'

'That was beginner's luck,' Felinde told him scathingly, 'this is the real thing!'

'This last list you gave me, they're tough nuts,' Pryce protested.

'I wouldn't be employing you to collect the money from them if they were easy pickings, now would I,' Felinde said derisively. 'I thought you were a hard man yourself, and not against using a bit of force when necessary.'

'I don't like violence.'

'Really?' Felinde studied the glowing end of his cigar contemplatively. 'You killed a man! That was why you were inside.'

Pryce shook his head. 'I threw a punch and he fell badly. It was an accident, I had no intention of killing him.'

Felinde scowled. 'In that case you are no use to me, so sling your hook!'

'I mightn't be any good as a debt collector, but I'd be first class at handling the bets,' Pryce argued.

Felinde selected a fresh cigar from a gold case and stared at him thoughtfully as he lit it. 'Can you prove it?'

'Willingly! When do I start?'

'Any time you like. Out on the street, as a runner. You bring in the bets and you get commission. It's the same set-up as on the debts you collected.'

'Bookie's runner! Dammo di, mun! It's against the law.'

Felinde blew out a cloud of smoke. 'Most things are.'

'What happens if I get caught?'

'With a record like yours you'd go straight back inside. I should think they'd take great delight in rapping it across you,' he added cynically.

Pryce wanted to refuse, but the thought of being completely penniless made him exercise caution. Refuse and he'd be back scavenging in bins, or begging on street corners.

'I'll give it a go,' he said grudgingly. 'Where do I start?'

Felinde stubbed out his half-smoked cigar. 'Anywhere you bleeding like. You've got the whole of Cardiff to pick and choose from. It's up to you, so get started! Shut the door as you go out,' he added dismissively.

Pryce stood his ground. 'You've got other runners. They must have their own patches. If I poach, there's going to be blue murder.'

Felinde shrugged. 'That's up to you, Pritchard.

You've just told me that you hate violence, so let's hope you can either talk your way out of things or else run fast.'

As he left the building Pryce knew he had reached rock bottom. He hadn't simply been sacked, he'd been given a suicidal option. If he went touting for bets, the man whose territory he was poaching would probably kill him. If he got away with that, but was caught working as a bookie's runner by the police, he'd be back inside. If that happened they'd show no mercy, and he'd be doing another stretch before he could blink an eye.

He'd been determined not to ask Sabrina for any help, but it now looked as though he had no alternative. She'd mentioned finding him work as a doorman at some club or other.

The thought of dressing up in uniform and bowing and scraping to people wasn't his idea of a worthwhile career. Yet, if that was the only way he was going to keep body and soul together, there was no alternative but to accept her offer.

He simply had to have a regular pay packet so that he could move into decent lodgings and buy some new clothes. Then, and only then, could he return to Pontdarw and find out if Rhianon would have him back.

Chapter Thirty-Two

'If I have to tell them where you live,' Sabrina said exasperatedly, 'once they hear it's a room at Old Megan's dosshouse they'd know right away that you were a down-and-out.'

'I realise that, but I'm planning to move into decent digs the moment I get my first pay packet,' Pryce argued.

Sabrina shook her head. 'It's no good. You won't get the job, or any job for that matter, not while you're living there.'

Pryce rubbed a hand over his unshaven chin. 'Well, can you get me an advance, or give me a loan, to tide me over for a few weeks . . . until I get my first pay?'

'No, I'm not going to do that,' Sabrina replied.

'Why not? I promise I'll pay you back.'

'It's not that. It's because I've already made you an offer, Pryce, and you've turned it down.'

He shook his head emphatically. 'I don't want to move in with you, Sabrina!'

'Why not? Don't you trust yourself alone with me?' she mocked, her eyes challenging.

He shrugged, but his eyes darkened ominously. 'Perhaps it's because I don't think I can trust you,' he countered.

She smiled up at him seductively, her hand resting on his arm. 'Most men would jump at the chance of sharing my flat with me.'

He shook her hand away. He knew what she was saying was quite true, but he wasn't most men. He stared at her, almost as if he was seeing her for the first time. She had every reason to be confident of her sexual allure. Slim yet curvaceous, with her shoulder-length glossy hair framing her face, luminous eyes, peaches-and-cream complexion and kissable mouth, she was most men's fantasy of the perfect woman.

Pryce knew, to his cost, that she was passionate. He also knew she was dangerous. He'd been ensnared once by her spell and paid the penalty.

He'd tasted those charms and knew only too well the risk entailed. He'd never completely obliterated from his mind the sound of her voice as she egged him and Hwyel on to fight, or the elation and excitement afterwards as they made love. It had been uncontrollable animal passion, and it had seared his mind.

He shuddered. Some men might embrace such feelings, but he'd felt ashamed and full of remorse the moment he'd regained his senses.

It had been lust, not love, and the last thing he wanted was a repeat performance.

'My offer stands,' Sabrina told him, cutting into his reverie of the past. 'Move into my flat so you have a decent address, and I'll make sure you are taken on as a doorman at the Dragon Club.'

'I'll think about it.'

She shrugged. She didn't offer him a drink or anything to eat, although she knew he must be starving. All she did was show him the door.

Frustrated and angry, he stormed out.

Outside, after the warmth of Sabrina's cosy flat, the cold November wind cut like a knife. There was an icy mist sweeping in from the Bristol Channel, wrapping itself like a clinging wet cobweb over everything. Pryce passed a hand over his face, then wiped it down his thin jacket. His clothes were so threadbare that they provided no warmth whatsoever, merely sufficient coverage to maintain decency.

The pavement beneath his feet was wet and slippery, and the holes in the soles of his shoes let in the damp and cold. As the wind whipped the thin material of his trousers against his bare legs he shivered.

Cold and hungry, he hurried back to his dingy room in the gloomy dosshouse that stank of cabbage, urine and the sweat of a dozen men who hardly ever washed or changed their clothes.

He pulled up sharp when he found he was unable to open the door to his room. He pushed, then put his shoulder to it. It couldn't be locked, none of the rooms had locks, only bolts, but they were on the inside of the door.

Old Megan claimed that none of her lodgers had anything worth stealing, so there was no need of locks. The bolts on the inside were simply to give them some protection, when they were in bed at night, from men coming home late too drunk to tell which room was their own. Bolting the door was a safeguard to make sure that you weren't stabbed to death in your sleep.

Angrily, Pryce cursed and shouted, then banged furiously on the door. Some drunken bugger had gone into his room by mistake.

The noise disturbed everyone else on the landing, as well as Old Megan. She came padding out of her kitchen on the floor below and yelled up at him to cut the din.

'Some silly bugger's in my room and he's bolted the door. I can't get in there,' he bellowed back down at her.

As he spoke the door swung open. A massive Nigerian filled the doorway. His white teeth gleamed like tombstones as he grinned at Pryce's anger and discomfort.

'Who the bloody hell are you, and what are you doing in my room?' Pryce demanded.

'Duw anwyl, there's a fool you are, Pryce Pritchard,' Old Megan puffed as she reached the top of the stairs. 'You've no room here any more, you haven't paid your rent, see!'

'Talk sense, woman,' he snarled angrily, 'I paid you last Friday.'

'And today is Friday again,' she cackled. 'Now get out before I wake up my Ivor and set him on you.'

'Ivor? That has-been!' Pryce said contemptuously.

Ivor, her thirty-year-old son, was all brawn and no brain. He lived with his mother, did all the heavy work around the place and acted as a bodyguard whenever she needed one.

'Don't trouble disturbing him, ma'am,' the Nigerian chuckled. 'Just stand out of my way and I'll soon deal with this unwelcome intruder.'

Before Pryce could speak or move he found himself picked up bodily, carried down the stairs and then tossed out into the road as if he was a bundle of rubbish.

By the time he had picked himself up the front door had been slammed shut.

Furiously he banged on it, but no one answered. Rage blinding him, he turned away as he heard Old Megan's raucous laughter coming from inside.

The cold bit into his bones, the fine mist was now a heavy drizzle, wet and freezing as it soaked through his clothing to his skin.

Sabrina merely raised her eyebrows and smiled superciliously when, half an hour later, he knocked on the door of her flat again. Wordlessly she ran him a hot bath and while he lay back in it, thawing out and luxuriating in its warmth, the tantalising smell and sound of sausages, eggs and fried bread sizzling and spluttering wafted in from the adjacent kitchen.

Refreshed and dry, wrapped in a fluffy pink dressing gown of Sabrina's, topped by a warm blanket, Pryce ate hungrily. Food had never tasted so good.

His plate cleared, he moved into an armchair in front of the glowing fire. With a contented sigh he accepted the large cup of strong coffee that Sabrina handed him.

Sabrina cleared away the remains of the meal and stacked the dirty dishes in the sink. Then she sat down facing Pryce, nursing her own cup of coffee.

She felt smug. Her plan had finally worked – although it had taken much longer for Pryce to capitulate than she had expected. Still, taking the night off had paid dividends. Aided by the co-operation of Old Megan and Felinde, matters had reached a highly satisfactory conclusion. Pryce had caved in at last.

Now that he had accepted her hospitality, she hoped that he would also be ready to resume their relationship. Her feelings for him were so intense that he filled her thoughts night and day. She wanted him. No matter how long it might take, she intended to win him and ensure that he put all thoughts of Rhianon out of his mind.

Pryce accepting her hospitality was only the first step in her scheme. She wanted so much more than that, but she wasn't too sure how to go about it.

'So what happened to the kid then?'

Pryce's unexpected question startled her.

She thought quickly, determined to win as

much sympathy from him as she could. She was tempted to tell him that Davyn had died, but she was afraid if she said that, he might simply dismiss the entire incident from his mind.

That wasn't what she wanted. To extract the maximum sympathy from him, she needed to pile on the agony, she decided. If she elaborated about the predicament she'd found herself in, she could make him feel so guilty that he'd do anything she asked of him.

She sniffed delicately. 'I don't want to talk about it,' she said in a strangled whisper.

He shrugged. 'As you wish.'

Realising he was going to drop the subject, she brought tears into play.

'It haunts me all the time,' she said, looking up at him pathetically. 'He was such a lovely baby, everyone said so.'

There was a mixture of pride and wistfulness in her voice as she added, 'Our little boy . . . your son!'

'So where is he? When you met me the day I came out of prison you said someone was looking after him. Was that the truth or did you finally manage to persuade Rhianon to go ahead and have him adopted?'

She buried her face in her hands, her shoulders shaking. 'There was no other way, I had to let him go . . . what else could I do?'

'What do you mean by let him go?'

'I tried to keep him, it broke my heart . . . I had to do it . . . it was what was best for him . . .'

'So what did you do? Put him in a home or have him adopted?'

'I let another woman take him,' she whispered, her face tear-streaked as she looked up at him. 'It was what Rhianon thought was best. He will be a toddler now, my own darling child . . . your son!'

Pryce frowned. 'That was what you wanted to do, though, wasn't it? Get him out of your life, put it all behind you and start afresh?'

'In the end it was what Rhianon thought I should do for the best,' Sabrina repeated, dabbing at her eyes with her handkerchief.

There was an uncomfortable silence, then she was suddenly racked by sobs and a torrent of tears coursed down her cheeks. Unable to stand her grief he pulled her into his arms, urging her to be calm.

'You did what you thought was for the best. I don't hold it against you,' he whispered. 'I can understand the dilemma you were in.'

She sighed deeply, struggling to stem her crying as she pressed herself into the warm comfort of his body. Clinging to him desperately, her shoulders continued to shake, but her sobs slowly decreased. Then she raised her face and her lips sought his.

'Please . . . kiss me, Pryce, to prove you forgive me. I didn't want to let him go because he was part of you, something so very precious to me. Rhianon insisted. She said it was better for all of us. I suppose I shouldn't have listened to her, but she's always been like a mother to me, so naturally I took her advice.'

Pryce hesitated, wondering how he could have got it all so wrong. He was sure that Rhianon had told him that she hadn't wanted to allow the baby to be taken for adoption, the last time she'd visited him in prison.

Wasn't that what they'd quarrelled about? She'd said adoption was what Sabrina wanted, but she thought the child ought to be looked after by his own family. Rhianon had talked about making a home for the three of them when he came out of prison. He was sure she had. Or had he simply imagined all that because it was what he wanted?

As Sabrina reached up with both hands and pulled his face down close to hers, he made no resistance. When her hot enticing lips found his he surrendered once more to the power of her passion, hoping it would obliterate for ever his dreams of being with Rhianon.

Chapter Thirty-Three

Pryce stared aghast, unable to believe what was happening inside the Dragon Club. It was dimly lit, plush, and packed to capacity as he had expected it to be. It was the clientele that made him gasp.

Most of the men wore smart suits, though a few were in naval uniform. The women's attire ranged from extremely low-necked dresses to skimpy shimmering shifts that left little or nothing to the imagination.

Many of the women were bedecked in fur stoles, feather boas, countless rows of dangling glittery necklaces or strings of pearls. It was as if they were trying to conceal their nakedness from the lewd prying eyes of their companions.

Against the thick fug of cigar and cigarette smoke he could see that a number of the men had already selected a woman for their evening's entertainment. Some of them weren't even waiting to take their women off to private rooms, but were physically mauling them in front of everyone.

When Sabrina had told him she could get him a job as a doorman at the Dragon Club, he'd assumed that it was a gambling den. He hadn't bothered to go and look at it. He had become so scruffy since living at Old Megan's doss-house that he knew if he paid them a visit he'd be turned away, and probably chased off the premises.

Now that he was inside for the very first time, he realised with amazement that the club where Sabrina had told him she worked as a hostess was nothing more than a high-class brothel.

Ten days holed up in Sabrina's cosy flat above the club, enjoying the warmth and good food, had made him feel like a new man. After a shopping trip at Sabrina's expense he looked like a new man as well.

The charcoal grey suit, the crisp white shirt and the plain red tie had been chosen by Sabrina, but met with his full approval. He'd also persuaded her to advance him enough money to buy a dark grey Melton overcoat and a dark grey trilby. These, together with his highly polished black brogues, completed his smart new wardrobe.

He felt respectable enough to go and visit Rhianon, but it was out of the question. When he'd tentatively suggested to Sabrina that they took a trip to Pontdarw over the weekend she'd bristled.

'In this weather! It's freezing! Far better if we stay here and you get your strength back, ready to start work on Monday.'

In clipped tones she'd gone on to remind him that Rhianon didn't want to see him ever again.

'It's because of the adoption. She thought you should have backed her on that. When you said it was up to me to make the choice, you were going against her.'

He looked confused. 'The child was yours, so I thought you had every right to make the final decision,' he told her logically.

'Rhianon didn't agree with that! I wasn't making the decision she wanted me to make, was I?'

He frowned, but said no more. He'd talk to Rhianon about it when he went to see her. It wasn't like her to be unco-operative, so he suspected that there might be more to it than Sabrina was telling him.

He knew he should consider himself lucky that Sabrina was doing so much for him as well as finding him a job. She pandered to his every whim, cooked him wonderful meals, was generous with the drink, and then sapped his strength with her possessive love-making.

He knew many men would have thought they were in heaven. Even when he was lying in her arms, though, completely sated after a passionate interlude, it was still Rhianon who filled his mind.

No one would ever replace Rhianon in his thoughts or in his heart. He desperately wanted to resolve the misunderstanding between them. It haunted him by day as well as by night. It was the only reason he had agreed to Sabrina's terms, to move in with her and to let her find him a job.

He'd known what she expected in return, but although he complied it was not what he wanted. Explaining that to her was impossible. He had never felt helpless in a woman's presence before, he thought, as he mulled over the situation he was in. Sabrina was not merely demanding, she gave herself to him so wholeheartedly, and she was so compelling in her approach, that he had found himself weakening and then submitting. After three years' abstention his sexual needs were so intense that he had capitulated guiltily to her charms.

Now that he had discovered where she worked, and realised what she'd meant when she said she was a hostess at the club, he felt uneasy. Perhaps Rhianon had been right after all when she had tried to oppose Sabrina's decision to have the child adopted? Could this false, brash existence perhaps be Sabrina's way of finding oblivion from the guilt she was harbouring?

Rhianon waited with growing impatience and anxiety for some word from Pryce. She couldn't understand his silence. She knew he was out of prison. Even if he didn't have any feelings for her after all this time, surely he would want to see his son?

It was only a couple of weeks away from Christmas, and she wondered if she should make the first move. Yet how could she when she had no idea where he might be living? She wasn't even sure if he was still in Cardiff.

There had been no news from Sabrina, either. Several times she wondered if she should go to Cardiff and see her, but she no longer knew if she was still living at the same address, and had no idea where she was working.

A few days later the problem of what to do about contacting Sabrina was resolved when Edwin Webster had another stroke.

'This one is far more severe, I'm afraid,' the doctor told her. 'He may not regain his speech or the use of his limbs. Can you continue nursing him at home or would you like me to have him taken into care? They won't admit him into hospital, so it would have to be the workhouse.'

'No, no!' Rhianon was almost as upset at the thought of her father going into the workhouse as she was by his stroke. 'No, he must stay here. I can manage,' she assured the doctor emphatically.

He frowned. 'Have you any close relatives to help you?'

'A sister, but she lives in Cardiff.'

'I see.' He looked thoughtful. 'I think it might be a good idea if you sent for her. Your father's condition is very grave. It is quite possible that it may deteriorate further during the next week, so she might like to see him while he can still recognise her.'

Shivers ran down Rhianon's spine at his words. She nodded numbly, her eyes fixed on the frail figure of her father, barely discernible beneath the bedcovers. He was now a shadow of the broad-shouldered upright man she remembered from her childhood.

Nothing had been the same for them since the fateful day of the fight between Pryce and Hwyel. The shame of being denigrated at Capel Bethel by Hwyel's father, and his name being struck from the list of lay preachers, had been a terrible blow for Edwin Webster.

His decline had accelerated rapidly after Sabrina had gone to Cardiff. Although he had been the one who said he never wanted her name mentioned in his house again, Rhianon was sure that if Sabrina had come home for good, and tried to make amends, everything would have returned to normal.

The trouble was, Sabrina was as stubborn as her father. Neither of them was capable of seeing the other person's point of view, or of ever admitting to being in the wrong. The word 'sorry' was not in the vocabulary of either of them.

It was probably too late now to build bridges, but she hoped that Sabrina would answer her call.

Surely she would and come and see her father for one more time so that they could be reconciled with each other, if only to allow him to die in peace?

The moment the doctor left she wrote to Sabrina, using the last address she knew and marking on it, 'Please forward if moved'. By using a postcard, rather than a letter, she hoped that whoever received it would read it and realise the urgency of the message.

It was Pryce, not Sabrina, who picked up the postcard and read the poignant message. He said nothing as he handed it to Sabrina, but waited impatiently for her comment.

When she merely dropped it on the table and went on eating her breakfast as though nothing had happened, he could contain himself no longer.

'We'll have to go, it's the decent thing to do,' he stated.

'We? What on earth do you want to visit my father for, even if he is dying? He never had a good word to say about you and I didn't think you thought very much of him, either.'

'Perhaps the time is right for me to make my peace with him,' Pryce said contritely.

'You think he would like to see you, do you?' She laughed derisively. 'If anything was going to finish him off, then a visit from you would certainly do it.'

'Rhianon might need some help with looking after him, if he's as ill as she says. We ought to go and find out,' Pryce insisted stiffly, ignoring her crude jibe.

She stared at him frostily. 'You're not suggesting that I should play the prodigal daughter and go home and help nurse him, I hope?'

He shook his head. 'No, I can't see that happening. I still think we ought to make sure, though, that the burden isn't proving too much for Rhianon. Since we are both working, perhaps we can offer to pay for someone to help her.'

'We can do that without traipsing all the way to Pontdarw!' She waved the flimsy piece of card in front of his face. 'There's such things as letters, you know.'

'Duw anwyl! Have you no heart, girl!' The temper he'd held in check suddenly erupted. His eyes became black flints and his mouth tightened into a grim line. 'What's the matter with you?'

'There's nothing the matter with me, but I can see that you have an overwhelming hankering to visit Rhianon,' she retaliated.

'And what is so wrong about that?'

'I'll leave you to answer that. Don't forget, though, that I've been the one who has stood by you. I was the one who was waiting outside the prison gates the day you were released. I'm the one who has shared her home with you, put clothes on your back, food in your belly and made sure you've got a decent job.'

Pryce ran a hand through his hair. 'I know, and I'm truly grateful!'

'Truly grateful!' she mimicked sourly. 'Oh yes, you're truly grateful. You've been happy to sleep with me too! Now, when there's the chance of seeing Rhianon again, you can't wait to dash to her side.'

'That's not quite true. I could have gone to

see her any time over the last two months but . . .'

'But you had no decent clobber to go in. You still haven't got the money for your train fare, unless I am prepared to give it to you! And when you do get paid at the end of the month,' she reminded him scathingly, 'you owe me a tidy wedge for the clothes you stand up in, as well as for all the food and accommodation I've provided for you.'

He nodded in agreement. 'I'm only too aware of all that,' he said curtly. 'I still feel we should do something to help Rhianon.'

Sabrina shrugged. 'I'll think about it. There's no rush.'

'From what Rhianon has written on that card, your father is in a pretty bad state and getting worse all the time.'

'So what are you implying?'

'That you should go and see him as soon as possible, of course!'

'I might. I wouldn't stay, though.'

'No one is suggesting you should. If we leave first thing in the morning and return late afternoon, we would be back in time for work.'

'I *said* I'll think about it.'

Pryce left it at that. He knew that to insist or try and push Sabrina into action would only make her resentful. She would then probably decide not to visit at all.

Sabrina knew she had to deal with the matter, but it wasn't easy deciding what to do. If she let Pryce come with her to Pontdarw, he was going to find out that the story she had told him about Davyn being adopted wasn't completely true. Adopted, yes, but not by a stranger, as she had led him to believe. Furthermore, she didn't want Pryce and Rhianon meeting up. She supposed it had to happen sometime, but the longer she could put it off the better.

She was very much afraid that once Pryce set eyes on Rhianon again, all the old feelings he had for her might be revived. After all the hard work she'd done to win him over, she had no intention of losing out to her sister.

Chapter Thirty-Four

His first sight of Rhianon sent the blood pounding in Pryce's head. She was exactly as he remembered her: beautiful, calm, her thick dark hair shining. Her warm welcoming smile stirred the very core of his being, sending a thrill, and a longing for her, right through him.

Hesitantly, murmuring a conventional greeting, he placed a hand on her shoulder and kissed her chastely on the cheek.

He ached to gather her into his arms, and hold her close. He longed to express all the passion that had built up for her inside him over the years. Instinct warned him that the moment was not right.

As he pulled back he studied her face, and was saddened to see the tiny lines beneath her lovely dark eyes. They were telltale signs of strain, and he guessed that they'd been caused by the problems she'd had to deal with over the last few years. To some extent, he thought reluctantly, he had been the source of many of those worries.

He would have liked nothing better than to be able to turn the clock back to the start of the miners' strike, that bright spring day three and a half years ago. The fight had released so much bad feeling, evil, lust, hate, that it had set off a landslide of disaster in all their lives.

The teaching careers that he and Rhianon had been struggling to achieve had been sacrificed, as had his dreams of their future together. Sabrina had been on the verge of marrying Hwyel, but those plans, too, had disappeared for ever. Everything had gone wrong from the moment he had landed that fatal punch and Hwyel had gone down and crashed his head against the curb.

Even Edwin Webster's life had been affected by the event. Almost overnight his position had changed: from being one of the most respected men in Pontdarw, he had become a pariah. The moment that Cledwyn Barker had turned against him, he had been ostracised by the rest of the townsfolk.

Religion had been such an important mainstay in Edwin Webster's life, and Pryce could understand what a bitter blow it must have been to be forbidden ever again to address the congregation at Capel Bethel.

'You've only just got here in time,' Rhianon warned her sister as they exchanged greetings. She knew her voice was sharp but she found it harrowing to see them together. 'You'd better come upstairs and see Father right away.'

Sabrina frowned. 'I need to thaw out first!' She unfastened her coat and held her gloved hands out to the fire. 'It was bitterly cold on the train, I thought that you'd at least have the kettle on,' she added crossly.

'It has boiled, so it won't take a minute to make the tea. I've got everything all ready so I'll do it right away,' Rhianon said quickly. 'Do you want to go on upstairs and see Father while the tea is brewing?'

'Stop rushing me. I've already told you, I'm shrammed right through. I need a cuppa first and a chance to get warm.'

Rhianon nodded. She turned away and began laying out cups and saucers for the three of them, together with milk and sugar and a plate of freshly made bakestones. Then she poured the boiling water into the teapot, set it down on the table and covered it with a tea cosy.

'Can you help yourselves? I must go back upstairs and see if Father is all right. Come on up when you are ready.'

By the time Sabrina finally came upstairs, Edwin Webster had slipped into a semi-coma and seemed to be unaware of her presence.

Tears trickling down her cheeks, Rhianon ran back downstairs to Pryce. 'I think he's dying!' she whispered anguishedly. 'Will you go for the doctor, please?'

Silently he nodded. Both of them knew there was little to be gained from the doctor's presence. Nevertheless, Pryce shrugged on his overcoat and rammed his grey trilby onto his head as he made for the door.

As Rhianon came back up to the bedroom,

Sabrina moved towards the window, covering her face with her hands. 'I can't stand this,' she whimpered. 'I can't bear to sit here at Dad's bedside and see him like this . . .'

'Then go downstairs,' Rhianon said sharply. 'Pryce will be back with the doctor at any moment, so you can open the door for them.'

As Rhianon had anticipated, by the time the doctor arrived it was too late. There was nothing more he, or any of them, could do for Edwin Webster.

Sabrina was in floods of tears, refusing to let go of her father's hand, throwing herself across the bed as she called his name over and over again.

When Pryce firmly moved her away she began berating Rhianon for not letting her know sooner that he was so ill.

Pryce watched with growing anger. He could see that Rhianon was truly upset by her father's death, and that Sabrina's performance was only adding to her distress. He wished there was something he could do to make the situation a little easier for her, and to relieve the tension that Sabrina was causing.

He desperately wanted to take Rhianon in his arms, smooth back her hair, kiss her brow, hold her and comfort her.

'Why don't you take Sabrina for a walk?' she suggested, when for the third time in as many minutes he asked if there was anything he could do. 'If you could get her out of the house for half an hour or so, while Maya Lewis is here laying my father out, that would be a tremendous help,' she explained sadly.

Since it was midday, he suggested to Sabrina that they might go for a drink.

'How can you be so insensitive! To go to the pub at a time like this!'

'I thought a drink might help to steady your nerves,' he explained. 'There's nothing stronger than tea here in the house, so going to the pub seemed like a good idea.'

'I'll make you another cup of tea instead if you would prefer,' Rhianon offered.

'No, no! Let's go to the pub. I need something to fortify my nerves. You've been expecting it to happen.' Sabrina gave a short dry laugh. 'It's probably a relief for you, but to me it is a terrible shock.'

'I do understand,' Rhianon said quietly. 'Don't hurry. Take your time, it will give me and Maya a chance to see to things here.'

Left on her own, Rhianon stood by the side of the bed, holding her father's cold hand. As she said her own goodbye to him she contemplated his life.

Widowed in his forties, he had refused outside help, but dutifully taken over the care of his two daughters himself. People had admired his devotion to his family, but, Rhianon reflected, she had been the one who had borne the brunt of the burden.

He'd expected her not only to act as

housekeeper, but also as a surrogate mother to her younger sister. He had treated them so differently. With her he had been strict and domineering, but he had doted on Sabrina, letting her twist him round her little finger. He'd idolised her and always been determined to ensure that she had the very best life could offer.

He had been a God-fearing man, a pillar of Capel Bethel. He'd been authoritative and hard to please. An unforgiving, unyielding man, his final years had been the bitterest of all. Banned from his beloved chapel, even his faith had brought him no comfort.

After kissing him on the brow, she dried her tears, then pulled up the sheet to cover his face.

'You should have left it all to me, cariad, and gone for a drink with Sabrina and that Pryce Pritchard,' Maya told her when she finally came downstairs after her work was completed. 'You used to be sweet on that Pryce once, didn't you?' she remarked as she accepted the cup of tea Rhianon had ready for her, and helped herself to one of the bakestones.

'He was a good friend,' Rhianon murmured non-committally.

After Maya left, Rhianon went back upstairs to take a last look at her father. Maya had done her work well. Dressed in a white shirt and his best dark suit, some of his old authority seemed to have been restored. He looked dignified, Rhianon reflected, like the man she had respected and obeyed.

'That sister of yours eventually turned up then,' Angharad, her next-door neighbour, commented when Rhianon went to collect Davyn. 'Only got here just in time by the look of things! I saw them arrive and the next minute I saw that Pryce Pritchard chasing off for the doctor. Where are they now then, gone back to Cardiff?'

'No, I asked Sabrina and Pryce to go out while Maya did what had to be done,' Rhianon explained.

Angharad sniffed. 'So they're both coming back to the house again then, are they?'

'Yes, any minute now.'

'See a difference in young Davyn, won't she! You can leave him here with me until after she's gone back to Cardiff, if you like,' she added shrewdly.

'No! That's kind of you, but I think they will both want to see Davyn,' Rhianon murmured, stretching out her hand to the child.

After she was back in her own house, Rhianon wondered if this was a wise move. Before she could change her mind and take Davyn back to stay with Angharad, she heard Pryce and Sabrina at the door.

Shyly, Davyn shrank back, clutching tightly at Rhianon's skirt, half-hiding behind her, as the two of them walked in.

Gently, Rhianon pulled him forward, holding his hand firmly, but not forcing him to move any closer to either Sabrina or Pryce.

There was a look of amazement on Pryce's

face as he stared at the child in silence. Rhianon saw the fury in Sabrina's eyes, and realised that her sister hadn't told Pryce that Davyn was here in Pontdarw or that she was looking after him.

'What the hell is he doing here?' Sabrina hissed furiously. She faced Pryce angrily. 'You know who this is, don't you! This is your kid,' she muttered resentfully.

He ran the palm of his hand over his chin. 'I don't understand! Exactly what is going on?' His question was directed at Sabrina, so Rhianon waited for her sister to explain.

The silence was so tense that Rhianon found she was trembling. Eventually Sabrina let fly at her. 'You did this deliberately to provoke me and make things difficult between me and Pryce,' she fumed, her lovely face contorted with rage.

Rhianon shook her head. 'Don't be ridiculous! Davyn lives here, you know that perfectly well.'

'He wasn't here when we arrived,' Sabrina scowled accusingly.

'No, Angharad from next door was looking after him. She collected him about half an hour before you came, to give me a break.'

'So why couldn't you leave him where he was until after we'd gone again?' Sabrina said sulkily.

'Her husband, Parry, is due home from the pit at any minute. Angharad has to get his bath and his meal ready for when he comes in, so it didn't seem fair to impose on her any longer.'

'It's not fair to spring this on me, either. You promised never to let Pryce know anything at all about our arrangement.'

'I haven't breathed a word to him. If you hadn't flown off the handle, he would never have known who Davyn was. You were the one who told him,' Rhianon pointed out.

'Don't talk so daft! You must think everyone's as twp as you are,' Sabrina sneered. 'Of course he'd know whose kid it was.'

'I think it's about time you told me the truth,' Pryce intervened. 'You said he'd been adopted. You told me how heartbroken you were at having to give him up. You explained you'd done it because you thought it was the only way he'd have a decent future. All of that is lies, isn't it, Sabrina? Go on, admit it.'

'There's no need to shout and bawl like a madman,' Sabrina protested tearfully. 'I did what Rhianon made me do. I wanted to have him adopted. I wanted to put it all behind me and start afresh. She was the one who wouldn't let me.'

'So you lied to me,' Pryce insisted. 'You never intended me to know that you'd kept him?'

'I didn't lie to you . . . not exactly, anyway. I'm not the one who has kept him. He has been adopted just like I told you. Rhianon has adopted him!'

'Duw anwyl! Is this the truth?' He looked from one to the other of them in disbelief.

Rhianon nodded. 'Yes, Sabrina is telling you

the truth. I adopted him because I couldn't bring myself to let your child be brought up by strangers,' she added quietly.

Pryce hunkered down in front of the little boy and held out a hand. 'Are you going to come and say hello to me?' he invited.

Davyn buried his face in Rhianon's skirt, then slowly peeped out from behind it. Gently Rhianon propelled him forward.

'Come on Davyn, say hello,' she encouraged. 'Say hello to your dadda.'

Chapter Thirty-Five

Pryce and Sabrina made the journey back to Cardiff in almost complete silence. Both of them were occupied with their own thoughts and though, to some extent, these ran parallel, neither of them were ready to share them.

Sabrina was furious about the way Pryce had discovered what had happened to Davyn. She supposed, looking back, she had been naïve to think that if Pryce accompanied her to Pontdarw, Rhianon wouldn't spill the beans.

Rhianon could have said that he was a neighbour's child and Pryce would never have known the difference, she thought irritably. Given the age of the boy, he might have been suspicious, but proving anything would have been another matter.

It had most likely been a deliberate ploy on Rhianon's part, she reflected angrily, or else sheer vindictiveness. She never approved of me wanting to have him adopted, she mused. She has always insisted that I ought to bring the kid up myself.

She stared out of the window at the darkening December landscape, and then smiled to herself as an idea came into her mind.

Perhaps that was the solution to keeping Pryce attentive. She'd seen the look on his face when he'd been playing with Davyn. He was besotted by him. She had found the answer to her problem, she thought triumphantly. If she took the child back, said she wanted them to be a family, she was pretty certain he would stay with her so that he could be with his son.

Pryce was also deep in his own thoughts, and like Sabrina's they centred on Davyn. It was the very first time he'd seen him, and he couldn't believe the child was his. He was utterly enchanting; so sturdy, handsome and brimful of mischief, already a little character.

Rhianon was doing a wonderful job of raising him. He looked the picture of health and already he was learning obedience and manners. He'd watched the way she'd encouraged the boy to speak to him, the gentleness of her voice when she'd reproved him, the love in her eyes and on her face as she took him in her arms.

There was a similar response from the child. It was obvious that Davyn adored her. The way he flung his arms around her neck and planted big wet kisses on her cheeks, the way he looked up at her for approval when he complied with what she asked him to do, told their own story.

Had things turned out differently, by now he and Rhianon would have been married, he thought sadly. Davyn could have been theirs and they would have been happily settled as a family, and living in their own home.

If Rhianon really had adopted Davyn, that might still be possible, he pondered. He would have to break free from Sabrina, find some other job, and get some money together. Only then would he be able to ask Rhianon if she was still willing to marry him.

Now that her father was dead and she was going to be on her own, surely she would give his proposal serious consideration? It would be good for Davyn to have a man in his life as he was growing up.

It was such a perfect solution that he felt elation building inside him. It would be a new start for him, as well as for Rhianon and Davyn. He couldn't wait to begin planning the next step. He was determined to make it work. He still loved Rhianon fervently, and he would happily spend the rest of his life making up to her for the heartache he'd caused her by his reckless behaviour.

It was raining when they reached Cardiff, and as they emerged from the railway station Sabrina made straight for the taxicab rank without saying a word to him. That she was the one to take the initiative riled him almost unbearably.

As he settled himself alongside her he felt like a kept man, and that made him still more furious. They were going back to her flat. He was wearing clothes she had paid for and within the hour he would be at the Dragon Club doing the job she had found for him, working more or less under her command.

His gorge rose. He hadn't spent three years in prison, atoning for the mishap that had resulted from her goading him and Hwyel to fight, to become her lackey. He squared his shoulders. No one dictated terms to him. His cellmates had recognised that and left him well alone. Or had it been his reputation as a killer that had made it easy for him to gain their respect?

He sighed, knowing he could not afford to upset Sabrina, not as matters stood at the moment. Yet he couldn't let things continue as they were. Now that he had seen Rhianon again he had no doubts that he still loved her deeply, and that Sabrina meant nothing to him.

He was determined to go back to Pontdarw on his own at the first opportunity, and find out how Rhianon felt about him. Out of respect for Edwin Webster he'd have to wait until after the funeral, of course. Ahead of that he would most certainly deal with the situation between himself and Sabrina.

He had no intention of letting their relationship develop as she seemed to think it would. He didn't love her, he never had. His moment of foolishness was behind him, and since she had made it plain that she didn't want their child, he would do whatever Rhianon would permit to make himself responsible for Davyn's welfare.

He had no idea what financial arrangements Sabrina had made with her sister for the child. It seemed obvious from the shabbiness of the house in Rhoslyn Terrace that whatever Sabrina was providing was nowhere near adequate.

They were already late when they reached the club, so there was no opportunity for them to talk before they started work. And by the time the club closed they were both far too exhausted to think clearly, let alone discuss such a complicated issue.

To Pryce's surprise, Sabrina was not only up before him next morning, but dressed and cooking breakfast when he walked into the kitchen at half past nine.

'You're up early,' he remarked. 'Something on your mind?'

She nodded, poured out a cup of strong tea and handed it to him.

'We've got to talk.'

'Yes, we have,' he said firmly. 'To start with . . .'

Before he could tell her that he had no intention of continuing as they were, that it was impossible for them to go on working together and living under the same roof, she interrupted him.

'Let me speak first! I know you want an explanation about Davyn. It's not the way you think.' She looked up at him from under lowered lids. 'I couldn't bear to let him go, because he was yours,' she said softly. 'That was why I asked Rhianon to care for him.'

He stared at her in perplexity.

'I've been sending her money each week,' she went on quickly. 'I've been meaning to tell you about it, but I was waiting for the right moment. I thought I ought to wait until you had found your feet and built a life for yourself.'

'And then you were going to explain everything?'

'Of course! I don't want to have any secrets from you!' She moved closer, laying a hand on his arm and smiling up at him.

He looked at her coldly. 'So what happens now? Do you want us to set up home together and then have Davyn back so that we all live together, and pretend to be the perfect family?' he asked sarcastically.

She sighed. 'I want us to live together, but I'm not sure that Davyn would fit in. It might be a problem while I'm still working.'

'So you weren't thinking of giving up your job and devoting all your time to your son?'

Her eyebrows shot up. 'Is that what you want me to be . . . a proper wife and mother?' she asked innocently.

He shrugged. 'I certainly think Davyn deserves a proper home, but I don't think it should be with you,' he told her frankly. 'You didn't even speak to him . . .'

'I couldn't! I love him so much that it would have broken my heart if he'd put his dear little arms around my neck and called me mummy!'

'I don't think it was very likely he'd do that,

366

do you? My bet is that he hadn't seen you for so long that he didn't know you from the wallpaper.'

'Pryce! How can you be so cruel?'

'The person he thinks of as his mother is Rhianon. That's clear from the way he looks at her and the way he does what she tells him. To take him away from her now would not only break his heart, but wreck his life as well.'

Sabrina pouted. 'Of course he knows her better than he does me, but that's because he's with her all the time.'

'And you'd take him away from her and destroy all that love and trust!'

Sabrina looked uneasy. 'I certainly don't want to disrupt his life and make things difficult for him. I know,' she clapped her hands together, 'we could let Rhianon come with him! As a sort of paid nursemaid,' she added brightly.

'To be under your thumb night and day, the same as I am?'

Sabrina bristled. 'I don't know what you mean! We are very happy, aren't we?'

'Are we?' His dark eyes were cold and unfathomable as he studied her face.

'We could be if you would put the past behind you,' she said sulkily. 'If you put both Rhianon and the kid out of your mind, we'd be able to build a life together.'

He stepped away from her, shaking his head firmly.

'Oh, come on, Pryce. Stop living in a dream

world. You know we can be good together, you know you want me as much as I want you.'

'That simply isn't true.'

Her face became angry, its prettiness distorted. 'You always were a selfish sod. You take whatever I offer and yet you give nothing in return.'

Pryce shook his head. 'Far from it! I am grateful to you for providing a roof over my head and finding a job for me, but I can't go on being indebted to you. Living here with you is not what I want . . .'

'No! What you want is Rhianon, isn't it?' she snapped. 'Don't bother denying it. I saw the way you were looking at her yesterday, and behaving like a lovesick schoolboy!'

Pryce made no attempt to deny her accusation. 'Then perhaps you understand the dilemma I'm in,' he said gravely.

'If you think I am going to stand back and wish you good luck you are very much mistaken,' she laughed scornfully. 'I've no intention of letting Rhianon get her claws into you again. I've taken you away from her once and I'll do it again. If you make any attempt to go and see her then watch out,' she railed.

'What good will that do? I've already explained that I don't love you, Sabrina.'

'I love you, though, and I want you. I'm even willing to have the child living with us if that's what you want; if that is what it takes to hold onto you. One thing I will not agree to is

Rhianon keeping him and the two of you setting up home together, so don't think for one minute that I will.'

Their argument lasted all morning, becoming ever more heated and bitter. When she found that he was determined not to stay with her, Sabrina castigated Pryce in every way possible.

Within an hour of starting work later in the day he was summoned to the office and told by Lorenzo, the Maltese manager of the club, that his services were no longer needed. 'You are not the sort of person we wish to employ at the Dragon Club.'

'I understand,' Pryce said grimly. He suspected that Sabrina was behind this move, so he didn't ask for an explanation, or put up a fight. In some ways it suited him, because it forced him into making the decision he knew was inevitable.

'Give me my money then and I'll be off,' he said calmly.

'Money?'

'Wages for the three nights owing to me.'

Lorenzo tipped back his chair and laughed in disbelief. 'You're getting no more money, you've been overpaid ever since you started work here. In fact, I would say you owe us money.'

As Pryce struggled to hold his temper in check, his hands automatically curled into fists.

Lorenzo was quick to notice and pressed a

bell hidden underneath his desk. Within seconds the door opened and two burly members of the kitchen staff were standing there. One of them was holding a long-bladed knife, which he waved menacingly.

Pryce raised both hands in submission. 'I'm going,' he said curtly.

'And remember to return that uniform you're wearing, it belongs to the club,' Lorenzo called after him. Pryce made no reply, but he felt his temper rising as he heard the gusts of laughter behind him.

He was quite sure that Sabrina had instigated his dismissal not only to humiliate him, but to prove her power. It was an attempt to make him change his mind and come to heel, but it only made him more determined to free himself from her clutches before she wreaked some even greater form of revenge.

Upstairs in Sabrina's flat, he took all the new clothes she had bought for him out of the wardrobe they shared, and folded them into a neat pile together with his uniform. Then he dressed in the thin shabby clothes that he'd been wearing when he'd come out of prison.

He counted up the money that was in his pocket. It was less than five pounds. As he left the warm comfortable flat and went out into the dank night, to start looking for some cheap digs, his spirits soared. For the first time in over three years he felt he was his own man.

He had no idea what the future would bring,

but he was determined that in time it would take him back to Pontdarw, so that he could be reunited with Rhianon.

With Rhianon and his son.

Chapter Thirty-Six

Edwin Webster's funeral was held on 30th December, a bitterly cold frosty Monday.

Sabrina attended, looking very chic and alluring in a sweeping black fur coat and a heavily veiled black fur hat pulled low over her eyes. To Rhianon's surprise she came alone.

'Pryce felt it wasn't right for him to attend since he isn't one of the family,' she explained. 'At least not yet,' she added with a simpering laugh.

Rhianon's heart sank. Ever since their visit ten days ago, she had been in emotional turmoil, haunted by mixed thoughts about Pryce. He had seemed so pleased to see her, and he had been so taken with Davyn, that it had wrought havoc with her feelings. She had allowed herself to contemplate the possibility that one day the three of them might be together.

A foolish fantasy was apparently all it was ever going to be, she thought morosely. What Sabrina wanted she usually managed to get, and there was no doubt at all in Rhianon's mind that her sister was infatuated with Pryce and determined to have him for herself.

Guiltily she pushed the matter from her mind. This was not the time to think about her own personal problems. Today her thoughts should be concentrated on saying goodbye to her father.

It was a simple funeral service. Apart from herself, and Sabrina, only a few neighbours were at the graveside. No one from Capel Bethel came to pay their last respects to the man who had once been a popular orator. The death of Hwyel Barker at the hands of a man who had been a friend of Edwin Webster's daughter had turned people against him. Though they preached forgiveness they had none in their own hearts, Rhianon thought bitterly.

In a way, she reflected, they were more responsible for her father's death than Pryce was for what had happened to Hwyel. Ostracising him as they had done had been a mortal blow for Edwin Webster.

He had lost all interest in everyone and everything after he'd been banned from his beloved chapel. He had grieved deep within himself, unable to believe that his congregation were capable of shunning him like this.

Sabrina barely spoke to the few neighbours who came to the house afterwards. The atmosphere was so frosty that one by one they quietly made their excuses and left.

'I'll just clear these things away and then I'll go and collect Davyn from Angharad,' Rhianon murmured as she put the used glasses and crockery on a tray. 'That is if you want to see him before you go home?'

'Leave all this clutter for the moment, there are other far more important matters that we have to discuss,' Sabrina said tetchily.

'About Davyn, do you mean?' Rhianon asked uneasily.

Sabrina frowned. 'No! About money . . . the money Dad has left!'

'He hasn't left any money! The only things of any value that remain are his gold watch and the diamond-studded fob on his watch chain.'

'I don't believe you! He must have had savings, money that you have been using to live on for the past two years?'

'No! I told you his savings were almost gone when you came some months back. We've had only his Lloyd George pension and the pittance I've managed to earn by doing knitting for Polly. That is until recently, when you started sending money for Davyn.'

'His pension and your pitiful earnings have not been enough for three of you to live on!' Sabrina said derisively.

'No, that's perfectly true. You can see for yourself that everything that was saleable has had to go. Even the pictures from the walls, and the few things that belonged to Mam! They've all gone. I told you that last time you were here, when you asked where all the ornaments were.'

'Surely you've not sold Mam's bits of jewellery, the ones that were in the ebony box on her dressing table?' Sabrina exclaimed crossly.

Rhianon nodded, looking pale and strained. 'Yes, and the box as well and also Mam's dressing table!'

'I don't believe you, you're lying! You're deliberately trying to deprive me of my share of what is rightly mine,' Sabrina scowled.

Rhianon shook her head. 'We were so hard up I simply had to sell them. That was why I accepted your offer so readily when you said you'd help by sending money each week. Surely you haven't forgotten?'

'Of course I remember that I promised to help out. I've been sending you money, haven't I?'

'Look around you and you'll see for yourself that what I'm saying is true. Now that Father is dead and we won't have his Lloyd George pension money, I shall probably have to sell his watch and fob to help put food on the table, and keep the room we live in warm enough for Davyn.'

Sabrina stared at her angrily. 'You are in this mess because you refused to do what I wanted and have that damned kid adopted,' she said petulantly. 'You're a fool, Rhianon! You've no choice now, though,' she added smugly, 'You can't afford to go on living here, paying the rent and keeping him, so you'll have to let him go after all.'

'No, never!' Rhianon faced her defiantly. 'I'll manage somehow. Even if I have to go out scrubbing floors, I won't give Davyn up. I won't let him suffer the indignity of going into a home or being adopted by strangers.'

'I can make you! He's my child, remember,' Sabrina pointed out triumphantly.

Rhianon shook her head, her dark eyes blazing. 'You're talking nonsense. He might be your flesh and blood, but you renounced all legal right to him when you signed the papers saying you were giving him over to me. I'll fight you in court over that if I have to.'

Sabrina chewed on her lower lip and tried to look contrite. She had to get Davyn back at all costs. He was the bait if she was ever going to control Pryce and keep him loyal.

When she'd persuaded Lorenzo to sack Pryce, she hadn't expected him to walk out on her. She'd intended his dismissal to make him more dependent on her. She'd been shocked when she'd found he'd cleared off and left behind all the clothes and everything else she'd bought for him.

If she took Davyn back to Cardiff with her, Pryce would return. He'd come running, and he'd stay, she had no doubt about that. Without Davyn, though, she knew that Pryce was lost to her . . . for ever.

'When I said I'd make you give him up, Rhianon, I didn't mean that he would go to strangers,' she murmured. 'I must have him back, though. I didn't want to tell you this, because I knew that at one time, before Pryce

went to prison, you were sweet on him yourself. The fact is, Pryce insists that he wants
Davyn back so that the three of us can be
together. I'm sure you can understand that he
wants us to be a proper family,' she added, with
a false smile of commiseration.

Rhianon stared at her sister, her senses reeling under the bitter news. She was aghast to
hear that she was about to lose at a stroke both
the man she loved and the child she adored.

'And is that what you feel is right?' Her eyes
searched her sister's face. She knew Sabrina
wanted Pryce, that she always had, but she still
couldn't believe she wanted Davyn as well.

'If that is Pryce's dream for the future, then
of course I feel it's right,' Sabrina told her.

'You mean you'll have Davyn living with you
in order to hold onto Pryce,' Rhianon said
contemptuously. Her voice rose angrily. 'You
feel nothing whatsoever for the child, admit it!
Yet you'll take him away from me, even though
you know how happy and contented he is here.
You want to take him back to Cardiff, like you
would a kitten or a puppy!'

'Now you are talking ridiculous!'

'No I am not. It's just a whim on your part,
Sabrina! What are you going to do if he doesn't
settle? I know quite well that you will soon get
tired of looking after him. So what happens
then?'

'What you are saying is complete rubbish,'
Sabrina blustered.

377

'No it's not. Davyn is staying here with me and that's all there is to it.'

'You've no choice! I insist on having him back,' Sabrina told her hotly, angry colour flooding her cheeks.

'Insist all you like, I'm not letting you take him,' Rhianon told her coolly.

'Not even if it's what Pryce wants?' Sabrina cajoled.

'I don't believe he knows anything about your plans. Let him come here and tell me to my face that it is what he wants.'

'And then will you let Davyn come to us?'

'When I hear from Pryce himself that that's what he considers is best for Davyn, then I'll think about it,' Rhianon confirmed.

Sabrina sighed dramatically. 'Why make so much fuss about such a simple request? I know I have picked a bad time to ask you – you are upset by the funeral and not thinking straight. Actually, I thought it would be a way of helping you, Rhianon. I'm sure you don't really want to be saddled with a small boy. With Dad gone you've got the chance to make a fresh start and pick up the threads of your own life, do the things you've always wanted to. You could go to college even, and become a teacher like you've always dreamed of.'

Rhianon shook her head firmly. 'Of course I am upset about Father, but it makes no difference to what I feel about Davyn.'

'You could still see him from time to time,' Sabrina wheedled. 'I really am thinking of what's best for you. Face it, Rhianon, he's not really your responsibility. You could be enjoying life, so why make such a sacrifice?'

'Because I love him!' she said passionately. 'I've watched over him every day since he was born, and I'm going to go on doing that until he is old enough to live his own life.'

'And deprive him of having a decent future, you mean, don't you?' Sabrina said sneeringly. 'Drag him up in poverty, never enough money for him to have the sort of possessions kids long to have, bikes and things like that. Probably he won't even have enough to eat, and he'll have to wear second-hand clothes.'

'He'll have all the love and care I can possibly give him. He'll feel secure and he'll know he's wanted. That is far more important than material things.'

'You're impossible. You're selfish, self-centred and bigoted,' Sabrina snapped. 'You've always been bossy. Look at the way you used to order me around when I was little!'

'Only to make sure that you came to no harm,'

'I can remember how miserable I was because of all the things you wouldn't let me do. At least I had Dad to speak up for me and take my side, but Davyn will have no one.'

'You only recall what you want to, Sabrina,' Rhianon told her wearily.

'Maybe! Anyway, are you going next door to collect Davyn or do I have to do it myself?'

Rhianon smiled. 'You can try your luck, but Angharad won't let you have him, Sabrina. She knows as well as I do that you don't give a twopenny damn for Davyn.'

'He's my child! Mine, and Pryce is his father, let me remind you,' Sabrina stormed. 'You're interfering and trying to cause trouble between us because you're jealous.'

'Think what you like, Sabrina. Your words have no effect on me. I know the truth and so do you. You would have had him adopted the minute he was born if I'd let you.'

Sabrina flounced over to the mirror above the fireplace and began titivating her make-up and patting her fur hat into place.

'I've no intention of arguing with you any more, Rhianon,' she said after outlining her mouth with a vivid red lipstick. 'There's other ways, but believe me I *will* have him back,' she vowed ominously.

'If Pryce wants him back then he must come here and tell me so himself,' Rhianon repeated, turning away.

'Will you listen to him?'

'I'll talk it over with him.'

'It's just a ploy to get him here, to try and get him away from me, isn't it?'

'If you are so certain of Pryce's feelings for you, and you both really want Davyn back, then surely that's a risk you'll be prepared to take,' Rhianon parried.

'There's no way you can wriggle out of it,' Sabrina told her confidently. 'He's my kid and I want him back and that's all there is to it.'

Chapter Thirty-Seven

New Year's Day 1930 was so cold that the streets were deserted. There was even a skimming of ice on St James Street canal, causing the gulls to squawk in distress as they landed and then slid uncontrollably along the surface.

Pryce's hands and feet ached and his teeth chattered with the cold. The skin on his unshaven face felt as though it had been stretched so tightly over his bones that it would crack at any minute.

He had spent the previous night huddled in a shop doorway. He'd been the butt for drunken revellers as they made their way home and he felt dirty and degraded.

He knew, from the tightness in his chest as he breathed in the freezing air, that if he slept out in the open again he'd either die of hypothermia or have pneumonia by the next morning.

It was not the sort of start for the new year that he had envisaged. He'd hoped that in 1930 things would take a turn for the better. He'd had dreams of convincing Rhianon of his love for her, dreams that they would be together again.

His prison sentence was behind him, and given a few more months to get on his feet he would have looked for something better than being a doorman at the Dragon Club anyway.

Once he'd achieved that, he'd start putting the rest of his plans into effect. The most important thing was to win Rhianon back. She must have some feelings for him still, he told himself, or she wouldn't be looking after his son.

His steps led him towards Cardiff General station, and he wondered what the chances were of taking refuge in the waiting room there. He couldn't even afford a platform ticket, so first of all he'd have to find some way of getting past the ticket collector.

He thought of saying he was meeting someone off the next train, but in his shabby state he knew that it would be difficult to convince any of the railway staff that it was true.

He hung around the station entrance with the idea of offering to carry someone's case onto the platform, but it seemed that none of the passengers travelling had any heavy luggage.

As he waited, a goods truck rolled by on the rails above his head, and that gave him a fresh idea. Scrambling up the scree at the side of the station he balanced precariously on the edge of the railway sleepers, trying to work out which platform he needed. Then he waited for the next empty coal truck that he knew would be travelling up to the Valleys.

* * *

The journey was dirty, dusty and bumpy. It was quite the most uncomfortable he had ever made. By the time he reached Pontdarw he felt bruised all over, and every bone in his body ached.

The truck slowed to snail's pace as they went through the station. When he realised that it wasn't going to stop he clambered over the side and jumped down onto the rails. As he hit the ground he felt one of his ankles painfully twisting underneath him.

Shivering and footsore he made his way into the town, wondering what to do next. In his present state he looked like a dirty old tramp, so Rhianon was hardly likely to welcome him with open arms, he thought ruefully. She might even shut the door in his face.

The tightness in his chest became more intense. He started to cough, a dry rasping spasm that left him gasping for breath, which led to even greater discomfort.

Wearily he made his way to Rhoslyn Terrace. He had no idea what he would do if Rhianon turned him away. If she did, then at least he'd be left in no doubt about where he stood with her, he told himself morosely.

As he knocked on the door a fresh spasm of coughing assailed him. He was spluttering and clutching his chest with both hands by the time Rhianon appeared. His face was haggard with pain and the words he had planned to say to her were lost as he panted for air, unable to breathe.

For a moment Rhianon didn't recognise him, he looked so gaunt and shabby. Then with a cry of surprise she grabbed hold of his arm and supported him as he stumbled over the doorstep.

Exhausted, he leaned against the wall, gasping her name. Slowly he sank to his knees as everything misted and swam before his eyes. Seconds later he passed into velvet blackness.

After that he knew no more until he woke up and found himself lying in a big bed in a strange room. A doctor was bending over him, examining him, sounding his chest and asking him questions he couldn't answer.

For several days Pryce lay wracked with cramps and fever. His laboured breathing, interspersed with bouts of coughing, left him limp and exhausted. Rhianon mopped his brow and gave him sips of diluted lemon juice and honey to soothe his raw throat.

Every time he opened his eyes they focused on Rhianon's face. It seemed to him that she was there at his side night and day. Either that or he was in the throes of some wonderful illusion, he mused hazily. He drifted in and out of consciousness, almost too weak even to swallow the soup she spooned into his mouth.

For Rhianon, Pryce's illness was extremely distressing. The doctor called every other day and prescribed a great many medicines that she couldn't afford. In desperation, knowing how essential they were for his recovery, she resorted to taking out a loan with a tallyman.

She felt bitterly ashamed of having to do this, but it was the only way she could afford all the medication Pryce needed, as well as feed herself and Davyn, and keep the house warm.

'You should have come and told me what was happening,' Polly scolded when she arrived one evening with some new knitting orders for Rhianon. 'I'm very surprised at you for having any truck with an old tallyman. You know you could have borrowed the money from me, you had only to ask.'

'How could I do that? You've been so good to me as it is,' Rhianon said awkwardly.

'That's what friends are for, cariad. They stick by each other when there's trouble, and help each other out. You and the little boyo are the nearest thing I've got to a family, and I'd do anything to help you. I thought you knew that!'

'Oh, Polly, I do, and I'm so grateful to you for all you've done for us. It is hateful having a tallyman calling each week. It would have upset my father, as he had no time for them. He always said they put people even deeper into debt because of the amount of interest they charged.'

'He was absolutely right, so why don't you accept my offer, cariad, and stop making such a fuss about it. Tell that old tallyman to get off your back. Repay him the money you borrowed immediately. You can settle up with me later on, when Pryce is back on his feet and things return to normal for you.'

'Well, if you're sure . . .'

'Of course I'm sure, my lovely. Here,' she opened her capacious handbag, took out a bundle of notes, and thrust them into Rhianon's hand. 'I came all prepared, see, cariad! I've got the takings with me. It will save me taking it to the bank tomorrow,' she laughed. 'Sing out, mind, if you need any more.'

Polly's money was a godsend. Even when she had put enough aside to pay back the loan she'd taken out with the tallyman, there was still plenty left for Pryce's medicines, and their everyday needs for the next few weeks. It meant that she would be able to buy nourishing foods to build Pryce up. He'd be back to his old self again in next to no time, she told herself happily.

She smiled ruefully, wondering if that was what she really wanted to happen. It had been wonderful having him there with her, and being able to care for him, and nurse him back to health.

He seemed so grateful, so content. She knew that from the look in his eyes, even though he was too weak to talk very much. She still didn't know why he had come to Pontdarw. Not unless Sabrina had sent him to collect little Davyn and take him back to Cardiff, she thought with dread.

She couldn't let him do that, she determined.

She'd have to find some way to talk him out of it the moment he was well enough to discuss the matter.

Still, Polly's generous help had taken one big worry off her shoulders. She'd face up to all the other problems when the time came to do so, she thought pragmatically.

Her relief was short-lived. When the tally-man called he was not prepared to let her repay the loan.

'You can only do that if you pay the full amount of interest that the money would have accrued over the two-year period for which it has been loaned,' he stated pompously.

He consulted his ledger, and Rhianon waited on tenterhooks as he made a great to-do about working out how much that would be.

'Surely that's not right? It's double the amount I've borrowed,' she gasped when finally he told her what the total was.

'That's what it comes to, missus,' he insisted, licking his stubby pencil.

'If I pay you all that I'll have no money left to buy food!' she exclaimed in dismay.

'Nothing I can do about it, missus. Those are the rules. Are you paying or not?'

'Well . . .' she hesitated. 'I'll have to think about it. Leave it until next time you call.'

She didn't want to worry Polly with her new problem, so she spent the time until the tally-man's next visit trying to work out what to do for the best. She hated debt. She even disliked having to borrow from Polly, but at least there was no exorbitant interest on that loan.

The result of all her calculations left her in no doubt that the best thing was for her to pay off the tallyman. She was going to take a firm stand and refuse to pay such an exorbitant amount of interest, though.

To her great relief Pryce was improving daily, and no longer needed special foods or medicine. He was still weak, but his unhealthy pallor had gone and his lethargic listlessness was replaced by a weak smile. He still tired very easily and slept a great deal. Nevertheless, whenever she was busy, he tried to keep Davyn amused.

Watching them together was like turning a knife in her own heart. They had bonded so closely. There seemed to be such a perfect empathy between them that there was no doubt about their relationship.

The weeks Pryce had been in her care had been some of the happiest she had known. The fact that he was under the same roof, and that he was sleeping in her father's bed, brought a wonderful feeling of contentment.

He was constantly expressing his gratitude for all that she did for him. His eyes seemed to follow her every move. It made her heart beat so fast that sometimes she had to find some excuse to leave the room.

She often wondered when he was going to open up and tell her what his feelings for her were. She thought perhaps he was waiting for her to speak first. She wanted to do so, but she was afraid of ruining their mutual happiness. There were moments when she felt an inner glow so glorious that it took her breath away.

If only time could stand still. If only Pryce and Davyn could both stay with her. If only they could be the happy family she dreamed about.

Whenever these thoughts came into her head she remembered her sister's words the last time she had come to Rhoslyn Terrace. Sabrina had left her in no doubt that she was determined to have Pryce, and that she intended using Davyn as bait to make him return to her.

Chapter Thirty-Eight

Pryce was improving so rapidly that he was no longer confined to the bedroom, but was getting up and coming downstairs each afternoon. His cough was practically gone, and he had lost the gaunt look that had worried Rhianon so much when he'd first arrived.

She was well aware that his eyes still focused on her whenever she was in the same room. If she looked at him, he would look away quickly, almost as if he was embarrassed. She found it very puzzling and she wondered what was going through his mind.

As much as possible she kept Davyn at her side, afraid that his constant chatter would tire Pryce. As he improved physically, however, Pryce spent more and more time each day keeping Davyn occupied.

They were as close as any father and son could ever hope to be, and she wondered how Davyn was going to react when it was time for Pryce to leave. More and more she worried about what would happen then. Would Sabrina insist that Pryce and Davyn should both be with her in Cardiff?

She wondered why they hadn't heard from

Sabrina. Several times she almost summoned up the nerve to ask Pryce, but her courage failed at the last minute. You've got both Davyn and Pryce here under your roof, so make the most of it and let sleeping dogs lie, she told herself.

She had other worries that were even more pressing. She still had to resolve the matter of the loan she had taken out with the tallyman. She rehearsed over and over in her mind what she was going to say to him. She was determined to be firm and show him that she didn't intend to stand any nonsense.

Her heart was in her mouth when she heard his distinctive rap on the front door. She found herself shaking and stammering as she blurted out that no matter what he said, she intended to clear the loan without paying any more interest.

'If you don't let me do that then I'll take matters higher and report you to your boss,' she told him.

He was a squat fat man, with red cheeks, a bristling moustache and small green eyes like dirty pebbles. Each time he spoke his tongue came out and licked his lips. After he'd made his deliberations, he would chew thoughtfully on his moustache, leaving it wet and shiny.

He listened to her diatribe, then shook his head. 'I told you last week, missus, that I don't do those sort of deals. If everybody wanted to pay me back after a few weeks where would I be? I'll tell you where I'd be, in Queer Street and broke the same as you!'

He laughed uproariously at his own joke. 'I tell you what, though.' He moved nearer until he was so close that Rhianon felt forced to take a step backwards into the hall. 'I could do a deal. As a special favour to you, but no one else must know. Understand?' He tapped the side of his bulbous nose with his pencil.

Rhianon gave a sigh of relief. It looked as though her resolve to stay firm was going to get her out of this unpleasant situation.

'Of course,' she smiled. 'I won't breathe a word to anyone else. I simply want to clear off my debt.' She gave a nervous laugh. 'I shouldn't have taken out a loan in the first place.'

He laughed with her. 'We all do things we shouldn't do at one time or another,' he agreed. He looked her up and down, licking his lips as he did so. 'I'd better come right inside then, hadn't I, since we don't want anyone else to know about our little arrangement.'

Before she understood the implication behind his remark, he was in the hallway and had slammed the door shut with his shoulder. 'Where's it to be then? Upstairs? I like a bit of comfort.'

As he tried to grab hold of her Rhianon struggled and pushed him away, trembling with indignation that he should take such liberties.

'Give over, woman. What the hell are you making such a fuss about? I'm only after a cosy cuddle and a bit of you-know-what!

Nothing to get yourself in a sweat about. I bet you give all the tradesmen a taste.' He laughed coarsely. 'Nice easy way for a pretty young woman like yourself to pay off the old bills, now isn't it!'

'Don't you dare come near me or try to touch me!' she warned. Sweat was trickling down the back of her neck and there was a sour taste in her mouth. As her fear mounted she shivered convulsively.

'Trying to get out of this as well as out of your arrangement about taking out a loan, are you?' he muttered contemptuously. 'Well now that you've got me all roused up this is one promise you can't backtrack on, let me tell you.'

As he made to grab hold of her again Rhianon let out an ear-piercing scream.

Pryce, who was sitting propped up in bed, reading a storybook to Davyn, heard the commotion and Rhianon's scream. In seconds he had thrown back the covers and was rushing down the stairs.

'Duw anwyl! Already got another bugger waiting for you,' the tallyman gasped. 'Up there in your bed all undressed and ready, you bitch! Leading me . . .'

He never had a chance to finish. Pryce's fist caught him square on the jaw, sending him reeling backwards. There was a sickening thud as the man's head hit the floorboards.

Rhianon felt sick as memories of an earlier fight blotted everything else from her mind. In an agony of fear she bent over the tallyman, trying to find out if he was still breathing.

Pryce pushed her to one side, knelt down and put his ear to the man's chest.

'Nothing to worry about,' he said as he straightened up, a look of relief on his face. 'He'll live.'

As he spoke, the man opened his eyes and shook his head as if trying to clear a mist from his eyes. Slowly he sat up, looking from Rhianon to Pryce uncertainly.

'Get up, mun, you're blocking the doorway,' Pryce ordered.

The tallyman scrambled awkwardly to his feet, grabbed his hat which had fallen off, and made for the door.

'Oh no you don't!' Pryce seized him by the scruff of the neck and pulled him back. 'You've got some paperwork to do first, I believe. Cancelling a loan agreement, if I remember? I was upstairs and I heard everything that was said, so don't try to renege on the deal.'

The man was shaking so much that his teeth were chattering. 'I . . . I can't do it unless you have the money,' he stuttered.

'Have you got it ready?' Pryce asked, looking questioningly at Rhianon.

She nodded and passed him an envelope with the money inside it.

No one spoke as the tallyman made out a receipt and handed it to Pryce. Pryce studied it carefully. 'Your writing looks a bit shaky to me,' he commented. 'I hope everyone at your office can recognise your signature, because we don't want to see or hear from you ever again. Got it?'

When the front door closed behind the man Pryce was so exhausted that he flopped down on the stairs, gasping for breath.

'I hope you haven't overdone things,' Rhianon said worriedly.

'A cup of tea and I'll be as right as rain,' he grinned weakly.

'I'll make it now. Do you need me to help you back to bed?'

Pryce shook his head. 'No, but you might have to finish reading the story to Davyn. All this excitement has left me short of breath.'

In the days that followed Rhianon watched over Pryce anxiously, and was relieved to see that the incident hadn't set him back at all. Now that his cough had cleared up he was well enough to get dressed and come downstairs first thing each morning.

Some of her joy was dimmed by the fact that when he was fully fit again he would doubtless be on his way back to Cardiff and to Sabrina, even though she had not once visited him the whole time he'd been ill.

There was still the matter of who was going to bring up Davyn, and she prayed that Pryce would listen to what she had to say and let him remain with her.

Finally, Rhianon could stand the suspense no longer. The three of them had spent a pleasant hour after tea playing a game before it was time for Davyn to go to bed. Pryce carried him upstairs and when he came back down Rhianon broached the subject.

'Look, Pryce, can we talk? About Davyn . . .'

He held up a hand to silence her. 'I've given the matter a lot of thought while I've been lying upstairs in bed all this time,' he told her. 'He loves you, Rhianon, and he's so very happy living with you that I want him to stay here where he is contented and secure. I'll support him, of course. Once I'm back at work you'll have no worries about money, I promise you.'

She felt her heart pounding. As much as she wanted Davyn to be with her, she'd hoped that Pryce might stay as well. Such was the warmth between them, she had begun to feel confident he would soon admit that his feelings for her were unchanged.

'Will Sabrina agree to such an arrangement?' she frowned, struggling to conceal her disappointment. 'When she came to the funeral she said that you wanted to have him back because you were planning to set up home for the three of you and . . .'

'Never!' Pryce exploded. 'Not in a thousand years! I never want to set eyes on your sister again.'

'Are you sure about this? Davyn does deserve to have a proper family, you know,' Rhianon persisted reluctantly. 'He needs a mam and a dad to give him security.'

'I know that!' Pryce agreed fervently. 'It's what I want for him more than anything. He could have them, too,' he said softly, 'if you were willing?'

Rhianon looked at him in disbelief. Was he saying what she thought he was? The words she'd dreamed about and yearned to hear for so long? The next moment her doubts vanished as he drew her into his arms. Gently he tipped her head back so that she was forced to look into his eyes.

'I do love you, Rhianon, I always have and I always will,' he murmured. 'Tell me that you still have feelings for me, that you can find it in your heart to forgive and forget all that has happened?'

'Oh, Pryce, of course I love you, I always have!'

Pryce groaned as his arms tightened. 'Ever since the fight with Hwyel Barker it's been like living in a nightmare. I've hardly dared hope that you would wait for me. Can we start afresh, cariad? I want us to be together so very much! I promise to take care of you, my lovely, for evermore,' he assured her, his voice breaking with emotion.

Tears misted Rhianon's eyes. 'Let's do as you say, let's start anew,' she breathed, her face flushed with happiness. 'To have both you and Davyn is the fulfilment of all my dreams.'

'Oh, Rhianon!' He kissed her, tenderly at first, then more hungrily.

She felt herself responding passionately. All the pent-up love and longing that she'd been holding in check since the day Pryce had been arrested could now be released.

Her heart thundered crazily. Knowing that from now on Pryce and Davyn would always be with her filled her with tremendous joy.

She said a silent prayer of gratitude that all the confusion and doubts that had been shadowing her life for so long, would now be gone for ever.

Chapter Thirty-Nine

Although her dearest wish to be reunited with Pryce had finally come true, Rhianon knew there were still many obstacles to overcome in the weeks that followed.

Neither of them were working, many of the people of Pontdarw, especially the Barkers, looked askance at Pryce living with her, and there was no guarantee that Sabrina would remain quietly in the background.

'The first thing we must do is put paid to all the gossip and get married,' Pryce told her. 'That is if you will have me, after all I've put you through?' he added contritely.

'Nothing would make me happier,' she told him softly. 'It's what I've dreamed of for so long – the first step in the fresh beginning we've talked so much about.'

They decided on the quietest wedding possible. Polly and Angharad Lloyd, Rhianon's next-door neighbour who had stood by her over the last difficult years, were asked to be witnesses at the simple register office ceremony.

Despite their new-found contentment, Rhianon knew that Pryce was just as concerned about their future as she was.

'I never want to work underground or be involved with the miners ever again,' he said firmly.

'So what will you do?'

He chewed on his lip thoughtfully. 'Well, more than anything I still want to be a teacher,' he admitted.

'If only that was possible,' Rhianon said wistfully. 'If only you'd been able to take your final exams, or we could afford for you to go back to full-time studying.'

'I had practically completed my coursework,' he pointed out. 'I was thinking that if I find a temporary job, I could carry on studying in readiness to sit the final exam.'

In spite of Rhianon's doubts, Pryce proved he was right. While he studied, he took any kind of casual work that came his way. Many of the jobs were menial ones, and the pay was so low that to a man of his ability it was insulting.

It also meant a hand-to-mouth existence for them. Rhianon had persuaded the landlord to agree to her taking over the tenancy after her father died, and she let out two of the rooms so that they had some money coming in for their basic needs.

Their excitement when Pryce finally qualified was somewhat dampened by a new problem. Where would he find a school to employ him? There was certainly no opening in Pontdarw.

'I wouldn't want to stay on even if you could teach here,' Rhianon told him. 'I'd sooner get right away. There's still such a lot of nasty gossip, especially about Davyn.'

'Well, does that really matter?'

She stiffened. 'You never know what children overhear when grown-ups are talking. Davyn might get bullied or teased once he starts school.'

Pryce insisted she was imagining it, but he knew from experience that so little happened in the mining community that such things did get chewed over and commented on, again and again, long after they should have been forgotten.

'Where do you fancy moving to, then?' he enquired. 'Or perhaps I should ask if there is anywhere you would rather not live?'

Rhianon shuddered. 'I'd rather not go back to Cardiff, too many bad memories, so don't apply to teach in any schools there.'

'Whew! That's a bit of a tall order, cariad! There's dozens of schools there! I'm more likely to find a teaching job in Cardiff than anywhere else.'

She shook her head. 'Too many unhappy memories for both of us, boyo,' she told him emphatically.

'It's a big city, cariad,' he argued. 'We needn't live anywhere near Tiger Bay.'

She didn't answer, but he could see the very thought of ever living anywhere in Cardiff troubled her.

It took several weeks and a number of

interviews before Pryce found a school interested in employing him.

'You're going to like this,' he told her excitedly when he read the letter confirming his appointment. 'It's a school in Porthcawl.'

'Porthcawl? Where's that? Not a part of Cardiff, is it?'

Pryce laughed. 'No, it's about twenty-five miles from Cardiff. Lovely spot, right on the coast. People go there for their holidays. It lies between Cardiff and Swansea. A great place for young Davyn to grow up in . . . and his brothers and sisters when they arrive.'

'You mean it's a seaside place?'

'That's right. Sea, sand and rocks. A really picturesque spot, you'll love it there,' he told her enthusiastically. 'I have to be ready to start work in less than two weeks, so we will have to begin making arrangements to move right away.'

'It's wonderful news, but such a big step, Pryce. We'll have to find somewhere to live . . .'

'That's all taken care of, all you have to do is start packing.'

Rhianon frowned. 'Taken care of? What does that mean?'

'There's a house that goes with the job!'

Their move was overshadowed by an unexpected visit from Sabrina. They could hardly believe their eyes when a sleek white Lagonda motor car drew up outside their front door.

'That's Lorenzo, the boss of the Dragon Club,

behind the wheel of that car,' Pryce exclaimed in amazement. 'What the hell does he want, coming all the way up here from Cardiff?'

As they watched, Sabrina stepped out and teetered over to their front door, her high heels clicking like castanets.

'You'd better open the door and let her in and maybe she'll tell us,' Rhianon said dryly.

Inwardly she was quaking. She was sure that Sabrina visiting them boded no good. Her greatest fear was that she had come to claim Davyn back.

As her sister came into the room, Rhianon picked the child up in her arms and held him protectively, burying her face in his soft hair. If Sabrina had decided she wanted him back then she'd find she had a fight on her hands, Rhianon vowed to herself.

Sabrina wasted no time on pleasantries. She refused Rhianon's offer of a cup of tea and at first she wouldn't even sit down.

'I'm here to let you know that Lorenzo has sold the Dragon Club and I am going to America with him, so I'll probably never see either of you again.' She looked round the shabby room, disparagingly. 'If we ever do come back to Cardiff on a visit I suppose I'll still find you here in this terrible dump.'

Neither of them answered her. It was as if by mutual consent they decided not to share the news of their change of fortune with her.

'Well, that's it then! I suppose it would be

asking too much to expect you to wish us well.'

'Not at all, I hope you both find the sort of life you crave,' Pryce told her gravely.

'Aren't you going to say goodbye to little Davyn?' Rhianon asked in astonishment, as Sabrina stood up ready to leave.

Sabrina paused. 'Who?' Her eyebrows lifted sardonically as her gaze rested on the child in Rhianon's arms. 'Why should I bother? He's your problem now, not mine!' she said dismissively.

As her sister turned away and headed for the door, Rhianon caught a glimpse of a tear sparkling on Sabrina's long lashes.

To find out more about Rosie Harris and other fantastic Arrow authors why not read *The Inside Story* – our newsletter featuring all of our saga authors.

To join our mailing list to receive the newsletter and other information* write with your name and address to:

> The Inside Story
> The Marketing Department
> Arrow Books
> 20 Vauxhall Bridge Road
> London
> SW1V 2SA

*Your details will be held on a database so we can send you the newsletter(s) and information on other Arrow authors that you have indicated you wish to receive. Your details will not be passed to any third party. If you would like to receive information on other Random House authors please do let us know. If at any stage you wish to be deleted from our *The Inside Story* mailing list please let us know.

Winnie of the Waterfront

Rosie Harris

Crippled by polio, young Winnie Molloy has little to look forward to in life. Her father, Trevor, adores her but she is neglected by her feckless mother, Grace.

When war comes Trevor is called up. He fears for Winnie and persuades Sandy Coulson to wheel her to school each day in a converted pram. Two years older than her, Sandy sticks up for Winnie and promises to be her lifelong friend.

But Grace is drinking very heavily and loses one job after another. To pay the rent on the one squalid room they are now living in she takes Winnie out begging until she is given a warning by the police. When Trevor is reported 'Missing Presumed Dead' Grace goes on a drinking spree, meets with an accident and dies.

And Winnie is left loveless and alone . . .

arrow books

**Order further Rosie Harris titles
from your local bookshop, or have them delivered
direct to your door by Bookpost**

arrow books